Salt of the Earth

Also by Michael Taylor

Eve's Daughter

The Love Match

Love Songs

Clover

Heart's Desire

Poppy Silk

MICHAEL TAYLOR

Salt of the Earth

Hodder & Stoughton

Copyright © 2004 by Michael Taylor

First published in Great Britain in 2004 by Hodder and Stoughton
A division of Hodder Headline

The right of Michael Taylor to be identified as the Author of the Work
has been asserted by him in accordance with the Copyright,
Designs and Patents Act 1988.

1 3 5 7 9 10 8 6 4 2

A CIP catalogue record for this title
is available from the British Library

ISBN 0 340 83056 5

Typeset in Plantin by Hewer Text Ltd, Edinburgh
Printed and bound by Clays Ltd, St Ives plc

Hodder Headline's policy is to use papers that are natural,
renewable and recyclable products and made from wood
grown in sustainable forests. The logging and manufacturing
processes are expected to conform to the environmental
regulations of the country of origin.

Hodder and Stoughton
A division of Hodder Headline
338 Euston Road
London NW1 3BH

ACKNOWLEDGEMENTS

With acknowledgements and thanks to the friendly and obliging management and staff of Davis Memorials of Cradley Heath, for their help and patience during my research and, not least, for their delicious cups of tea.

I

1856

The train escaped the tunnel's blackness, half obscured by a billowing veil of white steam, into the balmy sunshine of a late July afternoon. As soon as she heard the mechanical din of the locomotive, Lucy Piddock turned her head to watch, stepping back from the platform's edge. She urged her friend Miriam Watson to do likewise with a token pull on her arm. The engine and its unholy racket, offensive to the ears, passed them slowly, delivering its string of coaches to precisely where the rest of the passengers were waiting. As it groaned and hissed to a halt, Lucy smiled at Miriam, opened the door of an empty third-class compartment and allowed Miriam to step up inside before her.

'How did we manage to get about before we had the railway?' Lucy remarked as she and Miriam sat facing each other next to the window. The railway line had been open four years and the novelty of it, as well as the convenience, Lucy did not yet take for granted. 'We'd never have gone to Dudley before of a Saturday afternoon, would we?'

'Better than walking to Stourbridge,' Miriam agreed. 'It's a tidy walk to Stourbridge from Silver End . . . especially if you got a nail sticking up in your boot, like I've got.'

'I sometimes wonder if it's quicker to walk down to the other station below the castle or this one.'

'Depends where you am when you'm done, I reckon,' Miriam surmised. 'Which end o' the town you'm at. Neither one's close to the shops, but you don't have to put up with going through that dark tunnel if you go from this station.'

'That's true,' Lucy agreed. 'And it costs a bit less.'

She gazed out of the carriage window onto the platform, while Miriam took off her boot and rubbed her bunion where the offending nail was puncturing it. A young guard, smart in the livery of the Oxford Worcester and Wolverhampton Railway and wearing a cheese-cutter cap, checked the door to the compartment of the four-wheeled coach. He caught Lucy's eye through the window and smiled, giving her a waggish wink that made her insides churn, then pressed on to check the forward coaches.

'Did you see that chap, Miriam?' Lucy asked with a broad grin. 'The guard. I fancy *him*.'

'Trust you to fancy somebody you'll never see again.'

'Course I shall see him again,' Lucy said with a certainty that defied argument. 'He'll be coming back this way in a minute to get back in his guards' van.'

'Well, you ain't gunna get the chance to talk to him. The train'll be pulling out in a minute.'

Lucy shrugged. 'I only said I fancied him. I didn't say as I wanted to have a discourse about the weather, or whether the Queen and Prince Albert will have more children.'

'Ain't there no decent chaps where you work?' Miriam enquired. 'We'll have to get you fixed up with somebody soon, else you'll end up an old maid.'

'Chaps don't seem to fancy me, Miriam. I reckon I ain't pretty enough.' Lucy saw the guard returning and perked up at once. 'Aye up! Here he comes again. Have a peep at him.'

As he passed the window he turned and smiled once more, so both girls grinned and waved saucily.

'Well, *he* seems to think you'm pretty,' Miriam said. '*He* seems to fancy you. He was smiling at you, not me.'

'I bet he'd be a bit of a gig as well.' Lucy felt herself

2

reddening. 'I hope he gets off the train again at Brettell Lane.'

'Well, I ain't hanging about just to see if he does. Get yourself a local chap, Luce. That guard might come from Worcester or even Oxford for all you know. It'd be no good courting somebody from Worcester or Oxford. You want a chap to be where *you* am. Somebody who can sit with yer nights on the settle and tickle your feet for a bit o' pleasure and comfort.'

They heard a whistle, and the locomotive huffed, hauling them forward, slowly at first but soon picking up speed.

'Oh, I give up on chaps,' Lucy pouted. 'I never seem to get anybody. What's wrong with me, Miriam?'

'Nothing, you daft sod. There's nothing wrong with you. You *am* pretty, even if you don't think so. You got a good figure. You got lovely dark hair and big blue eyes.'

'*Pale* blue eyes!' Lucy repeated with exasperation. 'I wish I'd got brown eyes like you, or dark blue ones like a baby's. Pale blue eyes look that washed out. Even green eyes would be better than pale blue.'

'Be thankful for what you have got, Luce. A good many would be glad of your eyes and your looks.'

'Then if I *have* got decent looks why can't I get a chap? Have I got a dewdrop dithering off the end of my nose that I don't know about? Have I got a squint? Do I stink or something?'

Miriam chuckled. 'Course not. Anyroad, if you stunk I wouldn't come a-nigh you.'

'So what's up with me? I swear I'll step out with the first chap as ever asks me, even if he's the ugliest, vilest freak ever to have worn a pair of trousers . . . I will . . . I swear.'

Miriam laughed again. 'You ain't that desperate.'

'Yes, I am. It's all right for you. You got Sammy Osborne. And before him you had Jimmy Sheldon . . . and Lord knows who else before him. Lord knows, Miriam, you must've collected enough men's scalps to make a rug.'

3

'Oh, Lucy . . .' Miriam chuckled and sighed. 'Somebody'll come along and sweep you right off your feet.'

'And that's what I want. Somebody to come along and sweep me off my feet, before I'm stuck up a tree and too old. Before I have to start reading the deaths regular to see who's just become a widower . . . Oh, no,' Lucy added after a moment's pondering. 'On second thoughts I could never lower myself to go with a chap who's secondhand.'

'What's the rush? I sometimes think as men ain't worth the bother anyroad. They can't wait to bed yer, buying yer presents and giving yer all that fancy sweet talk just to get you there. And then, when they've had yer, they treat yer like flipping dirt.'

'I'm sure they ain't all like that,' Lucy said sceptically, and fell quiet.

The train rumbled over the high wooden construction that was Parkhead Viaduct and she gazed through the window at the busy network of canals that converged beneath it, and at the area's countless smoking chimney stacks, without really seeing any of it. She was deep in thought, grieving over the imagined monumental flaw in her looks or demeanour that rendered her positively repulsive to men. Even though no such flaw existed, Lucy was lacking in self-confidence because she firmly believed otherwise. This erroneous conviction compounded the problem, rendering her shy, which men interpreted as being 'stuck-up'. And what ordinary factory wench had the right or the reason to be stuck-up?

Lucy was not yet twenty years old and most of her friends the same age were courting. Some were even wed. This fact nagged at her, not incessantly, nor obsessively, but sometimes; and this moment was one such time. But when she was among her own friends and family, and not blighted by misgivings over her fancied inadequacies, she was good company, bright and amiable, and even threatened to be witty on occasions.

4

'I think I ought to try and get out a bit more,' she said to Miriam, releasing herself from her depressing daydream. 'I think I should try and mix more with folk.'

'You mean mix more with men,' Miriam corrected with a knowing look. 'I don't know what you'm worried about. Are you sure there's no men where you work?'

'None as I'd want. There's Jake Parsons who's too old, Bobby Pugh who's too ugly, Georgie Betts whose feet are too stinky . . . Then there's Alfie Mason who's got a wall eye and a hair lip . . . Oh, and Ben Craddock who never stops farting.'

'You'm too fussy.'

'I could afford to be fussier, if only chaps was falling over themselves and each other to ask me out.'

'What d'you do nights?'

'What is there to do nights? I generally sit with my mother picking my feet and pulling faces at the dog, while my father goes boozing up at the Whimsey.'

Miriam chuckled at the mental image. 'So why don't you go with your father up the Whimsey for a change?'

Lucy laughed with derision at the notion. 'Decent girls don't go to public houses.'

'They do if they work there. You could get a job nights serving beer. You'd meet plenty men.'

'Yes, all fuddled old farts . . . like my father.'

'Young chaps as well, Lucy. Hey, it'd be worth a try.'

'I doubt whether my mother would let me,' Lucy replied resignedly. 'You know what she's like.' She lapsed into deep thought again, considering the possibilities.

The train was drawing to a halt at Round Oak Station. When it stopped Lucy pressed her cheek against the window, looking again for sight of the chirpy guard. Those who had alighted made their way across the platform while others embarked, bound for Stourbridge, Kidderminster and beyond.

'Can you see him?' Miriam enquired, realising why her friend was scanning the platform.

'No, but I can hear his whistle.'

The train eased out of the little station. As it picked up speed down the incline towards Brettell Lane station, Lucy picked up her basket in readiness for when they would alight in just a minute or two.

When they drew to a halt at Brettell Lane, Lucy opened the door and stepped expectantly onto the platform. She looked longingly towards the rear, hoping to see the guard jump down from his van. She was not disappointed and lingered, adjusting her bonnet via her reflection in the carriage window for a few moments, hoping he might beckon her to go to him, or reach her before her tarrying seemed indecorous. But Miriam cannily took her arm and urged her to move. Lucy complied with reluctance as she glanced wistfully behind her at the guard. He smiled again and waved and she waved back, with all the coyness of inexperience manifest in her blue eyes.

'Come on, Luce, don't let him think as you'm waiting for him. Pretend you ain't bothered one road or th'other.'

'Is that the way to play it?' Lucy asked doubting her friend's advice. 'Shouldn't I let him see as I'm interested?'

'You already did. It's supposed to be the man what does the chasing.'

'But what if he don't?' Lucy asked ruefully. 'He needs to know as it won't be a waste of time chasing me.'

'Listen, if we go to Dudley next Saturday afternoon and catch the same train back, he's ever likely to be on it, ain't he? You can flash your eyes at him then.'

'I can't wait a week, Miriam.'

'Oh, don't be so daft. In a week you'll very likely have forgot all about him.'

*   *   *

The girls went to Dudley again the following Saturday and caught the same train back, but there was no sign of the guard. There was a guard, of course, but it was not the same man, to Lucy's crushing disappointment. They repeated the exercise the following three weeks, all with the same result, and poor Lucy realised she was never going to meet this man who had bewitched her, who had introduced a swarm of butterflies to her stomach.

'It's Fate,' Miriam told her flatly. 'You ain't meant to have him. If you was meant to have him you'd have seen him by now, and very likely have stepped out with him a couple o' times. You ain't meant to have him, Lucy. Anyroad, if we come to Dudley next week I want to catch an earlier train back.'

★ ★ ★

During high summer in Brierley Hill a breeze was regarded as a blessing. It not only cooled, but helped clear the air of the grimy mist and the sulphurous stinks perpetrated by the high concentration of ironworks, pits, firebrick works and bottle manufactories, whose chimney stacks belched out smuts and smoke like the upended cannons of an army in disarray. It was one such breezy summer evening in August 1856, the week following Lucy's final disappointment, that Haden Piddock, her father, was returning home from his labours at Lord Ward's New Level Iron Works, more commonly known as 'The Earl's', to his rented cottage in Bull Street. On the way he met Ben Elwell, carrying his pick and shovel over his shoulder like a soldier would carry a pair of muskets. Ben was not only a reluctant miner but also the eager landlord of the nearby Whimsey Inn in Church Street.

'I'll be glad to get me sodding boots off,' Haden commented. His clay pipe was in his mouth, held between his top and bottom teeth, which was amazingly no detriment to speech for, over the years, he had perfected the knack of conversing with

7

clenched teeth. The pipe, however, had gone out and Haden had not been able to re-ignite it. 'Me feet am nigh on a-killing me. As soon as I get in th'ouse, I'll get our Lucy to fetch me a bowl o' wairter from the pump so's I can give 'em a good soak.'

'Yo' need warm water to soak yer feet, Haden, lad. Otherwise you'll catch a chill.'

Haden turned to look at his mate, surprised he should feel the need to remind him of what was blindingly obvious. 'Yaah!' he exclaimed sarcastically. 'D'you think I'm saft enough to stick 'em in cold wairter, you daft bugger?' He took his pipe from his mouth and cursorily inspected the inside of the bowl. 'I'd get our Lucy to warm it up on the 'ob fust.'

'That daughter o'yours looks after yer well, Haden.'

'Better than the missus, when there's fetching and carrying to be done.' He tapped his pipe against the palm of his hand to loosen the carbonised tobacco, and allowed the debris to fall to the ground.

'Yo'll miss her when her gets wed.'

'*If* her ever gets wed,' Haden replied.

'I tek it then as yo' ai' coming for a drink now?' Ben said.

'No, I'll send our Lucy up with a jug to have wi' me dinner. I'll see thee later, when I'n finished me scoff and had a bit of a wash down.'

'Aye, well I don't expect I'll be shifting far from that tap room of ourn.'

'I don't envy thee, Ben,' Haden remarked sincerely as he slid his pipe into the pocket of his waistcoat. 'Yo' ain't content with swinging a blasted pick and digging coal out all day. Yo' have to serve beer all night an' all, to them buggers as yo've bin working alongside of.'

A smile spread over Ben's blackened face. The whites of his eyes sparkled and his teeth, which seemed dingy when his face was clean, seemed bright now by comparison. 'It has its compensations, Haden. I drink for free. As much as I've a mind to. And the missus brews a worthy crock, whether or no I'm behind her.'

'Her does, an' no question . . . And that reminds me, Ben . . . I've bin meaning to ask . . . Our Lucy wondered if you needed a wench to help out nights like. Her wants to get out more. It'd tek some of the load off thee an' all, give yer a bit more time to yourself.'

'Funny as yo' should mention it, Haden. Me and the missus was on'y saying yesterday as how we could do with somebody to help out. Somebody presentable and decent like your Lucy. Honest and not afeared o' work. How old is she now?'

'Coming twenty. Next September.'

'And still single? Still no sign of e'er a chap?'

Haden grinned smugly. 'Her's met ne'er a chap yet as matches up to her fairther, that's why. I doh think for a minute as her's short of admirers, though, but I reckon they'm all tongue-tied. Not like we used to be, eh, Ben?'

Ben cackled as he was reminded of his youth. 'No, we was never back'ard in coming forwards.'

'Anyroad, I want no Tom, Dick or Harry sniffing round our Lucy, so keep your eye on her for me, Ben, anytime I ain't there.'

'Bring her wi' yer tonight, eh? I'll get the missus to show her the ropes.'

'That'll please the wench no end. Yo'm a pal, Ben. A real pal.'

'How's your other daughter, Haden?'

'Our Jane? As happy as Ode Nick now as her's wed. I'm happy for her that he come back from the Crimea, even though he does have to get about on a crutch these days.'

'Better to walk on crutches than be jed and buried in some graveyard in Balaclava, I'd say. I tek it as he can still get his good leg over the wench, though.'

Haden guffawed. ' 'Tis to be hoped. He'll be getting boils

on the back of his neck, else. But there's no sign of e'er a babby yet. Mind you, there's no boils on his neck either.'

They had arrived at the corner where Haden turned off. He thanked Ben Elwell again for agreeing to take on Lucy as a barmaid, waved and went home.

Waiting by the entry was Bobby the shaggy sheepdog, named after Sir Robert Peel. Bobby lay with his nose between his paws and nonchalantly opened one eye when he heard Haden's footsteps approaching. When he saw his master he stretched, got to his feet and wagged his tired tail, anticipating being fussed.

'Christ, I bet you've had a bloody hard day looking after your mother, eh, Bobby?' Haden said, bending forward to ruffle the dog's thick mane. 'All that shuteye and lolling about. Christ knows how you keep it up.' The dog licked Haden's hand affectionately. 'Is your mother inside then? Has her fed yer?' He patted the dog and straightened up. 'It's all right for some, all rest and no work. I expect yo'll want some dinner off me now, eh?'

As he opened the door the smell of cooking welcomed him. He saw a pot of rabbit stew standing on the hob of the cast iron fire grate and knew that he would not go hungry. Lucy was standing half-dressed, tying up her long dark hair.

'Where's your mother?'

'I'm upstairs,' a voice called.

'What yer doing up there? It's time for me vittles.'

'I'll be down in a minute.'

Haden looked at his younger daughter as he tossed his snap bag on the settle. 'I had a word with Ben Elwell. He says if you go to the Whimsey tonight his missus will show you the ropes.'

'So he'll let me start working there nights?'

'And he'll keep his eye on yer. I want no drunken louts a-pestering yer. All right?'

'Yes.'

'Then it's settled. Lord knows what he'll pay yer, though. We never mentioned money.'

'I don't care. I'd do it for nothing, Dad.'

'No need to do it for nothing, my wench. Ben's fair. He'll pay fair. Now, get yourself dressed and fetch me some water so's I can wash me feet, our Lucy. When yo've done that, tek the brown jug wi' yer to the Whimsey and have it filled wi' beer . . . Here's sixpence . . .'

So Lucy, grateful that her father had had a word with Ben Elwell, went to the pump down the street and fetched water. Then, she took the brown jug from the cupboard next to the fire grate and stepped out into the early evening sunshine to fetch his beer.

★ ★ ★

The Piddocks sat down to eat, civilly and with all the decorum of a well-bred household, a habit which Hannah, Haden's wife, had imported and insisted upon. Her years employed as a housemaid in one of the big important houses in King-swinford, the adjoining parish, had instilled much domestic refinement into her, which the years and their own modest way of life had not diminished.

'I don't know as I hold with our Lucy serving ale to all them loudmouth hobbledehoys with their rough manners what get in the Whimsey,' Hannah remarked with maternal anxiety. 'No decent young woman should be seen in such a place. And will she be safe walking home at night?'

'I'll be walking home with her nights, I daresay,' Haden said, and shoved a forkful of rabbit meat into his mouth.

Lucy looked from one to the other. 'I'll be all right, Mother,' she affirmed. 'I'll come to no harm. They're not all rough folk that go to the Whimsey.'

' 'Tis to be hoped. But if ever you'm on your own and hear somebody behind yer, run for your life.'

'I will, Mother. I'm not daft.'

'I don't know what you'm a-fretting about, Hannah,' Haden said, as always dropping the initial aitch in his pronunciation, a universal habit in the Black Country. 'Things am quieter now than they used to be. I mean, there's nothing to get excited about any more – well, not at the Whimsey anyroad. There's no bull-baiting or cock-fighting these days to get folk excited. All right, there might be the occasional badger-drawing when the Patrollers ain't about . . . I remember Coronation Day—'

'Oh, spare us the details, Haden.'

'No, Mother, I'd like to hear,' Lucy insisted. 'My dad always comes out with some good tales.'

'Except I've heard 'em all afore, our Lucy. Too many times.'

'Well, I haven't. So tell us, Dad.'

Haden took a long quaff from his beer. 'It was June in thirty-eight,' he began again with a smile for his daughter. 'It started the day afore the Coronation of our young queen Victoria, God bless her. We'd heard that there was due to be a bear-baiting at the Old Bell up in Bell Street. The bear had been brought over from Wednesbury, and to keep him comfortable for the night they found him an empty pigsty. Next day, everybody as had got a bulldog – and that was a good many in them days – brought 'em along to bait poor old Bruin. So the bear-herd fetched the bear out o' the pigsty and led him over to the old clay pit. They drove an iron stake into the middle and put the ring at the end of the bear's chain over the stake, so as the animal could move about easy but not too far. Course, loads o' spectators lined the clay pit, a chap in a clean white smock among 'em.'

Bobby had installed himself at the side of the table near Haden and waited patiently with imploring eyes for a morsel to descend to the stone flags of the floor. But Haden was in full flow.

'As it happened, the ground had been softened by rain a day or two before, and as the kerfuffle started nobody noticed that the stake had come loose in the mud. I tell yer, there was plenty fun as them dogs baited the bear, but then it dawned on everybody that the bear had got free. We ran for our lives, and the poor bugger in the white smock fell over. He was rolled over umpteen times in the mud as folk trampled all over him.' Haden laughed aloud as he recalled it. 'He was a sight – the poor bugger did look woebegone.'

'Then what happened?' Lucy asked, wide-eyed.

'The saft thing was, the poor bear was as frit as everybody else, and run off back to the pigsty.'

'The poor, poor bear,' she said full of sympathy for the animal. 'I'm glad they put a stop to all that savagery.'

'Savagery?' Haden repeated. 'I've seen savagery. I've watched bull-baiting at the Whimsey – in the days when everybody called it "Turley's". Once, a bull gored a bulldog, pushing his horns right into its guts. He ripped it open and tossed it higher than the house.'

'Ugh! That's enough to put you off your dinner,' Lucy complained, turning her mouth down in distaste.

'Another time at a wake,' Haden went on, 'I watched a bull, that was maddened by the dogs, break free of his stake and cause havoc among the crowd. When they caught him they slaughtered him without a second thought and cut him up, and the meat was sold to anybody as wanted it at a few coppers a pound. Then they all trooped off to watch the next baiting.'

'I'm only glad it doesn't go on now,' Lucy said. 'Do you remember it, Mother?'

'I remember it going on. I'd never go and watch such things meself, though. But then I had you kids to look after.'

'Yes, they was rough days,' Haden admitted. 'We only had one parish constable in them days and he couldn't be every-where. Like as not he was paid to turn a blind eye, especially by the street wenches or their blasted pimps. But folk was poor and nobody had any education. They knew no better, knew no other life. These days, there's work about and while they'm still poor, they ain't as hard done by as they used to be.'

Bobby impatiently tapped Haden's leg with his paw to remind his master that he was still awaiting a morsel.

'Lord, I forgot all about thee, mutt,' he said, picking a thigh bone from his plate and tossing it to the dog. 'Here, that'll keep thee going for a bit.'

★   ★   ★

2

Arthur Goodrich, a man of average height and average looks, was twenty-five years old. He was a stonemason by trade, employed in the family firm of Jeremiah Goodrich and Sons, Monumental Masons and Sepulchral Architects. While Jeremiah, Arthur's father, tended to concentrate on the sepulchral design and construction side of the business in the relative comfort of the workshop along with Talbot, Arthur's older brother, poor Arthur, by dint of being younger and thus subordinate, was meanwhile generally despatched to the further reaches of the Black Country to effect the more menial, though no less skilled, work of cutting and blacking inscriptions on existing headstones in the area's sundry graveyards. For Arthur this was an eternal source of discontent to add to his many others.

Thus it was one Saturday morning in late September. Arthur, complete with a toolbag full of freshly sharpened chisels, several wooden mallets, a cushion and various other appliances of his craft, had been despatched early to the hallowed ground of St Mark's church in Pensnett, a good twenty minutes' walk even for a sprightly lad like himself. The apathetic morning had rounded up a herd of frowning clouds that matched Arthur's mood. He hoped that the rain would keep off, for today was the last cricket match of the season, against Stourbridge Cricket Club, and he had been picked to play.

He had been assigned two headstones to amend that day

and possessed a rough plan on paper of where they were situated within the graveyard. He located the first, a shining black grave, the granite imported at vast expense for the occupier's wife. The occupier had been a local claymaster, piously religious and a pillar of local society. Arthur put down his toolbag, sat on the grave and read the inscription to himself:

'*To the memory of Jacob Onions who passed away 15th October 1853.*

> *Farewell dear husband must we now part,*
> *Who lay so near each other's heart.*
> *The time will come I hope when we*
> *Will both enjoy Felicity.*'

Composed, obviously, by a grieving Mrs Onions, hoping for the better fortune of someday lying together again. Well, now that same grieving wife had joined her beloved husband, and Arthur was to append the inscription that confirmed it. He fumbled in the pocket of his jacket for the two pieces of paper that told him what words to cut on the relevant headstones. Just at that moment an ominous pain convulsed his stomach and he trapped the piece of paper under the grave vase so that he could clutch his aching gut. Within a few seconds the pain had gone.

Wind.

A decent breaking of wind would relieve it. He lifted one cheek experimentally but nothing happened, so he took the cushion from his toolbag, an essential item of kit when sitting or kneeling on cold graves for hours on end, and placed it on the grave beneath him near the headstone. He opened a jar of grey paint – some mystical kind that dried quickly and could be easily scraped off afterwards – grabbed a brush and daubed the area to be marked out with the lettering. While it dried, he located the other grave and performed the same task there. He read the inscription on that grave too.

'*In remembrance of Henry Tether who died in his cups 6th June 1840, a free spirit who in his lifetime would have preferred all spirits to be free.*' So poor Henry Tether had a partiality for drink. Perhaps it was the drink that killed him, for it was time to add the name of Henry's dear departed wife Octavia after sixteen years of widowhood. He left the scrap of paper that held the words for its appended inscription under its grave vase also, to save fumbling later for it in his pockets.

As Arthur made his way back to the first grave he was gripped again by the menacing pain in his stomach. Perhaps he was pregnant somehow and he was having contractions . . . No, that was plain stupid. He was a man, and men didn't give birth. Besides, he was not wed so how could he possibly be pregnant? Of course, it was something he'd eaten that had upset his stomach. He attempted to break wind again but . . . oh, dear . . . It was a mistake. Perhaps he shouldn't, for fear of an embarrassing accident.

He returned to the first grave and checked the paint. It was dry. It would not take long to mark out the lettering that was to be added, and nobody at the firm was as quick as him when it came to cutting letters. He picked up his blacklead to mark it out . . .

The pains in his gut returned . . . They were persistent now and he could hear a tremendous amount of gurgling going on there, as if there were some serious flaw in his intestinal plumbing. It was obvious he must hurry his work, for there were no privies within a quarter of a mile that he could discern. He dared not stoop to do it in the graveyard either, for it was on high ground, exposed to the passing traffic of Pensnett High Street, for all to witness. The vicar might appear like the risen Christ just at the crucial moment . . . it would be just Arthur's luck. So, in agony, he carried on marking out the letters and words, taken from the piece of paper he was working from.

He *had* to hurry. It was a matter of dire urgency that he hurry. He was desperate for a privy, for anywhere, hallowed ground if need be . . . Hallowed ground it would have to be, he decided . . . until a youngish woman, evidently a recent widow, accompanied by three of her children, tearfully presented themselves and a posy of flowers at a nearby grave. It would be the ultimate discourtesy to relieve himself in front of her at this moment. So he pressed on, cutting letters now as fast as he could, blunting one chisel and picking up another, till he had finished the first headstone. By this time his guts were about to burst. There was no time to complete the second headstone. He had to depart. Right now. This minute. He could return once he had procured relief. So he threw his tools into his bag and fled as fast as his tormented guts would allow. Clenching his buttocks stalwartly and with a fraught look upon his face, he strode across the graveyard and down the long winding path that led to High Street. If he didn't find a privy soon, Pensnett would be subjected to the foulest pollution every likely to strike it, an event that could become folklore for generations.

As he emerged onto the high road, behold, there was a row of houses in a side street opposite with an entry that led to a backyard. He must make use of their facilities without permission, for there was no time to seek it . . . and what if he did and they withheld their consent? . . . He could always knock on a door afterwards and confess his trespass, by which time it would be a done deed.

He crept up the entry and was relieved to find nobody in the backyard which served the terrace of four houses. He located a privy behind one of the brewhouses and burst the door open. It was a double-holer. Arthur had never seen a double-holer before. A roosting hen was perched on a shelf above and

Arthur impatiently removed the fowl to a squawk of protest. Just in time he managed to lower his trousers and perch over one of the holes . . .

Arthur was wallowing in the ecstasy of blissful relief for a minute or two afterwards, in no rush to move lest another bout of the vile stomach ache assail him, when the door opened. A woman about the same age as his mother entered.

'Mornin'.'

'Morning,' Arthur replied, more than a little taken aback.

'That's my side . . .'

'Oh . . . I beg your pardon.' With hands clutched embarrassed in front of him, he shifted across to the next hole and made himself comfortable again.

The woman proceeded to hitch up her skirt and positioned herself over the other hole. 'The sky's a bit frowsy this mornin', ai' it? 'Tis to be hoped we have ne'er a shower.'

' 'Tis to be hoped,' Arthur agreed tentatively, hearing the unmistakable trickle of spent water into the soil below them. He was uncertain whether to proceed with the conversation and prolong their encounter, or to say nothing more in the hope of curtailing it. Never in his life had he shared a moment like this with a complete stranger, nor anybody familiar either for that matter. He wanted to get off his seat and scarper, and allow the woman her privacy, but there was the hygiene aspect of his sojourn that had yet to be attended to. He glanced around him in the dimness looking for squares of paper.

Happily, he was released from his dilemma when the woman stood up and allowed her skirts to fall back.

'I'm mekkin' a cup o' tay. Dun yer want e'er un? I'll bring thee one out if yo've a mind.'

'No, thank you,' Arthur replied. 'That's very kind. But I'm just on my way. I just popped in for a quick one.'

'Suit yerself then, my son. Ta-ra.'

★   ★   ★

19

Arthur lived with his father, whom he hated, and his mother whom he felt sorry for, in a lane called Lower Delph, commonly referred to as The Delph, in Brierley Hill. His older brother Talbot had fled the nest to feather his own when he was married some five years earlier to a fine girl rejoicing in the name Magnolia. The family business had been founded by his father years ago and was conducted from the workshop, yard and stables which adjoined the house. Arthur was a man of many interests, but his big love was cricket.

The only cricket team he had access to play for was the one loosely attached to the old red brick church of St Michael, which he regularly attended on Sundays. The solemnity of Anglican worship and the richness of religious language appealed to his serious side. St Michael's cricket team played their home matches on a decently maintained area of flat ground in Silver End, adjacent to the railway line. Now Arthur was afraid that the acute bout of diarrhoea he'd suffered that very morning might manifest itself again on the cricket field, to his ultimate embarrassment.

'I've cut you some bread to go with this, my lad,' his mother, Dinah, said as she placed a bowl of groaty pudding and hefty chunks of a loaf before him at the scullery table. 'It'll help bung yer up.'

' 'Tis to be hoped,' Arthur said miserably, repeating the supplication he'd made perched on the seat of the Pensnett privy. He wore an exaggerated look of pain on his face to elicit his mother's sympathy.

'Your father's feeling none too well either.' She returned to the mug of beer she'd neglected while serving Arthur's dinner and took a gulp.

Arthur dipped a lump of bread into the stew-like morass. 'But I bet he ain't got the diarrhee, has he? You can't imagine what it's like being took short in a graveyard with no privy for miles.'

'There's ne'er a privy at the cricket pitch neither, but that ain't going to stop you playing cricket there this afternoon by the looks of it,' Dinah remarked astutely. ' 'Tis to be hoped as you'm well enough to knock a few runs without shitting yourself.'

' 'Tis to be hoped,' Arthur said again and grinned, thankful that his family were not so high-faluting that they could not discuss such delicate matters in plain English at the scullery table. 'I'm nursing meself so as I *can* play cricket this afternoon.'

'I wish I'd got the time to nurse meself,' Dinah said, and took another swig of beer. 'I'm certain sure as I've sprained me wrist humping buckets of coal up from the damn cellar.'

Arthur contemplated that it did not prevent her from lifting a mug of beer, but made no comment. 'I'd have fetched the coal up for you,' he said instead, and winced as if there were another twinge of pain in his gut. 'You know I would.'

'Never mind, you weren't here.'

'It's just a pity Father's too miserable to spend money employing a maid. You could have sent the maid to the cellar for coal.'

'A maid? He'll never employ a maid. He's too mean.'

'That's what I just said.'

Arthur finished his dinner, fetched his bat from the cupboard under the stairs and walked steadily and circumspectly to the cricket field, looking forward to the game against Stourbridge Cricket Club with a mixture of eagerness and anxiety.

★ ★ ★

St Michael's team lost the match. Arthur was the sixth man to bat, surviving the remaining batsmen who came after him. His team needed fifty-five runs to win and Arthur felt it was his responsibility to try and get those runs. But he experienced that dreaded loose feeling in his bowels again and had no option but to get himself run out when they still needed forty-eight, ending the team's innings. It turned out to be a false alarm, to Arthur's sincere regret at having thrown the match.

'I couldn't run,' he lamented to Joey Eccleston, with whom he had been batting at the end. They walked back together to the tent that was always erected on match days, to a ripple of applause from the attendant wives and sweethearts. 'I had the diarrhee this morning and I was afeared to shake me guts up too much for fear it come on again.'

'Well, we tried, Arthur,' Joey said philosophically and patted his colleague on the back. 'You especially. But we were no match for Stourbridge today. Next year, maybe. There's always next year. Next year we'll give 'em a thrashing . . . Coming for a drink after?'

'No, I'm due an early night, Joe. I promised my mother. My guts are still all of a quiver. I got to get myself better for work on Monday. The old man's already queer 'cause I didn't finish my job off this morning. Maybe I'll have a spot or two of laudanum to go to bed with.'

'It won't hurt you to come for a drink first. A drop of brandy or whisky would settle your stomach. You don't have to stop out late. It's been the last match of the season today. We'll all be going. You can't not come as well.'

They reached the tent and Arthur pulled off his old and worn batting gloves. 'I suppose it'll be regarded as bad form if I don't go, eh, Joey?'

'Sure to be. Anyway, you don't want to be seen as some stick-in-the-mud, or that you're mollycoddled.'

Arthur grinned matily. 'Me mollycoddled? That'll be the day.'

'That's settled then.'

'So where are we going for a drink?'

'We've settled on the Whimsey.'

★ ★ ★

22

The gentlemen of the church cricket team arrived at the Whimsey about eight o'clock, as the last embers of sunset were finally extinguished. Those who were blessed with wives or lady friends allowed them to attend and they occupied a room they called the parlour and chattered animatedly with each other, while the men stood in three groups in the taproom and got on with the serious business of drinking and analysing their defeat.

The Whimsey had opened for business in 1815, situated a couple of hundred yards below St Michael's church on the busy turnpike road where it was called Church Street. By the time Benjamin Elwell took it over in 1840 it was a well-established concern. Being a Saturday night the Whimsey was busy, and would get even busier. Already, the taproom was hazy with a blue mist of tobacco smoke from the men's clay pipes, and noisy from the voices of folk trying to be heard over the chatter of their neighbours.

'Pity you and Joey Eccleston couldn't keep up your innings a bit longer, Arthur,' James Paskin the team captain commented.

'I'm sorry, James,' Arthur answered guiltily, and took a quick slurp of his beer to avoid James's eyes. 'I was telling Joey – I had a bad bout of the diarrhee this morning and I was afeared of churning me guts up again on the cricket pitch, so I couldn't run very well. I didn't fancy being took short between the wickets.'

'Good Lord, I didn't realise,' James said with concern. 'In that case it was a valiant effort. Do you feel all right now?'

'Still a bit queer, to tell the truth.'

'Well, they beat us fair and square, Arthur. I didn't have a very good innings myself, nor did old Dingwell Tromans.'

'We'll do better next season,' Arthur said, although such optimism was normally alien to him.

Two youths at a table nearby had pulled the wings off two

23

bluebottles and were betting which would fall off the edge of the table first. Arthur turned his back on such brutal triviality and gazed around the room pretending not to notice, determined not to give the impression that he condoned their puerility.

'We might not have Dingwell Tromans next season,' James Paskin was saying. 'There's talk of him emigrating to America. D'you think you could take on the job of wicket-keeper, Arthur?'

At that moment, a girl with dark hair, slender and wearing a white apron, was slowly moving in his direction as she collected used tankards and crocks from the tables. She was not excessively pretty but, for Arthur, there was something powerfully alluring about her classic good looks and reserved demeanour. She possessed the most appealing, friendly smile, but also a look of shyness that struck a distinctly harmonic chord within Arthur, a sort of instant empathy. He watched her, fascinated, waiting to see her face again as she leaned forward to pick up more tankards. Then, just before she reached him, she turned and made her way back towards the counter, swivelling her body tantalisingly to avoid bumping into customers.

'Sorry, James, what was you saying?'

'About you having a go at wicket-keeping next season.'

'Oh . . . I wouldn't mind giving it a try . . . I've done a bit of wicket-keeping in the past, but I wouldn't say I was as good as Dingwell. But with a bit of practice, you never know . . .'

Suddenly Arthur was aware of a commotion behind him. Two dogs, one large, old and lethargic, the other a small, young and animated terrier, were snarling at each other under a table. The owner of the small dog lurched forward to grab it and knocked over his table in the process, sending several tankards of ale flying. They wetted not only the flagged floor but poor Arthur's good pair of trousers, and the coat of one other man. At once the indignation of the man, who was unknown to Arthur, was high, but mostly, it seemed, at losing his beer. Arthur, however, was largely unperturbed, realising it was merely an accident.

'I'll get thee another, Enoch, as soon as I'n gi'd me blasted dog a kick,' the offender said to his peeved acquaintance, righting the table. He went outside, taking his dog with him, its little legs dangling as he held it by the scruff of its neck.

The owner of the other dog managed to pacify his more docile animal, allowing it to lap beer from his tankard, and it resumed lying quietly at his feet, in a rapture of mild intoxication. Ben Elwell, who disliked such disruptive outbursts in his public house, was over in a flash to investigate, but it had already flared up and died. He saw the pool of beer frothing on the floor and called for a mop and bucket, and the slender girl with the dark hair and the white apron re-appeared to clean it up.

'Here, I'n got beer all down me coot,' the man named Enoch told the girl. 'Hast got summat to rub me down with afore it soaks through to me ganzy?'

'I'll bring you a cloth when I've mopped this up, Mr Billingham,' the girl answered apologetically. 'I'll only be a minute.'

As she cleaned, the owner of the offending terrier returned. 'I swear, I'll drown the little bastard in the cut if he plays up again,' he muttered, and asked whose beer he'd knocked over. He duly went to the bar to make reparations.

'Fun and games, eh?' James Paskin remarked to Arthur.

'That beer went all over my trousers, you know, James. I'm soaked through.'

'Ask the girl for a cloth.'

'Think I should?'

'Course.'

'I could catch a chill with wet trousers.'

'It ain't worth taking the risk, Arthur. Quick, before she goes.'

Arthur hesitated but, just as the girl was about to go, he plucked up his courage and tapped her on the shoulder. 'Excuse me, miss . . .' She turned her head and he saw by the light of the oil lamp hanging overhead that her face was made beautiful by wide eyes which were the most delicate shade of blue, full of lights and expressions. 'I . . . I got soaked in beer as well . . . Would you mind bringing a cloth for me?'

Had it been any of the regulars she would have taken the request with a pinch of salt, knowing it was an attempt at flirting, to get *her* to wipe their trousers. But there was something in the earnest look of this man that made her realise he was not preoccupied with such triteness. So she nodded and smiled with decorous reserve.

'I haven't seen her before,' Arthur said. 'She's quite comely.'

'Fancy her, do you?'

Arthur grinned self-consciously. 'Like I say, she's quite comely. She seems to have a pleasant way with her. Don't you think so, James? But I expect a wench like that is spoken for already. Is it the landlord's daughter, do you know?'

'Not that I'm aware of. I've not seen her in here before. Not that I'm stuck in here every night of the week, you understand.'

The girl returned and handed a towel to Enoch Billingham, apologising again for his being drenched. Then she turned to Arthur . . .

'You wanted a towel as well, sir?'

'Thank you . . .'

'Shall I hold your beer while you wipe your trousers?' she asked pleasantly.

'Thank you . . .' He began swabbing the spreading wet patch on his trouser leg, feeling suddenly hot. Just as suddenly he felt his bowels turn to water again and knew that he must

26

make another rapid exit. With intense agony he held himself, noticing at the same time that at least the girl was not wearing a wedding ring.

'What's your name?' he managed to ask. 'I ain't seen you in here before?'

'Lucy,' she said.

'You live local?'

'Bull Street.'

'Funny I've never seen you before.' Arthur was trying manfully to maintain a look of normality.

'Why, where do you live?' Lucy asked pleasantly.

'The Delph.'

'Fancy. Just up the road.'

Arthur was effecting some severe internal abdominal contortions coupled with heroic buttock clenching, in an effort to maintain not only his composure, but his self respect and his eternal reputation as well. He was desperate to keep the girl talking as long as he could, to try and find out more about her, but he was even more desperate to win the battle against his wayward bowels. It was a battle he was losing ignominiously, however, for without doubt he had to go.

'Yes, just up the road . . . You'll have to excuse me, Lucy . . .' He turned and fled.

'What's up with him?' Lucy enquired of James.

'Something he ate, I think,' James replied, being as discreet as he knew how. 'He's had a problem all day, I believe.'

Lucy chuckled. 'Poor chap. Well, he'll find nowhere to relieve himself that way.'

★　★　★

3

Sunday was another lovely day for mid September, a day when women kept open their front doors and sat on their front steps, gossiping with like-minded neighbours. They peeled potatoes and shelled peas which they would have with a morsel of meat for their dinners when their menfolk staggered back from the beer houses. Lucy strolled to the water pump carrying a pail. Bobby the sheepdog ambled wearily but proprietorially beside her, ignoring other animals that pointed their snouts at him and sniffed. Lucy tarried a minute or two with most of the women, pleased to comment on what beautiful weather they were blessed with, but said nothing of the dismal slag heaps and factory yards that rendered the immediate landscape squalid and colourless.

'It's a pity there ain't no fine houses with well-tended gardens in this part of Silver End,' she commented to one woman known as Mother Cope, who was smoking a clay pipe as she tearfully skinned onions in her lap. ''Cause the flowers, specially the roses, will still be in full bloom, and a sight to behold on a day like this.'

'If you want to see flowers, my wench,' Mother Cope replied, withdrawing her pipe from between her toothless gums, 'I daresay as there's a bunch or two in the churchyard you could gaze at, on the graves o' the well-to-do.'

Lucy returned to the house with her pail full of water and poured some into a bowl to give to Bobby, before using more to boil vegetables. At about three o'clock her father returned hungry from the Whimsey and the three sat down to their dinner.

'I reckon Ben Elwell could've done with your help again this morning, wench,' Haden remarked to his daughter.

'I've got too much to do here helping Mother of a Sunday,' Lucy answered. 'But he's asked me to work tonight.'

'Ar, well, there'll be some beer shifted tonight an' all, if the weather stops like this. Folk like to tek their beer into the fresh air and watch the world go by.'

'I only wish they'd bring back their beer mugs when they've done, instead of leaving them lying around for me to collect.'

'I reckon you've took to this public house working a treat, our Lucy,' Haden said with a fatherly grin. 'Her's took to this public house working, you know, Hannah. Who'd have thought it, eh?'

'Just as long as she keeps away from all them rough toe rags,' Hannah replied.

'Oh, they ain't all rough, Mother. There's a lot of decent, respectable men that come in for a drink. One or two even buy me a drink now and again.'

'As long as nobody expects any favours in return.'

She felt like saying that if there was somebody she liked the look of she might be tempted, but kept it to herself. 'D'you know anybody who lives down the Delph, Father?'

'The Delph? Why?'

'I just wondered. Somebody came in last night who I'd never seen before in me life, and he said he only lived down the Delph. You'd think you'd know everybody who lived close by. That's all. This chap was with a crowd that played cricket for the church, so Mrs Elwell said.'

'Lord knows who that might be. Fancy him, do yer?' Haden winked at Hannah.

'Not particularly,' Lucy protested. 'I only said it 'cause I think it's weird not ever knowing somebody, even by sight, who lives so close to us.'

★ ★ ★

As Sunday progressed Arthur Goodrich's self-willed bowels seemed to settle down. He attended matins at St Michael's during the morning with his mother, and they circumspectly sat in a pew at the back, lest he should have to dart out during the service. Mercifully, he was untroubled by any such need.

His brother Talbot came for tea with Magnolia and their small son Albert. The extended family, Jeremiah included, once more crossed the threshold of St Michael's for evensong. It was dark but warm when they finally emerged into the open air, and bats flitted in whispers between the tree tops overhead. Dinah and Jeremiah stopped to chat with some of the other parishioners by the light of a solitary gaslamp that hung over the main door, while the vicar, the Reverend Ephraim Wheeler, bid everybody a good evening with a shake of the hand and a benign smile, and looked forward to seeing them again next Sunday.

'I'm going for a drink afore we go home,' Talbot declared to Magnolia who was holding young Albert's hand as the lad stood beside her. 'I'll see you back at Mother's. Are you coming with me, our Arthur?'

'I think I got the piles,' Arthur answered ruefully. 'Me backside's that sore.'

Talbot rolled his eyes. 'It's because of the squits, Arthur. What ailments shall you be sporting tomorrow, I wonder?'

'It's your liver,' Magnolia stated sagely to her brother-in-law. 'It's what comes of eating kickshaws and other such muck. See as your mother gives you a dose of dandelion tea or summat. Or soda and nitre's good for you every now and again. That'll sort yer. It'll help to keep your system cool.'

'Me system's already cool,' Arthur replied morosely. 'That's the trouble. It's working in draughty graveyards what

30

does it. How can you keep in good humours if you'm always cutting and blacking letters in draughty graveyards, sitting on cold graves? I wonder I don't get pneumonia in me backside.'

'You can't get pneumonia in your backside,' Magnolia asserted.

'I can in mine. I'm forever catching a chill.'

'Is that what I can hear wheezing sometimes?' Talbot said with a grin.

'Oh, it's all right for you to mock, Talbot, stuck in a warm workshop.'

'Somebody has to do the work in graveyards, amending and adding inscriptions and what not,' Talbot replied. 'Anyway, it's skilled work.'

'You wouldn't know it from the wages. Anyway, I don't see you doing it very often. You're always in the workshop.'

'Designing and carving gravestones, me, polishing slate and marble . . .'

'It's always me what has to go to these terrible places.' He gestured with his hand to encompass in a frustrated sweep the very graveyard that now surrounded them.

'Count your blessings, our Arthur. At least you ain't got Father around you when you're out and about. But if you're dissatisfied, have a word with the old sod. Maybe he'll smile benignly upon you and start an apprentice who can do all them jobs.'

'Him? Smile? Benignly?' Arthur scoffed. 'Anyway, apprentices take time to learn. Years. And they cost money. That miserable old bugger won't spend any money, he's too tight-fisted. No, I ain't very pleased, Talbot.'

'Well, I'm off for a drink. It's up to you whether you come or not. But a drink might sweeten you up a bit.'

Then Arthur remembered the girl with the blue eyes who said her name was Lucy, and he suddenly brightened up.

'Why don't we go to the Whimsey? I went there last night with the lads from the cricket team. They keep a good drop o' beer. And it's on the way home.'

'All right, we'll go to the Whimsey. I'll ask Father if he wants to come.'

'No, leave him be,' Arthur said, not relishing the prospect of his father's company. 'Let him go home. I don't want him around me.'

'But you can ask him about keeping you away from church-yards.'

'It won't make any odds.'

Men were standing outside the Whimsey in groups, some leaning against the bay windows either side of the door, while some were squatting on the kerb. All were drinking, taking advantage of the evening warmth of an unexpected Indian summer.

'Shall we drink outside?' Talbot enquired.

'I'd rather go inside, in the saloon bar,' Arthur said decisively, driven by the possibility of seeing this Lucy again. 'I'll get the beer.'

He made his way through the small but crowded taproom towards the counter and waited his turn to be served. An older woman, supposedly the landlord's wife, was supping from a crock and serving drinks alongside Lucy. He watched them, trying to decide which one would get to him first, trying to catch Lucy's eye. When she saw him she smiled with reserve, and asked to serve him, making his insides flutter ominously once more.

'Oh, it's you,' she said, pleasantly surprised. 'You took off a bit quick last night. Are you all right now?'

Arthur grinned sheepishly. 'A lot better, thanks.' He was tempted to mention his suspected piles; it might elicit some sympathy. But he didn't know this girl well enough, and piles were a bit personal and private to talk about when you didn't

32

know somebody well . . . and might easily put them off. 'Three pints please, Lucy.'

'Fancy you remembering my name,' she said amenably, grabbing three tankards. She began to fill them from a barrel behind her. 'Are your trousers dry now?' she asked over her shoulder.

'Yes, thanks.'

'That's good,' she said, then placed the beers on the counter.

He handed her a shilling. 'Oh, and have a drink yourself.'

'That's decent of you. Thank you.' She handed him his change and he relished the brief moment when the tips of her slender fingers brushed his palm. 'Are you here with your mates again?'

'No, my brother and my father this time,' he replied, passing two foaming tankards to Talbot. 'We've just come from church. D'you go to church, Lucy?'

'Me? Not since my sister got wed at the Baptist chapel. No, I haven't got time for church. My mother goes regular though. To the Baptist chapel . . .' She turned to her next customer and began serving him.

But Arthur remained where he was, hoping to be blessed with some more conversation with this girl who appealed so much.

'Is that your brother?' she asked, evidently content to continue talking to him while he tarried, to his delighted surprise.

'Yes. His name's Talbot. And that's my father with him.'

'I've seen *them* about. Funny as I hadn't seen you till last night. Then I see you two nights running.'

'I know,' Arthur replied with a grin, his confidence growing, for this girl seemed easy to talk to, and not like the others. 'It's a funny coincidence, don't you think?'

She handed her latest customer his beer and took his money, still looking at Arthur. 'I bet my dad knows yours.'

33

'Oh? How's that, then?'

'He says he knows most folk round here. What's your name?'

'Arthur Goodrich. I'm a stonemason. The old man's Jeremiah. So who's your father?'

'Haden Piddock. He works at the Earl's. He'll be here soon. He generally comes for his beer about this time.'

'Maybe I'll recognise him. Does he go to church or chapel?'

The notion evidently amused her, for she laughed. 'My father? This place is *his* church . . . and his chapel.'

Arthur felt a tap on his shoulder. It was Talbot. 'Is she the reason you wanted to come here for a drink? The doxy?'

Arthur grinned sheepishly. 'She seems a decent wench.'

'Her's got long eyelashes, I'll grant yer,' Jeremiah remarked scornfully. 'But I'll tell yer this . . . As long as her can work, cook and bear babbies, the length of her eyelashes is of no consequence. Anyroad, her's Haden Piddock's youngest, unless I'm very much mistook.'

Arthur stepped back from the counter. 'You know Haden Piddock?'

'Oh, I know him all right.' Arthur noticed with awful disappointment the scorn in his father's tone.

'Well, I don't know Haden Piddock myself, Father, but his daughter seems a fine young woman.' He slurped his beer and avoided his father's look of disdain. 'And I ain't getting mixed up in some ancient feud you might have had with him.'

'Got your eye on her, have yer?'

'I might have. What's it matter to you?'

'Well, if you tek my advice you'll keep well clear of anything to do with Haden Piddock.'

'I was telling Father how you fancy a change from working in graveyards all the time, Arthur,' Talbot said, discreetly switching the topic.

'And I don't know what you expect me to do about it,'

Jeremiah said testily. 'Somebody has to do the stones in churchyards. We'd be better off employing somebody to work the forge and sharpen chisels. A handyman. But even a handyman will cost money and bring nothing in return.'

Arthur glanced back at Lucy, sorry that he had been dragged away from her, even more sorry that his father evidently didn't think much of hers.

'Did you hear what I said, Arthur?'

'I did, Father,' he said, turning his attention back to the old man. 'But I'd rather you employed another stonemason. It's bad enough in the summer with all the rain we get, but in the winter I might as well be a snowman. I'd rather work in the workshop. If you started another stonemason, I could.'

'And where am I gunna get another skilled stonemason in Brierley Hill?'

'Advertise,' Arthur suggested logically. 'There's bound to be somebody in Stourbridge or Dudley. Or even Kingswinford. But you'd have to pay him more than you pay me.'

'I got no sympathy with yer,' Jeremiah claimed. 'Respect is better than remuneration.'

'Well, I don't think so. Give me remuneration any day of the week. The respect will follow.'

'Listen to yer. Talking damned rubbish. We've all had to work in churchyards at some time, and it's done we no harm.' He coughed violently as if to disprove his own theory. 'And it'll do you none neither. You'll have to grin and bear it, our Arthur.'

Jeremiah turned to speak with another man he knew and his two sons drained their tankards.

'I hate him,' Arthur said venomously. 'Cantankerous old bugger.'

'Let's have another drink,' Talbot suggested. 'It's my turn.'

'Give me the money and I'll get 'em. I want another word with that Lucy Piddock.'

35

Talbot gave him a knowing look. 'You heard what Father said.'

'Sod him. I got no beef against this Haden Piddock, and I certainly ain't got no beef against his daughter. So why should I be obliged to uphold his petty prejudices? He evidently isn't about to do anything to help me. No, Talbot, I see a fine wench there, and if she's free of any attachment I might just try my luck.'

Talbot smiled matily and winked. 'Go on then, our Arthur, and I hope she's worth it.'

So Arthur approached the counter again. As soon as she was free, Lucy stood before him and looked into his eyes with a friendly smile.

'Same again?'

'Please, Lucy.' He leaned towards her. 'Can I ask you something?'

'Go on.'

'Are you courting or anything?' His heart was in his mouth, eager for her reply and yet dreading it.

Lucy smiled coyly and even by the dim lights of the oil lamps he perceived her blushing. 'No, I'm not a-courting anybody.'

'In that case, would you like to come out with me some-time?'

'If you like.'

Arthur felt a boyish gush of excitement, a whole gallon of joy, surge through him. 'Honest?'

'I just said so, didn't I?'

'When? What night don't you work in here?'

'Tomorrow?'

'Tomorrow then. About eight o'clock on the corner of Church Street and the Delph?

'Can we say half past seven? It'll be dark by eight and my mother won't want me to go off in the dark on me own, specially round here.'

He smiled. 'All right. Half past seven . . . Listen, I could walk you back tonight if you want.'

'No, it's all right. Me dad'll walk me back. He'll be here soon. He would've been here sooner but he fell asleep after his dinner and I reckon he hasn't woke up yet.'

'If he don't come, just give me the nod, eh?' Arthur responded gallantly.

★ ★ ★

A consignment of port decanters had been carefully packed with straw and laid in a wooden crate, which Lucy Piddock and her workmate Eliza Gallimore had been filling during Monday afternoon. Now, at last, it was time to go home. Lucy stood erect and placed her hands in the small of her back. She stretched to counter the effects of so much bending, then unfastened the pinafore she wore to protect her skirt and blouse which had been clean on that morning. In the high rafters of the glassworks' packing room two sparrows were squawking as they flitted from beam to beam in their squabble over a strip of bacon rind that one had picked up in the dusty yard outside.

The foreman, Job Grinsell, appeared. Job was a middle-aged man with a fatherly regard for Lucy.

'I see as you've finished that crate what's bound for Philadelphia,' he commented and peered inside it, cursorily checking it for any loose items.

'It's all counted and packed tight,' Eliza affirmed. 'I bet you'm dying to nail the top on for us, eh, Job? Lucy and me am going home now, ain't we Lucy? We've done our stint.'

Lucy picked up her cotton shawl from the hook on the whitewashed wall where she kept it and slung it loosely about her shoulders, ready to leave.

'Just steady the lid for me then, one of yer,' Job requested, 'and I'll do it for thee.'

'Sod off. It's past our knocking-off time. And Lucy ain't got time to hang about. She's got to pretty herself up. She's seeing a fresh chap tonight, ain't yer, Lucy?'

Lucy nodded.

Job looked at her intently. 'Hey, well, mind what yo'm up to.'

'You sound like my father,' Lucy said, and compliantly held the wooden lid in place while Job took a handful of nails and a hammer and fixed it onto the crate.

'I got daughters o' me own, my wench. I know what a worry daughters am.'

'Well, you need have no fears about me, nor the chap I'm a-meeting.'

Job guffawed derisively. 'And if I believed that I'd believe anything. I tell yer – watch what you'm up to. Just watch his hands.'

'Yes, sir,' she answered with a mock curtsey.

The weather that early evening was a delight. The sun shone with a rich yellow warmth as Lucy stepped into it from the dankness of the packing room and headed for home. She always walked to and from the factory by way of the railway line; it was much quicker than going the semi-circular route up North Street and down Church Street.

She pondered this Arthur Goodrich. They had spoken no more than a couple of dozen words to each other and she felt no particular excitement at the prospect of meeting him later. She quite didn't know what to make of him. The only reason she'd agreed to meet him was because it would actually be a bit of a novelty and better, she was certain, than being stuck in the house with her mother.

She wondered what she could possibly have said to Arthur that prompted him to ask her out. If she had set his heart aflame she had done it unwittingly, but he'd not had the same effect on her – and she doubted that he ever would. Lucy wanted somebody to sweep her off her feet. She needed

38

somebody she could fall hopelessly in love with, and Arthur was not the man. Oh, he seemed decent enough and even polite, but distinctly lacking in sparkle. She was certain she would have no competition from any other girl. Indeed, she would never be interested enough in him to worry about competition, he was so obviously anything but a ladies' man. Anyhow, she was sure he would treat her with respect, for he gave her the impression that he was a gentle person.

A train was coming up the line, huffing and volleying clouds of white steam and black smoke. Lucy stopped and stood still until it had passed, as close to the edge of the cutting as she could get. She fixed her eyes on the guards' van, just in case the man she'd taken a shine to the other day on the journey back from Dudley was working on it. But he was not, and she sighed. She would love to see him again, but it was as if he'd disappeared off the face of the earth. Maybe he was just a figment of her imagination after all. Maybe she'd merely dreamed about him and he didn't actually exist. As she continued walking she was beginning to wonder.

Her thoughts reverted to this insipid character Arthur and what reason she should give her mother and father for wanting to go out. Where would he take her? What should she do if he wanted to kiss her?

At last she reached the bridge over the railway at Bull Street. She clambered up the steep embankment and emerged onto the street, where she met Miriam Watson returning home from the firebrick works. They stopped to chat.

'I'm seeing somebody tonight, Miriam,' Lucy said, but there was no light of eager anticipation in her eyes. 'Somebody who came in the Whimsey on Saturday and Sunday night.'

Miriam grinned her approval. 'At last a chap. And is he handsome?'

Lucy shrugged. 'Not particularly, but he's better than nothing. He'll do till somebody handsome comes along.'

'Always supposing he wants to see you again after tonight, eh, Luce? You shouldn't take things for granted.'

'That's true.' She shrugged. 'Not with my luck. Maybe I won't suit him anyway.'

'Who is he? What's he do for a living?'

'He's a stonemason, named Arthur Goodrich. Me father says his family are well-to-do, but they're not rich or anything. Just regular churchgoers.'

'Oh, Lord!' Miriam rolled her eyes. 'You don't want anybody spouting religion at yer, Luce. If he starts that I should give him the elbow quick. He ain't a Methodist, is he?'

'No, church. He goes to St Michael's.'

'And what's he look like, this chap?'

'A bit ordinary. He seems to have some quaint ways about him as well, what I've seen of him so far. But he seems decent enough. He was wearing a nice clean collar on his shirt. At least he isn't rough.'

'Well, you don't have to stick with him if you ain't that fussed. But you did say as you'd go out with the first chap what asked you, even if he was the ugliest sod on earth, you said. Remember?'

Lucy laughed. 'I know I did, but he ain't that bad, thank God. At least I won't be ashamed if somebody sees me with him. It's just that I don't think it'll amount to much. I just don't fancy him.'

'Well, next time I see yer, don't forget to tell me how you got on, eh?'

'I won't. Anyway, I'd better go. Me belly's rumbling for want of something to eat.'

★　★　★

4

Arthur was particular about punctuality, but then he had a reliable watch in his fob pocket to assist him. Lucy, however, possessed no such device, and she was ten minutes late. Dusk was upon Brierley Hill and the sun, about to dip below the distant Shropshire hills, had daubed the western sky with intermingling hues of red, purple and gold that reflected in Lucy's eyes, setting them aflame. Arthur was moved by the effect. The air was mild, and the musky, smutsy smell of industry encompassed them, but was barely noticed.

'Have you been waiting long?' she asked, an apology in her tone.

'Only a minute or two,' he replied with easy forgiveness. He smiled, happy and relieved that she had turned up at all, for he had set much store by this tryst.

'Where are you taking me?'

'Well . . . Nowhere in particular, Lucy . . . I thought we might just go for a stroll. It's such a grand night for a stroll.'

'If you like,' she agreed pleasantly. 'Which way shall we go?'

'Which way d'you fancy?'

She shrugged. It was hardly a decision worth making and not one she'd been expecting to make herself. 'Oh, you decide.'

'Downhill, eh? Towards Audnam and the fields. We'll see what's left of the sunset as we go.' So they turned and set off in a tentative stroll.

A horse and buggy drove up towards Brierley Hill on the other side of the road, its wheels rattling over the uneven surface. The driver called a greeting to the lamp-lighter walking in the opposite direction, whose lantern was swinging from the ladder balanced across his shoulder. For the first few long moments neither Lucy nor Arthur could think of a word to say. The pause seemed ominous. Both realised it simultaneously and their eyes met with self-conscious, half-apologetic smiles.

'What have you been doing today?' Lucy asked, aware that maybe she ought to set some conversation in train.

'I had to go to a churchyard in Pensnett and finish an inscription to a headstone,' Arthur replied, thankful that Lucy had found something to say, for he was inexplicably tongue-tied. 'I should've done it Saturday but I couldn't.'

'Oh? Why was that?'

' 'Cause I had the diarrhee bad. I was taken short.'

She burst out laughing.

'It's not that funny,' he said, disappointed that she should appear to mock him so early on. 'Haven't you ever had the diarrhee?'

'Even if I have I'm not about to tell you. But it isn't the fact that you had the diarrhee I'm laughing at. I know you can't help that. It's just that . . .'

'What?'

'Well, the first time I saw you on Saturday night you had to run off afore you'd finished drying spilt beer off your trousers. I thought then as you'd been took short, and when I asked your mate what was the matter with you he said as how it was something you'd ate.'

He laughed with her, realising how ridiculous he must have seemed. 'So you guessed?'

'It doesn't take a genius to fathom it out. I hope you've got over it now.'

'Yes, thank the merciful Lord. I don't want another bout like that in a hurry, I can tell you. I've had a bit of toothache today, though.'

'Toothache? Maybe you'll have to have it pulled.'

'I'm hoping as it'll go away of its own accord. I don't fancy having it pulled. It's one of them big teeth at the back. They can be murder to pull out, they reckon.'

'Maybe it's just neuralgia,' she suggested.

They were approaching the canal bridge where Wheeley's Glass House stood with its huge brick cone that shielded from view the furnaces belonging to the same company. Over the bridge, on the other side of the highway was Smith's Pottery.

'So tell me what it is you have to do to describe a headstone,' Lucy said, not wishing to discuss Arthur's unexciting ailments for fear there were more, but veering obliviously onto a subject which had the same potential to assign her to woolgathering.

'*Inscribe*, Lucy, not describe.' Her error amused him and he smiled. 'I have to cut the letters into the stone or slate.'

'So you have to be able to read and write well?'

'Oh, yes. But I went to school, see? Can you read, Lucy?'

'Oh, yes, some. My father used to spend two shillings a week to send me to school when I was little. They taught me my letters. I can't read big words easy, though. But I can count, and do sums. I'm hopeless at spelling though. Hopeless.'

'Ah well, it isn't so important for a woman to be able to read and write, is it?' he said consolingly. 'Except maybe to write down a list of stuff you need to buy for the house.'

'I suppose not. All the same, it would be useful to be able to do it well.'

'Got any brothers or sisters, Lucy?'

'I got a sister – Jane – a bit older than me. She married

a chap called Moses Cartwright. He was a soldier in the Crimea, but they sent him home 'cause he got wounded. He'd been stuck in some makeshift hospital for weeks at the front.'

'No brothers then?'

'Yes, four brothers. All wed. One of them lives in Canada, so we don't see him any more. We don't see the others very often either . . . Come to think of it, they might as well all live in Canada . . . And you've got a brother, haven't you, Arthur? Any sisters?'

'Just one brother . . . He's wed to Magnolia –'

'Magnolia?'

'I know. It's a funny name for a woman.'

Conversation promised to flow naturally at last. They crossed the road at Hawbush Farm and turned into the footpath that led over fields to an area called Buckpool and eventually to Kingswinford parish. But it was getting dark and they would not have been able to see where they were going, so they lingered at a stile. Lucy perched herself on the top bar while Arthur leaned against it. By this time they were easier in each other's company, to Lucy's relief and surprise, for she found she was enjoying herself and actually liking Arthur.

Arthur complained how he and his father were always at cross-purposes, how he was expected to do the more menial tasks of stonemasonry and not the more glamorous ones of designing and building graves. It was obvious to her how it irked him.

'So why don't you leave home and find lodgings? Then you'd be out of his way.'

'I might. If I left home I'd have to leave the business as well, and that would show him good and proper.'

'What about your mother? Do you get on with her?'

'Oh, she's all right. It's just me father I can't stand. I feel sorry for her having to put up with him.'

'Is he that bad, Arthur?'

'He's a miserable old devil. It always seems to me that he's tried to do without love in his life, and that's what makes him so vile. It's almost as if he's made a little garden for himself, but if the family's love is sunshine he's certainly shaded himself from it. And he's planted this garden with bitter herbs, not beautiful flowers, yet he believes it's the whole world – that the whole world is like that. He's pig ignorant, Lucy. He never says "That's a good job you've done there, our Arthur", or "I'll pay you a bit extra for doing that, 'cause you was late getting back". Oh, not him. He's too tight. He wouldn't give you the drippings off his nose.'

'I don't think I'd want the drippings off his nose,' Lucy asserted, which made Arthur laugh. 'You make him sound vile.'

'He is vile.'

'Have you ever courted anybody before, Arthur?'

'Once. When I was about twenty. A girl from Brockmoor. There's some pretty girls in Brockmoor. But we split up after about six months.'

'And you never bothered since?'

'I never met anybody I fancied since . . . till I met you the other night.'

Lucy was touched by his sincerity. 'That's a lovely thing to say, Arthur. So what was it about me that took your fancy?'

He shrugged. 'I don't really know . . .'

'There must have been something,' she said, miffed that he could think of nothing.

'What I mean is, you aren't flashy,' he was quick to add, realising he'd unwittingly said the wrong thing. 'You've got such lovely eyes and such long eyelashes, though . . . and a lovely smile to match.'

Immediately Lucy was mollified. 'You think I've got nice eyes? I think they're a funny colour.'

'I've never seen eyes such a lovely colour. You've got a decent figure as well . . . and you have a nice way with you. I took a fancy to you as soon as I saw you.'

'I bet I'm not as pretty as that girl from Brockmoor, though,' she fished, relishing his compliments that boosted her confidence.

'She was only pretty, Lucy. But you're beautiful.'

Lucy's eyes twinkled in the half light. 'That's the nicest thing anybody ever said to me.' She slid off the stile and planted a kiss tenderly on his cheek. 'Thank you.'

In return he put his hand on her shoulder and touched her. It was the first time he had touched her in that way and his emotion was too pure for desire, too respectful for sensuality. 'You kissed me,' he said with astonishment.

'You don't mind, do you?' she replied, returning to her perch.

'Lord, no.'

Another awkward pause developed and Lucy realised that maybe she had been hasty, indecorous in kissing him, a regular churchgoer, when she hardly knew him.

'I'm sorry,' she said, relieving the tension. 'I shouldn't have done that. I bet you think I'm a proper strumpet. I'm not, though, Arthur. Honest I'm not.'

'Oh, I liked it, Lucy. I don't think you're a strumpet at all. You can do it again if you like.'

'I'd better not,' she replied with a laugh that to him sounded like a silver bell tinkling.

The last of the daylight had all but gone and a full moon was already high, sailing through wispy clouds. In the distance they could hear a locomotive puffing tiredly on its arduous journey up the incline towards the Brettell Lane and Round Oak stations.

'Tell me about your father,' Arthur suggested, eager to learn what he could that might give him an inkling as to why his own father evidently didn't admire the man. 'What's he like?'

'He's lovely and I love him,' Lucy answered simply. 'He's kind, he cares for us all. He wouldn't do anybody a bad turn – he'd rather help somebody.'

'What's he do for a living?'

'He's a shingler at the New Level ironworks. D'you know, Arthur, every time it's payday he buys me a little present? It might only be a quarter of cough drops, but he always brings me something.'

'That's being thoughtful,' Arthur agreed, and realised that here was a way he too could enhance his standing with Lucy. 'He sounds the dead opposite of my father . . . What about your mother?'

'Oh, she's a bit fussy. We only live in a little cottage, but it always has to be spick and span. She'd have a fit if she saw a silverfish in our house. Our clothes always have to be spruce as well. She'd have another fit if I went out in something that looked dirty or shabby.'

'Well, every time I've seen you, Lucy, you look nice,' Arthur remarked. 'So she must be a good influence.'

'I just hope I can be like her if I ever get married.'

'I hope, Lucy – if I ever get married – I'll be lucky enough to pick a wife like that.'

Whatever was being implied, however inadvertently, and whatever was being likewise perceived, seemed to put paid to their conversation entirely and they remained unspeaking for long embarrassed seconds, until Lucy thought of something to say to divert them.

'Can you ride a horse, Arthur?'

'After a fashion. It isn't my favourite method of transport though. Awkward, stupid animals, horses. I don't feel comfortable on a horse. Not since I fell off and broke a rib.'

'You didn't!'

'I did.'

'Well, you're a real knight in shining armour and no mis-take,' she laughed, 'falling off your horse.' It was just like him to do that, she thought.

'I'd rather drive our cart and have the nag in front of me. The worst he could do is take fright.'

'You drive a cart?'

'Course I do. It's what we lug our stone and masonry around with.'

'I fancy riding on a cart. I've never ridden on a cart in me life.'

'Honest?'

'Honest.'

'Maybe one of these days I'll take you for a ride.'

'Mmm, I'd like that, Arthur . . . You ain't got a carriage, have you, by any chance?'

'A carriage? God's truth, who d'you think we are? Lords of the manor?'

'I was only wondering. It doesn't matter. A cart will do. As a matter of fact, a cart will do nicely . . . I'm getting off this stile, Arthur. I got pins and needles in my bum . . . Shall we carry on walking?'

'If you like. Let's walk to Stourbridge. It's a light night with the moon as bright as it is.'

So they walked to Stourbridge and back, chattering away, getting to know each other in the process. On the way, Arthur claimed he was parched and they stopped at the Old Crown Inn on Brettell Lane before he returned Lucy home. They stood on the corner of Bull Street, within sight of the Piddocks' cottage, but at a respectful distance.

'I've really enjoyed tonight, Lucy, talking and walking with you,' he said sincerely. 'How about you?' In the scant moon-light he discerned her smile.

'Yes, so have I.'

'Can we meet again then?'

'If you want,' she agreed. 'When?'

'How about tomorrow?'

'I help out at the Whimsey tomorrow.'

'Well, I could come and walk you back after.'

'My dad will walk me back. Let's leave it till a night when I'm not working.'

'When's that?'

'Thursday.'

'That's the night of my bible class.'

'Oh.'

'But I could meet you later.'

'How much later?'

'Just after nine, say.'

'My mother wouldn't let me out that late. She reckons I should be abed by then.'

'What if I call for you?'

'And let you meet my mother?' He saw the look of doubt in her eyes. 'I don't know, Arthur. I haven't told her about you.'

'What then?'

She shrugged. 'I don't know.'

'How about Saturday afternoon? Or Sunday?'

'Saturday afternoon I sometimes go to Dudley with my friend Miriam. I could meet you Sunday afternoon though.'

'It's a long time to wait, Lucy. Nearly a week. I'll have forgot what you look like by Sunday.'

She shrugged again. 'Maybe your toothache will have gone by then.'

'It's gone already,' he said brightly. 'Maybe I'll come to the Whimsey one night when you'm working. Just to say hello.'

She shrugged. 'It's up to you.'

'You don't sound very bothered,' he suggested.

'I just don't see the point. I won't be able to walk home with you. Not with my father there.'

'But I'll see you Sunday at any rate, Lucy. Does three o'clock suit?'

'Yes. And thanks for asking me out, Arthur.'

She sounded sincere, he thought, and was encouraged. 'It's been my pleasure . . .' He grinned like a schoolboy. 'And thank you for the kiss earlier. I shan't be able to sleep for thinking about it.' He turned and went on his way, euphoric.

★ ★ ★

Arthur could not help himself. So taken was he with Lucy Piddock that he could not sleep properly at night for thinking about her. He fought the urge, but found it impossible to keep away from the Whimsey any longer, where he knew she would be. He would have gone on the Tuesday, the evening after their first tryst, but had the sense to realise that he might appear too keen. If he'd had even more sense he would have known he should keep away altogether and let Lucy wonder why he hadn't been nigh, let her watch the door every night to see if the next customer entering would be him. But Arthur was unacquainted with the foibles of young women and how to better gain their interest. So, on Wednesday evening at about nine o'clock, just two nights after their outing, he sauntered into the taproom, his heart a-flutter, aching to see again this delightful girl who had turned his world upside down.

'Oh, it's you,' Lucy remarked when she saw him standing at the bar waiting to be served.

'Hello, Lucy.' He grinned amiably, but was deflated by what he perceived as aloofness in her greeting. 'A pint please.'

She held a tankard under the tap of a barrel and placed it, full and foaming, on top of the bar before him. 'What brings you here?'

He handed her tuppence ha'penny. 'Well, I've a right to come in here if I'm of a mind,' has answered defensively. 'But the real reason I came was to see you.'

50

'But you can see I'm working, Arthur. I thought I wasn't seeing you till Sunday.'

'I just wanted to come and say hello.' He smiled again perseveringly.

Lucy turned and afforded a polite smile to her next customer, however, a young man who had a confident bluster about him. Arthur leaned on the bar and lifted his tankard to take a drink, watching her and the young man. Her almost-blue eyes seemed even wider by the glow from the lamps that hung from the ceiling, and that look of ethereal gentleness and perilous vulnerability they exuded wrung his heart with longing and a desire to be her guardian angel for eternity. This was how true love felt, this delightful yet sickening feeling that filled his breast, that made his heart hammer inside and his head swim with emotions. It was a sensation that neutralised all physical, gastronomic hunger, save for his raging hunger for her love. He felt no physical lust, no carnal desire for her, for to engage in such activities would be to violate her, and how could he violate somebody so soft and gentle, so innocent and susceptible? Even if she were to consent, which was unlikely.

Lucy smiled coyly at the young man with the confident bluster and he made some comment to her, which Arthur was fortunately unable to hear through the high ambient noise. Then the man turned to his mate who was standing behind him and made a gesture that signified a dark and dangerous lust for the girl. Arthur was incensed, indignant and utterly resentful of the man for having elicited an innocent smile from Lucy with his contrived ingenuousness. He prayed silently that she was not so gullible as to be unable to see through it. Yet what could he do? He was not a fighting man. And even if he was, he was not certain of his standing yet with Lucy. He had no prior claim on her, save for this searing love he felt that so far had not been entirely reciprocated, nor yet showed

51

many encouraging signs. This, he realised for the first time in his life, was how it felt to be jealous, and it was not a feeling he enjoyed.

Nobody else was clamouring to be served just then and Lucy turned to Arthur, moving along the bar to stand closer to him and so obviate the need to shout. 'How's your toothache, Arthur?'

'It's come back,' he said and rubbed his cheek gently to indicate where the pain was centred.

'Oh.' He had a short nose hair protruding from a nostril and Lucy focused on it irrevocably. 'Where've you been working today?'

'Netherton. I had to work on a stone in St Andrew's churchyard.'

'Pity the weather's turned, eh?' She could not detach her eyes from this obnoxious nose hair, and yet she longed to. It was so off-putting.

'You're telling me! The wind blows up there at the top of Netherton Hill like it does in St Michael's graveyard up the road. I swear I've caught a chill.'

'Maybe you should have an early night then,' she suggested, in the hope of avoiding any embarrassing situation later with her father present. 'Have a nip of brandy and get yourself tucked up in bed all nice and warm, and sweat it out.'

'I thought I'd wait and see if your father comes in. If he don't, I'll walk you home.'

'He's here already,' she said, and nodded towards a group of men playing crib at a table behind him.

'Oh? Which one's your father?'

'The one scratching his head under his hat.'

'Maybe I should make myself known to him, Lucy . . .'

She felt a pang of apprehension at the notion. 'What for?'

'To tell him I'm walking out with you.'

This Arthur was taking too much for granted, and much too soon, but she hadn't the heart to tell him so. 'Maybe if you bought him a drink . . .'

'A good idea, Lucy,' he beamed, encouraged. 'If you pour it, I'll take it to him.'

'I don't think he'd take too kindly to having his match interrupted. Better if I beckon him, then he'll come over when it's finished.'

Lucy signalled her father and she continued making small talk with Arthur between serving customers. When Haden had finished his crib match he stood up.

'Arthur,' Lucy said hesitantly. 'First I've just *got* to tell you . . .'

He looked at her anxiously, fearing she was going to let him down badly, that she was about to shatter his dreams by confessing she was already promised to another. 'What?'

'You've got a little hair sticking out down your nose.'

'Oh,' he exclaimed brightly, grinning with relief. 'Have I?'

'It's driving me mad . . . Your left nostril.'

He found it and gave it a yank, then tilted the underside of his nose towards her for inspection. 'Better?'

'Yes, better,' she said with a smile of gratitude. 'Look, here he comes. I'll pour the beer that you're buying him.'

Haden Piddock presented himself at the bar, his old and crumpled top hat shoved to the back of his head. Arthur was instantly aware of his presence, a hefty man, big chested, but not running to fat. He sported a big droopy moustache and mutton-chop sideboards. His smouldering clay pipe was clenched between his teeth.

Lucy shoved a tankard of fresh ale in front of him. 'This young man wanted to buy you a drink, Father,' she said and tactfully moved away to collect empty tankards while they became acquainted.

Haden looked at Arthur suspiciously. 'That's decent of yer, son. To what do I owe the honour?'

Arthur felt a tickle inside his nose where he had pulled out the offending hair. He sneezed violently. 'Oops. Sorry about that, Mr Piddock. I just pulled a hair from down me nose.' He sneezed again. 'To tell you the truth, I think I might have a chill coming an' all.'

'Sneedge over the other way next time, eh, son?' Haden suggested pointedly. 'I ain't too keen on it tainting the beer what you very kindly bought me.'

'My name's Arthur Goodrich,' Arthur said, stifling another sneeze with a violent sniff. 'I wanted to make myself known to you, 'cause me and your Lucy have started walking out together.'

'Oh?' His eyes searched for his daughter. 'Since when?'

'Well . . . Since Sunday night.'

'As long as that?' Arthur thought he detected irony in Haden's tone, but he missed the look of sardonic frivolity in his eyes. The older man lifted his tankard. 'I wish you luck, lad.'

'Thank you, Mr Piddock.'

Haden took a long drink. 'It's news to me about anybody stepping out with our Lucy . . . Did you say your name was Arthur?' Arthur nodded. 'I'd have appreciated you having a word with me fust, so's I could've run me eye over thee . . .'

'Oh, I would've, Mr Piddock, but I didn't know who you was. Anyway, I'm here now. I thought it only right and proper that you know.'

'Well then . . . Tell me about yourself, young Arthur. I hope your intentions towards me daughter am decent and honourable.'

'Oh, yes, Mr Piddock,' Arthur replied vehemently. 'I'm a churchgoing man. A regular worshipper at St Michael's and at Mr Hetherington's Bible class. I believe in honour and virtue

54

and clean living, Mr Piddock. Lucy's honour is safe with me. Safe as the safest houses. You need have no fears.'

'Well, I'm glad to hear it. 'Cause so sure as ever anything amiss happened to our Lucy, and it was down to thee, I'd separate ye from your manhood.'

Arthur winced at the terrifying prospect. 'Like I say, Mr Piddock. You need have no fears.'

'Good.' Haden lifted his tankard and emptied it. 'Here, let me buy thee a drink now, just to set a seal on our under-standing, eh? Same again, lad?' In Lucy's continued absence he called Ben Elwell's wife to serve him. 'What do you do for a living, young Arthur?'

Arthur told him.

'Goodrich, did you say your name was?'

'Yes. Arthur Goodrich.'

'Then you must be Jeremiah's son?'

'You know me father?'

'I do, the miserable bastard.'

'Oh, I agree with you a hundred per cent.' Arthur said. So there was some antagonism between Haden and his father.

'I knew your mother, see.'

'Oh? How d'you mean?'

'Well, lad, I used to be sweet on your mother years ago, when she was Dinah Westwood.'

'Honest?' Arthur guffawed like a regular man of the world at the revelation. It was obviously the reason his father had such little regard for Haden Piddock.

'Oh, aye. Not that your old chap had got much to fear from me. I was never high and mighty enough for your mother, being only an ironworker. Her father had a bit o' property, I seem to remember, so nothing less than a stonemason, a skilled craftsman, was good enough for Dinah Westwood.'

'Yes, she is a bit high-faluting, me mother,' Arthur agreed amiably. 'Puts on her airs and graces when she's out.'

55

Haden guffawed amiably. He quite liked this son of Dinah Westwood, despite who his father was. 'And who wouldn't put on airs and graces if they was used to owning property?'

'Owning property is all well and good, Mr Piddock, but the inside of our house is nothing to shout about. Be grateful that me father got her and you didn't, else you'd be forever tidying up after her, especially if you was of a tidy nature.'

Haden laughed at Arthur's candour, and Mrs Elwell put the two refilled tankards in front of them. Haden paid her and turned to Arthur.

'Well . . . It done me a favour in the long run, young Arthur, and you've confirmed it. I started courting Hannah not long after that, and Hannah is a tidy woman. Very tidy. Hannah's Lucy's mother, you know.'

'I hope to make her acquaintance some day.'

'And so you might, lad. All in good time, I daresay. So I expect you'll want to walk our Lucy home after, eh?'

Arthur beamed. 'If it's all the same to you, sir.'

'Aye, well just remember, I'll be right behind thee, so no shenanigans.'

'No shenanigans, Mr Piddock, I promise. Thank you.'

★　★　★

Arthur was pleased with the progress he'd made in establishing himself so soon with Lucy's father. That evening, he walked her home proprietorially, leaving Haden behind in the Whimsey.

'I like your father, Lucy.'

'I told you he's a decent man.'

'He is, and no two ways. Maybe I'll meet your mother soon.'

'Soon enough, I daresay, at the rate you're going.'

They were approaching Bull Street where Church Street levelled out like a shelf before commencing its long descent into Audnam, the stretch known as Brettell Lane.

'Shall I come and meet you tomorrow after me Bible class?'

'It'll be too late, Arthur.'

'But your father knows we're walking out together.'

'I'd rather wait till Sunday to see you, like we arranged.'

'What about Friday? I could come to the Whimsey again and walk you home.'

'I'd rather wait till Sunday, Arthur,' she persisted.

Arthur sighed. 'I want to be with you, Lucy,' he said softly. 'Don't put palings up around yourself as if you was some special tree in a park.'

'I'm not,' she protested mildly, but touched by his tenderness.

'Well, it seems to me as if you are.' He thought painfully of the young man with the confident bluster whom she'd served earlier. 'Do you see some other chap some nights?'

'No, I don't,' she replied, as if he had a damned cheek to suggest such a thing.

'So why don't you want to see me sooner than Sunday?'

' 'Cause I feel that you're rushing me, Arthur. I don't want to be rushed.'

'You mean you're not sure about me?'

'Yes . . . No . . . Oh, I don't know . . . I mean, I like you and all that . . .'

Arthur sighed again frustratedly. 'But?'

'But I've only known you a few days. You can't expect me to be at your beck and call when I've only known you a few days. It takes longer than that.'

'I'm sorry, Lucy,' he said pensively. 'I suppose you're right. It's just that I'm a bit impatient . . .' He looked at her in the moonlight, his heart overflowing with tenderness. He reached out and took her hands, holding the tips of her fingers gently. 'Haven't you ever wondered whether your perfect mate would ever come along, Lucy?'

'Oh, yes, many a time,' Lucy answered quietly, content that it was the simple truth.

'Well, Lucy, I feel that you're my perfect mate . . . I know it's a bit soon to be professing love and all that, and I'm not . . . not yet . . . 'cause I might yet be wrong. But it's what I feel at this minute. And knowing what I feel at this minute, I get impatient and hurt that you keep putting me off so as I can't be near you.'

'Oh, Arthur . . .' Lucy realised right then what agonies he was suffering on her account, and felt ashamed that she should be making another person unhappy – another person who held her in such high esteem. If the situation were reversed she would not relish being made unhappy. But she really was not sure of what she might feel for Arthur in the future that she did not feel now, and it was no good saying she was. She *did* need time to discover. Maybe, given time, she might grow to love him; he was a deserving case, he seemed a good man. But she didn't *fancy* him enough, and she had to fancy somebody before she could commit herself. Why wasn't he that man in the guards' van on the railway? If only he was that man, she would want to be with him every night that God sent, especially if he was as gentle as Arthur.

'But how can you feel like that, Arthur, when you've only known me five minutes?' she asked. 'You don't know anything about me. I might not be worthy of your . . . your tender feelings.'

'In the long run, Lucy, you might turn out to be right. I only said, it's what I feel now.'

'You're a really nice chap, you know,' she said sensitively, and meant it.

'I am as I am, Lucy. I can't help the way I am, no more than you can help the way you are. But I'll heed your words. I'll make myself wait till Sunday to see you again . . .'

'It'll be for the best,' she agreed, and stepped forward with a smile and planted a kiss briefly on his lips. 'I'll see you Sunday then, like we arranged. Here at three.'

Arthur felt the use drain out of his very being at the touch of her lips on his as he watched her walk away, a silhouette in the darkness. It was such a fleeting but a blissfully tender moment, a moment he would never forget, whatever might befall them.

* * *

5

Jane and Moses Cartwright lived in a tiny rented house situated on a steep hill called South Street. It was no great distance from Haden and Hannah Piddock's equally humble abode, but to visit his young wife's mother and father was a trouble for Jane's husband, since he had to do it on a crutch. Moses had received a gunshot wound in his leg during the siege of Sebastopol, which had shattered the shin bone. His leg had consequently been amputated below the knee, and Moses was still not certain which had been the more traumatic of the two terrifying experiences, the shell wound or the amputation. But at least he had survived both, and he lived to tell the tale. Indeed, he loved to tell the tale. He told it well to Jane Piddock on his return to England. He had courted Jane before he went to war and she was heartbroken when he went. His returning minus half a limb did not deter Jane and she agreed to marry him, despite the fact that everybody said he would be unable to work. She still had her own job moulding firebricks at the fireclay works. She could keep them both on the little money she earned, with a bit of help from her father.

That Thursday evening, they ventured slowly to Bull Street, as they had begun to do on a regular basis since Moses had returned from the Crimea. The light was fading and, at each step, Moses was chary as to where he planted his crutch lest he found a loose stone on which it might slip and upset his balance. They arrived at the Piddocks' cottage without mishap, however, and Moses was accorded due reverence and made to rest on the settle in front of the fire.

'Our Lucy, pop up to the Whimsey and fetch we a couple o' jugs o' beer,' Haden said when his older daughter and son-in-law arrived.

'I will if you give me the money,' Lucy answered.

So Haden handed her a sixpence, whereupon she duly found the two jugs and ran to the public house. When she returned, he thanked her and shared the beer between them all, pouring it into mugs.

'How's that gammy leg o' yourn, Moses?' Haden enquired and slurped his beer.

'It's bin giving me some gyp today, Haden, and no question. D'you know, I can still feel me toes sometimes, as if they was still on the end o' me leg. You wouldn't credit that, would yer?'

'Well, at least you ain't got no toenails to cut there now, eh?'

Moses laughed generously. 'Aye, that's some consolation.'

'There's plenty of talk about the Crimea and that Florence Nightingale,' Hannah said as she darned a hole in one of Haden's socks. 'I bet you happened on her when you was lying in that hospital in the Crimea, eh?'

'I was nowhere near Florence Nightingale, Mother.' Moses referred to Hannah as Mother, but to Haden by his first name. 'Nor any hospital for that matter. Her hospital was at Scutari, miles from where we was.'

'So who looked after yer?'

'There was a kind old black woman they called Mother Seacole.'

'A black woman?' Hannah questioned, looking up from her mending.

'Ar. All the way from Jamaica. A free black woman at that. She crossed the ocean just to help out when she heard

61

about the sufferings at the Battle of the Alma. Her father was a Scotsman by all accounts, a soldier. She knew a thing or two about nursing anyroad. Anyroad, she set up a sort of barracks close to Balaclava, and she nursed me there and a good many like me. She used to serve us sponge cake and lemonade, and all the men thought the bloody world of her. I did meself.' Moses smiled as he recalled the woman's kindnesses. 'But that Florence Nightingale and her crew would have nothing to do with her, everybody reckoned. Stuck up, she was. I could never understand that . . . It was 'cause Mother Seacole was a black woman, they all said . . . Anyroad, that Florence Nightingale was generally treating them poor buggers what had got the cholera or the pox in her hospital. And there was thousands of 'em, I can tell yer. We lost more soldiers to cholera than we did in the Battle of the Alma, they reckon.'

'Did you ever see anything o' the Battle of Balaclava?' Haden asked.

'Not me, Haden. But I heard tales from them as did. Bloody lunatics them cavalry of ourn, by all accounts.'

'I'd hate war,' Lucy said. 'I can't see any point to it.'

Haden looked at his younger daughter with admiration. 'Our Lucy's a-courting now, you know.'

'Courting?' Jane queried with an astonished grin. 'It's about time. Who'm you courting, our wench?'

'I ain't courting,' Lucy protested coyly.

'Well, she's got a chap who reckons he's a-courting her.'

'Arthur Goodrich bought you a tankard o' beer to get on the right side of you, Father. I've seen him once or twice, but it don't mean I'm courting serious.'

'So what's up with this Arthur Goodrich?' Jane enquired.

'Oh, he's decent enough, our Jane, and respectable. I'm sure he'd be very kind and caring, but I just don't fancy him.'

'You mean he ain't handsome enough?' Jane prompted.

'Handsome is as handsome does,' Hannah opined, and withdrew the wooden mushroom from the inside of Haden's mended sock. 'I married your father for his ways, not his looks. I'd never have married him for his looks. I'd never have found 'em for a start.'

Lucy chuckled at her mother's disdain and her father's hurt expression. 'Poor Father.'

'I married you for your money, Hannah, but I ain't found that yet neither. I wonder who got the best o' the bargain.'

'You did, Haden. You got me. All I got was you.'

'He does strike me as being a bit of a fool, that Arthur, now you mention it, our Lucy,' Haden pronounced. 'Although he seems harmless enough. But fancy him thinking he can have you when you got your sights set on somebody who's handsome enough to become a national monument. As if looks mattered, like your mother says.'

'They matter to me,' she answered quietly.

'Then, 'tis to be hoped as you grow out of it, our Lucy,' Jane said in admonishment.

Lucy was at once conscious that Jane had agreed to marry Moses when he was not only very ordinary looking, but also physically mutilated, without one leg, without hope of work or anything approaching prosperity.

'Every chap can't be handsome, the same as every wench can't be beautiful,' Jane continued. 'Looks am only skin deep anyroad. What more can you want from a man other than he be decent and honourable and caring? You want somebody who'll look after you, and who you can look after in turn. Contentment is in being comfortable with somebody, our Lucy, not worrying about whether he's got looks enough to turn other women's heads. And you can be sure that some women would move hell and all to get their claws into that sort when your back's turned, just because he's blessed with an 'andsome fizzog.'

'I never looked at it like that,' Lucy admitted quietly.

'Then p'raps it's time you did.'

'He sneedged into me beer, that King Arthur,' Haden proclaimed. 'I dain't take very kindly to that. Said he'd got a chill coming.'

Lucy giggled. 'He's always got something coming. The very first time I ever saw him he had to run off because he'd got the diarrhee.'

The others laughed.

'Maybe he's got weak bowels,' Hannah said. 'There's none of us perfect, like our Jane says.'

'I wonder what his ailment will be when I see him Sunday afternoon?'

'You'm seeing him Sunday afternoon?' her mother queried. 'Then you'd best bring him for tea. I'd like to meet this Arthur.'

'But that'll only encourage him, Mother.'

'It sounds to me as if he's worth encouraging, our Lucy. I was beginning to wonder if you'd ever find a chap.'

'There's nobody handsome enough nor perfect enough for our Lucy, Hannah,' Haden said sardonically. He turned to Lucy. 'What if he was the handsomest chap in the world and he still had the squits the fust time you met him? Would that put you off him?'

'Oh, Father!' Lucy protested, and everybody laughed. 'Can we find something else to talk about?'

★ ★ ★

Next day, Friday, Jeremiah Goodrich was tempering re-sharpened chisels in the forge. Hard stone, like granite and marble, rapidly blunted the tips of the steel tools and they had to be heated in the forge till they glowed red, then quenched in cold water at a fairly precise moment in their cooling in order

64

to harden them properly. As he withdrew several from the flames he heard a tap at the door and looked up to see who it was. The abominable animal that vaguely resembled a sheep-dog stirred beneath the workbench and pointed its snout in the direction of a well-dressed man in expensive clothes who was standing in the doorway glowering.

'Mr Goodrich?'

'That's me.'

'My name is Onions. James Onions.'

The man was well-spoken and his name was recently familiar to Jeremiah. 'How can I help thee, Mr Onions?'

'I have a complaint. A rather serious complaint.'

'Nothing too painful, I hope?' Jeremiah said flippantly. 'Mebbe you should be seeing a doctor, not me.'

'I suppose I should have expected a frivolous reply,' Mr Onions responded, 'in view of the nature of my complaint.'

'Which is?'

'My wife called in here a matter of a couple of weeks ago to request that you add an epitaph, following the death of my mother, to the grave where she and my father, who passed away three years ago, are buried.'

'I think you'll find as the work's bin done, Mr Onions, if you'd like to go and check.' Jeremiah walked over to a high desk strewn with paper and started rummaging through them for confirmation.

'I have checked, Mr Goodrich, which is why I'm here.'

'St Mark's churchyard in Pensnett, if I remember right,' Jeremiah murmured, browsing. 'So what's the nature of your complaint? The work's been completed like I said. Course, if you've come to pay for it, I ain't made out the bill yet, but I can soon remedy that.'

'Let me save you the trouble. I'm paying no bill until a brand new headstone is installed on the grave.'

'A brand new headstone?' Jeremiah scratched his head, mystified as to what could be so wrong that a brand new headstone would be justified.

'Precisely. A brand new headstone. I have a note here of the inscription my family wanted putting on that headstone, Mr Goodrich . . .' He felt in his pockets and drew out a piece of paper. 'No doubt you already have a note of it still, somewhere . . .'

'If you can just bear with me a minute, while I find it . . .' Jeremiah rootled about again. 'Ah! What's this?' He adjusted his spectacles and scrutinised the piece of paper. '*To the memory of Jacob Onions who passed away 15th October 1853.*' He looked at his irate visitor. 'That the one?'

'That's the one, Mr Goodrich. If you would be so kind as to read on . . .'

'*Farewell dear husband must we now part, who lay so near each other's heart. The time will come I hope when we will both enjoy Felicity.*' Jeremiah looked up questioningly. 'A fine sentiment, Mr Onions.'

'The inscription we intended adding was also a fine sentiment, Mr Goodrich. But do you realise what we have ended up with?'

'I can see what you was supposed to end up with . . .'

'Excellent. Then you will realise that what we ended up with, and I quote, "*Here also lies the body of Octavia Tether, obliging wife of Henry. May she be as willing in death as she was in life*", is not entirely supportive of my father's spotless reputation. You have put him in bed with another woman, Mr Goodrich, and my family is not amused. Worse still, you have no doubt despatched my honourable, devoted and alas dear departed mother to the bed of Henry Tether.'

'Our Arthur!' Jeremiah exclaimed with vitriol. 'He did it. I'll kill him, the bloody fool. I swear, I'll kill him.'

★ ★ ★

66

'I'm going for a drink in the Bell while you get the dinner ready, Mother,' Arthur said as they stepped out of the sacred dimness of St Michael's redbrick hulk into the sunshine of a late September noon. 'It'll give me an appetite. I seem to have lost me appetite this last couple of days as well as this cold I've got.'

'I'll boil some nettles up in the cabbage, our Arthur,' Dinah said sympathetically. 'Nettles always help to keep colds and chills at bay. Your father could do with it as well. I'm sick of seeing him bad all the while.'

Only Dinah accompanied Arthur to church that Sunday morning, since his father, Jeremiah, was at home in bed feeling out of sorts and very sorry for himself. Not that he was an ardent churchgoer; he would always seek some excuse to avoid Sunday worship.

'By the way, I'm going out this afternoon, Mother.'

'Oh? Do you think you'm well enough?'

He forced a grin. 'I'd have to be dead not to go. Anyway, I'm hoping as your nettles will perk me up a bit.'

Arthur left his mother and exited the churchyard by the Bell Street gate while she took a different way, walking with another woman down the broad path that spilled onto Church Street. He entered the Bell Hotel and ordered himself a tankard of best India pale ale which he took to an un-occupied table close to the fireplace. A man whom he knew did likewise, nodded a greeting and sat on a stool at another table. Arthur blew his nose on a piece of rag he took from his pocket, and sniffed. This damn head cold. He'd picked it up from that blustery graveyard at St Andrew's in Netherton. By association, his thoughts meandered to that pair of head-stones in Pensnett churchyard where he'd mixed up the inscriptions. Of course, it was because he'd been taken short while he was doing them. He'd not been concentrating. And how could he when his bowels had been about to explode?

67

Well, it would cost him dear, for his father was adamant that he pay for new ones himself as punishment. Nor would he be paid for cutting the letters, and he'd better get them right this time.

He stuffed the rag back in his jacket pocket and pondered Lucy Piddock instead. This day had been a long time coming and he'd been counting the hours till he could see her again. It seemed ages since he'd last seen her, and he was by no means sure she cared anything for him at all. But he was hopeful that at least he might have her father on his side.

Four men approached. Two were familiar.

'D'you mind shifting along the settle, mate?' one of them said. 'We'n got a crib match.'

'Glad to oblige,' Arthur replied amenably. He removed his tankard from the table as he shifted along the bench that lined the wall on one side of the room and placed it on the next. 'Are you playing for money?'

'There's no point in it unless yo' am,' was the pithy reply.

Arthur watched as they began their play, amazed that grown men could become so absorbed in something which he considered so trivial. He finished his beer, stood up and made his way to the bar for another. When he'd got it he turned around to go back to his seat only to see that somebody else was occupying it. The room was filling up so he decided instead to stand by the bar and quietly finish his drink there. Most of the patrons he knew, some only by sight, but those he was better acquainted with merely nodded. He watched, envious of the banter they shared, and it struck him that nobody was bothering to engage him in conversation. Not that he minded right then; he sometimes found it difficult to converse with folk, especially when he was nursing a cold or toothache, and so preferred to be left alone anyway. He leisurely finished what remained of his beer and slipped out to go home, unnoticed by anybody.

It was strong beer they brewed in Brierley Hill and it had gone straight to Arthur's head. It was on account of the head cold, of course. Two drinks didn't normally affect him. It did the trick for his appetite, though, for now he was ravenously hungry, feeling weak and wobbly at the knees.

Arthur sliced the joint of pork Dinah had roasted in the cast iron range in the scullery, while she drained the cabbage and the potatoes.

'I could do with a maid,' she complained, shrouded in steam. 'Nobody ever thinks of any help for me.'

'Tell Father.'

'Your father wouldn't pay out good money for a maid,' Dinah said. 'Mind you, he has a lot of other expense . . . Here, our Arthur . . . Take his dinner up to him. He wants to see you anyroad.'

'Shall I take him some beer up?'

'No,' Dinah snapped. 'Why waste good beer on him? I'll finish it meself.'

Arthur did as he was bid. He found Jeremiah lying flat on his back, his eyes closed and his hands pressed together as if in supplication. He opened one eye when he heard Arthur enter the room.

'What'n we got for we dinners?'

'Pork.'

'Blasted pork! Your saft mother knows as pork serves me barbarous. So what does her keep on giving me? Blasted pork! It's a bloody scandal. It's a bloody conspiracy. I swear as her's trying to see me off.'

'Well, when the time comes I'll do you a nice headstone, Father,' Arthur replied, inspired by the thought.

'Oh, ar? Then mek sure as yo' get the inscription right this time.'

'Oh, I'll dream up a good one for you. Anyway, I apologised

for that one,' Arthur said defensively. 'I told you, it was the time I was took short.'

'Well, sometimes I think you've bin took short of brains, if you want my opinion.'

'I wasn't concentrating, I told you. My mind was on other things.'

'Be that as it may, you owe me compensation for making me look such a fool.'

'Compensation? What do you mean, compensation? I've already agreed to pay for two new headstones out of me own wages.'

'I want you to collect a debt this afternoon,' Jeremiah said, making a meal of sitting up in bed so that he could take the old wooden tray on which his Sunday dinner was presented.

'What debt?' Arthur asked suspiciously. 'And why this afternoon?'

'I want you to fetch some money off a customer called George Parsons. Money he's owed me too long. He'll be expecting you, but he reckons he'll be gone out by three o' clock.'

Arthur handed Jeremiah the tray. 'But I'm supposed to be going out this afternoon, Father. It's been arranged all week. I'm meeting somebody at three and it's two already, and I ain't had me dinner yet.'

'Well, it can't be helped.' Jeremiah picked up his knife and fork and began hacking at the pork that served his system so badly. 'It's money I've been trying to get hold of for ages. If I was well enough I'd go meself, but I ain't, and there'll be no other chance till next Sunday. He works away, see, does this George Parsons – Stafford way. He only comes home of a Saturday afternoon.'

'But, Father, I've arranged to meet somebody and I'm not going to let them down. Anyway, where's he live, this perishing George Parsons?'

70

'Pensnett. Near to Corbyn's Hall. I'll tell you the address.'

'But I shan't have time to go there.'

'Damn me!' Jeremiah exclaimed huffily. 'After that stupid sodding blunder you made last week . . .' He shook his head ruefully. 'After all I do for you, and you can't run one little bloody errand for me. You ought to be ashamed of yourself, our Arthur. Anyroad, it's firm's money. It's for your own benefit as it's collected. When I'm dead and gone . . .'

'Tell me the damned address then,' Arthur said with exasperation. It was typical of his father to spoil whatever he'd planned. 'I ought to charge you commission for debt-collecting.'

Jeremiah told him the address and Arthur went downstairs disgruntled. If it took longer than he thought he was certain to miss Lucy. So he bolted his Sunday dinner and left the house without even having any pudding, losing no time in putting a hastily formed plan into effect. He didn't want to give Lucy the impression that he didn't care or that he was unreliable. Already the ground was slipping from under his feet where she was concerned. He must not make matters worse by any perceived disregard for her.

Corbyn's Hall was a couple of miles away, too far to walk there and back in the time allowed. The only answer was to go on horseback. He harboured a distinct dislike of riding and horses. Or was it merely a dislike of their own wretched horses? He seemed to hold no sway with them, even when he drove the cart. But the weather was fine for a ride and, at a steady trot, he should be there and back in the three-quarters of an hour that were left. Just about enough time to get back and meet Lucy.

The equine stock of Jeremiah Goodrich and Sons, stone-masons and sepulchral architects, comprised two sturdy but ageing mares whose terms of reference suggested that they generally hauled the cart, for they were seldom ridden. They

71

were the equine embodiment of lassitude, long-developed artfulness and not a little spite. Arthur took down a set of reins from the stable wall and forced the bit into the mouth of one of the mares called Quenelda. Quenelda was the older and scruffier of the two, but usually the most co-operative, a quality Arthur had taken into account. Quenelda's mane sprouted only in places, like sparse tufts of grass poking through a neglected pavement. He coaxed the horse outside and mounted, but without a saddle since he didn't have time to find it and tack up. But the horse's sharp-edged back and broad girth elicited concern for his manhood and the potential for damage to it.

Seated on the horse, he looked around him assessively, first gazing towards Withymoor, then across the valley to Audnam and Stourbridge in the opposite direction to that which he must go. His fingers clutched the reins tensely as a barge and attendant bargee glided as one along the Stourbridge Canal, drawn by a hack as unattractive as his own. The bargee was singing some unsavoury ditty as he headed for the Nine Locks where doubtless he would get his belly, and his wife's, filled with ale.

Arthur pulled on the rein. 'Gee up, Quenelda!' As the horse turned around he looked up the yard and onto the Delph in anticipation.

But Quenelda had ideas of her own. Sunday was her day of rest, and long years of experience had led her to recognise the sabbath's inactivity. If man did not work on the sabbath, then she did not work on the sabbath either. The mare thus made her way back to the stable with no regard for Arthur who was tugging manfully at the reins. Passing through the stable door, Arthur was not quick enough to duck, by dint of the alcohol he had consumed, and ended up banging his head and acquiring a nasty cut across his eyebrow. Angry and frustrated, he got down from the horse and dabbed the cut with the rag from his pocket.

'Listen, you,' he snorted impatiently, punching the animal hard on the nose, 'we'd better sort out who's gaffer here.' He grabbed a stick for good measure and led the horse out again. When he mounted Quenelda she made for the stable once more. 'The other way, you varmint.'

Arthur hit the mare on the rump with the stick, and pulling hard on the reins, he succeeded in turning her around, but she veered again crab-fashion towards the stable. Cursing bitterly, he lashed at the horse's rump once more. As far as Quenelda was concerned this was the limit. She reared up on her hind legs in an attempt to unseat him. Arthur saved himself by grabbing one of the tufts of mane and gripping his legs tightly around her belly. It was a war of wills. For what seemed like an eternity Arthur clung on while Quenelda was bent on throwing him off. While he could hold on to her sparse mane Arthur felt secure enough . . . but his hands were becoming sweaty with the exertion, and the tuft was becoming slippy. He lost his grip.

It became desperate. Quenelda reared up high and whin-nied, beating the air with her front hoofs. Arthur snatched at the mane, held on and righted himself just in time, as much to save messing up his best Sunday clothes as to avoid hurting himself more.

'You won't get the better of me,' he rasped determinedly. 'Enough of your vile behaviour.'

The mare spun round and round on her hind legs and Arthur caught sight of their conjoined shadow spinning beneath him. But he had no time to study the aesthetics of shadow dancing, for his legs had become tired and weak, aching inexorably from perpetually pressing into Quenelda's sides for grip, and he lost hold. He felt his body twist around violently while the mare bucked and pranced with all the vigour of a whirlwind. In frantic desperation he reached out and grabbed what he thought was the patchy mane to save himself from falling to the ground and hurting himself. In that same instant, the mare was under the impression that she had at last thrown her rider and returned all four feet to the ground. Arthur quickly realised that his position on the horse was quite unorthodox and, at that precise moment, beheld his mother emerging from the scullery wiping her hands on a towel.

'Th'oss'll think yo'm saft sitting the wrong road round.'

'I don't care much what it thinks.'

'What yer doing with her?'

Arthur sighed with impatience at having to explain. 'I'm trying to teach her the gentle art of wrestling, Mother,' he answered with measured sarcasm. His collar was agape from the tussle and his waistcoat had parted company with his trousers, leaving his shirt half hanging out.

'Couldn't you find ne'er a saddle?'

'I thought I hadn't got time to look.'

'Hold on . . .' Dinah went into the stable and came back lugging an old mildewed saddle. 'Get down.'

He got down.

'Put this hoss back in the stable and fetch out the other un.'

'Why?'

'Cause this'n's took umbrage at thee, that's why. Yo'll do no good with this'n today.'

'Oh.' Arthur did as he was told and emerged from the stable leading Roxanne, an equally tatty mount.

'Now fasten this saddle on her,' Dinah said. 'Roxanne won't mind you trying to ride her. I'll help you, shall I?'

'I'd be obliged.'

Together, they saddled up Roxanne and Arthur mounted the mare, but gingerly. To his immense relief, this mare made no fuss and actually responded to his signal to go. He rode out of the yard and was on his way.

They did the journey to Pensnett at a steady trot that shook

Arthur's dinner and his beer about somewhat. He contemplated the tussle with Quenelda. He had stuck doggedly to the task of making the mare see who was master. Horses were like women. If only he could apply the same resolve to women. If only he could apply it to Lucy Piddock.

6

Lucy Piddock waited and waited for Arthur Goodrich to show up. She reckoned she'd been waiting a good quarter of an hour before she realised it was futile to wait any longer. Evidently she'd put him off with her indifference when he walked her home on Wednesday. Well, who would have thought it? Yet who could blame him? If she returned home now and had to tell her folks that King Arthur – as her father had started calling him – had not turned up she would be a laughing stock. Jane would say that it served her right for being dissatisfied with him just because he didn't have the looks of a god. So would her mother. Her father would think it the funniest thing out and would guffaw for the rest of the afternoon and possibly into the night as well.

It was a dirty trick, not turning up when you'd arranged to meet somebody. All morning she'd worked hard, getting her domestic chores done while her mother was at the Baptist chapel, so that she could spend the afternoon with him. Well, he obviously didn't deserve it, the charlatan. All the time this Arthur must have been stringing her along . . .

But she remembered his words on Wednesday night, that he believed he'd found his perfect mate in her. It was a gloriously tender moment and, if she was honest with herself, it had registered in her heart. She'd thought about those words a lot, his sincerity, his reserve. Of course, after what she'd said to everybody, it would be hard to say now that she'd changed her mind about Arthur, but he had definitely gone up in her

76

estimation. It was a pity he was not going to show up now to reap the benefit.

So she waited a little longer, hurt and disappointed. Yet the longer she waited the hurt and disappointment diminished and were replaced by agitation. If he had the gall to turn up now after keeping her waiting so long, all he would get would be her scorn. She adjusted her shawl ready to cross the road back to Bull Street, determined to wait no longer.

As she looked up the hill towards the church she spied a mangy horse going at a tidy canter, the rider waving his hat like a lunatic. She could hear him calling something, warning everybody that the animal had taken fright and he had lost control, she supposed. But, as he got closer, she could see that the madman was none other than Arthur Goodrich. Torn between her pique at having been kept waiting for so long and a natural curiosity that must be satisfied as to what the hell he was up to, she stood waiting for him to reach her, unsure quite how she should behave towards him now.

'Whoa!' he yelled and there was a clatter of hoofs on the cobbles as the forlorn mare scraped to a halt. Arthur was out of breath. 'Sorry I'm late, Lucy.'

'It's too late to be sorry,' she replied, deciding to manifest her scornful side. 'I'm going back home.'

'Oh, wait, Lucy.' He sounded irritated and impatient at what he deemed unreasonableness. 'If you knew the trouble I've had you'd be *very* understanding. I didn't *mean* to keep you waiting. I've gone through hell and high water to get here on time.'

'You didn't get here on time.'

'I know that. But I still went through hell and high water.' He dismounted and stood before her. 'I had to run an errand for my old man. He's bad abed.'

'What's up with him?' she asked indifferently.

'God knows. With any luck it'll be terminal.'

'I thought you didn't like riding horses,' she said, softening.

'I don't. I loath and detest the bloody things. Damned stupid animals. But if I'd walked I'd never have got here.'

'What've you done to your eyebrow? It's cut and bleeding.'

'I know.' He put his fingers to it gingerly.

'Let me have a look at it.'

Obediently he bent his head forward and she inspected the wound, putting her gentle fingers to his temples. He felt a surge of blood through his body at her warm touch.

'I think it'll be all right,' she said softly. 'It needs a smear of ointment on it. How did you do it?'

'I banged my head on a lintel.'

'Banged your head on a lintel?' she repeated, incredulous. 'You aren't that tall.' He explained in detail how it happened and her pique melted away with her peals of laughter. 'I've never known anybody like you for getting in the wars,' she said. 'It's one calamity after another with you.'

'So do you forgive me, Lucy . . . for being late?'

'Oh, I suppose so.'

'I won't do it again.' He sniffed audibly.

'You've got a cold.'

'I know. A stinker.' He snivelled again to emphasise the fact.

'So where are you taking me? And is the horse going to play gooseberry?'

'If it's all the same to you, Lucy, we'll take the horse back together and put her in the stable. After cricket practice last evening I went rabbit shooting over Bromley, and there's a brace of the little buggers I want to give you for your mother. They'll make a fine dinner.'

She smiled appreciatively. 'That'll please her. Thank you, Arthur. I'll give one to our Jane.'

As they made their way towards the Goodriches' house and yard Lucy explained about the poverty in which Jane and her new husband lived, on account of his handicap.

'She's a brave girl, marrying somebody lame like that,' Arthur commented, leading the horse by its halter.

'She loves him,' Lucy conceded. 'But I'd think twice about marrying a cripple.' She shuddered at the thought. 'I don't think I could do it.'

'But he's a hero, Lucy. He was fighting for queen and country. He has to be admired. And your Jane is his just reward for his self-sacrifice. Besides, love overcomes all.'

They arrived at the yard and Arthur tacked down while Lucy looked about her at the separate stacks of both cut and unhewn stone, the slabs of marble and slate, the various urns and vases that would end up adorning graves.

She patted Roxanne's long, dappled face. 'He's a scruffy devil in't he, this horse?'

'He's a mare, Lucy.' Arthur grinned with amusement at her failure to recognise the fact.

'He's still a scruffy devil, mare or no. Don't nobody ever groom him?'

'You can come and do it, if you're so concerned.'

'Would I get paid?'

'By my old man?' Arthur lifted the saddle off the mare and turned to take it into the stable. 'You'd be lucky to get a kind look,' he said over his shoulder and pointed resentfully to an upstairs window. 'You'd have to catch him on one of his better days, and they're few and far between.'

He backed the mare into the stable, made sure she was settled and emerged into the sunshine to shut the door behind him with a self-satisfied grin on his face. 'That Quenelda was a bit fidgety when I went in there just,' he said smugly. 'She knows I ain't standing no more messing off her. Come on, Lucy, let's go in the house. You can meet my mother.'

'D'you think I should?'

'Yes, course. I want her to meet you.'

It was a large house compared to the tiny cottage that Lucy

and her family lived in, but it was by no means grand. Her own mother would have a fit if she walked into this hallway and saw all the clutter, the unswept flags, and the dust that lay like a dulling film over the wooden furniture. Lucy felt like taking a duster and a tin of wax polish to everything to freshen it up, to try and eliminate the dusky smell that pervaded the place.

They found Dinah in the parlour peeling an apple into her lap, a tumbler of whisky within easy reach. Her mouth dropped open when she saw a pretty girl at her son's side.

'Mother, this is Lucy Piddock. Lucy's my girl, and I brought her home so you could meet her.'

'I wish to God I'd a-knowed yo' was bringing a wench back here,' Dinah admonished. She rose from her seat, grabbing the apple peel to save it falling on the floor. 'I'd have put me a decent frock on and done me hair. He never tells me nothing, you know . . . Did he say your name was Lucy?'

Lucy nodded and smiled uncertainly, afraid that Arthur had not chosen a good moment to present her to the unprepared and disorderly Mrs Goodrich.

'Never mind about your frock, Mother,' Arthur said. 'We ain't come to see you in a mannequin parade. We've come to get a couple o' them rabbits what me and our Talbot shot yesterday. I said I'd give a couple to Lucy for her mother.'

'Do I know your mother, Lucy?' Dinah asked trying to show an interest in this vaguely familiar face. She put down the apple, together with its cut peel and the knife she was using, on top of a news sheet that lay on the table beside her.

'No, but you used to know her father,' Arthur replied for her, with a look of devilment.

'Oh? Who's your father, then?'

'Haden Piddock.'

'He used to be sweet on you, didn't he, Mother?' Arthur was grinning inanely.

'Haden Piddock . . . By God, that was a long time ago.'

Lucy noticed the instant softening in Mrs Goodrich's eyes as she recalled the lost years. Maybe, all those years ago, there had been a spark of something between her father and this woman. She could hardly conceive of him giving her a second glance now, but she might have been a pretty young thing once. It was such a shame, Lucy thought, that age and the years eventually robbed everybody of any gloss and sparkle, which was generally at its brightest around the age of twenty . . . in women anyway. Some men never sparkled at all though. You only had to look at Arthur . . .

'Well, fancy you being Haden's daughter. I tek it as you'm the youngest.'

'That's right, Mrs Goodrich.'

'Well, why don't you stop and have a drop o'summat to drink? I got a nice bit o' pork pie on the cold slab an' all, as I'm sure you'd enjoy. It was made from one o' Mrs Costins's pigs up the Delph . . . and you look as if you could do with feeding up a bit.'

'No, we ain't stopping, Mother,' Arthur reasserted. 'We've only come to get the rabbits. But Lucy can come another Sunday, eh, Lucy?'

Lucy nodded politely. 'Yes, I'd like to.'

Arthur went to the brewhouse and returned with four rabbits wrapped in old newsprint. 'There's two for your mother and two for your Jane,' he said proudly.

'How many did you shoot?' Dinah asked, as if he might be giving too many away.

'Eighteen. Me and Talbot had nine apiece.'

'It's very kind of you, Arthur,' Lucy said sincerely. 'Thank you. My mother and sister will be ever so pleased.'

Arthur smiled, delighted that he'd earned some esteem from his girl. 'Come on, we'll go and deliver 'em now, eh?'

'I can see now why he was in such a rush to get out afore,' Dinah said, looking incisively at Lucy. ''Cause he'd arranged to see you, young Lucy. He was getting into a tidy pickle with that cantankerous old mare we'n got when he knew he'd got to run an errand for his father.'

'How is Mr Goodrich?' Lucy enquired. 'Arthur tells me he's bad a-bed. What's the matter with him?'

'Mrs Costins's pig,' Dinah replied matter-of-factly. 'He had some pork yesterday. So sure as he touches a bit o'pork it's all over with him. When I went to fetch his plate after his dinner I swear as he was praying to the Lord, asking Him to ease his suffering.'

'He should be ashamed troubling the Lord of a Sunday afternoon for the sake of a bit o'wind,' Arthur remarked acidly, 'when a dose of bicarbonate of soda would set him straight.'

'I'll tek him some up after,' Dinah said.

'No, let him suffer.'

'Our Arthur's got no respect for his father, you know, Lucy. Am you sure you won't stop and have a bit o' pork pie? It's beautiful. I doubt whether I ever med better. I'm sure as the good Lord must've bin in the oven with 'em a-Friday when they was a-baking.'

'I told you, Mother, we're going now.'

Dinah gazed at her visitor critically. 'But look at the wench, our Arthur, her could do with feeding up a bit. A bit o' me pork pie would do her the world o' good. Am yer sure yo'm all right, young Lucy? You look pale to me, an' all.'

'I feel perfectly well, Mrs Goodrich—'

'Well, I'm glad to hear it. Mind you, I've heard it said as pale folk am often the healthiest, though they mightn't be the handsomest . . . But it's better to be healthy than handsome, I always say. Mind you, him upstairs is neither . . . Shall I cut a piece o' me pie to take to your father? He could have it for his snap tomorrow at work.'

'That would be ever so kind, Mrs Goodrich . . .'

* * *

'So this is Arthur,' Hannah Piddock said, standing up to welcome the young man who had seen fit to start stepping out with her youngest daughter. She looked him up and down circumspectly. 'Well, he ain't as bad looking as you made him out to be, our Lucy. I expected somebody with a face like a bag o' spanners.'

'I never said any such thing,' Lucy at once countered, embarrassed that her mother should have been so tactless as to repeat in front of Arthur what she had said.

Arthur looked first at Lucy, then at her mother, and grinned sheepishly. 'I know I'm no oil painting, Mrs Piddock. I couldn't blame Lucy for saying so.'

'Arthur's given us some rabbits, Mother. Haven't you, Arthur? Two for us and two for our Jane.'

'And there's plenty more where they came from,' he said stoutly. 'My brother and me often go shooting 'em over Bromley.'

'That's ever so kind, Arthur. Why, our Jane will be ever so grateful an' all.'

'It's no trouble, Mrs Piddock. I understand her husband can't work. I'm glad to help out.'

He looked about him. The room was tiny with a small cast-iron range in which a coal fire burned brightly, a polished coal scuttle stood to one side. The mantel shelf above was edged with pristine white lace. On it stood two small crock urns, one at each end, and in the middle a sparkling mirror hung. In front of the hearth was a wooden settle with chenille covered squabs neatly placed. A rocking chair was set beside it turned in towards the fire, and in it dozed Haden Piddock after his drinking spree at the Whimsey. Under the window that looked out onto the street, stood a small square table covered in a lace-edged cloth, and three chairs set around it. All modest and unassuming, but its unsullied cleanliness and cosiness struck Arthur. Nothing was out of place, and it all looked invitingly spruce and bright, unlike his own home.

'Arthur's mother's sent some of her fresh pork pie for me father's snap,' Lucy said.

'That's very thoughtful of her, Arthur. Be sure to thank her for me.'

'I will, Mrs Piddock.'

'That's a stinking cold you've got there, young Arthur. Let me give you a drop of hot rum with some sugar in it.'

Arthur grinned with appreciation. 'That sounds too good to miss, Mrs Piddock.'

'Well, one good turn . . . And I warrant as it'll make you feel better.'

Haden woke himself up with a sudden rasping snort, and looked about him disorientated for a few seconds. 'Well, I'm buggered,' he said and rubbed his eyes. 'It's King Arthur . . .'

'He's a king and no two ways, Haden,' Hannah declared. 'He's bought us some rabbits for a stew, and his mother's sent yer a lovely piece o' pork pie for your snap.'

'His mother, eh? . . . What's that he's a-drinking?'

'Hot rum and sugar.'

'I thought I could smell rum. I'll have some o' that, an' all, our Hannah.'

★ ★ ★

On the afternoon of the last Saturday in September Lucy Piddock and Miriam Watson decided to treat themselves. They took the train to Wolverhampton to visit the shops, a rare and exciting excursion. The journey took them through the Dudley Tunnel, when all was suddenly converted to blackness. The insistent rumble and click-clack of the iron wheels, traversing the joints of the iron track, took on a gravitas that was not only unheeded in daylight but augmented by the close confines of the tunnel. The two girls clutched each other for reassurance, lest they were each suddenly ravished by one of the occupying male passengers, even though they looked so ordinary and so harmless by the light of day.

'Lord, I hope this thing don't come to a stop while we'm in here,' Miriam whispered. 'What if the roof fell in and half of Dudley was to come crashing down on us?'

'You're full of pleasant thoughts,' Lucy murmured. 'I wish you wouldn't say such things. You scare me.'

'What if one o' these Johnnies here jumped on we?'

'I thought you liked men.'

'I don't mind 'em if I can see 'em. But it'd be just my luck to get the ugly un. And there must be nothing worse than realising you've had the ugly un when all of a sudden it gets light again and you've imagined you bin with the handsome un.'

However, they soon emerged into daylight at the new Dudley Station, which was still only half built. The train stopped to disgorge passengers and take on others before it resumed its journey through a stark and bewildering landscape of factories, pits and quarries interspersed with small impoverished-looking farms. Brown smoke swirled into the air from chimney stacks which were sprouting like bristles on a scrubbing brush. At Wolverhampton Low Level Station the locomotive hissed to a halt, and the coaches behind it nudged each other obsessively in their commitment to line up behind it.

The two girls stepped down from their third class accommodation onto the paved platform. There was a distinctly autumnal nip in the air, a sudden and drastic change from the Indian summer they'd enjoyed hitherto. As Lucy pulled her shawl more tightly round her shoulders as protection against the blustery wind, she instinctively glanced behind her towards the guards' van. It was just possible that *he* might be on duty. But evidently he was not and, disappointed, she returned her attention to Miriam who had been telling her in hushed tones about the scandal of her cousin being put in the family way by a young lad of thirteen.

'Serves her right,' Miriam said as they walked out of the station. 'She must've bin leading him on, showing him the ropes if I know her, the dirty madam. I mean, you don't expect a lad of thirteen to know all about that sort o'thing, do yer? A wench, yes, but not a lad. Lads of that age am a bit dense when it comes to that sort o' thing.'

'So how old is this cousin of yours?' Lucy asked.

'Twenty-six. It's disgusting if you ask me. Mind you, she's nothing to look at. You couldn't punch clay uglier. She's got a figure like a barrel o' lard an' all, and legs like tree trunks. Couldn't get a decent chap her own age, I reckon.'

'So is she going to marry this young lad, Miriam?'

'It's what everybody expects, to mek an honest chap o' the poor little sod. Mind you, if I was his mother I'd have summat to say. I'd tell him to run for his life and not come a-nigh till he was old enough to grow a beard that'd hide his fizzog and save him being recognised.'

'So you think it's her fault?'

'I do, and no two ways. But who in their right mind would want to get married anyroad, let alone to her? Do you ever want to get married, Luce?'

'Yes, some day . . . to the right chap.'

'But the Lord created us all single, Luce. If He'd wanted us to be married, we'd have been born married. If you look at it that way why fidget to get married? Why rush to bear a chap's children and his tantrums?'

'I ain't fidgeting to get married,' Lucy protested. 'But some day I'd like to be married. If I loved the chap enough. If I was sure of him.'

'You can never be that sure of men. Look at my Sammy. You'd think butter wouldn't melt in his mouth, but show him a wench in just a chemise and he'd be after her like a pig after a tater.'

'I reckon I could be sure of Arthur.'

'Then he's the only man alive you could be sure of. But tell me, Luce, 'cause I'm dying to know . . . do you love this Arthur?'

Lucy smiled diffidently and shook her head. 'No, I can't say as I do, Miriam. But I do like him. I wasn't bothered at first, but I like him now despite all his quirks. There's something pathetic about him that makes me want to mother him. And me own mother's as bad, or as mad – she's took to him as if he was her own. Our Jane as well. Ever since we took 'em them two rabbits he'd shot she thinks there's nobody like him. There must be something about him.'

'What about your father? What does he think of him?'

'Oh, he thinks he's a bit of a joke. He thinks Arthur's quaint and a bit too gentrified, and he's puzzled as to why he should bother with the likes of me. Well, he's quaint all right, but he ain't gentrified at all. He's just a stonemason working in his father's business. His father ain't gentrified either from what I can make out – and his mother certainly ain't.'

'So . . . he's got a trade, and you can be sure of him,' Miriam mused. 'Well . . . It seems to me that he's as good a catch as you'm ever likely to get . . .'

'If only I fancied him . . .'

'Oh, fancying's nothing,' Miriam declared. 'When you'm lying with him in the dark just imagine it's that guard off the railway you keep on about.'

'I don't lie with him in the dark, Miriam,' Lucy protested. 'I don't lie with him at all.'

'No? Well, I daresay you will sometime . . .'

Wolverhampton's Low Level station was blessed with platforms that were long and wide to prevent overcrowding. The single span roof was an impressive construction of iron and glass. There was a grand entrance hall with booking offices, the company offices, waiting and refreshment rooms. The whole blue brick pile was not too far distant from the shops, and soon the two girls were in a warren of narrow streets teeming with folk and horses hauling carts or carriages. An omnibus drew up alongside them as they were about to cross the street and disgorged its passengers. Soon, they were surrounded by haberdashery shops, furniture shops, tailors, cobblers, bakers, an ironmonger's, silversmiths and gold-smiths, an apothecary and a host of butchers; and that was only in one street. As well as the many licensed premises Lucy saw a printing works, hollow ware workshops, a saddlery, a chandlery, a corn merchant and a blacksmith. They wanted for nothing in this town. On a corner of one street a man was roasting chestnuts, and the eddying smoke from his cast-iron oven made Miriam's eyes run until they had moved upwind.

'I want to find me a decent Sunday frock from a second-hand shop,' Miriam said. 'Sammy says as how he'd like to see me in summat different of a Sunday afternoon.'

'I'll have a look as well, Miriam. Now I'm stepping out with Arthur I ought to make an effort. Specially of a Sunday. Just so long as it's cheap.'

Lucy and Miriam scoured the secondhand shops and, in a back street called Farmer's Fold where they were content that they'd happened on one that offered good value, they each found suitable garments. As they emerged into the street they espied on the corner an ancient black and white timber-framed building, which evidently served as a coffee house. They decided they needed refreshment, and rest for their tired feet before the walk back to the station, now some distance away. Duly refreshed and giving themselves plenty of time, for they were not sure how long it would take them, they left the coffee house carrying their new secondhand clothes with them.

As they entered the station, a man wearing a guard's uniform was walking in front of them and Lucy's heart went to her mouth. She nudged Miriam.

'There's that guard,' she whispered excitedly.

'How can you tell? He's got his back towards us.'

'Miriam, I can tell. Of a certainty. Oh, I wish he'd turn around so I could see his face.'

The guard hailed a porter coming towards him and they stopped to talk. Lucy tugged at Miriam's sleeve and they loitered very close to where he stood.

'You should be ashamed, Luce,' Miriam quietly chided. 'You've got a perfectly decent chap and you'm hankering after *him*.'

'But he's so lovely, Miriam. Oh, me legs am all of a wamble now that I've seen him. I'll have to see if he smiles at me again. I wonder if he'll be on our train?'

'There's one way to find out . . .' Miriam stepped brazenly up to the guard. 'Excuse me, where do me and me friend catch the train to Brettell Lane?'

The guard looked at Miriam, then to the friend she referred to. He smiled in recognition. 'Hey, I've seen you before, eh, miss?' Lucy nodded and felt herself go hot as her colour rose. 'I could never forget a face as pretty as yours.'

'We normally go to Dudley of a Saturday afternoon,' Miriam said, ignoring his compliment to her friend, 'but today we thought we'd treat ourselves and come to Wolverhampton. The trouble is we don't know the place, and we forgot what time the train goes as well.'

The guard took his watch from his fob and smiled. 'It leaves in a quarter of an hour, ladies. That's the one, standing at the platform over there, being hauled by locomotive number two . . .' He pointed to it. 'I'll be working on that train, so I'll keep me eye on you. Where d'you say you want to get off?'

Lucy found her voice. 'Brettell Lane.'

'Brettell Lane. Live near the station do ye?'

'Not far. Bull Street. Just across the road.'

'I'll surprise you one day and pop in for a quick mug o' tea, eh?' he teased.

'You'd be welcome.'

'Her chap wouldn't be very pleased though,' Miriam wilfully interjected, and received an icy glare from Lucy for her trouble.

'Oh, aye,' he grinned. 'Here, let me carry your bags and I'll take you to a nice comfortable coach . . .' He bid goodbye to the porter and turned back to Lucy. 'Here, give us your bag, my flower . . .'

'It's all right,' Lucy said. 'I can manage, it's no weight.'

'No, I insist . . .' He stood with his hands waiting to receive the two bags and Lucy handed them to him, blushing vividly again. 'So what's your name?'

'Lucy Piddock. What's yours?'

'Everybody calls me Dickie. What tickets have you got, Lucy?'

'These . . .'

'Third class. Well, I reckon we can do better than that for you. Here . . .' He opened the door to a second class compartment and winked at Lucy roguishly, which caused her insides to churn. 'We'll install you in second class, eh? More comfortable, and more space to stretch your pretty legs. Nobody'll be any the wiser, but if anybody should say anything refer 'em to Dickie Dempster. Here y'are, Lucy, my flower . . .' He offered his hand and helped her up into the coach, then handed up her bags. 'Have a comfortable journey and I'll come and open your door for you to make sure you'm all right when we get to Brettell Lane.'

'Thank you, Dickie,' she said politely. 'But are you sure we'll be all right in second class?'

'Trust me.' He winked again, then turned to Miriam. 'Now you, miss . . .' He handed her up, closed the door and waved as he went on his way.

Lucy sat on the upholstered seat and put her head in her hands, unable to believe what had just happened. Her face had turned red when she looked up, wearing an expression of elation and astonishment, at Miriam. 'Oh, I've gone all queer, Miriam. You know, I get the strangest feeling that he fancies me.'

'Fancies you?' Miriam scoffed. 'I'll say he fancies you. He never so much as looked at me. He didn't offer to carry *my* bags, did he?'

'Oh, I hope he asks to see me again when he opens our door at Brettell Lane.'

'And if he does, what about Arthur?'

'I ain't *married* to Arthur – nor ever likely to be,' Lucy protested. 'I ain't promised to Arthur.'

On the journey back Lucy was full of Dickie Dempster. She giggled and speculated wildly on what might happen when they arrived at Brettell Lane station.

'If he don't ask me out, should I ask him, do you think?'

'I do not,' Miriam answered emphatically. 'Act like a lady, for Lord's sake. Don't get throwing yourself at nobody. It's the road to ruin. What's the matter with you? I've never seen you like this before. You'm like a bitch on heat. Your mother would be ashamed of you.'

'But it's fate that we met again, Miriam. Don't you see?'

'Twaddle! It's nothing o' the sort, Lucy. It's a coincidence. Nothing more. The trouble wi' you is that you've bin starved of a chap for too long. Get that Arthur up the churchyard and lie him down on one o' them graves and make a man of him.'

'Ooh no, not Arthur. Besides, the churchyard is the last place *he'd* want to go, seeing as how he spends half his life in

91

churchyards already. Anyway, I'm not getting my bum all cold on the freezing slab of somebody's grave. Not for Arthur . . . For Dickie I might though.'

'Then take poor Arthur somewhere else. Over the fields by Hawbush Farm. Give him a good seeing to. And once he's given you a good seeing to, you won't look at e'er another chap again.'

'And I was starting to take to Arthur as well,' Lucy said dreamily. 'Now I'm all unsettled again.'

'Lucy, just forget this Dickie Dempster,' Miriam chided. 'Be satisfied with what you've got.'

As the train slowed to a stop at Brettell Lane Lucy waited with bated breath for Dickie to come along and open the door for them.

'I ain't waiting,' Miriam exclaimed, deliberately teasing. 'I'm opening the door meself.'

'No, wait. Wait just a minute, Miriam.'

Miriam rolled her eyes.

'Just a minute . . . Please . . .'

Dickie's beaming, handsome face was soon framed in the window of the door. He opened it and stood aside, then offered his hand to help Lucy down.

Again she blushed to her roots, smiling self-consciously. 'Thank you, Dickie.'

'My pleasure, Lucy.' He turned to Miriam to help her down next. 'Happy to be of service. Thank you for using the Oxford, Worcester and Wolverhampton Railway,' he added in an amusing parody of formality.

Reluctant to move, Lucy seemed stuck fast to the platform. 'How often are you working on this train?' she asked.

'Well, nearly every day. The time depends on me shift.'

'I'll look out for you. I'll wave if I see you.'

'I'll look out for you, Lucy.'

'If I knew when you was coming through our station I could

bring you a bottle of tea and something to eat, ready for when you stop.'

'Oh, aye,' he said doubtfully. 'That'd be good, but it'd upset the station master. Do you work, Lucy?'

'Yes.'

'Then you'm most likely at work the same hours as me.' He drew his watch from his fob and looked at it. 'Look at the time,' he said with a smile. 'This train has got to be going else we'll never get to Worcester. Like I say, I'll keep me eye open for you.' He winked again.

Lucy winked back saucily. 'I'll keep me eye open for you as well.'

He scanned the train for open doors then skipped back along the platform to his guard's van. Lucy heard his whistle and, as the train began moving forwards she stopped to wave, disappointed that evidently nothing was going to come of this encounter after all.

'Why did you let him know as I've got a chap, Miriam?' Lucy asked, frowning as they walked along the platform to the gate. 'I bet that's why he didn't ask to see me.'

'You don't want to see him,' Miriam replied, looking straight ahead. 'He'd be no good for you.'

'I don't know how you can say that. You don't know him.'

'Neither do you, Lucy . . . But I know you.'

★ ★ ★

7

Arthur made it to the Whimsey just before nine that evening. He immediately searched for Lucy across the room, and saw her serving an elderly customer. She had a soft, dreamy look in her blue eyes, a look which enchanted him just as surely as if a spell had been cast on him by some benign love witch. He approached the bar.

'How do, Lucy. You do look nice.'

She smiled serenely. 'Thank you, Arthur, it's nice of you to say so,' she said, taking money from the elderly man.

'She does, don't she?' he said to the man who was standing beside him waiting for his change.

The ageing customer crinkled up his rheumy eyes and nodded. 'Her meks me wish I was young again. But still, I'n had my day. They say as every dog has his day, and I'n had mine – more's the pity.'

Arthur nodded his acknowledgement of the man's reply and grinned matily. He turned to Lucy. 'A pint please, Lucy. And have a drink yourself.'

'Thank you, I will.' She filled a tankard and placed it on the bar. 'How's your cold today?'

'Oh, much better . . .' He handed her the money. 'But I've hurt me back lifting a slab of marble.' He put his hand to the small of his back and grimaced as if in pain.

'How did you do that?'

'Me and our Talbot was fitting a new counter top at Mr Guest's shop this morning – you know, the haberdashery. I

94

tried to lift it on me own, but it was too heavy. Now I'm in agony.'

'Maybe you'd best not stay here then,' she suggested. 'Maybe you should go home and rest.'

'No, I'll be all right. What time's your father due?'

'Any minute.'

Another customer came and stood at the bar seeking service, and Lucy served him before turning to Arthur again.

'So you've done nothing this afternoon?' she queried. 'On account of your back.'

'Yes, I have. I went and had me likeness taken in Dudley.'

'Had your likeness taken? I bet that cost a fortune. Did you have that same look of agony on your face?' she asked impishly.

Her irreverence amused him. 'I'd like you to have yours taken, so's I can look at it when I'm home and you're not with me. I forget what you look like sometimes and it drives me mad. If you had your likeness taken it would remind me.'

She laughed self-consciously and wiped the top of the counter with a cloth. 'How can you forget what I look like?'

'By trying too hard to remember, I reckon. I think about you a lot, Lucy . . . Anyway, you can have a copy of my likeness when it's done. You never know, you might take to it.'

She smiled, endeavouring to hide her conscience at both her inability to reciprocate his feelings and her eagerness to yield hers to Dickie Dempster, should he ever ask. 'Look, I'm getting busy, Arthur,' she entreated. 'I can't talk now, or I'll get into trouble. I'll see you later.'

Haden Piddock appeared just at that moment, accompanied by another man. 'Why, it's King Arthur.' He turned to his companion. 'Arthur's a keen cricketer, you know, Enoch. You know what he calls his bat?'

'What?'

'Excalibur . . .'

The two men guffawed.

★ ★ ★

'I'll see you tomorrow afternoon, shall I?' Arthur suggested as he and Lucy stood outside the Piddocks' cottage after walking her back.

'Oh, Arthur, I don't know . . .'

'What d'you mean, you don't know? Don't you want to?'

'I need to set one or two things straight . . .'

They were standing about a yard apart and Arthur was itching to get close to her, to take her in his arms.

'About what?' he said quietly, dreading hearing what she was about to say.

Lucy shrugged, sighing profoundly. 'It's just that . . . I don't want you to think I'm leading you on, Arthur,' she whispered guiltily. 'I know that you're keen on me . . .'

'I am keen on you. So?'

'Well . . . I think you're keener on me than I am on you.'

'Then you should be flattered,' he said, outwardly undaunted by her reticence, but inwardly agonised.

'But I don't want to hurt you, Arthur. It's the last thing I want. You're such a decent, gentle chap.'

Arthur emitted a great sigh. 'Well, you're hurting me just by saying such things. If I'm such a decent, gentle chap why are you holding back from me? I don't understand, Lucy. I think the world of you . . .'

'I know you do, Arthur. That's what makes it all so difficult . . . But I think it's best if we don't see each other for a bit.'

'Why?' he protested. 'I only see you a couple of nights in the week and Sunday afternoons as it is. It's not as if I get the chance to get fed up of you . . . or you of me, come to that.'

'But it might be best for you,' she said, his best interests at

96

heart. 'If I find myself missing you, I'll know I've only been fooling myself. I'll know better how I feel.'

'Are you sure there ain't somebody else you'm seeing on the quiet, Lucy?' he said perceptively.

'I swear, Arthur. I ain't seeing anybody but you.' It was actually no lie, but how could she confess she was preoccupied with another man who actually knew nothing about her devotion, and possibly cared even less. She would seem so stupid.

He plucked up his courage and wrapped his arms around her, hugging her to him. To his relief and encouragement she snuggled to him like a kitten, laying her cheek on his shoulder.

'You poor, mixed up madam,' he said softly, accidentally tilting her bonnet as he nestled her to him.

'Careful, Arthur,' she complained. 'You're knocking me bonnet askew. Oh, that's typical of you.' She straightened it, tutting to herself at his unwitting clumsiness, which marred even his feeblest attempts at romance.

'Sorry.' He could have kicked himself for his ineptitude. 'I didn't mean to knock your bonnet over your eyes. Are you all right now?'

'Yes,' she said stepping back from his awkward embrace.

'Good . . . Well, if you ain't seeing anybody else, what do you do on Saturday afternoons?' he asked, returning to the problem in hand. 'I mean, even Saturday afternoons you don't want to see me.'

'I generally see my friend Miriam . . .'

'I don't know this Miriam, do I?'

'Not that I know of, but you might.'

'What do you do when you see her?'

'We go somewhere. Generally Dudley. We went to Wolverhampton today on the train.'

'Wolverhampton? What's the point of going there?'

'To have a look round. I bought a new Sunday frock in Wolverhampton.'

'Oh, a new Sunday frock.' He grinned hopefully. 'Then you'll have to meet me when you're wearing it, so's I can have a gander at you.'

He caught her flattered smile in the spilled light from a window, and was again heartened.

She shrugged resignedly. Arthur was not going to be easy to shake off. 'But what about your poorly back?' she asked.

'It don't stop me walking, does it? Nor will it stop me working next week either . . . more's the pity.'

'All right,' she agreed softly, relenting.

'And you'll wear your new frock for me?'

'Yes, all right. Where shall we go?'

'Depends on the weather, I expect. If it's fine we could walk to Kingswinford over the fields.'

'But not if it's cold and raining.' There was a plea in her voice.

'Then I'll take you to a few graveyards so you can see what it's like working there in the cold and wet.'

'No, you won't,' she declared emphatically. 'So where will you take me?'

'I'll think of somewhere.'

★ ★ ★

Arthur spotted an opportunity to inveigle himself into Lucy's heart as he sat in the Bell Hotel after church the following Sunday morning. A man, whom he knew vaguely, was show-ing a very young mongrel pup to another customer, and they were bartering for it.

'I'll give thee a shilling,' Arthur heard the second man say.

'Two and a tanner and the mutt's yourn,' replied the first man.

'Two and a tanner for a mutt? No, a bob's me limit.'

'But its mother's got a lovely nature.'

'So's mine. But what d'you know about it's fairther?'

Arthur stood up with his tankard of beer and made his way

towards the men. 'Excuse me, but if this gentleman don't want the pup, I'll give you a florin for it,' he said hesitantly.

The second man looked at him curiously. 'If yo'm saft enough to pay that much for a mutt, then yo'm welcome.'

'Two and a tanner is what I'm asking,' the seller reaffirmed, instantly able to recognise somebody bent on making a purchase. 'I'll not budge on that.'

Arthur sighed. Two shillings and sixpence was just too much, especially in view of the extra expense he was committed to because of the two wrongly inscribed headstones he'd had to pay for. Besides, he would look a fool if he bid higher when the other man was only prepared to spend a shilling. 'Ah well,' he said. 'That's all I'm prepared to pay.' Disappointed, he moved away from the two men to resume his seat.

'Fair enough,' the seller called after him. 'I'll tek the little bugger home with me then and drown it, like I drowned the other four out the litter. I kept this'n 'cause it was the strongest, but if nobody wants it . . .'

Arthur turned around, a look of astonishment on his face. 'You wouldn't drown it, would you?'

'It'd cost money to keep it. Course I'd drown it.'

'But then you'd have neither the pup nor any money for it,' Arthur argued logically.

The man shrugged. 'That's up to me. Why should it concern you?'

'Because there's no logic in it. I've just offered you two bob, but rather than accept it, you'd rather drown the poor little mite. I hope you can sleep in your bed at night,' he added indignantly.

'I hope you can sleep in yourn,' the man replied with equal resentment, 'when for an extra tanner you could have saved it.'

Arthur smiled in acknowledgement of the way the owner of the puppy had turned the tables on him. He felt in his pocket and pulled out a handful of coins, counted out two shillings

99

and sixpence, and offered the money. 'Here . . . I couldn't have the poor little thing on me conscience for the sake of another tanner.'

The exchange was made, the man pocketed the money and, with a self-satisfied grin, turned to the second man. 'It generally works, does that ploy,' he said quietly.

Arthur held the little bundle of fur in one hand and stroked its head gently with the other. 'I know somebody who'll just love you,' he said softly to the puppy.

★ ★ ★

That afternoon, he put the puppy in his jacket pocket and walked to Bull Street, trying to imagine Lucy's delight at seeing it. As he approached the Piddocks' cottage, Bobby their sheepdog sauntered up to him sniffing suspiciously.

'I got a little pal for you,' he murmured to the old dog. 'Just you wait and see.'

He tapped on the door and Lucy opened it with a smile. 'I thought it would be you,' she said. 'Come on in.'

'Is that your new frock?' he asked, stepping over the threshold.

'Yes,' she answered expectantly. 'Do you like it?'

'The colour I like, it matches your eyes. I like the shape of it as well, but it could never outdo those blue eyes of yours, Lucy.'

'But do you think it looks nice?'

'I think you look lovely in it, yes.'

'You do say lovely things sometimes.'

Inside, the smell of dinner still lingered, but as usual, the place was clean and tidy. Haden came in from the privy, greeted Arthur and sat on the settle.

'How's your back?' Hannah enquired of Arthur.

'Tolerable, Mrs Piddock, thank you.'

'Would you like me to rub it with some goose grease? That would ease it, I reckon.'

'That's very kind, Mrs Piddock, but I'd better not. I've got a clean vest on today.' He turned to Lucy. 'I brought you a present, Lucy,' he said proudly and felt in his jacket pocket. With a broad grin, he pulled out the warm bundle of fur.

'Oh, look!' she shrieked with delight, carefully taking the animal from him. She put it to her cheek and felt its soft fur warm against her face. 'Oh, isn't he beautiful? Oh, thank you, Arthur.'

Haden, facing the fire grate as he sat on the settle, could only hear what was going on behind him. 'What's he bought thee?' he asked, turning around.

'A puppy, look . . . and he's beautiful.'

'A puppy?' Haden grinned. 'Let's have a look at him . . .' Lucy handed the little dog over to her father. 'This dog's a bitch,' he exclaimed with obvious disappointment.

'It doesn't matter,' Lucy said with a laugh of joy, taking the puppy back. 'I still love it.'

'And in no time it'll be in pup itself and we shall have a house full o' bloody pups, most likely from that dirty bloody Bobby we got outside.'

'Oh, I doubt that,' Hannah countered. 'Our Bobby ain't got it in him.'

'What are you going to call it, Lucy?' Arthur asked.

'I don't know. I think you should choose a name, since you bought her. Can you think of anything?'

'Well, she likes being tickled, by the looks of it. Why not call her Tickle?'

'Tickle,' Lucy mused. 'Yes, I like that.'

'Tickle!' Haden mocked, rolling his eyes. 'Fancy calling a bloody dog Tickle.'

Lucy sat down and played for ages with the puppy in her lap. Arthur watched, revelling in his newly won glory. Hannah, meanwhile, boiled a kettle and made a pot of tea while Haden and Arthur talked about the new fireclay works that was being built near Silver End and the increased employment it would bring.

As she fondled the puppy, Lucy was in her own world. She pondered her relationship with Arthur. Never had she met a kinder, more well-meaning man, and she felt guilty that she could not find it within herself to reciprocate his obvious devotion. She was fixed by her dream of eventually winning the love of a handsome young man. He did not have to be wealthy; she did not aspire to wealth. She would be perfectly content living in a little cottage, like Jane her sister did, romantically cuddled up with this handsome new young husband she craved, in front of a homely fire. And what did her ideal man look like? That was easy. He had to look like Dickie Dempster.

Try as she might, she could not purge her mind of Dickie Dempster and thoughts of them eventually being together. She lay awake at night and imagined him in bed with her, engaged in passionate embraces and hungry kisses, which almost left her breathless. She imagined the manly scent of him, his firm skin rubbing gently on hers. She stroked her inner thighs, her breasts, and made believe he was doing it, and left herself ever hungrier for him. Dickie Dempster was becoming an obsession and it was not fair. It was certainly not fair on Arthur, for in every other way Arthur would be an ideal mate for a gentle soul like herself. He was not only kind and thoughtful, but he made her laugh with his unwitting antics. When he told her about his adding the wrong epitaphs to the two graves in Pensnett churchyard she howled with laughter. And so did he; they laughed together so much. When he told her about the trials and tribulations with the horses she could picture him in her mind's eye, and it tickled her for days afterwards. If only she could feel desire for Arthur, this same desire she felt for Dickie Dempster, he would be exactly right for her and she could make a commitment to him. But she did not feel desire so ardent, nor would she ever, so she could not commit herself. Arthur was not handsome, Dickie Dempster was. Dickie possessed a sort of animal magnetism that for her was overpowering, Arthur did not.

It was nature's way.

If she had never cast eyes on Dickie, then things between her and Arthur might already be vastly different. But they were not. She was aware that poor Arthur would believe she was hard and unemotional, but that wasn't the way she was at all. Deep down she was as soft as this little puppy, which she was stroking in her lap. There were so many things about Arthur that she liked, that maybe she was even beginning to love, but she really did not relish the thought of serious physical contact with him. It held no appeal. But if Dickie Dempster touched her, she knew her heart would melt and run, like the cold hard iron ore as it melted in the Earl's furnaces.

'Have you fed the puppy?' Hannah asked Arthur.

'I gave it a saucer o' milk afore I left home,' he answered. 'The poor little mite drank it all. It must have been thirsty.'

'I'll give it some more, and find it a bite to eat as well. I bet it's hungry.'

'Oh, no!' Lucy suddenly exclaimed, and stood up, holding out her skirt.

'What's up?' Arthur enquired.

'It's just peed over my new frock.'

★ ★ ★

8

1857

Winter came and went, and those few months saw little change in the lopsided courtship between Lucy Piddock and Arthur Goodrich. She held back, unwilling to commit herself, saving herself for the elusive Dickie Dempster, who might at any moment come along and sweep her off her feet. She had seen him only a couple of times, and then only from afar when she had been walking either to or from the glassworks along the railway line, and he had been in the guards' van of a passing train. Both times he'd spotted her and waved, and she'd watched his thrilling smile disappear into the distance. The second time he'd even blown her a kiss. But at no time had another opportunity to speak to him presented itself. Her Saturday trips with Miriam had produced no further encounters either.

So, as winter turned into spring and spring turned into summer, Lucy's interest in Dickie Dempster actually waned, and she began taking Arthur a little more seriously, even though his minor ailments, whether real or imagined, were a continual source of irritation to her.

Arthur was not insensitive to Lucy's greater amenability and it made him happier. Lucy agreed to see him more often and he became more relaxed with her. He made her laugh with little anecdotes of his working life and his contentious en-counters with his father. His account with Lucy was greatly enhanced when, in the spring, he actually persuaded his father to employ Moses Cartwright as a general hand, grooming the horses, greasing the cart's axles, cleaning up, tending the forge and sharpening chisels. This very act of kindness for a crippled war hero precluded any possibility of an increase in wages for himself, although Arthur made no mention of that to Lucy. He was content to help out somebody he liked and admired, who was becoming a sort of mentor with his infinitely vaster experience of the world and its ways. Moses and Jane, too, were grateful for his intervention, for their own existence was materially improved by this singular act of compassion.

But Arthur's relationship with his father was one facet of his life that did not improve. Apart from the consensus over Moses, Arthur disagreed with every other deed and notion of the old man. It reached the point where Arthur dreaded getting up on workdays, he hated returning either home or to the workshop at night, for every encounter with Jeremiah ended up in an argument. What Arthur failed to realise was that he and his father were in many ways alike, both prone to complaining about their ailments, both lacking in patience with each other, both eager to denigrate the other.

Arthur had contemplated leaving home. It began to dawn on him that marriage to Lucy would serve him well in that respect, if she could be so persuaded. She would, after all, have to give up her two jobs to become his wife. He would rent a house and they would live under the same roof together. They would sleep in the same bed, and the prospect of that thrilled him. Marriage would also offer the ideal escape from the stressful conflicts with his father – at home anyway.

The problem was, it was as yet too soon to be contemplating marriage. Arthur had known Lucy little more than six months and in those six months their courtship had never been intense. Even kissing was hardly commonplace, so anything beyond kissing was distinctly out of the question, for the immediate future anyway. Not that Arthur was unduly concerned. He still considered it important to respect Lucy in that way, and not to assail her femininity with assaults on her virginity, even though the notion of what he might find under her skirts was utterly appealing, arousing, and caused him many a sleepless night. But her father had threatened unspeakable things, should anything untoward result from any such immorality.

Nevertheless, he would gently broach the subject of marriage, to try and draw her out, to ascertain whether or not she was agreeable, at least in principle. He would have to pick his time, of course. You could hardly introduce a subject with such vast implications when the object of your affection was preoccupied with something else, but he would mention it somehow. First, though, he would seek the advice of Moses Cartwright who was familiar with the quirks of the Piddock family's womenfolk.

★   ★   ★

Moses proved to be very effective and diligent in his work at the premises of Jeremiah Goodrich and Sons, Monumental and Sepulchral Architects. Despite his handicap, he had perfected a method of keeping himself balanced and upright on one crutch, while maintaining the freedom of at least one arm to enable him to do the tasks expected of him, like grooming Quenelda and Roxanne, cleaning the windows and tending to the forge. One Friday afternoon in July when Arthur returned to the workshop he found Moses in the yard lugging a bucket of coke inside for the forge.

'Let me carry that for you, Moses.'

'Nay, Arthur. I'm capable, and it's what I'm paid to do.'

'Is the old man inside?'

'No, he's gone into the house. I reckon he's finished for the afternoon now.'

'Good.' Arthur followed Moses inside.

'So's Talbot. I've been making meself busy waiting for you to come back and lock up. Got much on tomorrow, Arthur?'

'A trip to Kidderminster. We've been asked to put an inscription on a new stone pulpit we made.' He placed his toolbag down on a workbench. 'So make sure I've got plenty hardened and sharpened chisels, Moses.'

'Aye, there's plenty done. Would you like me to put 'em in your bag ready for morning?'

'Yes, better to do 'em now, I reckon. I'll need an early start in the morning if I've got to catch a train to Kidderminster. I expect it'll be gold-leafed as well, so I'd better make sure I got plenty gold leaf.'

'How's your thumb where you hit it with the mallet?' Moses asked.

'Oh, still sore as a boil . . .' As Arthur put a few sheets of the precious gold leaf into his bag. 'I've got damned toothache now as well. I'm always getting the damned toothache . . . It drives me mad.'

'Sounds to me as if you should get it pulled.'

'Pulled?' Arthur said scornfully. 'I ain't getting it pulled. I'd be in even more agony than I am now if I had it pulled. No, I'd rather keep me tooth.' He paused a few seconds, watching Moses operate. 'Moses, I've been meaning to ask your advice . . .'

He ceased shovelling coke into the small furnace and regarded Arthur expectantly. 'You want my advice?'

'Yes.'

'What about?'

'About Lucy.'

'About Lucy?'

'Yes . . . Sit down for five minutes, Moses . . . Are you in a rush to get off?'

'Not particularly, 'cept Jane'll have me fittles ready afore long.'

'Well, I won't keep you long, Moses.'

Moses sat down on the dusty old wooden chair. 'I don't

know as I'm qualified to give advice about Lucy, you know, Arthur.'

'Well, it's not so much about Lucy as about me and Lucy together. I've a notion I'd like to marry the wench, see, and it's your advice on how to go about broaching the subject as I need.'

'Oh, I see,' Moses answered, with a broad grin. 'Just ask her outright. Just say, "Listen, Lucy, will you marry me?".'

'Is that how you asked Jane?'

He shrugged nonchalantly. 'More or less. I asked her afore I went to fight in the Crimea though. But we thought it better to wait till I got back afore we went and did it, for fear I didn't come back and med a widder of her. If I never come back she'd have a better chance of marrying somebody else if she was a spinster and not a widder, we reckoned.'

Arthur nodded his understanding. 'But I get the notion that your Jane thinks more o'you than Lucy thinks o' me.'

'Oh? How d'you work that out?'

'It's how I perceive you. She looks at you with such love in her eyes, Moses. I never see that for me in Lucy's eyes.'

'But Lucy thinks the world of you, all the same.'

'Do you know that for sure? Has she ever said so?'

'Not in so many words, Arthur . . . But in the way she talks about you, especially to Jane, it's obvious.'

'She's never told me she loves me.' Arthur looked down at his swollen thumb, which he was twiddling agitatedly around his good one, as he sat on the workbench next to his toolbag.

'Have you ever given her the urge to?'

'How do you mean, Moses? I don't think I follow.'

Moses threw his hands out in a gesture of frankness. 'Have you ever bedded the wench?'

Arthur looked astonished at such a direct and personal question, which compromised Lucy's integrity. 'No, and I don't think it would be the right thing to do afore marriage, Moses.'

Moses laughed at Arthur's prudery. 'Well, maybe that's your problem, Arthur. Wenches always respond better to a man once he's given 'em the benefit of a good poking. Maybe that's what Lucy needs – a good poking.'

'But, Moses, I wouldn't dream . . . Did you give Jane a good . . . you know . . . poking – pardon my asking – afore you got married?'

'Aye, course I did. Many's the time. Afore I went to the Crimea. I had to give her summat to remember me by.'

'But she didn't get pregnant?'

'No. But wenches don't necessarily get pregnant every time you give 'em a poke, else there'd be millions o' babbies running around all over the place. You have to pull your old man out in time.'

'Do you still bother to pull it out now you'm wed?' Arthur asked, intrigued.

'If she's due for a fall of soot I don't bother.'

'Pardon me for asking, Moses . . . but how do you manage to do it now with only half a left leg?'

'Well, I use the rail at the foot o' the bed to give me a bit o' purchase. Having only one good leg don't hamper me a bit, I can tell you.' He winked waggishly.

'Good. I just wondered . . . Anyway, you think that's what I should do to Lucy?'

'If she's averse to a poke she'll be the first wench ever. My advice is, give her a good poking regular, and she'll be eating out of your hand.'

Arthur smiled resignedly. 'I never thought it right and proper, Moses, and I still ain't sure as I believe you, but—'

'Listen, Arthur, if *you* don't do it, somebody else'll beat you to it. Wenches am like that. They'm fickle till they've had the benefit of a good poking. They'll go for the chap as gives 'em a good poking every time, mark my words . . . Has Lucy ever bin poked afore by anybody, d'you reckon?' Moses asked guilelessly.

'Lord, no. I'd stake me life on it.'

'No, I wouldn't have thought so either. So get in there first, eh? Wenches never forget their first poke, and they love the chap as did it forever after.'

'Are you sure, Moses?'

'Ask anybody.'

★ ★ ★

Having finished his work, Arthur made his way back to Kidderminster station, pondering his own behaviour while he'd been working on the church pulpit, now completed. All morning he'd suffered agonies, his toothache throbbing as if he were afflicted with some sort of dental gout. It had caused him to be rather curt with the vicar of the parish who came to see how he was getting on. Arthur brooded over how sorry he was for that, and for being so offhand with the maid who had trundled across the churchyard from the vicarage to bring him a mug of tea, just because there was not enough sugar in it. She was a pretty girl, inoffensive, and did not deserve his abruptness. If only he could have bothered to explain the agony he was in.

He hoped the train would not be late. He was due to play cricket that afternoon at Netherton. He was the team's wicket-keeper now, a very responsible position in the team. He'd trained hard and was becoming quite adept. If only this nauseating toothache would go away . . .

The train steamed in from Worcester and Arthur clambered awkwardly into the first available third-class compartment, lugging his bag with him. He heaved it onto the luggage rack above then flopped forlornly into a seat, scanning his travelling companions assessively. They were three in number, and none seemed interested in him. Two were gazing out of the window at the sunshine and the third was reading a news sheet.

He felt in his jacket pocket and pulled out a small green bottle containing laudanum. Just a couple of drops would numb the pain entirely and he would have some respite. He did not habitually take laudanum, but once in a while at bedtimes, when the pain was intolerable, he might take a drop or two for it helped him sleep as well. He opened the bottle, surreptitiously glancing again at his fellow passengers, and allowed a few drops to drip onto his tongue, before he pushed the cork back in and returned it to his pocket.

As the train chugged on he thought about Lucy. Last night, when he went to the Whimsey and walked her home afterwards he could not pluck up the courage to mention his thoughts of marriage. Indeed, there was no great rush. There needed to be a decorous amount of time between starting courting and getting wed, and a decorous amount of time had not yet passed. Perhaps Christmas would be a good time to get wed, always assuming Lucy agreed to it. It would also be nice to be in a position where he was sure of a positive answer. Perhaps Moses Cartwright had a point when he advocated giving Lucy a good poke. If it truly were to ignite a passion for him and establish her lifelong devotion, as Moses suggested it would, then perhaps he was being foolhardy in not pressing for it. But how did you go about it? How did you go about seducing the love of your life before you were married, when hitherto you had endeavoured to be honourable and decent? If he tried suddenly to play the role of the amorous seducer after all these months of passive courtship, would he look a fool? Would he appear plausible? Besides, he should have asked Moses for some clue as to where such an initiation could take place, for Arthur was bereft of ideas.

His toothache was mercifully easing away, and he was beginning to feel warm, comfortable and relaxed as the train rattled on through countryside as pleasant as anywhere in England. The laudanum was doing its work. Arthur closed his eyes, leaned his head back against the headrest and tried to imagine himself in a soft feather bed with Lucy. Yes, that was not beyond his ability to imagine. But contriving how to get her there was causing him some concern. He could never persuade her into bed at their little cottage in Bull Street, for Hannah was generally in residence even if Haden wasn't. He might be able to effect it at his father's house, providing he could get his mother out of the way; preferably on a day when his father was at work . . . But then Lucy would be at work as well . . .

Maybe he could bribe Moses to lend him his and Jane's bed one evening . . . Or Haden's and Hannah's . . . He could go up to Haden and say, 'Hey, Haden, I want to give your daughter a good poking, so let me borrow your bed.' Haden would be very understanding and say, 'With the greatest of pleasure, my lord king. And would you like me to bring you a pot of tea and some crumpets afterwards to refresh you both?' Oh, Haden could be very accommodating at times. Imagine if he presented himself at Talbot's house and started divesting Lucy of all her clothes in front of Magnolia, she too would be very understanding and hospitable and say, 'Oh, let me help you, Arthur.' Then she would take her own clothes off and make sure she joined Lucy and him in her own marital bed while Talbot did a spot of letter cutting in his place at some churchyard or other.

But wouldn't it be a good idea if they could dress in the same colours as the place where they were, like polar bears in snow. Then it would look as if they weren't there. They could get up to all sorts of antics if they were so well disguised and nobody would be able to see them. If they each had an outfit the same colours as his mother's parlour furniture for instance, folk would come in and have a look around and not even know they were there, and they would be able to poke to their heart's content undetected. They could dress in greens and browns and blend into the countryside, looking as if they were parts of hedges and stiles. On a Sunday afternoon with Lucy in her blue muslin dress and him in white cricketing trousers, they hardly looked like a hedge or a stile; you don't see many hedges or stiles made out of blue muslin or white flannel. They could even paint each other with a woodgrain effect and poke about on a pew in church . . .

Perhaps he could go to the vicarage and ask the vicar if he would lend him *his* bed, for services rendered in the cricket team. 'And is this young woman a member of my flock?' the vicar would say spouting mouthfuls of communion wine over the curate. No, your highness, but her mislaid grandmother used to make lovely dripping. The trombone was her downfall though. That and sitting up all night trying to bleach the parrot lest the minister thought it too gaudy . . . when he came for his weekly poke . . . Ha-ha . . . When he came for his poke . . . When he . . .

★   ★   ★

Lucy and Miriam decided that a trip to Dudley would be the thing to do that Saturday afternoon, since it was such a lovely warm day. As they sat waiting on a bench for the train at Brettell Lane station they gossiped about this and that.

'I heard as Penina Baggott has just buried her ninth,' Miriam said, and drew her mouth down at the corners to emphasise the gravity.

'Fancy,' Lucy replied with equal solemnity. 'How old was it?'

'I ain't sure. They've never been wed, you know, her and that chap of hers. He just rented a house and she just moved in with him. Scandalous it is, I reckon.'

'And me. I believe in marriage, Miriam. I mean, you can't share a house with a chap and not expect to have his kids, can you? And I think you should only have kids when you'm married.'

'It's bad enough him playing the fiddle of a night,' Miriam declared. 'He's a keen fiddler by all accounts. I mean, you wouldn't want e'er a fiddle a-squawking round you when you'd still got eight kids all a-squawking an' all, would you?'

'It'd drive you potty,' Lucy agreed.

'I'd leave him, with all that row going on.'

They heard the railway engine panting hard as it approached the station, and stood up in readiness.

'I wonder what happened to that guard you used to fancy, Lucy?' Miriam remarked. 'We ain't seen him for ages.'

'Months,' said Lucy. 'Last time I saw him was in the winter.'

'P'raps he's left and found other work.'

'Who knows? Maybe he's emigrated.'

The train pulled into the station with its usual mechanical squeals, clanking of buffers and the attendant acrid smells. As it drew to a halt Lucy, out of ingrained habit, looked to the rear at the guards' van, just in case Dickie Dempster was on duty, when she saw him.

'Miriam, he's here!' She nudged her friend excitedly. 'He's just getting out the brake van. Hang on, I'll have to speak to him.' She waited a second or two, and he spotted her.

'I thought you was dead,' he said amiably when he reached her. 'I ain't seen you for ages.'

'I was just saying the same thing to Miriam.' Lucy sounded breathless. 'Have you altered your shift?'

'Swapped it around. I start earlier and finish earlier. That's why I ain't seen yer. I finish about two. This is me last trip today. When I get back to Wolverhampton, that's me done. I shall get meself in front of a nice tankard of ale when I walk out o' Low Level station. Where are you bound for, ladies?'

'Dudley.'

'Pity. I'd have took you for a drink if you was going to Wolverhampton.'

'That would've been nice,' Lucy said, looking at Miriam for her agreement.

' 'Cept we've already bought our tickets to Dudley,' Miriam interjected.

'Pity,' he said again. 'But why don't you make it Wolverhampton next week, eh? I'll be on the same train. Catch it and I'll meet you off, eh? Then I'll treat you to a drink.'

Lucy's blue eyes sparkled with verve and she blushed to her roots. But she was not going to let this opportunity pass. Of course, nothing would come of it, but she had dreamed of this for far too long to allow it to pass her by now. 'Yes, all right,' she said and her smile was dazzling. 'We'll be on this train next Saturday. We generally catch this one.'

'Good.' He took his watch out of his fob and glanced at it. 'This carriage, ladies?'

It was second class and Lucy giggled. 'If you say it's all right, Dickie.'

'Course it's all right.' He opened the door and let them in. 'Have a good trip and I'll see you next week.'

'We're looking forward to it already.'

Dickie Dempster slammed the door to and waved, then scanned the train for stragglers and doors left open before he hurried back to his guards' van. Once more the girls heard the familiar shrill sound of his whistle signalling the engine driver that it was safe to recommence their journey.

'I shan't go for a drink with him,' Miriam declared.

'You won't?'

'No, you can go on your own. It's what you want anyroad. You don't want me about, Lucy. I'd only be in the way and spoil your fun.'

'But Miriam, I don't think I should go and meet him on my own. He'll be expecting us both.'

'No, it's you he's interested in, not me.'

Lucy sighed. 'But I'd feel guilty going on my own. After all this time, I'd feel I was being untrue to Arthur.'

'Well, I reckon that depends on your intentions, Luce. I mean, if you want your seeing this Dickie Dempster to be something more, then yes, you'd be being untrue. But if it's just being polite, and politely accepting his invitation, then you ain't. So which is it?'

'I don't know, Miriam. I honestly don't know.'

'So it's goodbye, Arthur,' Miriam said.

★ ★ ★

9

D ickie Dempster's eyes lingered on Lucy Piddock as she
and Miriam Watson walked up the ramp from Netherton station at Blowers Green, which took them to the road into
Dudley. He had a good view of her from his guards' van.
There was something about her reserved nature that appealed,
reserve that complemented her elegance. She was tallish with a
straight back, and the outward demeanour of a young woman
of quality. At least, she was the closest thing to a lady he was
likely to encounter again. Her waist was small and he fancied
holding her in his arms and feeling her warm slenderness
pressed against him.

Still watching, he turned the wheel that let off the brake as
the train eased towards the tunnel. By the time his van was
disappearing into it, veiled in swirling smoke and steam, she
was crossing the bridge over the railway and she waved. Of
course, he returned the gesture gladly, a broad grin fixed to his
handsome face. Pity he would not be on the return run. It
might just coincide with hers.

All the way to Wolverhampton Low Level Station he
pondered this Lucy Piddock. There was an innocence, a
naivety about her that he itched to exploit. He had no doubt
that if ever he could entice her between the sheets, it would be
her first time. And he could teach her so much, mould her into
what he wanted her to be, a sensuous, willing lover.

At the terminus, the train ground to a halt and those
passengers who had remained on it disembarked. He watched

them head for the exit in a human swarm, some hurrying, some strolling. The summer air was shrill with the sibilant noise of steam escaping under pressure, and voices hailing each other over the top of it. When Dickie was sure the train had emptied he called a porter to off-load the parcels and freight they were carrying and then made his way, his snap bag over his shoulder, to the stationmaster's office to sign off.

'Fancy an hour's overtime, Dempster?' William Humphries the stationmaster asked from behind his desk.

'Doing what, sir?'

'Cording hasn't turned in, and the coaches you just brought in are due to be oiled and greased and the wheels checked. They'll have to be shunted into the far siding. I'd like you to supervise it ready for the wheelwrights, and then check all the shackles and coupling chains.'

Ironic, he thought. It was just as well that Lucy Piddock had not agreed to go with him when he'd finished work; she'd have a long wait. 'That's all right by me, sir,' he replied. 'Do you want me to do it straight away?'

'Yes, get the train away from the platform,' said Humphries. 'Just tell Baxter the engine driver what's going on.'

Dickie nodded. 'I will, Mr Humphries.'

He went out into the sunshine and headed for the engine. Standing beside the two massive driving wheels which were as tall as he was, he yelled to the engineer over the engine's noise. The driver turned and cupped his hand to his ear.

'We gotta shunt the train into the far siding,' he shouted, gesturing with his hands to make himself understood.

The driver nodded and Dickie stepped up onto the footplate with his snap bag. He watched as the driver turned a valve and, with a series of ear-splitting huffs, the powerful locomotive began slowly, smoothly moving backwards. Buffers clanked resonantly as the string of coaches nudged each other in turn at the gentle shove, followed by the squeal and creak of chains and shackles while the couplings took the strain as they drew to a halt again. Dickie gestured to the signalman in the box to change the points, and the train inched slowly forward, coming to rest on the far sidings, as requested by the stationmaster.

'Had anything to eat or drink lately?' Dickie enquired.

'Nothing since we left for Worcester,' the boilerman answered.

'Nor me, and I'm half starved. I'm going to eat me snap afore I do anything else. What about you pair?'

'We've finished for the day,' Baxter said, shutting the engine down. 'I'll have my snap at home.'

'It's all right for some,' Dickie jibed good-humouredly. 'Are you working tomorrow?'

'Day off tomorrow. I'll be shepherding the kids to chapel and then Sunday school, I daresay.'

'Chapel, eh? I didn't realise you was such a regular Christian, Georgie.'

'Wesleyan, me, Dickie. Through and through. You ought to try it sometime.'

'No, chapel ain't for me, mate. I'd rather be in the alehouse.'

The three men stepped down from the footplate one after the other, the driver last so that he could check that his steam pressure was decreasing. Georgie Baxter and Trudle the fireman made their way across the railway track while Dickie sat beside it sunning himself. He took out his dinner and his bottle of tea from his snap bag and ate, thinking again about Lucy Piddock, while the engine's hissing gradually diminished. He hoped he would not be called upon to do overtime next Saturday when he was due to see her.

He finished his snap and stuffed the wrappings inside his bag and laid it back on the footplate. He would pick it up when he had finished checking the couplings in the absence of Cording. He'd have a word with Cording, make sure he rolled up for work next Saturday. No doubt the bone-idle bastard had drunk too much beer last night and had woken with a thick head. He tended to be a bit unreliable, did Cording.

Dickie began working backwards from the engine's tender, checking the centre couplings and the side chains, ensuring none were broken and that they were all securely fastened. He looked at the flanged wheels cursorily, solid and unbreakable, and marvelled at this age of the railway in which he was privileged to live, with all its brilliant feats of British engineering that led the rest of the world. All seemed fine and it took him about half an hour to check all the couplings down the whole length of the carriages. Done, he turned around, ready to collect his snap bag from the footplate.

As he walked along the side of the train he thought he saw a man sitting in one of the third-class compartments and stopped to investigate. Dickie peered through the window of the compartment. The man was quite still, unmoving, not even breathing as far as he could make out, and deathly white. Possibly dead. Dickie's heart suddenly started beating fast at the discovery. Just what had he stumbled across? What if there had been a murder on the train when he was in charge of it? He tapped the window hard to try and wake him up, just in case it was somebody who had fallen asleep and gone past his station. But the body did not stir. The face had the sickly pale hue of the dead. Whoever he was, he must be dead, poor sod.

Ignoring his snap bag, Dickie raced across the tracks towards the company's office and rapped urgently on the stationmaster's door.

'Come in!'

'There's a body in one of the third-class compartments,' Dempster uttered breathlessly. 'In the train we shunted over to the far sidings.'

'A body?' William Humphries stood up at once, alarmed at

hearing such news. 'You're sure it's a body and not somebody sleeping, Dempster?'

'I tried to wake it by hammering on the windows, Mr Humphries, but to no avail.'

'Is it male or female, this body?'

'Male, sir.'

'I'd better take a look. Come with me, Dempster. Show me where it is. I don't like the sound of this.'

So Dickie Dempster ran back across the tracks to the sidings, William Humphries following hard by, puffing and panting from the heat and his excess weight. They stopped at the carriage that held the body, and Dickie pointed it out.

'Jesus Christ!' Humphries exclaimed under his breath. 'The last thing we want on the Oxford Worcester and Wolverhampton Railway is for somebody to have been found dead in one of our coaches. Especially at our station, Dempster. It won't look very good in the news sheets.'

'Maybe he's been murdered, sir.'

'Jesus Christ! Murdered?'

'It's a possibility, sir. He looks very pale, as if he's been suffocated or strangled.'

'Well, I can't see any blood . . .'

'Shall I go inside the compartment and feel if he's still warm, sir?'

'Better not, Dempster,' Humphries exclaimed decisively. 'We'd better call in the police. Let them deal with it. If it's a murder it's outside our jurisdiction. We must be sure. Until we know for sure we must not touch the body, nor go anywhere near it. What if the poor soul has died from some contagious disease? We'd have to fumigate everywhere.' He put a handkerchief over his mouth and nose for protection, alarmed at his own frightening suggestion. 'Come on, Dempster. Somebody will have to go and fetch a couple of bobbies.'

'I'll go, sir.'

'Good man.' They leapt down from the carriage and shut the door. 'Meanwhile, Dempster, I'll have the train cordoned off. In fact, I'd better get the whole station cordoned off. Nobody must come near until the police have investigated thoroughly.'

'I'll be as quick as I can, Mr Humphries.'

So Dickie ran to the police station and Humphries organised some of the station workers and engineers to cordon off the train. While they waited for the police to arrive the men speculated wildly on the unfortunate victim inside, and invented fabulous notions of how the poor devil might have met his fate.

'Just imagine,' somebody said, 'the murderer stepping calmly down from that compartment and then calmly walking out of a station along the line as if nothing had happened.'

'He might have left the train at our station,' another conjectured. 'We might have a murderer in our midst in Wolverhampton.'

'I bet he owed money,' yet another theorised. 'Murders am generally over somebody owing money.'

'Or over women,' the first suggested.

'Aye, or over women.'

And so it went on until Dempster got back twenty minutes later with two bobbies in tow.

'He's still dead, I take it?' Dickie asked inanely.

'Once you'm dead you'm dead, mate,' one of the policemen, a sergeant, stated with all the wisdom of authority. 'We'd better go in and have a look at him, and see if there's any evidence of foul play.'

Dickie Dempster opened the door to the compartment and followed the two policemen in. They peered at the body and one of them gently prodded it with his forefinger, then gently placed the backs of his fingers against its brow to assess its temperature.

'He ain't been dead long,' the sergeant who was full of authoritative wisdom declared, bending down to inspect the body more closely. 'Rigor mortis ain't set in yet.' He raised the arm of the corpse and let it drop. 'He's cold, poor bugger, but he ain't as cold as he would have been if he'd been dead a couple of hours.'

Humphries the stationmaster joined them. 'Do you suspect foul play, Sergeant?'

'Hard to say, but we can't rule it out. There's no injuries as I can see, no marks on his neck where he might have been strangulated . . . He could have been suffocated though.'

'That's what I said,' remarked Dickie. 'He might have been suffocated.'

'I wonder if he's got a ticket?' Humphries said. 'Can one of you policemen feel in his pockets. It'll tell where he boarded the train.'

The younger officer withdrew a ticket from the fob pocket of the corpse's waistcoat and handed it over. He handed it to Humphries who scrutinised it.

'Kidderminster.'

'Well, there's nothing for it but to send for the coroner,' the sergeant pronounced. 'It'll be up to the coroner to ascertain the cause of death. I wonder who the poor bugger is . . . We'd better check his pockets . . .'

Just then, the other policeman, a younger man, happened to glance up and spotted a tool bag in the luggage rack above. 'Aye up!' he ejaculated. 'He's got a bag o' tricks up yonder, look . . .' He reached up, retrieved it and opened it up.

'Chisels . . . A mallet . . .' the sergeant said, rummaging. 'And what's all them sheets o' gold? Think that's what it's over . . . gold?'

'With all them chisels and that mallet, I reckon he'd been up to no good anyroad,' the younger officer said. 'A thief or burglar, I wouldn't be surprised, with all them tools. They use 'em for picking and breaking locks and padlocks, you know. Vile people.'

'Hmm . . .' The sergeant turned pensively to Mr Humphries. 'Let's get the coroner, Mr Humphries. Can you arrange for a couple o' porters to carry the body to your office on a shutter or something?'

'Yes, I'll organise it straight away, Sergeant.'

'If you could keep it there till the coroner arrives.'

'It won't start to smell or anything, will it?' Humphries queried, his face an icon of aversion.

'The coroner shouldn't be that long, Mr Humphries,' the sergeant replied reassuringly.

The police sergeant departed and more railway workers left their posts, accompanying the porters who were carrying a shutter, to hurry over the railway tracks so they could get a peek at the corpse of the vile young burglar who had come to a sticky end on one of their trains. Then when they had loaded the body onto the shutter they trooped in slow procession, bearing it with all the solemnity of a state funeral, and deposited it with the silent reverence accorded the dead, across the desk of Mr Humphries.

'I can't say as I like having a dead person on my desk,' Humphries said with distaste.

'Upsets you, does it, sir?' Dempster said.

'Makes me feel creepy. I'm a bit tickle-stomached about death.'

'It don't bother me, Mr Humphries. Would you like me to stay here with you till the coroner comes?'

'That's decent of you, Dempster. Thank you. If you're sure you don't mind.'

'I'm in no rush, Mr Humphries. Glad to help out.'

The coroner, a weedy little man, eventually arrived with another policeman. He doffed his tall hat and introduced himself as Mr Eccles. His beard and moustaches made up for hair he lacked on top of his head. 'I trust this is the body?' he said with professional gloom.

'Yes, this is it, Mr Eccles,' Humphries replied. 'The police seem to think he's been suffocated. Mixed up in some criminal goings on, they suspect. Everything points to him being a professional burglar. But I wonder if he died of some contagion.'

'Any identification?'

'Not as yet.'

'Did they look for any in his pockets?'

'Not fully, but we found his rail ticket.'

'We must identify him before any inquest.' Eccles said impatiently and rooted clumsily through the pockets of the deceased man. He withdrew a small green bottle and held it up suspiciously. 'Hmm . . . Poison, I'll wager. Looks to me as though the silly fool might have poisoned himself. Suicide looks a distinct possibility. Pity the police didn't find this.'

While everybody was looking at the small green bottle, they heard a strange blowing of lips, not unlike the sound a horse makes. All eyes were suddenly upon the corpse as it opened its eyes and looked about itself with a dazed, puzzled look.

'Lord! Where am I?' it said.

The coroner detached his eyes from the remaining policeman to look at Humphries, then at Dempster and then at the animated corpse, with a look of both disbelief and frustration to add to his natural cheerless disposition. 'Pardon me, but you are supposed to be a dead person, sir, whom we are trying to identify.'

'Identify? Well, there's no mystery about me. My name's Arthur Goodrich.' Arthur propped himself up on his elbows and looked about him confused. 'I can't believe I'm dead. Where am I?'

'In the stationmaster's office at Wolverhampton Low Level station,' Humphries replied, an expression on his face depicting shock and relief simultaneously. 'We were of the opinion you were dead, Mr Goodrich. We had shunted our train into sidings to be serviced and checked, when Mr Dempster here noticed you in a carriage. We could not rouse you and presumed therefore that you were dead. We found this bottle of poison on your person.'

'Poison? What poison? That ain't poison, it's laudanum. I took some when I got on the train at Kidderminster. It must have knocked me out. What time is it?'

Dempster looked at his watch. 'It's twenty to four.'

'Twenty to four? Oh, no, I've missed me cricket match.'

The coroner shifted his weight from one foot to another in agitation. 'Is that all you can say for yourself after all the trouble you've caused us, Mr Goodrich?' he said bleakly. 'I have been fetched from my home just to attend to you, a live person who foolishly knocked himself out with an excess of laudanum. The police have been unnecessarily interrupted from their important work keeping the peace in the town, the station has been shut for fear of an outbreak of some infectious disease, the stationmaster has been detained here unnecessarily, as has this other gentleman from the railway, and all you can say is a trifling "Oh no, I've missed my cricket match". Do you realise the trouble you have caused, Mr Goodrich?'

'How could I know?' Arthur answered defensively. 'I was asleep.'

'Well, now that you have woken up, might I suggest that you find your way home.' The coroner picked up his bag and put his hat back on his bald head. 'I'll bid you good day, gentlemen.'

'He's a bit prickly,' Arthur said resentfully, 'him with the upside-down head.'

'Hardly surprising,' the stationmaster replied, 'the trouble you've caused. Where are you from, Mr Goodrich? We know you travelled from Kidderminster.'

'I live in Brierley Hill.'

'There'll be a train calling at Round Oak and Brettell Lane in half an hour, Mr Goodrich. Perhaps you be good enough to be on it.' He turned to the guard. 'Dempster, would you take Mr Goodrich for a cup of tea or something and make sure he's quite fit to travel before he embarks on another of our trains?'

'I will, sir.'

'Thank you.' William Humphries sat down in his chair, sighed profoundly, and buried his face in his hands as Dickie Dempster led Arthur Goodrich out of his office.

'This way, Mr Goodrich,' Dickie Dempster said sympathetically. 'I imagine it must be a bit of a shock waking up like you did and finding yourself in a strange place, surrounded by strange folk, all prodding you about.'

'You have no idea,' Arthur replied. 'What did you say your name was?'

'Richard Dempster. Folks call me Dickie.'

'Well, thank you for taking care of me, Mr Dempster. I take it you work for the railway.'

'Yes, I'm a guard. It was me that found you. Look, here's the tea room. Let's sit you down and I'll get you a cup of tea, eh? I could do with one meself as a matter of fact.'

'You're very kind, Mr Dempster. Not a bit like that rude chap. Who was he?'

'Only the coroner.' Dickie laughed as the farcical nature of what had happened dawned on him. 'You were a bit of a celebrity for a while this afternoon, Mr Goodrich,' he went on, guiding Arthur to a table. 'You could have been world famous. Christ, there was a hell of a flap when we thought we'd got a corpse on our hands. Sit down, eh, Mr Goodrich? How do you feel now?'

'A bit drowsy, to tell you the truth.' Arthur sat down. 'You would as well, after a dollop of laudanum. I took it 'cause I'd got toothache.' Arthur exercised his bottom jaw up and down and from side to side experimentally. 'It seems to have cured it . . . for the time being, at any rate.'

'Fancy something to eat as well?'

'I wouldn't mind, to tell you the truth. I'm feeling a bit peckish. It's a while since I ate.'

'How about some pork pie?'

'Perfect.'

Dickie called a waitress who took their order, then turned his attention to Arthur. 'You was supposed to see a cricket match this afternoon then?'

'I was supposed to play in one. I'm the stumper in our local team. I hope I haven't lost me team place because of it. I feel bad about letting the lads down.'

'Never mind. You didn't do it intentional, like, did yer?'

'Course not.'

'Besides, laudanum makes you drowsy, and I reckon you wouldn't be in any fit state to play cricket. Especially as stumper.'

'No, maybe not,' Arthur agreed. 'I'd be black and blue where the ball kept hitting me. To tell you the truth, everything seems distant. I feel as if I'm in another world, detached from this one but still a part of it. Maybe I *am* dead after all, Mr Dempster. Maybe I'm in that nether world between this one and the next.'

Dickie laughed amiably. 'That's the laudanum, I expect.'

'I shan't do it again – take that stuff when I'm travelling by train. I feel such a fool now . . . But I was in such agony with toothache.'

'I shouldn't worry,' Dickie Dempster said. 'I don't suppose the coroner had much else to do this afternoon, bar tending his roses. The important thing is, you'm all right. You ain't dead after all.'

They fell silent for a few seconds, during which time the waitress brought their pot of tea and wedges of pork pie.

Dickie poured the tea while Arthur tucked into his food ravenously. He finished it before he spoke again.

'I enjoyed that.'

'Want some more? It's on the railway.'

Arthur shook his head. 'No, I'd better not, thanks. I'll just finish me cup of tea, then I'll get out of your way. You've been very kind, Mr Dempster. Thank you for that.'

'Oh, I've done nothing,' he replied dismissively. 'Anybody would do the same.'

Arthur sugared his tea and stirred it. 'You say you're a guard on the railway, Mr Dempster?'

'Yes. I've worked this railway ever since it opened in fifty-two.'

'Then there's every chance I might see you again. If you ever get the chance, call in to see me at Jeremiah Goodrich and Sons, Monumental Masons and Sepulchral Architects.'

'Struth, that's a bit of a mouthful. I'll never remember that.'

'Stonemasons, then. We're up the Lower Delph in Brierley Hill.'

'Is that what all them tools are in your bag, then? For working masonry?'

'Course. What did you think they was?'

'The policemen what came thought they was for picking locks. They thought you was a burglar. If you'd bin alive, they'd have nicked you.'

'It's a good thing I was dead then, eh?' Arthur said, and grinned impishly. He finished his tea. 'Just goes to show how stupid our policemen are. Hardly blessed with the finest brains.'

'Which is why they're only policemen, eh, Mr Goodrich?'

Arthur nodded his agreement with a grin. 'I'll be off then, Mr Dempster. Thanks again for taking care of me.'

'It's no trouble. I'll see you safely to the train. I'll get you a ticket first, though.'

'It's all right, I'll get me own ticket.'

'But it's on the company this time, Mr Goodrich.' Dempster winked. 'Their treat. Let's make sure it's first class, eh?'

'Good Lord,' Arthur grinned once more. 'First class . . . Well . . .'

★　★　★

10

'You damn fool. Fancy taking laudanum just as you've boarded a train. It stands to reason as you'll fall asleep.' Jeremiah Goodrich had just been told of his son's misadventure on the way back from Kidderminster. 'Pity they didn't leave yer overnight in one o' them big long sheds with all the rats and mice. That might have brought you to your senses at last.'

'But I had toothache,' Arthur argued. 'It was murder.'

'Murder!' Jeremiah scoffed. 'There'll be murder done in this house unless you pull yourself together. I've never known such a useless muff in all my born days. To have had the police and the coroner out . . .' The old man shook his head in derision. 'Did they have e'er a doctor out to thee?'

'Not that I know of.'

'Ah, well, stands to reason,' he scoffed. 'If they'd had e'er a doctor to you he'd have had you certified for sure, and they'd have locked you up in the workhouse . . . And it'd be the best place for yer.'

It was always the same. Sunday morning in the Goodrich household and Arthur had just returned from the Bell Hotel after church. Dinah had returned before him and related Arthur's tale to Jeremiah meanwhile, and he had huffed and tutted as the story unfolded.

'If I didn't have to go and work in damned cold churchyards all the time, there'd very likely be no need for laudanum, nor anything else for that matter,' Arthur complained spiritedly,

131

' 'cause I doubt if I'd get all the toothache and chills as I get. Working in graveyards is affecting my health.'

'Poppycock!' Jeremiah rasped angrily. 'Working outdoors is healthy. It's good for the constitution—'

'Yes, look what it did for you, Father. Ill all the time. I don't want to be like that. I hate feeling bad.'

'You should be grateful. You should be grateful you've got work that's light and easy. You should be grateful as you ain't digging coal or fireclay, or navvying on the railways.'

'You reckon? I might earn more money doing that.'

'Y'ain't worth more money,' Jeremiah hissed. 'You bone-idle bugger.'

Arthur looked his father squarely between the eyes. 'Then, if that's the case, find somebody else to do your graveyard work, and see if they'll do it for the same money. I've had my fill.'

'Listen to him, Dinah. He never stops moaning.'

'I do wish you two would stop arguing,' Dinah intervened. 'You'm like cat and dog, the pair of you, at each other's throats all the while. I get no peace in this house when you two am together.'

'Well, you'll have all the peace in the world soon, Mother, because I'm going. I mean it. I can't stay here and have to put up with this all the time.'

'Going?' she queried. 'You can't go. You ain't got nowhere to go to.'

'I'll find somewhere. I'll find lodgings . . . and work. Somewhere where they'll appreciate me. Somewhere they'll appreciate what I do.'

Dinah turned to her husband angrily. 'See what you'm doing, Jeremiah? You'm driving him away with your cantankerousness.'

'Oh, he won't go nowhere, Dinah – more's the bloody pity.'

'Oh? Then we'll see,' Arthur said defiantly and left his mother and father to argue it out between them.

He really had had enough. It was time to move on, time to get away from his father's oppression and exploitation. Never had Jeremiah acknowledged that Arthur was anything but a lackey in the family business. Never had he shown him affection, only ever derision. Never had he thanked him for work he'd done, never had he praised him when praise was deserved and indeed appropriate. It could have made all the difference. Even when he was a little lad his father was always remote, distant. The old man seemed to treat Arthur as a nuisance, somebody he was responsible for, but accepting the responsibility with immense reluctance. It was no wonder that Arthur was lacking in confidence, that he found it difficult to make friends, that he was always afraid people would react off-handedly towards him. He'd had a lifetime of being shunned, turned away, ignored. Well, it was time to let the miserable old bugger see that his younger son could make his own way in the world, that he did not have to rely on the family firm, that he did not have to rely on an antagonistic father for a roof over his head and for money in his pocket.

Neither would he dine with them today. He would go where he knew he could count on some genuine affection and hospitality, as well as a decent Sunday dinner. He would go to the Piddocks' cottage. Besides, he had an apology to make to Lucy.

Lucy was sitting on the front step of the cottage peeling potatoes in the sunshine. Bobby, the ancient sheepdog was lying at her feet, paying scant attention to the frisky Tickle who was licking his ear attentively.

'Well, look who it isn't,' Lucy said with some disdain when she saw him. 'I thought you'd left the country.'

'Sorry I didn't see you last night,' he said morosely. 'I wasn't well.'

'Wasn't well?' she said, with mock surprise. 'That's unlike

you, Arthur. So what was it this time? Ear-ache, toothache, backache, leg-ache or face-ache?'

'I ain't asking for sarcasm, Lucy,' he replied, feeling sorry for himself, 'and neither do I expect ill temper from you – I have enough of that at home. I had a really peculiar day yesterday.'

'Oh, well I didn't, I had a very nice day.' Her tone held a defiant edge of truth. 'And it was all the better for not seeing you.'

'I came to apologise.'

'You can apologise all you want.'

'And something else . . .'

She looked up at him and rolled her eyes impatiently. 'What?'

'I'm leaving home. I can't stand it there any longer. I'm moving out, Lucy . . .'

'Moving out?' Her eyes had an interested look in them now, a look that told him that there had been pretence in her impatience and she was concerned after all.

'Yesterday was what triggered it. This morning was what decided it.'

'I've finished the spuds now,' she said, and stood up. She picked up the pan into which she had put her peeled and cut potatoes. 'Pick up the bowl for me, please, Arthur. Let's talk inside.'

He picked up the bowl of peelings and followed her inside. 'Is your father here?'

She turned and smiled. 'Don't be daft, he's gone to the Whimsey. Mother's back from chapel, though.'

'Morning, Mrs Piddock.'

'Morning, young Arthur,' replied Hannah Piddock. 'How's this? We don't expect to see you of a Sunday dinnertime.'

'He's leaving home,' Lucy advised. 'Or have you left already, Arthur?'

'I would leave today if I'd got somewhere to go.' He hoped that it didn't sound as if he were asking to be taken in, for that was the last thing on his mind. 'I wouldn't mind some Sunday dinner, though, if you can spare some.'

That amused Hannah. 'Course you can have some Sunday dinner, my son. We got a bit o' pork. Tommy Banks slaughtered one of his pigs in the week and he sold us a nice bit o' pork.'

'I like a bit o' pork,' Arthur said agreeably. 'Thank you, Mrs Piddock.'

'D'you want me to do anything else, Mother?' Lucy enquired.

'No, I can manage. Sit down with Arthur.'

So they sat together on the settle and looked at each other, each waiting for the other to say something. It was Lucy who began.

'So what happened yesterday?'

'I had toothache—'

'You and your toothache . . .'

'But it was really bad, Lucy. It was so bad I had to take some laudanum to relieve it . . .' He told her what had happened.

'So you woke up at Wolverhampton Low Level to find the stationmaster, a policeman and the coroner all there, thinking you were dead?' She laughed at the absurdity of it all. 'Only you could do all that, Arthur. I bet you looked a proper fool.'

He shrugged. 'I don't care whether I looked a fool or not. I couldn't help it. I fell asleep on the train. I would still have been there now, I bet, if they hadn't been a-prodding me and feeling in me pockets to find out who I was . . . or to pinch my money.'

'I never heard anything like it,' Lucy said. She turned to Hannah 'Have you ever heard anything like it, Mother? He's the limit.'

'I remember your father once having too much beer one Sunday dinnertime and not waking up till the Tuesday morning. He missed a day's work.'

'But you didn't get the coroner out, did you?'

'Oh, no, there was no need. I knew he wasn't dead. I could hear him snoring.'

'Anyway,' Arthur went on, 'there was one chap who worked on the railway as a guard and he looked after me. A chap named Dickie Dempster—'

'Dickie Dempster?'

'Yes.' He looked up at her questioningly. 'Why? D'you know him?'

'No, no, I don't know any Dickie Dempster . . .' Lucy was glad that Arthur seemed not to notice her blushes at hearing the name.

'Well, he was kind. He took me for a cup of tea and something to eat in the tea room after. He seemed a decent chap. I was grateful to him.'

'Oh . . .' Lucy nodded. 'Yes, he sounds a decent chap . . . whoever he is . . .'

'Anyway, Lucy, when I got back home late yesterday afternoon, I still felt groggy from the laudanum, so I went to bed to sleep it off, and I didn't wake up till early this morning. That's why I didn't get to the Whimsey last night. That's why I didn't come to walk you home after.'

'Oh, it's all right, Arthur,' Lucy replied absently. Suddenly she was immersed in thoughts of Dickie Dempster and how she was to meet him next Saturday.

'Then, it all blew up this morning,' Arthur continued, oblivious to her thoughts. 'Me father called me all the silly buggers under the sun. We had a right argument. I told him, if I didn't have to go working in all these cold and damp graveyards I wouldn't be suffering with colds and toothache and everything else that afflicts me. He never says thank you, well done our Arthur, kiss my arse, nor nothing . . . Sorry, Mrs Piddock, I didn't mean to swear—'

'Don't worry, Arthur, I'm used to it,' Hannah replied, prodding cabbage leaves into a pan of water.

'I could earn double what I get working somewhere else. So I've decided I'm leaving, Lucy.'

'So where will you go?'

'I haven't decided.'

'Oh,' Lucy said, half in shock, half in relief, for if he were not around she could openly conduct an affair with Dickie Dempster, if things were to progress that far.

'Anyway, I was thinking,' Arthur continued. 'It'll be your birthday in early September. You'll be twenty-one. It only wants six weeks. I thought that in six weeks I would've found work and a house to rent, wherever I end up. I thought we could get married and you could join me . . .'

'Oh, that'd be nice, our Lucy,' Hannah proclaimed as she hovered over the hot cast-iron range, before Lucy could get a word in. She dried her hands on a cloth and stood in front of the couple, smiling gleefully. 'Twenty-one's a lovely age to get wed, you know. Neither too old nor too young. You'd make a lovely bride.'

Lucy stood up, as if to unshackle herself from the confines of marriage to a man she was by no means sure she loved. 'I don't know as I want to get wed, Arthur,' she said quietly. 'It's nice to know you think so much of me, but . . . But I don't know as I want to get wed . . .'

Arthur flashed a look at Hannah, a look that was a plea for help. 'What do you think, Mrs Piddock?'

'I think you'd make a lovely husband for our Lucy, Arthur . . . But it's up to her whether she accepts you or not.'

He looked intently at Lucy. 'So why don't you want to wed me, Lucy? I'd be a good husband. I'd look after you.'

'Yes, you would,' Lucy responded sincerely. 'I know you would. But I'm not certain I'd be a good wife.'

'You'd be the best wife any man could have.'

Lucy shook her head. 'If I was sure I loved you . . . I'm not sure that I love you . . .'

'But we've been courting nigh on a year.'

'Ten months . . . on and off.'

'So you must feel something for me, else you wouldn't have wasted ten months of your time.'

Lucy shrugged and her expression was one of painful regret. 'I'm just not sure, Arthur. Even after ten months I'm not sure. Oh, I like you . . . course I like you. I think the world of you . . . But that isn't enough. It isn't enough to get wed on.'

'I intend to go miles away from here, Lucy,' he said, as if it were a threat. 'That's why I ask you to marry me. So as we can still be together.'

'It makes no difference how far away you go.'

'Oh, I bet it will,' Hannah asserted with some confidence. 'She'll miss you if you go, young Arthur. When you've been gone a week or two she'll soon realise how much she misses you.'

'But I'd like her answer now, Mrs Piddock.'

'I've given you my answer,' Lucy said quietly.

'But it ain't the answer I want, Lucy.'

'It's the only answer I can give.'

Arthur looked at Hannah again beseechingly. 'What can I do to make her say yes, Mrs Piddock?'

'Nothing,' Hannah replied flatly. 'You'll just have to wait for her to come to her senses. If you want my advice, Arthur, you'll leave her be. She'll soon come to her cake and milk when you've gone. She'll soon change her mind.'

★　★　★

Sunday dinner was a subdued affair as far as Arthur, Lucy and Hannah were concerned. Arthur picked at his food fussily. He was always a pernickety eater, worried that too much fatty gravy brought on indigestion or cabbage gave him the wind, all of which irritated Lucy. Haden, however, was merry after an adequate intake of beer and he spouted forth volubly on various issues that concerned himself, oblivious to the emotions, doubts and certainties which, prior to his return home, had beset his wife and daughter over Arthur. And the other three were glad of his rumbustious chatter, for it adequately camouflaged the intensity that had befallen them in his absence; the intensity of a worthy young woman in her prime, reluctant to be a bride because she was clinging to her own secret hopes and dreams; the intensity of her would-be groom, whose previous two days had been so miserably eventful, but whose life was now rendered meaningless because of her rebuff. Afterward, Haden made himself comfortable in the rocking chair, and drifted off into his usual inebriated Sunday afternoon snooze.

'Shall we go for a walk, Lucy?' Arthur suggested, when the object of his devotion had finished helping her mother clear up. 'It's a lovely afternoon.'

'If you like,' she agreed, content awhile to be away from her mother's further inevitable advice to Arthur.

They ambled along the canal while the hot July sun beat down on them, heading towards the industrial melancholy of the Old and the New Level Ironworks, that still spouted forth columns of unsavoury brown smoke and broke the Sunday silence with irreverent clatters. For the first few minutes they spoke little, each lost in their own thoughts. Arthur grieved inwardly over his failure to elicit a positive response to his unromantic but eminently practical proposal of marriage. Lucy, meanwhile, suffered genuine pangs of guilt that she could not requite Arthur's love. She could only look forward romantically to next Saturday when she would be in the company of Dickie Dempster, with whom she had been secretly, guiltily and iniquitously in love for nearly a year.

It went against her nature to deceive and it bothered her deeply. She was well aware that Arthur was a worthy contender, for she had debated his vices and his virtues with herself and others on occasions too numerous to recount. Much as she hated turning him away and hurting him, she hated even more the hypocrisy of pretence. She was determined to pursue happiness in the other direction, that of Wolverhampton and Dickie Dempster. She owed it to herself. She could not sacrifice herself on the altar of marriage for a man she did not love. It was not that she was being deceitful in the obnoxious sense, she was rather following her instinct that true love was beckoning from this other direction, love that would be fulfilling, fine and virtuous. She was not interested in living life any other way. This was the only direction in which she could allow herself to be drawn. The purity of the concept of the relationship she envisaged with Dickie Dempster was driving her, and she knew it was good because Nature was prompting her, thus Nature decreed it.

'Have you got any idea where you'll go?' Lucy asked him, conscious as ever of the silence between them.

He shrugged sullenly. 'I dunno. Far, far from here . . . to try and forget you, Lucy . . . Maybe I'll go to the coast. I fancy living by the sea for a while. Something different. It would do me good to breathe fresh sea air for a change . . . It would do you good as well,' he added as an afterthought.

'I can't leave my mother and father,' she replied, seizing another excuse. 'I couldn't go anyway.'

'Your brother did.'

'And it broke their hearts. I couldn't do that to them.'

'Yet you can break mine . . .'

They were ascending the towpath at the Nine Locks, a spectacular stretch of the Stourbridge canal that seemed to rise to eternity. A flotilla of narrowboats with smoking chimney pipes sat low in the murky water of the lower basin, loaded to the gunnels with coal, fireclay or ironstone, waiting their turn to go through the locks. Towing horses, weary and unkempt, grazed speculatively on the sparse vegetation while the bargees and their wives slumped with easy abandon in the sunshine, taking advantage of the rest.

'I've never been anything other than honest with you, Arthur,' Lucy said defensively. 'You've known from the start how I have and haven't felt. I never made you any promises. You know I didn't.'

'Yes, I know. But you don't have to be head-over-heels in love to marry somebody.'

'I do.'

'Well, I shan't give up with you. It's a certain fact as I can't stay here and let my father rule my —'

'And I admire you for that, Arthur,' she interrupted. 'You *should* get away. It'll be the making of you. You've been held back all the time by your father . . . It shows you've got pluck.'

'I shan't give up on you, Lucy,' he said again. 'I shall write. D'you promise to answer my letters?'

'Course I do,' she replied tenderly. 'Course I shall answer them. Just remember I'm not the best writer in the world.'

He laughed at that, looking into her soft eyes. He wished he could drown in those blue pools, so liquid, so clear. It would be such an exquisite death.

'Moses said I should give you a good poking.'

'Moses said what?' Her tone was a mixture of mocking laughter and indignation.

Arthur grinned with embarrassment, at once realising he'd been foolish in uttering something so utterly stupid. But . . . in for a penny . . . 'He said if I gave you a good poking, you'd be eating out of my hand.'

After a few uncertain moments she laughed, seeing the

absurdity of such a notion when applied to Arthur. 'Well, you never did, did you? . . . So I'm not.'

'You mean . . .'

'Oh, I don't mean anything, Arthur.'

'Yes, you do. You mean you would have let me?'

'Maybe,' she teased. 'If you'd tried hard enough. You didn't try.'

'So let's try now.'

He grabbed her by the waist and pressed his lips on hers, but she wriggled free of him, laughing.

'It's too late now. Besides, there's folk about . . .'

'But, Lucy . . .'

'It's too late, Arthur. If I change my mind about you when you've gone away . . .'

'Then how shall I know, if I'm a hundred miles or more away?'

'I'll let you know . . .'

'How?'

'When I write.'

'Promise?'

'I promise.'

'Can you spell "poke"?'

She thumped him playfully on the chest and laughed. 'You're the limit, Arthur Goodrich,' she said.

★ ★ ★

Next morning Arthur was as good as his word. He packed a bag with his things, took all his money and said goodbye to his mother. She tearfully bid him farewell, begging him not to go, but aware that he had no alternative if he wanted peace from his father, who she knew had never tried to understand his son.

'Don't forget to write,' Dinah said emotionally.

'As soon as I've found some lodgings,' he replied, and kissed her goodbye.

Sadly he made his way to Brettell Lane station, undecided

142

as to where he should go. If he went one way he would go to Wolverhampton. Not far enough away. The temptation to return to see Lucy would be too great. He had to make himself inaccessible. He was beginning to pin his hopes on an old adage, that absence makes the heart grow fonder. But being away from Lucy would no doubt have a greater effect on him than it would on her. So he must go the other way, anywhere, far from Brierley Hill and his father. He consulted the Bradshaw railway guide, to check the time of the next train to Oxford, then bought a ticket. When he reached Oxford he would review the situation.

★ ★ ★

11

Each day of that week seemed like a decade for Lucy as she waited with enduring patience for the time when she would at last be alone with Dickie Dempster. Yet, conversely, it seemed no time since she had last seen Arthur. The weather turned that week and the rain came in warm summer showers that were soft and fine, drenching everything. Gazing absently through the window of their cottage she watched the broken gutterings of nearby buildings douse the bright dandelions beneath, which thrived stubbornly in the hard ground against the redbrick walls. She wondered how Arthur was, where he was; he was not in Brierley Hill anymore, because he would have been to see her. She was conscience-stricken that she had turned him away, remorseful that he was no longer around. She couldn't help but worry over him, couldn't help but feel a guilty sadness that she had been unable to be what he desperately wanted her to be, driven instead to explore the alternative on offer, although it was an eternity coming. With two days to go Lucy considered it time she spoke to Jane, and called to see her on her way to the Whimsey. Moses was out, which meant the sisters could speak confidentially and frankly.

Through Moses's working at the Goodrich's workshop, Jane knew of Arthur's going away, and she wondered how much of his decision was to do with Lucy's illogical inability to commit herself.

'You've let a good man go,' Jane remarked as they sat

drinking tea in the Cartwright's cottage. There was no condemnation in her tone, just regret.

'I know,' Lucy admitted softly. 'The truth is, our Jane, the same day I first cast eyes on Arthur, I saw this other chap I liked. It was earlier in the day, when Miriam Watson and me were coming back from Dudley on the train, and as soon as I saw him I knew he was the one for me. Ever since then I've wanted nobody else. He was my destiny and I just knew it. But then Arthur came along, and I was flattered at his attention, so I agreed to see him 'cause he was there, and I was tired of being by meself. I never saw this other chap again for months and months, and I suppose me and Arthur fell into a sort of half-hearted courtship, never serious . . . Then one day, when we went to Wolverhampton, this other chap pops up again and I'm all of a fluster at seeing him. This time we spoke, and he told me his name was Dickie Dempster. I couldn't get him off my mind after that, and I knew then that it was wrong to lead Arthur on, or let him think I was at all interested when I was really only interested in Dickie. But you know Arthur, our Jane. He hangs on like a limpet to a rock, and I hadn't got the heart to tell him I didn't want him, although I meant to. Then, last Saturday, I met Dickie again and he asked to see me this Saturday . . .'

'So it's handy that Arthur's gone,' Jane commented wryly.

'But it's a coincidence, Jane. I would've gone to meet this Dickie whether or no. Arthur had another row with his father and decided to leave home. He was desperate to get away – had been for ages . . . He asked me to marry him.'

'Yes, I thought he was about to from what Moses told me.'

'Well, he said if I married him we could go away together. I turned him down – because of Dickie Dempster . . .' Lucy sighed profoundly. 'Do you think I'm wicked?'

Jane sighed also and looked at her younger sister, her eyes brimming with sisterly sympathy. 'Just foolish, I reckon, our bab. Young and foolish. 'Cause nothing might come of you seeing this Dickie Dempster, and you'll have lost Arthur. You know the old saying – a bird in the hand is worth two in the bush . . .'

'I'm really mixed up,' Lucy confessed. 'Now that he's gone, I . . . I wish he hadn't . . . I worry about him, Jane. I hope he'll be all right. I feel it's all my fault.'

'Arthur will survive, our Lucy,' Jane counselled. 'And better than most. I know we'm all afeared that he's a bit soft, but I reckon he's a sight tougher than any of us give him credit for, and a lot brighter up top. And if you don't want him, our Lucy, let's hope he meets some other decent young woman, wherever he's gone, who'll care for him as much as he'd care for her.'

'But don't condemn me for seeing Dickie Dempster,' Lucy beseeched. 'I did see him before I saw Arthur, and I think I fell in love with him the minute I set eyes on him. I've got to see if there's a future with him. I just have to . . . Don't you think I should?'

'Yes, I do,' Jane responded gently, touching her sister's arm reassuringly. 'You have to follow your heart, our Lucy. If you don't you'll regret it for the rest of your life. And there's no point in living your life in regrets. But if it's all for nought and there's nothing to show for it at the end . . .'

'Then I'll be as I was before . . . By myself, growing into an old maid. But I have to see what happens,' she repeated earnestly. 'Nothing ventured, nothing gained . . .'

★ ★ ★

Saturday finally arrived. The morning dragged on interminably and Lucy was frequently looking at the clock in the packing room as she wrapped and packed finished glassware. Eliza Gallimore, her workmate, commented how distant she seemed, but Lucy just smiled enigmatically and looked at the clock again, and listened to the rain drumming on the roof and thunder crackling all around. When it was at last time to go home she hurried along the railway line to the Bull Street bridge through the deluge of rain, and entered the cottage with water dripping off her.

'There's a letter here what came while you was at work,' Hannah said with a knowing smile. 'I bet it's from Arthur.' She handed it to Lucy.

Lucy regarded it intently. Her name was clearly written on the envelope in ornate swirls.

'Aren't you going to open it and see?'

'I haven't got time now, Mother. I'll read it on the train.'

It was a rush to get ready. Lucy had to dry her hair, redo it, and change her undergarments before she could even think of putting on her best frock and best bonnet. Even her stockings were soaked through from the downpour. Hurriedly, she ate her dinner, put the unopened letter in her reticule and went out again, anxious not to miss her train.

Mercifully, the rain had eased off, and she stepped over the puddles of Brettell Lane as she headed for the railway station on the other side of the road. She bought her ticket and pondered Arthur again. He would almost certainly have come to the station to begin his journey to wherever it was he was bound for. No doubt his letter would reveal all.

Lucy heard the train chugging up the line from Stourbridge, and looked to see steam emerging in powerful vertical blasts from the engine's tall funnel as it came into view through the grey murk. She shuffled back from the edge of the platform and waited for the carriages to draw to a halt, all the time peering anxiously towards the guards' van. If Dickie wasn't in it she would die.

Then she saw him. He jumped out of his van, a smile as ever on his handsome face, and her knees suddenly felt weak. It seemed like an age before he actually spotted her, but when he did he waved and ambled nonchalantly towards her.

'You ain't forgot me then,' he said with a wink, which knotted up her insides.

She shook her head and smiled bashfully, feeling herself blush. 'No, I haven't forgot you, Dickie.'

'Good. Hey, you look a treat, Lucy. Nice enough to eat, you know that?'

'It's nice of you to say so.'

'Here, let me see you into a second-class compartment, eh?' He winked again and handed her up into a coach, then beckoned her close to him. 'When the train stops at Wolverhampton Low Level, just find a seat on the platform and wait for me to come to you,' he whispered secretively. 'I have to sign off and everything, afore I can leave.'

She nodded her acknowledgement and smiled again, then sat near the window so that she could catch glimpses of him when they stopped at all the other stations along the way. Second-class compartments were more spacious and more comfortable than third class and Lucy glanced at the two other passengers she was sharing with, a man wearing a tall hat and a woman in her thirties, very decently dressed. Neither acknowledged her and Lucy felt uncomfortable, even unworthy to be travelling with them, but she gathered up her self-esteem and endeavoured not to appear overawed.

Dickie's whistle blew and she felt the train's gentle movement forwards, picking up speed only slowly as it gasped and hawked up the long incline to Round Oak. She was excited, itching to be alone with Dickie, wondering where he would take her, what they would talk about, what she would discover about him. She was desperate for him to like her enough to ask to see her again. Then she thought of Arthur, and remembered his letter in her reticule. She fished it out, opened the envelope and began to slowly decipher the elaborate twists and twirls of his fancy handwriting. It read:

My dearest Lucy,

And so I have begun a great adventure, embarked on not entirely out of choice, but out of necessity. For you who have such a loving and amiable relationship with your own father, it must be hard for you to understand how I can feel the way I do about mine. But already I feel free of his wearisome oppression and am much more content. My one abiding regret is that you are not with me, but the hope dearest to my heart is that you will change your mind and we can soon be joined in Holy Matrimony. In this, I beg you to consider the possibility more.

As you can see from the address I find myself in Bristol. When I caught the train on Monday morning I did not know where I would end up, so I bought a ticket for Oxford. Oxford is such a splendid place, full of beautiful architecture and I thought I might stay there. The view of the city from the railway as you enter the station is magnificent and it must be one of the most beautiful places on Earth. The Spires and Domes of the Churches and Colleges make you catch your breath and there must be plenty of work for a Stonemason like myself there. But it would have been too convenient in Oxford to just get on a train and go back home. So, while I sat and ate my snap I decided I must travel further afield. Hence, I went on to Didcot, and from there on Mr Brunel's original broad gauge Great Western Railway to Bristol. I found nice lodgings with a Mrs Hawkins, a very respectable widow.

Bristol is not as beautiful as Oxford, I reckon. I haven't had much chance to explore very much yet, but it must be an interesting city with its famous sea-faring history, and I dare say it holds plenty of delights in store.

Yesterday I went to see a Mr Pascoe about work. He is a builder and was advertising for a stonemason on good pay to do restoration work on a Church called St Mary Redcliffe, said to be the most beautiful parish Church in the Kingdom.

I went and had a look. It is magnificent and very different from our own redbrick Church in Brierley Hill! It used to have a spire but it blew down in a gale nearly four hundred years ago, and now they are talking about rebuilding it. I shall be happy to accept work doing up the church if Mr Pascoe offers it me, but I won't know till Monday. There could be work here for years if I want it.

I have not been keeping too well this week, what with the toothache coming back again and long bouts of hiccups which makes me feel sick the longer it goes on. I had a sore throat Wednesday and thought I had a chill coming, but that seems to have subsided, for now at any rate.

I am missing you terribly, Lucy. It would be the greatest treat imaginable if you could see your way clear to paying me a visit in Bristol if only for a short stay. I could arrange for good lodgings for you, which I would pay for; and I could show you around. I am sure you would like Bristol very much. Please think about it. And please reply to my letter as soon as you can. I long to hear from you, to know that you are all right and that your family are well. I would also deem it a great favour if you could find time to visit my mother and tell her that I am well and, for the time being at least, living in Bristol. I'm sure she'll be worried about me and I don't want to write there yet in case my father thinks I'm trying to wheedle my way back home, because I'm not.

Your ever loving
Arthur Goodrich

Lucy folded the letter, put it back in her reticule and withdrew a spotless white handkerchief. With a swift hazy glance at her travelling companions to check they weren't watching, she wiped tears from her eyes that for some stupid reason had accumulated there while she was reading.

★   ★   ★

At Low Level Station Lucy did as she'd been bid and found a seat on the platform where she could wait for Dickie Dempster. He saw her primly awaiting him and waved before he disappeared for some minutes. She watched the comings and goings of fellow travellers, wondering what they were doing there, where they were bound for. The rain had gone and the sun was hurling intermittent shafts of brilliant light through the mist of smoke and steam that lingered under the single-span roof in a perpetual swirl. At last he came, carrying a snap bag and wearing his usual amiable smile. She rose to greet him, also smiling expectantly.

'I hope I ain't kept you waiting too long.'

'You haven't at all.'

'It's a good thing you didn't come last week, you know. We found some chap asleep in one of the carriages – on the train we'd travelled in – when we'd shunted it into the sidings over there . . .' He thumbed in the general direction. 'We thought he was dead, poor sod. He caused a tidy commotion.'

'Fancy,' Lucy replied with a grin, doing her best to feign surprise. 'But I expect you get lots of funny folk on the trains.'

'Well, this chap was funny all right. It turned out the fool had took laudanum when he set off from Kidderminster and it sent him to sleep.'

'I should think it would,' Lucy agreed. 'What a nit!'

'But he was all right after. I took him for a cup o'tea and had a chat with him. He turned out to be a stonemason . . . from your neck of the woods, as it happens. Name of Goodrich. D'you know him?'

Lucy shook her head. 'I don't think so,' she answered, avoiding Dickie's eyes, believing it more expedient to lie than admit to knowing such a fool.

'Come on then, eh? I'll take you to the Old Barrel at Boblake. It ain't far to walk. At least it's knocked off raining now.'

He took off his guard's cap and stuffed it in his bag, and began walking briskly. Lucy had her work cut out keeping up with him as they left the station. The sun was bursting through fractured clouds. Its shimmering brightness reflected off the wet surface of the road and roofs, making them both squint.

'Are we in a rush?' Lucy asked. 'I can't keep up with you.'

He turned to her and grinned. 'Sorry. I'll slow down . . . That better? I always walk quick. It never occurs to me that other folk mightn't. So what've you been a-doing with yourself this week?'

'Oh . . . Just working . . .'

'That all?'

'What else is there?'

'I got the impression from your mate that you had a chap, Lucy . . .'

'Did have – after a fashion.' Their eyes met as they walked and she smiled shyly. 'He's gone.'

'Gone?' he queried. 'You mean you sent him packing, or he left of his own accord?'

She uttered a self-conscious little laugh. 'Of his own accord,' she replied economically.

'Then more fool him.'

Lucy shrugged as a signal of her indifference to Arthur. A dray was being driven by, close to where they walked, and she stepped back so as not to be showered by the overspray from its wheels, which clattered over the cobbles and precluded them from hearing each other until it had passed.

'I can't imagine anybody wilfully giving you up,' Dickie said when they could resume their conversation. 'A pretty girl like you.'

'Such flannel!' she chuckled. 'I know very well that I'm not pretty.'

'Then you know nothing, Lucy.' He turned to look at her again. 'Such eyes! I've never seen eyes the colour of yours.

And such long lashes. But there's more to you than just your eyes, I reckon . . .'

'Oh?' She felt herself blushing again. 'Such as?'

'I shan't tell you now.' He smiled mysteriously. 'I'll tell you some other time.'

Some other time. That suggested they would meet again, and Lucy's heart turned somersaults.

Before too long they reached Boblake, an old and decrepit street in the centre of the town. On the corner, where it adjoined a narrow road called Bell Street, stood an ancient black and white building, its top storey leaning over drunkenly.

'That's the Old Barrel,' he informed her. 'My mate keeps it.'

'It's old, Dickie.'

'Tudor, they reckon. But the welcome's good. So's the beer.'

Despite it being hardly a spruce area, she was with Dickie Dempster, so she did not mind the decrepitude, nor the ill-kempt street women who eyed her up with envious and resentful looks because of her decent frock and her handsome companion. Inside the Old Barrel the ceiling was low and the rooms were small, not at all like the Whimsey. He led her into a snug which was devoid of any customers, but which was clean and cosy even though it was empty. In the small fireplace flames lapped like tongues around one large solitary lump of coal. It was so perfect it might almost have been reserved for their private use.

'I'm glad they've lit a fire today,' Dickie commented. 'It's been chilly for July. What d'you fancy to drink, Lucy?'

'A small crock of beer, please.' He left her alone while he went to a hatch to fetch their drinks. When he returned, she said, 'Are you not courting somebody, Dickie?'

Her directness amused him. 'Me, courting?' Tantalisingly, making her wait for his answer, he took a swig from his beer and wiped his lips on the back of his hand. 'I just finished with somebody, Lucy, and that's the God's honest truth. I daresay if I was still a-courting her I'd be hurrying back to her right now, instead of sitting here with you.'

She breathed a sigh of relief at his answer. The question had been occupying her for some months, and with unbearable intensity during the past week.

He leaned forward, grabbed the poker and started prodding at the lump of coal to break it up. A stream of sparks flew up the chimney. 'Tell me about your family,' he said.

When she'd finished telling him she said, 'Now tell me about yours.'

'Not much to tell, Lucy. I got a mother, a father, two brothers and five sisters. Two sisters are older than me, three are younger. Me two brothers are younger.'

'So you're the third child.'

'Yes, the third. And the oldest of the lads.'

'Are many of them married?'

'I got four sisters married and one brother.'

'How come a brother younger than you is wed afore you?'

Dickie laughed. ' 'Cause he found somebody he wanted to wed afore me, I reckon. She's a nice wench an' all.'

Lucy wanted to ask whether he felt *he* would ever get married, but realised it would have sounded probing, maybe even presumptuous, and might easily have put him off, if he considered she was trying to lead up to something. After all, she hardly knew him yet.

'Tell me about this girl you've just finished with,' she said instead.

'Not much to tell. She says she wants me back. Keeps coming round after me, trying to persuade me to get back with her.' He shook his head resignedly. 'But I ain't interested no more.'

'What's her name?'

He shrugged. 'What does it matter what her name is?'

'Well, then you could refer to her by her name,' Lucy said logically.

'Myrtle. She's called Myrtle.' He lifted his tankard and took another draft.

'Is she pretty?'

'Yes. Very pretty.'

'And what sort of things does Myrtle say to you when she comes and tries to get you to go back with her?'

'You want to know the top and bottom o' Meg's arse, Lucy,' he answered with a grin.

She could have kicked herself for being so stupid as to ask such things. Probing, prying, as if she were already established in his heart and in his life. Of course, it was nothing to do with her what poor heartbroken Myrtle said to him. She must try and curb her inquisitiveness. But she would love to have known the strength of her competition.

'Tell me about that chap who you found in the sidings,' she said, anxious both to change the subject and to find out whether Arthur had mentioned anything about her, which Dickie was not revealing.

'I felt sorry for him, poor chap. He seemed a bit of a muff, but I couldn't find it in me to dislike him. I think he was grateful when I took him for a cup of tea and a slice of pork pie afterwards, and talked to him. He was a bit awkward at first, as if he wasn't used to company, but after a bit he loosened up.'

'Did he say whether he was married, or courting, or anything like that?'

'He never said, and I never asked. He didn't look like he was married. Still being looked after by his mother, I should say, if his manner was anything to go by.'

'Oh.' Lucy was glad of the information. At least Dickie had not made any connection between herself and Arthur. 'But how can you tell by looking at a man whether he's married or not?'

'It was difficult to tell with him, 'cause he had the careworn look of a married man with all the troubles of the world on his shoulders. But he was just too callow, too unworldly for a married man his age.'

'So marriage makes a man careworn, does it?' she asked feigning mild indignation, picking the weightier of the two notions to discuss.

'The way I see it, Lucy, half the women in the world marry a man 'cause they see him as the exact opposite of what he really is. Then, when they've found out that he ain't what they think – that he's just the way he always was to everybody else – they spend the rest of their lives punishing him by trying to change him. Then, when they've changed him and moulded him to their ideals – if he's daft enough to go along with it, that is – they walk all over him. Consequently, half the marriages in the world are unhappy ones.'

'I wouldn't try and change a man,' Lucy protested defensively. 'If I like what I see in a man, why should I try and change him?'

'No man is perfect. A woman will always find some flaw in a man, something she wants to change, whether or no.'

'You could say the same about women. No woman is perfect.'

'Some are more perfect than others, I grant you,' he answered with an admiring smile that suggested plenty. 'Some are prettier than others.'

'I think prettiness can be a curse, although a good many would say it's a blessing.'

'How do you mean, a curse?' Dickie asked.

'Well, a girl who is pretty can generally attract the man she wants, which might be seen as a blessing. But maybe she'll attract men she doesn't want as well, men who'd be no good for her. That's where the curse arises. So, in some ways, while I wish I was pretty, in other ways I'm thankful I'm not . . .'

'I wouldn't say you'm not pretty, Lucy.'

'I'm not pretty, Dickie,' she said earnestly. 'I know I'm not pretty.'

'Like I said, you know nothing. You've got the most beautiful eyes. Crystal clear, they are. Like a baby's.'

'So it's been said before. But I'm not pretty.'

'There's something about you, all the same . . .'

'What?'

'Some . . . some fascination, a certain allure . . . I don't know how to describe it without offending you. And yet at first glance you always look so aloof, so stuck up.'

'I'm not stuck up, Dickie,' she laughed. 'You know I'm not stuck up.'

'I know it, 'cause I took the trouble to speak to you. But to folk who don't know you, you *look* stuck up. That's all I'm saying.'

'So what's this *fascination*, this *allure* you reckon I've got?' she fished.

'Promise you won't hit me?'

'Why should I hit you?'

'You might, if I'm too blunt. If I'm too blunt for somebody who seems stuck-up . . . like you.'

'No, I won't,' she chuckled. 'Just tell me . . .'

He finished off his tankard of beer and licked his lips, smiling at her waggishly.

'Well? . . .'

'Well . . . you'm so damned beddable, Lucy Piddock, and I fancy you like hell. I'm dying to get you between the sheets. Just dying to . . . And I will, you know . . .'

She gasped, not knowing how to respond, flattered that he desired her in that way, indeed grateful that he did, but apprehensive of the prospect and certain that she ought to register some indignation for the sake of propriety.

'And it won't be just one good rogering either,' he

continued. 'I get the feeling I could never get me fill of you. And once you'd got the taste for it . . .'

'I don't know what you expect me to say to that, Dickie Dempster,' Lucy said, breathless and embarrassed at such an astonishingly frank admission. 'But I'm not a girl like that and it's only fair to tell you. I didn't come here today with anything like that on me mind. I have to tell you, to save you getting the wrong idea about me. Nothing could have been further from my mind when I said I'd meet you. I've always believed that a girl should wait till she's married for that sort of thing . . .' She was babbling on disjointedly, disorientated at receiving such an outlandish proposal. While she was anxious to protest her chastity she did not want to lose his interest.

He smiled and placed his hand on hers reassuringly. His firm but gentle touch stirred her insides alarmingly, and there was a warmth in his eyes that made the blood course through her veins and her head throb.

'Don't look so worried,' he whispered, as if in a hot conspiracy of hearts. 'But why wait till you'm married to enjoy the natural pleasures God created for men and women? It'll happen whether or no, and you'll want it to. I can't say where or when, but we'll be partners in the blanket hornpipe sooner or later. When you'm ready that is, Lucy, my love . . . But I ain't gunna rush you. I just hope as you'll want to see me again after today . . .'

'Oh, yes,' she said unhesitating.

'Good.' He put his arm around her waist and drew her to him. 'I hoped you would.' He bent his head and kissed her on the lips, a long, lingering kiss. 'I'm head over heels for you, Lucy. Have been for ages. I can't wait till the next time I see you.'

'But please don't think as I'd be easy.'

'Course I won't. I don't want you to be easy.'

'Good.' She smiled and there was a warm light in her eyes. 'So when's it likely to be that we meet again?'

'One of the nights, eh?'

'Depends which night. I work some nights in an alehouse called the Whimsey.'

'I can only manage Wednesday night next week. I'm doing some work for our Sarah . . . one of me sisters.'

'But I work Wednesday nights,' she said, her disappointment obvious. 'Damn! . . . But to hell with it, Dickie. I'll take the night off, or swap it for another night.' She beamed up at him. 'So that's all right.'

'I'll come over to you then,' he said. 'I'll get on a train to Brettell Lane. You can meet me at the station.'

'Course I will. Just tell me what time and I'll be there . . . So do you like working on the railway?'

'I wouldn't work anywhere else.'

★   ★   ★

12

Tuesday 21ˢᵗ July 1857

Dear Arthur,

Please forgive my awfull handriting its not as pretty as yours. I got your letter Saturday when I got back from the glass works. I am glad you found nice lodgings and I hope this Mrs Hawkins is looking after you well. I did as you asked and went to see your mother Sunday afternoon. I gave her your adress and she says as she will get Talbot or Magnolia to write to you for her. We had a nice long talk and she says how she was serprized and glad as you stood up for yourself agenst your father at last but sory as she could not prevent you going away. Your father was abed asleep after his Sunday dinner and not well again I believe so I didn't see him but your mother said as how he misses you and he's having to send your brother Talbot to do the letter cutting on the graves which he don't like at all but I think our Moses is a big help and he is keen to lern letter cutting as well our Jane says. I think that sort of work would sute him and I'm sure he cud do it if he put his mind to it.

I'm glad as you like Bristol, Arthur it sounds a lovley place and I hope as you have been lucky enuff to be given work on that lovley church you rit about I'm sure you will make a very good job of it because I know how carefull you are. As for visiting you for a few days I don't know about that it would be very nice to visit you but I can't see my

160

way clear on account of work and how my father would take it if I said I wanted to go to Bristol for a few days on my own to be with you.

I hope as your tooth acke is better, and your soar throte. I spect you will end up having it pulled wether or no if you want some peace from it, and a good thing an all.

As for us getting wed, Arthur, I don't think it would be good for you to set much store by that. Its not as if I don't like you because you no I do but I don't want to get wed. I told you all this before your went. So if you meet another nice young woman in Bristol I shant be offended. Our Jane says as how you deserve the love of a nice young woman who can look after you and cherish you better than me. All the same it will be nice to here from you from time to time to tell me how you are going on. I hope you make your fortune in Bristol, Arthur, My mother and father send there love.

Your ever faithful servant

Lucy Piddock

*   *   *

Sunday 26th July 1857

My dearest Lucy,

It upset me greatly to hear that you would not be offended if I took up with another young woman in Bristol. You seem to disregard my love for you as if it's a fly landed on your shawl to be cast off with a swipe. Well I can assure you, Lucy, it's no such trivial thing. I only hope you can understand the hurt it causes me when you say such things, because I could never inflict any such hurt on you. Then you sign yourself off as my ever faithful servant. Well you are not my servant, Lucy, nor ever likely to be, although I hope and pray you will be ever faithful, as I shall be to you.

You will doubtless be pleased to hear that I am now working for Mr Pascoe. I went to see him Monday as arranged and he told me I could have the job at seven and

161

six a week more than my father was paying me. That's a handsome rise and more than covers my lodgings. I am working on the St Mary Redcliffe church I told you about with another stonemason called Cyril Chadwick a bit younger than me who seems a decent sort, trying to restore it to its former glory. By the way, he has a sister the same age as you.

Mrs Hawkins my landlady is a good cook and she makes me some very tasty dinners and puddings, except for something she calls sillybub or sillybubble or something. I can't stand it, so when she isn't looking I give it the cat who seems to like it.

The other night I went ferreting with Cyril Chadwick but we caught nothing. I bought a ferret off Cyril for four shillings but he has to look after it for me, because Mrs Hawkins won't let me keep it at my lodgings. That reminds me, could you ask my mother to send me my cricketing things. She could send them by rail and I could collect them from Bristol Terminus. There is a cricket team down here I could get in with, but not if I haven't got any gear and I don't see the point in buying new when I have already got some.

The weather here has been very fine and quite warm and I don't mind working outside when it's like that. I have a sniffly cold now which makes me feel very cross, especially when the weather is so warm. Also I cut my finger badly on a chisel. My toothache isn't too bad at the moment.

Well, Lucy, I still miss you no end and I hope you miss me. Don't forget to ask your father if you can come and visit me here. I know you would like it and it would be such a change for you to stay in Bristol for a few days. There's plenty to see and we could even go to Bath for the day. Mrs Hawkins would put up some sandwiches to take with us I'm sure. I haven't been to Bath myself yet, but the trains run

there regular so it wouldn't be any trouble getting there and
back. Only like going from Brierley Hill to Wolverhampton
and back. I bet you would like Bath. Please write to me
soon.

Ever yours
Arthur

★   ★   ★

Sunday 2nd August 1857

Dearest Lucy,
I haven't had a letter from you since last time I wrote so I
hope yours and this one will have crossed in the post. I hope
you can persuade your father to let you come to Bristol. Ask
your mother to have a word with him. If you are strapped
for money I could send you a post office order. You must be
due for a few days holiday from the glass works, I bet. When
you do come here I have decided to buy you an engagement
ring. I am earning good money now and I can afford a
decent engagement ring for you, what with my savings and
all. There is a very good jewelry shop here what you would
like. We don't have to get married though till you are good
and ready, but it would be nice to be engaged all the same.

I still haven't heard about my cricket things so can you go
and have another word with my mother and ask her to send
them, but to let me know when so as I know when to pick
them up from the Terminus.

I have been invited to tea at Cyril Chadwick's house this
afternoon. His mother asked him to ask me to go. Maybe she
feels sorry for me living in lodgings. I daresay I shall meet
his sister who still lives at home. I believe her name is
Dorinda and she is said to be quite pretty.

At least my cold is better and my poorly finger is healing
nicely. I think the air down here suits me. I hope you are
keeping well, and also your mother and father and Moses
and your Jane. Well, Lucy, I'd better go and get ready to

*visit the Chadwicks now. Give everybody my best wishes
and give Tickle a tickle for me, and I hope your letter will
arrive in tomorrow's post. If not, please write soon. I miss
you terribly and I'm thinking about you all the time.*

Ever yours
Arthur.

★ ★ ★

Sunday 9th August 1857

My dearest Lucy,

*Why have you not written? Have I upset you in some
way? If I have, I never intended to but I apologise just in
case. I am worried sick about you, not having written. Are
you poorly or what? Maybe you have written and your
letters have got lost in the post. Perhaps you should check
what address you are sending them to. Anyway, thank you
for asking my mother to send my cricket stuff. I picked it up
from the Terminus yesterday.*

*I've had a busy week working. On Tuesday Cyril and me
were working on some statues of the Disciples set in the
outside walls of the church trying to spruce them up, and he
fell off the scaffolding. He swears one of them Disciples
pushed him. I think he put his shoulder out but nothing
worse than that. When you think about it it could have been
a lot worse. I had a very nice time last Sunday when I went
to his house for tea. His mother and father are very nice and
his unmarried sister Dorinda is such a pretty girl, I can't
think why she's still a spinster. Anyway, Dorinda herself
suggested I go to tea again today and her mother didn't seem
to mind her asking me. At least I'll be able to see Cyril
because he hasn't been to work since his accident.*

*There's not much else to report. The weather has been fair
and warm, Mrs Hawkins continues to give me syllabubs a
couple of times a week (I found out what they're really called
and how to spell it) and I continue to feed them to the cat,*

although I think even the cat is getting tired of them now. I shall have to tell her I'm not that fussed. A nice apple pie wouldn't come amiss for a change like those your mother makes.

I really am quite content living down here in Bristol, Lucy. The only thing that upsets me is not being able to see you. I do miss you so much, so please be sure to write and let me know how you are and what you are doing. If you were here with me as my wife my contentment would be complete, but I can't stand the not knowing. If I don't hear from you soon I shall have no alternative but to return to Brierley Hill to see what's wrong, but I could do without having a day off work so soon after starting. Give my fondest wishes to your family.

Ever yours,
Arthur.

★ ★ ★

Wednesday August 12th

Dear Arthur

I'm sorry I haven't rote but I've been ever so busy what with work at the glass works and the Whimsey and everythink. I'm glad you got your cricket things after all. It prooves I asked your mother to send them. I still don't know about coming to visit you in Bristol Arthur, I don't think it would be a very good idea though so maybe you should forget all about it. I daren't ask my father because I no what he wood say and what with work and everythink I can't see my way clear. Anyway, it sounds as if you have good companey in the pretty Dorinda to worry to much about me. We are not betrothed to one another remember so it might be a good idea for you to take up with Dorinda while you are in Bristol if you like her. I woodnt mind at all and I woodnt blame you neither. She might be just what you need and she is from a nice family and all by the sounds of it.

165

I hope your friend Cyril gets better soon after his accident he sounds very nice. It's a good thing it wasn't you Arthur what got hurt else you might have had to come home to be nursed speshaly if you'd got hurt bad.

Your father hasn't been keeping well at all by all accounts. I spect you've heard from your Talbot or his wife anyway letting you know. I don't know what's up with him Moses didn't know and your mother didn't tell me. Still I don't think its anything bad enough for you to have to come back home. Mind you I can't see you wanting to come back just to see him after the way you've talked about him rotten and the way he treated you.

My mother says as how she misses the rabbits you used to catch for us. Moses says he'll try and catch some but he woodnt be too steady with a gun I don't think on account of him only having one leg to keep him steady and our Jane isnt very happy over him trying. She says what if he falls off his crutch and shoots hisself in his good leg then she'd have a right game with him so I don't think as Moses will go out shooting rabbits and he surely woodnt be any good at rustling pigs or even sheep.

Anyway I'd better close now Arthur as I'm writing this in my dinner time because I'm going out tonight for a change. Don't worry if you don't hear from me all that often. It's not that I don't care about you Arthur its because I have to much to do.

Yours very truly
Lucy Piddock

★ ★ ★

Thursday August 13th

Dearest Arthur,
I expect this is a surprise hearing from me so soon after my last letter, but there's somethink I wanted to say to you that I really mean. I do like you a lot Arthur and I admire

166

you. You are honest and decent and you've always cared for me much more than I deserve. I know it better than anybody and I am thankful for it. Any normal girl wood be potty to give up the chance of being your wife and our Jane thinks I'm potty for turning you down. But the truth is, I've met somebody else who I like a great deal and I am very serious about him. I haven't told my father yet but my mother knows and she thinks I'm potty as well.

So if you really like this Dorinda you wrote about then don't feel bad about seeing her reglar as she sounds like a very nice girl and if she's as pretty as I am potty then why not. You could do worse by the sounds of it and I know she could do a lot worse than to hitch up with you.

Please write to me from time to time to let me know how you are going on and you can even send me an invitation to your wedding if you ever deside to get married to the lovely Dorinda.

Arthur, I really think this wood be for the best. I know you will be disappointed in me and annoyed but in the end you will thank me. I don't think I could ever have been any good for you and it wood be rong of me to hold you back from happiness with another young woman more deserving than me. I wish you well.

Your friend for ever
Lucy Piddock

★ ★ ★

Friday 14th August 1857

My dear, dearest Lucy,

I have just got in from work and Mrs Hawkins has just handed me your letter. I can scarcely believe what I have read. Lucy, I am heartbroken. I cannot describe how I feel. I suppose I should not be surprised really, the way you've never been able to commit yourself to me properly. I always hoped and prayed that in time you would, but evidently it is

167

not to be or you are not giving it enough time. I feel so helpless being so far away from you and unable to do anything to try and persuade you otherwise. I know it was my own decision to leave home, and you know why, but I did it believing you would agree to us being wed once I was settled. Now my dreams are shattered.

Lucy, my own darling, you are the least selfish person I ever met for not begrudging me happiness. I want you to be happy too but I want you to be happy with me and not without me. Truly loving somebody means wanting them to be happy whatever way they choose, and if you are not able to be happy with me, I love you too much ever to begrudge you any happiness at all. Life is too short to harbour grudges, so I hope you and this new chap of yours will be very happy.

As for the lovely Dorinda as you call her, well it never crossed my mind to ask to see her while I thought you and I were courting. She's a very nice girl, but I would never lead her on knowing there was to be nothing at the end of it for her, just because I was in love with somebody else – you!

Well, Lucy, I wish you well despite my being so upset. I hope and pray you will change your mind, that you will realise you miss me and want to be back with me. I yearn for that day. Write to me anyway from time to time and let me know how things are in Brierley Hill. If I find myself back there on a visit I shall come and knock on your door and say hallo. Until then, take very good care of yourself.

My love forever
Arthur.

13

The first Sunday in September was dull and overcast. Autumn had arrived too early, bringing a dramatic change from the fine weather of August, which had ripened the barley in the fields around Brierley Hill. Lucy had risen early as usual, to help Hannah make breakfast, to clean and to make beds before she went to chapel. Haden had gone to see Jane and Moses, bearing a pheasant, one of a brace that had come his way. So Lucy took advantage of the time by herself to reflect. She sat on the settle, kicked off her boots and put her feet up, her back resting against one of the side wings. Through the squares of glass that made up the small window she could see out onto Bull Street. A cart clattered past, of no consequence.

Lucy inspected her fingernails cursorily. Packing glassware into crates did not help in the struggle to keep them in good condition but, although uneven, at least they were clean due to their often being in water. How nice it must be to live the life of a lady of leisure and have pretty nails, and nothing more to worry about than what dress you were going to wear for dinner, or whether the maid had cleaned the silver cutlery properly.

The fire spat, diverting her attention. Her pale blue eyes were drawn to the glowing coals and she stared, deep in thought, into their glimmering flames, turning them into grotesque faces. One such image reminded her of Arthur. It had been six weeks since he had left, driven out of house and home by his father's relentless abuse, and still he popped persistently into her thoughts. It had also been six weeks since her first arranged meeting with Dickie Dempster. Since that day she and Dickie had been regular companions a couple of times a week. She had changed her Wednesday nights working at the Whimsey to Thursday to accommodate him, and continued to meet him on Saturday afternoons at Wolverhampton Low Level, where he persisted in taking her to the Old Barrel at Boblake. Dickie had finally admitted that the room they always occupied he reserved specially for them, so they could be alone together. There they kissed and cuddled and laughed and sighed, and drank beer till it was time for her to go. Yesterday they had tarried long, leaving it till the very last minute to return to the station, just in time to get the six o'clock train back to Brettell Lane.

'What time's the next train?' she asked, always reluctant to go.

'Ten to eight,' he replied without hesitation.

'Damn. I'd never get to work in time.'

The station was busy, but that did not deter them from standing dangerously close. She held her face up to him, poised for a kiss, and he obliged. She felt the lush softness of his lips again which matured into a deep, probing, hungry kiss, one that would have to keep her going till next Wednesday. The guard on duty, Fred Cooke, whom Dickie knew well, gave them a low wolf-whistle as he walked past carrying his flag. They broke off, and Dickie grinned waggishly at his friend.

'All right, Fred, the lady's going now. I'll just see her into a carriage, then you can let the train go.'

'Sorry to rush you, mate,' Fred said in a head-shaking show of mock regret. 'Must keep the trains running to time, Dickie. You know the rules.'

Thus Lucy reluctantly left him so that she could return

home and get herself ready for serving beer at the Whimsey, to customers who often seemed ungrateful and abrupt, and who were not aware of the tenderness and desire she had experienced during the whole of the afternoon with the man she loved more dearly than she had ever thought possible.

It crossed her mind that now she had achieved this ambition of finding the man of her dreams there was no longer any point in working at the Whimsey, of putting up with their brusqueness. She had taken work there merely temporarily, to put herself on display, to attract a suitable man. As it turned out, all she had attracted there was Arthur Goodrich, an insignificant prize. Indeed, the Whimsey had not provided the man of her dreams at all from its clientele. But the railway had. And what changes the railway had brought her. What a difference it had made to her life.

Some things had not changed, however. This settle on which she was relaxing, for instance, was the same settle she had known since childhood. She knew intimately every knot in the panels of its backrest, every tiny scratch in the varnish of its curved arms, as surely as she knew her own face. The same cast-iron fire-grate before her seemed to have adorned that one wall of the cottage since time began, and she knew every blemish on its surface at least as well as she knew every tiny mole on her own body. There were the treasured trinkets her mother had collected over the years, prized and cleaned and steadfastly returned to their appointed place on the mantelshelf week in week out, month after month, year on monotonous year. Through her sadness, through her joy, through the tediousness and even the excitement of life, through her torments through her pleasures, these things had remained constant, unchanging, and unaffected by the perpetual tide of events that influenced her. No, some things never changed.

She had inevitably changed, along with the seasons and the

years. She had changed just like the frost in winter, which formed its fancy crystal patterns on the window panes, then melted and disappeared with the inevitable thaw. She had changed like the sky changes from clouds and greyness to vivid sunshine and blueness, then back again, with a monumental certainty, and yet with such frustrating unpredictability.

In the distance she could hear the coarse huff-huff of a locomotive and she pondered anew how the coming of the railway had changed her life. Without it she would never have known Dickie Dempster, would never have cast eyes on his gloriously handsome face. But for the railway to broaden her horizon she might well have been content to live the rest of her life with Arthur Goodrich, evolving by default into his wife, unaware of the more desirable match which had lain latent, awaiting discovery. So it must be with many women who willingly succumb to the first man who comes to claim them, without troubling themselves to look further afield. She had seen and fallen in love with Dickie Dempster from further afield, a consequence of the railway's construction. Both were immutable, which convinced her that this romance with Dickie was preordained, that it was meant to be.

Arthur, poor soul, had written again. Perhaps he would always write. Maybe he would never be able to let go. She regretted that, but it made no difference. Her destiny was set. She would marry Dickie; she knew it with a certainty. How could she ever have committed herself to Arthur, good and kind as he was, when all the time she knew unquestionably where and with whom her true fate lay? Self-sacrifice, for the sake of the uninvited love of another – however persistent – was not part of her temperament. Much as she hated to hurt Arthur, she hated the hypocrisy of pretence more. The white-hot heat of her love for Dickie Dempster was both truth and beauty, and she would settle for nothing less.

She was half expecting another letter soon from Arthur, to

wish her well on her twenty-first birthday next Saturday. Why couldn't he see where his best interests lay and try his luck with this Dorinda in Bristol? Then she need not feel so guilty about him.

The latch clicked and the door to the street opened. Lucy turned to look and saw Haden's bulk filling the doorframe.

'Nothing to do, our bab?'

'I was just having a rest . . . thinking.'

He tapped his pipe into the fire grate and inspected the empty bowl. 'Missing King Arthur?'

'No, I'm not. That's just it, Father, I don't miss him at all.'

'I never thought as you would. Whilst he's a decent enough lad, I never thought he was stalwart enough for you, our Lucy.'

'It's nothing to do with him being stalwart or otherwise . . .'

'Oh? What then?' Haden was filling his pipe anew from his leather tobacco pouch as he stood with his back to the fire.

'Didn't Mother tell you?'

'Tell me what?'

Well, this was as good a time as any to let her father know the real reason she did not miss Arthur. He would hear of it soon enough anyway from gossip, if he hadn't already. 'I finished with him. I'm seeing somebody else.'

Haden looked up from his task, surprise evident in his eyes. 'Your mother never said. Who's the lucky chap this time?'

Lucy told him.

'Dickie Dempster, eh? And he's a steady chap, is he?'

'Like I say, he's got a good job on the railway as a guard.'

'I'd like to meet him, our Lucy. I'd like to satisfy meself that he's a straight sort of a lad.'

'Oh, he is. Straight as a die. I shall marry him, Father, I know I shall.' She grinned, grateful he had not mocked her over her new love.

'Has he asked you yet?'

She smiled wistfully. 'Not yet.'

'Then don't count your chickens. I should hate for me favourite daughter to be hurt.'

'I always thought our Jane was your favourite daughter,' Lucy goaded, content either way.

'I mean that you'm me favourite daughter still living in this house . . .'

Lucy pouted, lowering her eyes, in a pretence of sulking at his teasing.

'Hey! Our Jane!' Haden exclaimed. 'Christ, that's just reminded me. Her's just told me as her's having a bab.'

'A baby?'

'Yes. I tell you, it's a load off me mind. I was starting to get worried as there was summat up. What with Moses being a cripple and that.'

'You mean she's pregnant?' Lucy's feet were on the floor at once and she stood up animatedly. 'She's having a baby?'

'That's what I just said, in't it? I'm supposed to tell you and your mother.'

'Oh, Father, I shall have to go and see her.' Lucy reached down for her boots and put them on, stooping down to fasten the laces. 'Right away. Maybe I'll meet Mother coming from the chapel and we can go together.'

'What about me dinner?' Haden queried, alarmed.

'Oh, your dinner might be a bit late. Stay a bit longer in the Whimsey, that's the answer.'

'Hang me! I wish I hadn't told you now till we was having we dinners. At least I'd have bin sure o' getting some.'

★ ★ ★

'Our Jane, Father's just told me you'm expecting,' Lucy said as she had burst excitedly into their cottage in South Street. 'When d'you reckon it's due?'

Jane was hovering over her own fire-grate about to turn the pheasant somebody had poached, which was roasting in the oven at the side. She looked up at her younger sister and smiled contentedly. 'I reckon I'm about three months, our Luce. So sometime in March, I would've thought.'

'D'you want a boy or a girl?'

'I ain't bothered one way or the other. Whatever it is, it'll be loved.'

'Oh, our Jane, I'm that excited. Have you thought of what you might call it?'

Jane chuckled. 'I ain't gi'd it a thought. There's plenty time to sit and think about such things.'

'What does Moses think? I bet he's pleased.'

'Pleased? He's like a dog with two bones. But you'd expect him to be, eh?'

'Oh, I would. Where is he?'

'At the Whimsey. He said he'd meet Father there. I daresay they'll have a few extra to celebrate. I just hope as he don't fall off his crutch and hurt hisself. By the way, did you see that Dickie yesterday?'

'Yes,' Lucy sighed. 'Now I have to wait till Wednesday to see him again. I was thinking, it might pay me now to finish working at the Whimsey so as I have more nights free. I can't survive on seeing him just twice a week. What do you think, our Jane?'

'I don't know. Shall I ever get to meet him? Till I've met him I shan't know what to think.'

'Father wants to cast his eye over him as well. I'm meeting him at the station Wednesday. So I'll take him to meet Mother and Father then . . . I'm head-over-heels, you know, our Jane.'

'I know you are. That's what worries me.' Jane stooped to grab hold of the sizzling tray in the oven with a folded cloth. She turned it around and the glorious aroma of roasting game filled the tiny room. 'If you want my advice, don't give up working in the Whimsey altogether. Cut it down by a couple of nights by all means, but don't make yourself too available for this Dickie chap, else he might get tired of you quick.'

'But I want to be with him every hour, every minute that God sends.'

'Struth, our Lucy, you *have* got it bad. Temper it.'

'But it's been such a long time coming, our Jane. It'll be a longer time going away.'

★　★　★

The unsettled weather of the weekend became settled again and the rest of September looked set to remain still and fair. Wednesday evening arrived and, beneath a sky daubed with every vivid hue from red to gold, Lucy hurried to the station to meet Dickie. As the locomotive that brought him wheezed and its line of carriages clanked to a halt, her pulse raced in anticipation of being with him once more. Despite all the carriage doors being thrust open simultaneously, she immediately spotted him stepping down from a second-class carriage and her legs turned to jelly. When he saw her and waved, his glorious smile put even the sunset to shame.

As soon as he reached her he put his arm around her waist and she snuggled her head against his shoulder with a smile of eager affection.

'The train's late,' she commented softly.

'About five minutes,' he agreed. 'There was a bit of a problem at Priestfield. A coupling came adrift, but the guard on duty replaced it.'

'Anyway you're here.' She beamed up at him and her eyes were soft lamps with the reflection from the low swollen sun. 'I've missed you.'

'I've missed you, Lucy.'

They turned and walked towards the station's exit and she linked her arm through his fondly.

'Shall we walk along the cut or over the fields?' he asked. There were certain connotations in the question. Earlier in their courtship it had been their habit to stroll along the canal of a Wednesday evening, but lately they had sauntered over the fields towards Kingswinford, inevitably stopping to lie down in the long grass and enjoy delicious long kisses that worked them both up into a frenzy of desire, as yet unsatisfied.

'My father wants to meet you,' she answered rolling her eyes, half embarrassed at having to report Haden's request. 'I think he wants to know that I'm in good hands.'

'You're in the best hands.' He turned to her and grinned.

'I know it, Dickie, but *he* needs to be convinced. So we'll walk along the cut first. Then I'll take you home. With any luck he'll get tired of waiting and go up the Whimsey.'

'I don't mind meeting your father, Lucy. We could go to the Whimsey as well if you've a mind. I wouldn't mind a quart of ale with your father. I'll pay me corner.'

'We'll see. If we get on the towpath at Meeting Lane, we could come off at the Nine Locks then get to our house by walking down the Delph. I just want you to myself for a while first.'

Meeting Lane was narrow with high walls on both sides, and was like walking through a channel. Lucy and Dickie took advantage of the concealment it afforded by giving each other hugs and squeezes, and stopping for a half dozen playful kisses before they met the canal.

The water winked and glinted in the dying sun and strolling beside it was a pleasure, despite the ever-present chimney stacks and factory walls that lined the other bank. Ducks waddled circumspectly out of sight as soon as they were aware of the couple, and a drake that was nonchalantly bobbing up and down on the water took off in a panic, disturbing the industrial silence with the natural whoosh of water and the sudden flapping of powerful wings.

'I've been thinking, Dickie . . .'

'What?'

'That I should give up working a couple of nights a week so that we can be together more. I want to be able to see you more than just twice a week . . .'

'I suppose it depends what nights.'

'Why? Are there some nights you can't see me?'

He shrugged. 'Some, I suppose . . .'

'How about Saturday nights? I'd like to see you Saturday nights.'

'But we already see each other Saturday afternoons.'

'I want to see you Saturday nights as well, Dickie.'

'But that's me cribbage night. Anyway, I bet the gaffer at the Whimsey can't spare you Saturday nights.'

'I don't care whether he can spare me or not,' Lucy pouted. 'It's up to me, not him.'

They disturbed a rat which scuttled away. Then, two dirty, half-naked and barefoot children rose up with guilty expressions from behind a clump of thistles and tall grass, and also ran away in a departure similar to the rat's.

'What they up to, I wonder?' Dickie said. 'Maybe I should go after 'em and give 'em a clip round the ear apiece.'

'Leave them be,' she replied, anxious not to lose the thread of their conversation. 'They was just trying to start a fire, I daresay. You know what kids are like.'

'I know what some kids are like. *They* were a couple of proper little toe rags.'

'Oh, never mind them. So you don't want to see me Saturday nights?'

'I didn't say that. Course I want to see you. I want to see you as often as I can. But it ain't always possible, is it? I mean, what if I have to change me shift? I do sometimes.'

Lucy sighed frustratedly. 'If you have to change your shift I understand. As long as you're not seeing that Myrtle . . .'

'Myrtle?' he scoffed. 'You know I'm not seeing Myrtle.'

'Good. 'Cause if you are, Dickie, I'll stop seeing you. I'd never stand for that.' It was an empty threat, issued in desperation. Lucy knew well enough that if he was still having anything at all to do with Myrtle, she would have neither the courage nor the conviction to stop seeing him. She would have no alternative but to put up with the anxiety and the heartache and compete, using every feminine wile that she could muster to overwhelm any such competition.

'I wouldn't expect you to stand for it, Lucy,' he answered soothingly, calmly, to her immense relief. 'That's why I would never do that to you. I've told you before a dozen times – Myrtle means nothing to me any more. It's been months . . .'

'But she keeps trying to win you back.'

'I know she does, but she's not winning me back.'

'Do you promise me that, Dickie? Do you swear?'

'Course I do.' His voice was butter, creamy and smooth. 'It's the gospel truth, Lucy. I swear.'

She squeezed his arm in recognition of his consideration and smiled up at him, tears trembling on the long lashes of her wide blue eyes. 'Kiss me again,' she pleaded, forcing tears back, and turned herself in to him in anticipation.

He took her in his arms and kissed her again, ardently, lustfully, thrusting himself against her. 'Jesus God, I want you, Lucy,' he breathed as soon as they broke off.

'Honest?'

'Honest,' he repeated solemnly, as if it were an oath. 'D'you remember what I said to you that first Saturday afternoon? How I swore I'd bed you?'

She nodded, her forehead resting on his shoulder, unable to look up at him lest he could see through her clear eyes and read her sensual thoughts.

'I don't know how I've kept my hands off you this long. But I don't intend to wait much longer . . .'

She knew it was time. Indeed, she yearned for the moment.

'I'm glad, Dickie,' she whispered. ' 'Cause I don't want you to wait any longer . . . But not here. Not tonight.'

'No, not tonight.' There was a hint of humour in his voice. 'Shall you be all right Saturday?'

She caught his meaning and nodded again, still unable to meet his eyes.

'Good.' He lifted her chin and smiled caringly into her soft eyes. 'I love you, you know, Lucy. That's why I want you so much.'

She returned his look, with all her commitment shining through, tenderness brimming through the watery tears that still quivered on her lashes. 'If you love me only half as much as I love you, I'll be content,' she said.

'No, Lucy.' He shook his head. 'You wouldn't. Anyway, I love you twice as much as that . . . Come on, dry your eyes and let me meet your father. I should hate him to think as I'd been making you cry.'

* * *

14

On the Friday before her birthday, as she returned from the glassworks, Lucy met Miriam Watson who was approaching from the opposite direction, also on her way home. The two girls saw each other almost daily returning from work, but their Saturday trips out to Dudley and Wolverhampton had been curtailed because of Lucy's intimate assignations, which naturally took priority.

The mercurial September weather had failed to fulfil its promise and there was a light drizzle. The heavy clouds threatened more to come.

'I'm sick to jeth of this weather,' Miriam said at once, charily looking up at the grey sky. Her very words were a form of greeting, dispensing with the usual hellos and how-are-yous, taking for granted their amity, and understood as such. 'I'm sick to jeth of getting shit all over me shoes and up the hem o' me frock an' all. It's a pity them damned hosses cor' drop their loads in the fields for a change. Anywhere but the sodding roads. I wouldn't mind, but when it's fresh the stink's enough to blind yer.'

Lucy chuckled. 'You've had a good day then, I take it.'

'Lousy. Look at the state o' me.' Miriam looked herself up and down frustratedly. 'I'm gunna find me a different job. This work in the fireclay works is too mucky. Is there anythin' going at the glassworks?'

'I don't know, Miriam. I'll ask for you tomorrow, if you like.'

'Would yer?'

'Yes. I'll let you know next time I see you.'

'Am yer off a-courting again tomorrow afternoon, Luce?'

Luce nodded and smiled. 'Course. I wouldn't miss my Saturday afternoon for the world. That and Wednesday nights are the only times I can go a-courting.'

'Why don't this Dickie take you a-courting of a Sunday afternoon, like any normal chap?' Miriam asked pointedly. 'You always used to see Arthur of a Sunday afternoon, din't ya?'

'Dickie plays cribbage of a Sunday dinnertime when he isn't working. By the time he's had a few tankards of beer he's too tired to come out of a Sunday afternoon.'

'What of a Sunday night then?'

Lucy shrugged. 'I don't like to press him. He's got brothers and sisters who he's close to, as well as his mother. I think they all like to get together of a Sunday night. I don't like to press him, Miriam.'

'Have you met his family yet?'

'Not yet. He says he's going to take me, but he hasn't yet.' She smiled brightly, masking her frustration. 'When we get together we'm too wrapped up in one another to worry about his family.'

'Lucky you,' Miriam remarked. 'He must be bringing out the woman in you good and proper . . . Anyroad, I've had such a lousy week, Luce, I'm coming with you to Wolverhampton tomorrow. I want some new things to cheer meself up.'

Lucy looked concerned that her tryst which promised so much was in jeopardy.

'Oh, don't look so worried. I'll leave you at the station and mek me own way into the town. Then I can meet you again after and we can get the train back together.'

She smiled with relief. 'Oh, all right. I normally get the six o' clock from Low Level, on account of working at the Whimsey on the night.'

'That'll do,' Miriam said. 'I want to find me some new boots and have another look in that clothes broker's we went in afore.'

Lucy herself would have liked to do the same, but her commitment to Dickie would not allow it. 'So shall I meet you at the station tomorrow dinnertime?'

'Yes, I'll be there. Usual time, eh?'

'But I shan't wait if you ain't there when the train comes,' Lucy warned.

Miriam grinned. 'I din't expect as you would.'

*   *   *

Although it was her birthday, Saturday began like any other day for Lucy Piddock. She left for the glassworks at half past seven and trudged along the railway track battling a stiff and very cool breeze. In her basket she carried a few cakes which her mother had baked so she could celebrate with her work-mates during their morning break. She was mindful that now she had reached that age when she and Dickie could be wed without the need to seek her father's permission, and it afforded her an enlivening feeling of independence. She was a woman at last, fully fledged and free to do as she pleased, as long as she did not stray too far beyond the unbending bounds of convention. At work, the time passed slowly as it always did when a tryst with Dickie was im-minent. She yearned for the time when they would be man and wife, when their being apart would only be during the hours he was at work, and not the endless days she had to endure now. Life now was spent fondly reminiscing, reliving their brief times together, and patiently looking forward to the next.

When it was time to go, she hurried home along the railway track to get ready to meet Dickie.

'There's a parcel come, our Lucy,' Hannah informed her as soon as Lucy walked through the door. 'Jack Mannion dropped it off. It come up by rail this morning to Brettell Lane station, special delivery from Bristol.'

'From Bristol?' Lucy repeated. 'It'll be from Arthur. Oh, what's he done now?'

The parcel, long and thin, had been given pride of place on the scrubbed wooden table and lay awaiting Lucy's attention.

'Open it, and see what it is.'

'I haven't really got time, Mother. I'm due out in half an hour.'

'Off to see Dickie?'

'Yes.'

'Well, it'll only take a minute to open the parcel.'

'He shouldn't be sending me parcels. It's not as if we're courting . . . or ever was in any serious way.'

· 'Well, I reckon he thought you was, our Lucy, whatever you say now. And he's ever likely to be very fond of you still.'

Lucy cut the string that tied the box together and opened it up. 'Oh, the fool,' she gasped. 'What did he have to send these for? Have you ever seen such beautiful red roses?' She withdrew them from the box and, holding them by the stems, she sniffed them.

'I'll put them in a vase for you, our Lucy, if you'm in a rush,' Hannah offered. 'Aren't they beautiful. They must've cost a fortune. Is there no note with 'em?'

There was a note in the box also. Lucy picked it up and opened it. She read it to herself. '*Thinking of you on your birthday,*' it read simply.

'It was a lovely thought,' Hannah said. 'I wonder if that Dickie will be as thoughtful?'

'I expect so,' Lucy answered, somewhat indignant at what her mother was implying.

Ever since Dickie had been presented to Hannah and Haden, Lucy had the feeling that they were not overly impressed. They had said nothing – to her at any rate – had made no comment at all about him, in fact. If they liked him she felt sure they would have said so. After they met Arthur they were always talking about him; even though sometimes it was irreverently, it was always with affection. Lucy could not understand why it should be so, when Dickie was such a jovial and amiable person. Well, it was up to them what they thought. She was twenty-one now and could do as she pleased. It was nothing to do with them any more how she conducted her love life. She cared not whether they approved or not.

★   ★   ★

Both Miriam and the train were on time. Dickie Dempster, on duty, made a great fuss of Miriam when he saw her, and settled the two girls comfortably in a second-class compartment as usual.

'Why don't he stick we in first class?' Miriam enquired when he'd gone.

'Maybe he'd get into trouble if anybody found out we'd only paid for third-class tickets,' Lucy reasoned in a whisper, even though there was no other person occupying the compartment.

'Not if we said as we'd cheated and he knew nothing about it.'

'Then they'd ask us to pay the extra, Miriam. It's a tidy difference.'

'I hadn't thought o' that,' Miriam admitted.

Lucy could not reconcile in her mind why Miriam should not be satisfied travelling second class when it had cost them each only the price of a third-class ticket. 'Do you like Dickie?' she asked after a pause.

'Like him? D'you mean fancy him?'

'No. Do you like him? As a person. I get the feeling me mother and father don't.'

'Either way he ain't the type I'd go for, Lucy,' Miriam

answered without hesitation. 'I ain't so sure as he's the right type for you either, if you want my honest answer.'

'Course he's the right type for me, Miriam. He's exactly the right type. If he wasn't the right type I wouldn't be courting him. Still, I suppose I can always count on *you* to give me an honest answer.'

'I liked that Arthur better.'

'Oh, he was a proper nit, Miriam . . . Still is . . . He sent me a box of roses for my birthday. They're beautiful and no two ways, but why would he want to waste money sending me roses all the way from Bristol?'

'Out of respect?' Miriam suggested. 'Out of politeness? Because he still thinks a lot of you?'

'Because he's a nit, Miriam. Because it cuts no ice with me any more.'

'I hope as he meets a *decent* young woman, Lucy,' Miriam said cuttingly.

'So do I. Save him sending me roses all the way from Bristol.'

With Lucy feeling admonished they fell silent again, each looking out of opposite windows at the shifting landscape. Perceiving the disadvantage to their friendship of airing their differences for too long, their silence amounted to a tacit acknowledgement of their diametrically opposed opinions on both Arthur and Dickie.

'Did you find out if there was any work going at the glassworks, Lucy?' Miriam asked, breaking the awkward lull.

'I asked, but there's nothing at the moment.'

'Oh.'

After another long pause, Miriam said: 'I forgot to tell you . . . D'you remember I told you about me cousin Penina what got into trouble with a thirteen-year-old lad?'

'Yes . . .' Lucy looked at her friend with renewed interest, aroused from her daydream.

'Well, it turns out as it mightn't have been the lad after all. Her'd been having it off with the lamplighter unbeknownst to anybody.'

'Oh, I'm glad for the poor little chap, Miriam,' Lucy replied sincerely. 'I thought about him a lot.'

'So did the little soul's mother when her found out. Her went round to our Penina and paled her round the yed with a broom handle. There was hell to pay . . .'

★ ★ ★

Miriam walked with Lucy and Dickie as far as Boblake, where they went their respective ways, arranging to meet at Low Level station in time to catch the six o'clock. Dickie escorted Lucy into the Old Barrel again and bid her sit in the side room they always occupied while he fetched them drinks. He returned clutching a bottle of gin, two crocks to drink from, and a bouquet of red roses.

'Oh, red roses!' she cooed, taking the flowers from him. 'Oh, Dickie, they really are lovely. When did you get these?'

'Yesterday, when I finished work. I brought them here for Nancy to look after till you came today. I'm glad you like 'em.'

'Like 'em, I love 'em. Here, let me give you a thank-you kiss.' She placed them down.

He put the gin and the crocks on the table alongside the roses and held her by the waist. Their lips met in a long, lingering caress.

'You don't know how much these roses mean to me,' she breathed.

It was such a relief that she could show her folks and Miriam that Dickie was no less thoughtful than Arthur Goodrich. It meant a great deal, and justified her faith in him. She sat down, happy, expecting him to sit beside her.

Instead he held out his hand, and gestured her to get up again. 'We're not staying in here. I got a better room organised for us. There's another birthday gift I want to give you . . .'

She smiled and a look of anticipation flashed across her bright eyes. 'Oh? Where?'

'Upstairs.'

'Upstairs?' she queried.

'One of the bedrooms. It's ours for the afternoon. Come on, bring the roses with you. Follow me . . .'

She followed him up the narrow back stairs that seemed to creak very loudly, announcing to the patrons and staff in the bar below where she was being led. At the top of the stairs he stopped and felt in his pocket for a key. When he found it he thrust it into the lock of one of the doors and opened it. He let her go in first.

She looked around her while he locked the door from the inside. The room reeked with a damp, musty smell. It was small, the walls were crooked and the varnished wooden floor was uneven. Lucy laid her roses down on a tallboy that occupied one corner and moved over to the window, one frame of which was open a little. It looked out onto Boblake. Below, a cart was being driven past, and a group of jabbering youths had congregated, obviously undecided as to where they should partake of their next beer. Lucy watched them move on.

'D'you like the room?' Dickie asked, coming up behind her and putting his hands to her waist.

'It's a bit small.' She leaned back against him, enjoying the warmth from his body at her back. 'It's almost as small as my own room at home.' She glanced at the bed. It was obvious she was going to end up there, and yet her only qualm was whether the sheets were fresh and clean. If they were not, she would be reticent about getting between them, but nothing else would inhibit her. 'At least there's no dust lying about. Somebody's been and dusted.'

Beside the tallboy stood a wooden chair with a wicker seat. Almost in one corner of the room stood a fireplace jutting out from a crooked chimney breast, but no fire had been laid.

'Let me take your bonnet off for you.'

She turned around biddably in his arms and tilted her face up to him. He undid the ribbons of her bonnet and placed it gently on the chair.

'Let's have a sip of gin now, eh? I'm parched.' He uncorked the bottle and poured a large measure into each crock. He took one and handed it to her. 'Cheers!'

She sipped it, looking intently into his eyes over the rim of the crock.

'Oh, those eyes,' he said with intense feeling. 'I've never known such eyes.' He downed his gin in one and refilled it before turning to her again. 'Here, let me take your shawl . . .' He folded it carefully and placed it over the back of the chair. 'There . . .'

'You're very neat,' she commented wryly. 'You remind me of my mother.'

He laughed at that. 'I'm not sure where I should put this though . . .' He was unbuttoning the front of her cotton frock as she stood before him compliantly. 'When I've divested you of it.'

She lowered her eyes, embarrassed, her long lashes seeming to sweep the curve of her cheek. He took her chin gently between his thumb and forefinger and tilted her face to his again, then kissed her on the lips. Her lips parted and allowed his tongue ingress, which sent the blood swirling through her body. She could taste the gin he had just swallowed, sweet and hot.

'I want you, Lucy,' he breathed. 'I want you bad.'

She squeezed him tight. 'I'm yours, Dickie.'

His hands were inside her bodice but his attempts at caressing her breasts were thwarted by the thin but very significant barrier of her chemise.

'I want to undress you.'

'It might be easier if I do it myself.'

'You're not held together with corsets and ribbons are you, Lucy?' he asked, and there was a genuine look of concern in his expression.

'I should hope not,' she replied. 'Even if I could afford to be.'

He grinned. 'Then it shouldn't be too difficult.'

'All the same . . .'

So she began to peel off her clothes, aware of his eyes on her.

'Don't stand and watch me, Dickie . . .'

'Sorry . . .'

He turned his back to her and began unfastening the jacket and waistcoat of his guard's uniform. By the time he had finished and was undressed Lucy was standing naked watching him. She had wondered how he might look without his clothes and she was not disappointed. He tapered beautifully from his broad shoulders into his narrow hips and small backside. His legs were well-formed, sturdy and somewhat hairy. He caught her looking at him.

'I thought you wanted no peeping.'

She grinned devilishly. 'I didn't want you watching me. I didn't say anything about me not watching you.'

'All the same,' he replied, hurling her own expression back at her. 'I'm getting a good eyeful now . . .'

As he turned around she could see him standing proud. He was bigger than she had imagined and she did not know whether that was a good thing or a bad thing.

'That thing's sticking up for the weather,' she remarked with a flippancy she certainly did not feel, in an effort to take some intensity out of the situation.

'Sod the weather, it's sticking up for you,' he responded, and his voice was thick with desire. 'Come here, let me feel you . . .'

At once they fell into a passionate embrace and the feel of his skin on hers was like nothing she had ever imagined. His hands roamed over her relentlessly, lingering here, teasing there. He seemed to know so many ways of touching her that fuelled her desire for him. Quickly she had to put aside any sense of modesty and virtue she was clinging to as he caressed her in her most private places. She hoped that while he was doing all these perfectly improper things to her, he was retaining some sense of esteem for her. She prayed that this freedom she was allowing him now would make him appreciate how much he meant to her; that she did not allow it because she was wanton, but because she was profoundly in love; that love engendered and condoned this sort of behaviour.

They slumped onto the bed in their frenzy of passion, then had to interrupt proceedings while Lucy pulled back the sheets and slipped between them. She thankfully noticed in passing that they were clean and fresh. It was a strange bed, though, a bed that must have been occupied by many people over time, some no doubt engaged in similar antics.

Dickie smiled at her, reassuring her, and at the same time admiring her. His hands resumed exploring her again, everywhere. They were in the small of her back, then gliding over her hips. Next he was cupping one cheek of her bottom and gently squeezing it. Lucy reciprocated hardly at all, quite afraid of doing the wrong thing. Aware that she must not appear cold and disinterested, however, she raised both arms and flung them around his neck, coaxed his face to hers and kissed him. Now there could be no misunderstanding. His knee prised her thighs apart and she closed her eyes as he rolled onto her.

'You ain't done this afore, have you?' he whispered into her ear.

She opened her eyes and smiled at the ceiling. 'Never. I've been waiting for you.'

'Are you sure you still want to?'

'Why? Would you stop if I asked you to?'

'Do you want me stop?'

She grinned, half embarrassed, half ashamed, totally self-conscious of lying there in that strange bed, naked beneath him. 'No, Dickie, I don't want you to stop. I love you too much. We've come this far . . .'

'I'll be gentle. I'll try not to hurt you.'

'You make it sound like . . . like having a leg cut off.' She thought of Moses and the pain he must have endured.

He kissed her again briefly, looked down at her and grinned. 'It shouldn't be anywhere near as gory. But then you never know . . .'

It was strange, she thought as she felt him hard against her softness, pressing for entry, how all the girlish things that a man finds attractive – demeanour, elegance, grace, virtue, flattering clothes as well perhaps – were all abandoned in this unseemly spreading of legs. Yet Dickie was so excited by it.

'Give me your hand,' he said. She let him have it and he guided it down between his own legs. 'Feel him . . . Go on, feel him . . . Hold him gently . . . Now move your hand up and down . . .'

'Oh!' she exclaimed, not without some surprise. 'He feels all lovely and soft and smooth on the outside, but all hard on the inside.'

'If he was hard on the outside he'd hurt you. But he won't. See?'

He pushed into her determinedly. She imagined herself being stretched as she felt a sharp pain, and sucked air through her teeth momentarily. But it was transient, certainly nothing compared to the exhilaration of giving herself to this man whom she had loved from near and far for so long. He muttered how sorry he was that he'd hurt her after all, but she was not interested in his apology. There was no need, and she would rather he hadn't bothered. She just wanted him to fill her up inside, and began moving against him the better to accommodate him. Soon they were locked deep together in a mesmerising rhythm that brought a warm glow within her, which seemed to emanate from the centre of her body and radiate to the extremities of her limbs. Its growing intensity elicited a series of gasps. This . . . it was all an enchanting yet utterly stupefying sensation . . . So this was the ultimate expression of love given and received. And she was so grateful for the chance to experience it.

★   ★   ★

15

Arthur Goodrich had established his lodgings in a part of Bristol known as Totter Down, a quaint fairytale village of steep tangled streets, stepped razor-backed rooftops and excellent views over the city and the countryside. Mrs Hawkins, his landlady, was as good as a mother to him. She did his washing, cleaned his room and changed his bed regularly. She fed him conscientiously with good nourishing food and was not deterred by his finicky attitude to some of the things she presented. The house, which she had inherited on the death of her husband, lay on a hill just off the Bath Road, and was within easy walking distance of the church of St Mary Redcliffe.

On account of the variety of restoration tasks in which he was involved, Arthur had discovered a renewed enthusiasm for his craft in the employment of Mr Pascoe. Every morning, with a good breakfast inside him, Arthur approached the church and would look at the stump – all that remained of the spire – and try to imagine it in all its lofty architectural splendour before it collapsed. Then, typically, he would speculate mentally on the mayhem that must have followed the collapse, whether anybody was maimed or killed because of it.

To his immense satisfaction, Arthur shared a rapport with the young man with whom he found himself working, Cyril Chadwick. Cyril was a year or two younger but their affinity had not diminished with their increasing familiarity. The

reverse had happened and their friendship had actually flour-
ished. To Cyril, Arthur sounded quirkily different. At first, he
could barely understand what his new workmate was saying
because of his strange incoherent accent and unfamiliar expressions, but he soon grew used to it. Arthur, conversely, was
amused by Cyril's soft Bristol burr, and the pair regularly
teased each other about their respective cadences. It was not
simply their different accents that helped to bond them,
however; they shared a similar sense of humour yet, more
significantly, both had been unlucky in love. Consequently,
they found some comfort in confiding to each other their
innermost thoughts. They often met at night, sometimes
drinking in the local public houses, and bared their respective
souls after a few tankards of beer.

Cyril Chadwick was the son of a mine manager from
Bedminster. He had opted to take up the craft of stonemasonry as a youth, and had helped in the rebuilding of St
John's, his local church just to the south of East Street, the
main road through the parish. The Chadwicks' house was
situated in a better part, and owned by the Bedminster North
Side Colliery, which in turn was owned by a Mr William
Goulstone, a churchwarden of St John's. Hence, the family
attended that place of worship regularly.

Arthur was not particularly impressed by Bedminster. It
had obviously evolved from a village, judging from some of
the quaint buildings that remained, but in its present state
it reminded Arthur of Brierley Hill. In terms of immediate
landscape it vied with Brierley Hill for squalidity and quite
possibly beat it. Bedminster certainly possessed uglier and
higher slag heaps, which the recent proliferation of coal mines
within its parish bounds spewed out indiscriminately, even
onto East Street. Cyril assured Arthur that coal was bringing
greater prosperity to Bedminster's inhabitants, half the male
population of which were said to be employed in mining.

Arthur asked at what cost; East Street, he pointed out, was in part already lined with unsightly grey slag heaps.

Shortly before Cyril met with his accident falling off a scaffolding, he had invited Arthur home to take Sunday tea with his family. John Chadwick and his wife Catherine made Arthur welcome and Catherine, like Mrs Hawkins his landlady, also recognised Arthur as something of a lost soul, and so began to regard him as another potential son who needed mothering. It was on the first of these visits that Arthur met Cyril's sister Dorinda.

Cyril had mentioned already that Dorinda was a pretty girl, but he had said it with a brotherly disdain that somehow devalued her looks in Arthur's expectation, so that he anticipated meeting a girl of no more than merely pleasant visual appeal, and there were plenty of examples of the like in Bristol. However, when he actually met Dorinda and saw how strikingly lovely she was, he was in hallowed awe of her beauty.

That particular Sunday afternoon Arthur was thrust centre stage and his performance surpassed by a mile his own meagre expectations of himself. He was natural, amusing, relating tales of his life and exploits in the Black Country, encouraged by Dorinda's spontaneous laughter and obvious enjoyment. The Chadwicks were tickled with his strange accent and loved to hear it. He proved such a likeable success that Dorinda suggested that perhaps Mr Goodrich might like to return next Sunday, upon which the kindly Mrs Chadwick had no option but to confirm the invitation.

Arthur was, of course, still preoccupied with Lucy Piddock's refusal to take up his serious offer of marriage. It seemed perfectly reasonable and sensible that they should get wed. They had known each other for nearly a year and, even though she claimed that she did not love him enough, it was hardly a viable excuse for he loved her enough for both. Besides, she would inevitably come to love him in time. As

Moses her brother-in-law had explained, all she needed was a good poking on a regular basis to concentrate her attention and her emotions. Arthur was thus convinced that a good poking would have worked wonders, and he still might engineer the opportunity if only he could convince her to visit Bristol and stay for a while with him, in one of the many pleasant inns the city boasted.

After Lucy had written and told him she was no longer interested, Arthur was naturally devastated. His first reaction had been to return to Brierley Hill to talk some sense into the girl, to make her realise he was in earnest with his proposal of marriage and that such earnestness was not to be trifled with. Not only that, he was certain he could offer her a comfortable and secure future. But Cyril suggested that such a move would not only be futile, but would occupy valuable work time, and possibly might lead Lucy to perceive him as both immature and pompous. So Arthur, after some days of thought, decided that Cyril might be right.

By which time, he'd begun to realise he'd been existing without seeing Lucy for a month already. He had missed her, of course, but he was surviving; life continued. She was perpetually in his thoughts, but during that time away his emotions and his disappointment were becoming less intense. Over the ensuing weeks and months he began to realise that what was niggling him was not so much her actual refusal to wed, but the principle of it. He had loftily offered her the chance to venture into that honourable estate, ordained for the mutual society, help and comfort that the one ought to have of the other, both in prosperity and adversity. Of course, what he had also offered, although it had remained unspoken, was the likelihood of their having sons and daughters, since marriage was also ordained for the procreation of children. What ordinary working girl, the daughter of a humble ironworker, had the brass-bound effrontery to spurn such an offer, especially when it was earnestly made by the son of a self-made monumental mason and sepulchral architect, albeit a modest one in terms of professional and commercial achievements.

Thus it was that Arthur began to develop a greater regard for Dorinda Chadwick, though he knew it must remain distant and unspoken, for what girl, as beautiful as she was, would be interested in the likes of him?

Dorinda was twenty-three years old, intelligent and single. Although she'd had one abiding romance with a young naval officer, that affair had come to a dismal and unanticipated end when he'd returned to port two years earlier and claimed he had married a Maltese girl while he'd been away. The disappointment brought her considerable heartache and a heightened mistrust of all men thereafter.

Until Arthur came along.

In Arthur, she saw the exact opposite of her perfidious naval officer. She saw an ordinary man, but honourable, reliable and down to earth. If not endowed with great masculine beauty, he was not altogether repulsive. She found him amusing too but, perhaps more importantly after what she had suffered, she felt she could trust him. Arthur was too honest in his self-portrayal to be either devious or deceitful. He possessed the added attraction of being almost a foreigner, and thus sufficiently 'different'.

★ ★ ★

In the early spring of 1858, some seven months after his own disappointment over Lucy Piddock, it was arranged that Arthur should come to tea again one Sunday and perhaps accompany the family to evening service at St John's. The hurt had gone by this time. He could think and talk about Lucy without pain. He was free of the acute emotional stranglehold she'd had over him, and he looked forward to freshly feasting his eyes on the lovely Dorinda once more. The last time he had seen her was before Cyril Chadwick had recovered from his accident and was still laid up at home. So he strolled along to the Chadwicks' home dressed in his Sunday best and a new tall hat, and presented himself at their front door.

Dorinda answered the bell.

'Oh, Miss Chadwick . . .'

'Good afternoon, Mr Goodrich. You look surprised to see me.'

'Well, I was expecting the maid –'

'Well, you've got me instead.' Her smile was brilliant. 'Sorry to disappoint you.'

'No, I'm not disappointed, Miss Chadwick. Honest I'm not.'

She looked like a goddess who had swooped down to earth to lure some adoring Endymion. Her dress, all in white, served only to enhance the almost supernatural effect of her dazzling loveliness. She seemed enveloped in a haze of snowy clouds and shimmering moonbeams, the pure whiteness of which set off the brilliance of her copper hair and her green eyes. Arthur looked at her mesmerised.

'Oh, come in, Mr Goodrich,' she cooed in her delightful Bristol drawl. 'It's so lovely to see you again. How've you been?'

'Oh . . .' He was about to deliver a bulletin of his recent ailments, but wisely thought better of it. 'I've been well enough, thank you. How about you?'

'Seldom better. We've been looking forward to seeing you again, Mr Goodrich.'

'I wish you'd just call me Arthur, you know, Miss Chadwick.'

'Very well . . . If you'll call me Miss Chadwick.' She giggled deliciously. 'No, I was only jesting. Of course you can call me Dorinda.'

He smiled rentatively, for he was not sure how to react to her jest. 'Thank you, Dorinda.'

She led him into the sitting-room where the family waited. Mrs Chadwick, big and buxom, got up from her seat, her stays creaking, and offered her fat face. Arthur planted an exaggerated and rather noisy kiss on one cheek. Mr Chadwick, thin and scrawny by comparison, stood up and shook Arthur's hand cordially, as did Cyril even though he saw Arthur every day of the week at work.

'Please sit down, Arthur,' Dorinda said.

These people were not like the sort he was used to. Mr Chadwick was an important person at the mine; they employed a maid and lived in a house that had four bedrooms as well as a garret in the loft for the maid. It was clean and tidy, with soft drapes and decent furniture. Vases of freshly cut daffodils neatly arranged adorned a whatnot and a pianoforte. Comfortable chairs with soft cushions were abundant, there was a table with a pristine chenille cloth draped over it, and a print of the young Queen Victoria and Prince Albert graced one recessed wall.

Talk at first was about the mine and how fortunate Cyril was, having chosen to avoid working in any capacity in mining.

'Not being bright enough to become a manager, nor stupid enough to become a miner, has stood Cyril in good stead,' his father proclaimed approvingly. He sucked on his clay pipe and the filaments of tobacco in it glowed momentarily. 'Becoming a stonemason was a sensible move. The lad will never make a fortune, but at least he might derive some spiritual satisfaction from the craft.'

'I might even try my hand at sculpture one day,' Cyril declared. 'I do b'lieve I got an artistic streak in me.'

'How about you, Arthur?' Dorinda quizzed. 'Would you like to try your hand at sculpture perhaps?'

Arthur shook his head. 'I have enough trouble carving letters,' he replied unpretentiously.

She laughed with approval at his beguiling self-derision. 'I'm sure you're far too modest, Arthur.'

'Oh no, it ain't a question of modesty, Miss Dorinda, it's a question of ability.'

'So what are you good at?'

Arthur pondered the question for a few seconds, all eyes on him. 'Cricket? I'm all right at cricket . . . Shooting rabbits . . . Carving the wrong inscriptions on headstones,' he added with a boyish grin of embarrassment.

'Oh, do tell us . . .' Dorinda pleaded, anticipating a chuckle.

'I daren't. It's a bit . . . indelicate . . .'

'We're not such prudes,' Mrs Chadwick affirmed. 'I'm sure we'll not be too shocked.'

So Arthur told about the time he got the two inscriptions mixed up in Pensnett churchyard and his being taken short. It only served to enhance his standing with the Chadwicks, who liked him the more for it, and especially Dorinda whose mirth lasted until the family migrated to the dining room.

Tea was served, with sandwiches and cakes and . . . a syllabub.

'Don't you like syllabub?' Mrs Chadwick asked when she could see that Arthur was reticent about having any.

'No, I don't care for syllabub at all, sorry . . . Mrs Hawkins, my landlady, used to make lots of syllabubs, but I always ended up giving them the cat when she wasn't looking. But even the cat turned its nose up at them in the finish. So I had to tell her I didn't like them.'

'It's a wonder the cat wasn't perpetually inebriated,' Mr Chadwick said, laughing. 'Especially if she used spirits in them, as well as wine.'

'The cat used to act a bit queer now you mention it, Mr Chadwick,' Arthur said straight-faced. 'It used to jump about after its own tail, then fall over.'

Everybody laughed.

'Syllabubs are very popular in these parts. Not so in the Black Country?'

'Oh, I daresay, but I never heard of them till I came to Bristol.'

'Such a sheltered life you led, Arthur,' Dorinda remarked. 'A situation we'll have to remedy.'

The nights were drawing out and it was not yet dark when, after tea, the family and Arthur put on their respective shawls, mantles, hats and bonnets and walked to church, battling a stiff breeze. Arthur placed his best top hat under the pew and Dorinda made sure she sat next to him. From time to time during the service she turned to look at him with admiring smiles as he sang familiar hymns with enthusiasm. He sat half listening to Reverend Eland's sermon, half concentrating on returning Dorinda's heavenly smiles. When the service was over and the choir and clergy were in procession returning to the vestry, Dorinda leaned towards him.

'Would you like to go for a walk after the service, Arthur?' she whispered conspiratorially. 'I quite fancy a bracing walk afterwards, but I don't suppose anybody else will.'

'All right,' he answered without hesitation. 'If your mother and father and Cyril have got no objection.'

Dorinda beamed at him with her big green eyes. 'Oh, leave that to me.'

* * *

The day had been bright and remained dry, but the wind was funnelling briskly up East Street, making it feel colder than it should. The party walked back to the Chadwick family's abode, when Dorinda announced that she and Arthur were going to continue to walk for a while.

'If you've got no objection to me walking with Dorinda, that is,' Arthur, to his credit, was quick to add as a qualifier.

'Perhaps Cyril would like to go with you,' Mrs Chadwick suggested out of a sense of propriety.

'It's too chilly for me,' Cyril affirmed.

'Very well,' Mrs Chadwick conceded. 'But I urge you not to tarry too long in this dreadful wind. You neither of you want to catch a chill. Are you going to be warm enough, Dorinda?'

'Yes, Mother.'

They turned and walked on.

'In any case I have my blubber to keep me warm,' Dorinda said to Arthur when they were out of earshot of the others, who stood and watched them go.

'What do you mean, blubber?' Arthur asked puzzled.

'My fat.'

'Your fat? What fat? You ain't got no fat. You're all nice and slender.'

'Oh, at the moment,' Dorinda said, a look of sad resignation clouding her face. 'But look at the size of Mother.'

'But she's your mother. All mothers are fat . . . Well, not all, but most.'

'But I don't want to be fat. I don't want to grow into a stout middle-aged woman like she is. That's why I don't eat very much. I want to stay thin.'

'I don't see as you've got anything to worry about, Dorinda. You've got a lovely face anyway.'

'Oh, I know I have. I don't dislike my face at all . . . But my figure isn't exactly everything that I'd wish – or rather it is right now. What I mean is, it's in danger of becoming much stouter than I'd wish . . . Can you think of any more sorry sight than seeing a woman's pretty face stuck on the peak of a mountain of flesh, like a perfect peach perched on top of a Suffolk Saddleback. It's such a waste of a pretty face . . . But it will be my fate, I suppose.'

'But you might take after your father,' Arthur suggested rationally. 'You can't say as he's fat. Far from it, he's like a lath. I mean to say, Cyril isn't fat either. He's more like your father in that way.'

'But he's a man. All the women on the Williams's side – my mother's side of the family – end up fat. And so shall I.' Dorinda sighed profoundly. 'And men don't give birth neither, do they, Arthur? If I ever get married I shall refuse to have any children. If I were forced to have a whole host of children, I should end up so fat that I'd overflow on both sides, and wobble like an egg custard every time I moved . . . It's not funny, you know, Arthur . . . Do you dislike fat women?'

'No. You can't have too much of a good thing.' He smiled at her reassuringly, proud of his response. 'Some of the nicest women I have ever known are fat. Take Mrs Hawkins for –'

'But a fat woman is hardly likely to be the object of a man's desire when seeking a wife.'

'Maybe that would depend if she's got money or not . . .'

Dorinda sighed. 'Then it is my fate to end up plump and penniless. I have no money, Arthur. My family are certainly not wealthy, you know.'

'Well, I for one wouldn't be looking for wealth in a woman, Dorinda. I can make my own way in life. I'd never depend on a woman for money.'

'And you wouldn't mind if she was fat?'

'I wouldn't marry anybody fat, but I don't think I'd mind if she got fat when she was older. It'd show as she was well-fed and content.'

'I'm sure that's why Philip – that's the navy chap I was engaged to – went off and married somebody else. Because he knew I'd get fat. I understand his Maltese wife is a petite little thing . . . and always will be, no doubt. No doubt he thoroughly inspected *her* mother before he committed himself, to make certain that fatness didn't run in the family.'

'I think he must have been a letter or two short of an inscription to have let go of you, Dorinda,' Arthur declared sincerely, which elicited a look of satisfaction from his beautiful companion. 'I wouldn't have done it.'

'A letter or two short of an inscription?' she queried, wishing to be sure what it meant.

'Short of brains,' he explained.

'Oh, I see.' Dorinda beamed at him, her large green eyes alight with admiration. 'Do you really think so, Arthur?'

'I would never have given *you* up . . . A girl like you . . .' Arthur's heart was beating fast. Even he was perceptive enough to see where this could lead if he didn't muck it up by saying something stupid.

'Oh, Arthur, wouldn't you?' By the light of a gas lamp he could see the look of tenderness in her eyes.

'No, I wouldn't.'

Dorinda linked her arm through his, and he at once felt that he was important to her, which elicited a warm glow inside him. 'Cyril told me that you had a disappointment with a girl . . .'

'He told you, did he?'

'Yes. I felt quite some sympathy. You and I are like souls, I believe, Arthur. We've both been wronged.'

'Yes . . .' he answered pensively, reminded of Lucy.

'Were you very much in love with the girl?'

He nodded. 'I idolised her.'

'Tell me about her.'

'There ain't much to tell . . . She's just an ordinary girl. She works at a glassworks in Brierley Hill where I come from. Her father's an ironworker, her mother goes to chapel regular . . .' He shrugged. 'She was decent enough . . . Nicer than most in her quiet, reserved way . . .'

'Was she very reserved?'

'She sort of made it hard to get close to her. Made it hard for me, anyway. Not the next chap who comes along though, I reckon.'

'But she was special to you.'

'Oh, yes, she was very special . . .'

'Was she pretty?'

'I suppose she was, yes. There was certainly something about her . . . She had the most beautiful pale blue eyes . . .'

'Hmm . . . I don't think I like blue eyes in a woman, you know, Arthur. Especially *pale* blue. Women with pale blue eyes can be so cold and aloof.'

'D'you think so?'

'Yes, I do,' she answered decisively.

'Well, I suppose she was a bit aloof.'

'Then it proves my point, you see . . . Was she slender?'

'Yes, but no more slender than you are.'

'But is her mother fat?'

'Well, I wouldn't call her fat . . . But she ain't thin neither.'

'Hmm,' Dorinda uttered thoughtfully. 'So what happened?'

Two seafaring men were engaged in a drunken argument outside a tavern on the opposite side of the street. Arthur and Dorinda quickened their step to be shot of their shouting and foul language.

'I fell out with my father,' Arthur continued when they'd passed them by. 'All my life he's never paid me much attention, except to moan and have a go at me. I couldn't take it any more, working with him as well as having to live with him, so I decided to leave and make me way elsewhere in the world. I just had to get away. I thought it was as good a time as any to ask Lucy – that's her name, by the way – to marry me, so as we could be together all the time. But she said she wasn't interested in getting married –'

'Oh, but she must've been mad!'

'Then, a month after I'd gone, she wrote to tell me she was seeing another chap and she was keen on him.'

'She's off her head . . . Oh, poor Arthur . . .' She gave his arm an affectionate squeeze. 'Well, it's her loss. I wouldn't have let go of you. I'd have clung to you for dear life, no matter what.'

He smiled at her sheepishly, hardly able to credit what he was hearing. 'D'you mean that?'

'Oh, I do,' she said with emphasis. 'I think you're such a decent, gentle soul. Oh, looks are all well and good in a man, but not that important. Not like they are for a woman, I always think. So, although you are no Adonis, Arthur, you'd be an excellent catch. I'm sure your Lucy must have been mad to let you go.'

'But if she didn't feel strongly enough about me . . .'

'It sounds to me that you're making excuses for her, Arthur. You are still very loyal to her, aren't you? Would you still be loyal to her if you and I were walking out together?'

'You mean if me and you was a-courting?'

'Yes, that's what I mean.'

'Lord, no,' Arthur was quick to deny. 'If you and me was a-courting, Dorinda, I'd be loyal to you. I wouldn't give her a second thought.'

'That's so nice to hear.'

'Well, she had her chance . . .'

A silence fell between them when Arthur was tongue-tied. He perceived well enough that Dorinda might be offering herself to him, and he was so inordinately flattered and overwhelmed that he did not know how to take this situation that vital single step further. When there was no response from him, Dorinda had no option but to believe that he was not particularly interested in her after all. So they walked on as if nothing significant had been said. Arthur looked up at the sky self-consciously, feeling more and more foolish and inept because he knew momentous words *had* been spoken, and it was up to him to acknowledge the fact. He quickly realised that if he didn't ask her outright, she would feel slighted and he would lose his chance with this lovely girl.

'Dorinda,' he uttered tentatively. 'I . . . I'm not one for making fancy speeches and things like that, but . . . but would you consider . . .? What I'm trying to say is . . .'

'Are you about to ask me to be your girl, Arthur, by any chance?'

He smiled, half embarrassed, half terrified of being rejected. 'If . . . Only if you're prepared to consider it. I'd be that privileged if you'd be prepared to think about it . . .'

'Oh, Arthur!' she stopped walking and held on to his arm proprietorially, turning to him. She looked up earnestly into his eyes. 'Nothing would make me happier. *I'd* be the privileged one. Of course, I'd be honoured to be your girl.'

'Honest?'

She laughed. '*Dear* Arthur. You sound as if you don't believe me.'

'It's just that . . . Well, I hardly expected—'

'Goodness . . .' She giggled infectiously. 'I hope you're not regretting it already.'

'Oh, no. I'm . . . I'm . . . God, I'm so pleased, Dorinda. Should we go back and tell the others as we've started courting, d'you think?'

'Oh, no, not yet. Let's walk along the New Cut. We don't have to rush back. If we rush back I shan't have you to myself, shall I?'

★ ★ ★

16

One Saturday afternoon during that same windy March of 1858, Moses Cartwright struggled up South Street's steep incline, hobbling on his crutch. It was a day of low racing clouds and flurries of rain, and a booming, blustering wind that strove to separate him from his only means of physical support. He cursed his ill luck at having lost a perfectly good leg fighting a war that he regarded now as folly, and too expensive in human lives and limbs. He reached the top, and a hail of dirt and small twigs met him as he turned the corner panting from the exertion. From where he was now, on Church Street, it was all downhill and he expected to quicken his pace. He pulled up his collar for protection. Smoke was being torn from the tops of chimneys by the vicious wind and hurled into the swirling oblivion of the low clouds. Folk with any sense at all would avoid going out on a day like this unless they had a pressing purpose. But life for some required them to go out. Moses nodded cursorily to such folk, some of whom he knew, unwilling to stop and talk however, because he *had* a purpose and there was no time to lose.

He reached the Piddocks' cottage. Neither of the dogs were about. Unusual. They had some sense after all, those dogs, hiding somewhere from the storm. He tried the door, lifted the latch and opened it.

'Hannah!' he called. No reply. He called again. Still no reply. He tried yelling for Lucy, but Lucy did not reply either . . . Out . . . Damn. Just when he desperately needed them.

He closed the door behind him and ventured back into the squalling rain that was creating fleeting, transparent butterflies on the back yard, and called again as he approached the privy. There was no reply from the privy either. He lumbered back to the street. Behind the roar of the gusting wind he heard the whistle blast of a locomotive and watched its column of steam forced up from the cutting as it left the station, only to be scattered in the boisterous wind. That's why Lucy wasn't at home. She would be aboard that train on her way to do her courting in Wolverhampton. But where was Hannah? He knew where Haden would be, in the Whimsey. But Haden would be no use at all, more hindrance than help.

He could not afford to hang around. He turned himself around on his crutch and headed back home to South Street as fast as he could, arriving panting for breath.

At the bottom of the narrow bending staircase of his cottage he left his crutch and sat himself on the bottom-but-two step, then shoved himself upstairs on his backside.

'Am yer all right?' he called to Jane.

'Quick, Moses,' she called back in some anxiety. 'The pains am a-coming quicker now.'

He scuffled urgently up the last few rough wooden steps and stood up on his one leg using the stair rail to haul himself up.

'There's nobody in at your mother's.' His face was an icon of angst. 'Lord knows where your mother is, but I bet any money as Lucy's gone a-courting with that dirty Dickie.'

Jane's face was contorted in her agony. 'Put some water on the hob to boil, Moses,' she uttered through clenched teeth. 'You'll need some to clean up after. Then see if you can find somebody to help. P'raps Mrs Goodrich, or the old woman from next door.'

'Mrs Goodrich has got her work cut out tending to the old

man, Jane. It wouldn't be fair to drag her away.' He shook his head sombrely. 'An' I ain't having her from next door anywhere a-nigh either, the dirty old bugger. I ain't a-gunna leave yer, Janie. Not now. If it comes to the put to, we can bring this babby into the world weselves. You know what has to be done. I'll be here to do it.'

'Then put some water to boil,' she gasped. 'And plenty of it.'

Moses got down on his backside again and slid down the stairs. He picked up his crutch, lurched over to the fireplace and lifted the kettle off the hob. There was water in it but not much. He nestled it securely onto the coals, then picked up the pitcher Jane always used and stumbled awkwardly through the door, back into the wild wind and rain, heading for the water pump in Silver End. Jane's waters had just broken, enough to fill a bucket, he reckoned. If he'd known water was needed he would have fetched it sooner, but he did not know. Anyway, why should he know? It was sod all to do with men. Birthing was women's work and he'd expected that a woman would be present now to do it. The fact that there wasn't meant he'd have to fulfil the duty himself, but he would do it gladly for his Jane.

He reached the pump and laid his crutch against it while he pumped with one hand and held the pitcher beneath the water's flow with the other. He struggled to carry the laden pitcher using one hand, and a couple of times he had to stop to relieve the strain on his wrist. When he arrived back at his cottage he topped up the kettle that was already steaming, and called up to Jane once more.

'Quick, Moses,' she yelled back.

He shuffled his way hurriedly up the stairs again. He saw that Jane had kicked away all the bed clothes and she sat propped up against the brass bedstead clutching the sheets, her nightgown around her backside, her legs apart and her knees up. She was grimacing, her hair was awry and her knuckles were white as she gripped the bedrail in her absolute agony.

'How close is it?'

'Lord knows,' she gasped and winced with the pain. 'But I hope to God it's quick.'

'Does it hurt?'

'Oh, no . . . it's like being on a bloody picnic,' she rasped and screwed her eyes up. 'Course it hurts.'

He grabbed his other crutch, the one he kept against the stairs rail in their bedroom, and plodded over to her. He leaned it against the wall and sat on the bed with her.

'I swear it's coming,' she shrieked.

'Is there summat you have to do to help it out?'

'I'm supposed to push.'

'Well, push then.'

'I *am* bloody pushing!' Beads of sweat were forming on Jane's forehead. 'Put another towel under me, Moses.' She relaxed as the spasm receded. 'Make sure it's a clean one.'

Moses got up from the bed again, sought his crutch and a clean towel from a drawer, and returned. 'Lift your arse up.'

Jane complied entirely without inhibition.

'What a sight,' he declared, attempting humour to lighten the situation. 'It's enough to put yer off your dinner.'

'You've bin quick enough after it till now,' she replied, and her face brightened with an amused smile. 'Dirty devil.'

'Well, I was trying to shove summat in there afore. This time you'm trying to shove summat out. There's a world o' difference.'

'I'm trying to shove out what you let in,' she said wryly, taking advantage of the temporary lull in her contractions. 'Remind me never to let you do it again.' She looked at him sideways, which evoked a smile from Moses.

Their banter relieved the tension and they remained quiet, unspeaking for a few minutes while he watched his suffering wife intently. The wind and rain were lashing the window panes and Moses wondered whether the roof would come off. Jane had her eyes shut and he anxiously watched her face contort again as the agony of pain passed over her. He shuffled across the bed to sit beside her and held her in his arms comfortingly.

Jane let out a shriek.

'Shove,' he whispered into her ear.

She gripped his hands tight that were held against her bare hips. 'I'm shoving,' she groaned. 'Oh, Lord!'

'I wish I could suffer this for you,' he said quietly. 'I'd do it gladly.'

'I wish you could as well . . . *Oh, Christ!* . . .' She gripped his hands with a renewed strength, digging her nails into his flesh, shrieking with the torment of pain. 'You wouldn't believe the agony,' she said presently.

'You'm being very brave, our bab,' he gently consoled. 'You'm doing well . . .'

This went on for some time, and Moses wondered whether the child was ever going to make an appearance. He listened alternately to his poor wife's harrowing screams and the wind whistling through the joints of the window frame. The squalling rain, which spattered the panes in spasms, were coming and going like his wife's contractions, and with comparable vigour. As daylight began to fade, Jane informed him that she could feel the child almost there.

'Come round and look,' she gasped.

Moses unhanded her and shifted down the bed. 'Christ, I can see its little head.'

'Little?' Jane whimpered. 'You could've fooled me.'

'What shall I do?' Moses exclaimed, in a sudden panic of excitement. 'I think I'm gunna faint.'

'Don't you *dare* faint,' Jane hissed through her teeth. 'I need you to help. I'm trying to shove it out before my hips are torn apart . . . For God's sake, grab hold of it gently and pull . . .'

He watched, mesmerised as the little being emerged into the world all wet and greasy. Its tiny face, what he could see of it, was all purple and pinched. He leaned forward and lifted the child, inspecting it, checking that God had blessed it with a full set of limbs, fingers and toes. It felt slippery and he was worried he might drop it, and it was still attached by some fleshy-looking rope to Jane. The little bundle began to cry, weakly at first, but more robustly within a very few seconds. Jane was smiling now. Moses was smiling at her. He had never seen such a look of pure joy on her face. Her arms were outstretched, waiting to receive the baby in her arms. His baby. He shuffled across the bed, holding the child as if it were the most fragile, the most precious thing in the world, and placed it on Jane's belly. At once she embraced it.

'It's a girl,' he said inadequately, his voice taut with emotion. 'It's a girl, Janie.'

Moses was sure he was going to cry. Tears filled his eyes. Never had he seen anything like this. Nothing so sublime, so wondrous. He had seen soldiers dying in screaming agony in the Crimea, had witnessed too many fine decent men prematurely departing this world. But he had never witnessed a new life coming into it before, and it was a stunning, emotional experience. It filled him with immeasurable joy, with hope for the future. This was the start of a new phase in their lives. A baby was another mouth to feed, an added responsibility, but it was a responsibility he welcomed with all his heart. His lack of a leg would be no handicap. He would continue to overcome it as he had before, but with a greater determination now that he was the father of a beautiful new child. His responsibility.

He shuffled to Jane's side and put his arm around her. 'You did well, my flower. I'm that proud of you.'

She laughed happily. 'So did you.'

'I din't do anything. I felt no pain, 'cept for the agony of watching you going through it.'

'You was here with me.'

'Course I was. There was nowhere else for me to go.' He gave her a loving squeeze and looked into her eyes, peaceful now, content. 'Thank you for giving me a perfect little daughter.'

'You gave it to me first. I just looked after it while it grew inside me.'

'What do we do with that cord?'

'We cut it, and tie it off. The rest of it's due to come away from me any minute.'

'I'd better get a knife then.' He moved to get up from the bed.

'A sharp one, Moses. And make sure its been washed in hot water and soda . . .'

'Lord, the water . . . I bet as it's all boiled away by now. I bet the kettle's buggered an' all.'

★　★　★

At about half past seven, when it was getting darker Moses, lying alongside Jane, listened for the sound of the child's breathing. There was a hush everywhere. After the frantic ravings of the gale it was as if a blanket had fallen over everything, muffling all sounds. He could hear Jane's breathing as she slept, drained of strength after her excruciating pushes and exertions. A late shaft of sunlight shot from behind a cloud, painting the tiny room a rich shade of orangey-red. Moses leaned over to the chest of drawers that stood under the window, and looked with wonder at his beautiful daughter lying in the half-open top drawer that was her crib. The baby licked her lips with a tiny pink tongue and rubbed one closed eye awkwardly with a tiny fist, and tears filled his eyes again at the wondrous enormity of what had come to pass that day.

He roused himself and went downstairs. The fire needed making up, but he lit a spill from it and ignited two oil lamps, one of which he would take with him upstairs. He placed coal from the coal bucket on the hearth onto the fire and poured water from the pitcher into the kettle, whistling as he worked. He heard the door latch rattle and turned to see who it was. Haden entered, with Lucy behind him. They were on their way to the Whimsey.

'Any sign yet, Moses?'

'Sign? Sign o' what?'

'Of e'er a babby, yer fool.'

'Oh, a babby . . . Funny you should mention it . . . One just happened to pop out this afternoon.' He grinned, unable to keep up his sarcasm any longer. 'A little wench.'

'You mean, our Jane's had the bab today?' Haden's old eyes sparkled with the reflection of the oil lamp as he looked at Lucy for her reaction.

'This afternoon, like I said.'

Lucy shrieked with excitement and headed for the stairs. 'Are they both all right? Can I go up and see?'

'Why didn't you send for Hannah?' Haden asked.

'I did. I went down to fetch her, but there was nobody in.'

Haden nodded. 'She'll go saft when she knows. She went to Stourbridge, and our Lucy went t'Ampton to see Dickie bloody Dempster . . . Can I go up and see the bab an' all?'

'If you've a mind, Haden.'

'Then I'll trot back 'um and tell Hannah.'

'Oh, our Jane, she's beautiful,' Lucy cooed, peering into the top drawer of the chest at her new niece. 'Can I hold her?'

'Course.'

Gently, Lucy lifted the child and pressed her to her bosom.

'She's so tiny, our Jane. Look at her little fingernails. Oh, our Jane, isn't she beautiful? Has she fed yet?'

Jane nodded. 'She finished about a half hour ago.'

'So who was here when you had her?'

'Just Moses.'

'Just Moses?'

Jane nodded again. 'He was a brick. He coped as well as any midwife. 'Cept when he nearly fainted. I had to threaten him then.' She grinned with pride.

Lucy looked at the baby with instant love. 'I wish she'd open her eyes so I can see them. Oh, anytime you want me to look after her, our Jane, just say the word . . . Have you decided what to call her yet?'

'We ain't thought about it properly.'

'Dickie likes the name Julia.'

'Yes, that's nice. It's funny how the old-fashioned names come round again.'

Haden appeared at the top of the stairs in the bedroom.

'Hear that, Father?' Lucy said. 'Moses delivered the baby.'

'Moses?' Haden queried with a look of surprise. 'He's got more guts then me.'

★   ★   ★

The courtship between Lucy and Dickie Dempster continued to flourish. She slavishly went to Wolverhampton every Saturday afternoon, and their routine never varied. They continued to visit the Old Barrel in Boblake and he would pay for an upstairs room where they spent the afternoon in bed making love ardently and with ever-increasing finesse. Lucy's hope that he might take her somewhere else afterwards was a forlorn one; once he was sated he had no further use for her. So they went their separate ways homeward, Lucy to catch the six o' clock to be in time for work at the Whimsey, he to do whatever it was he chose to do on a Saturday night.

Wednesday nights he continued to travel to Brettell Lane

where she met him off the train and they would go for walks, or sit in a public house drinking beer – the Bell Hotel was a favourite. Sometimes they even sat with Hannah in the Piddocks' cottage. It all depended on the weather. Monday nights had been added to the agenda lately; it was an added opportunity to be together and Lucy welcomed it with all her heart. With their heightened desire rampant, every occasion to express it was a bonus. They made love vertically against the wall, hidden in some recess along the canal when it was dark and they were undetectable. Sometimes they writhed in long grass over the fields if it was dry and the wind not too chilly. Dickie only had to touch her and she wanted him . . . and he knew it.

The subject of marriage had been alluded to, mostly by Lucy. She had asked him questions as to his feelings on the subject and she had been encouraged by his responses. Maybe they could think of marriage, he'd said, when they'd been courting a couple of years. If she ever became pregnant, he said he would do the right thing by her. Meanwhile, of course, it made sense to be careful, and he was careful. It would be folly, he told her, to invite trouble by allowing yourself to be so overwhelmed with passion that you forgot yourself and were unable to withdraw in time.

So far they'd had a couple of scares when Lucy, normally regular, was a week or so late. Thankfully, both turned out to be false alarms, but it focused Dickie's mind on the realities of life even more, and he began to take his responsibilities even more seriously. The stigma if he made her pregnant would be unbearable, she told him, even if they married as soon as she realised she was carrying. Think of her poor mother, what she would have to put up with, a regular chapel-goer. Her father, too, would have something to say . . .

But all these enforced restrictions on their ardour, and the curtailment especially of Dickie's pleasure through *coitus interruptus* – since it was intensely more gratifying to climax inside the object of your desire than over her belly – only served to heighten their mutual lust. And Saturday afternoons they looked forward to immensely, if only because they had a soft warm bed in which they could lie together, at ease and in relative comfort. Much preferable to dusty fields with unspeakable insects wriggling beneath you, or rough brick walls to lean against while you stood up to do it, all the time peering about you to make sure no ganners were watching. A comfortable marriage bed would be the perfect answer to all these hindrances, Lucy realised.

A taste of it was put before them when, towards the end of May, Jane asked if Lucy would be prepared to look after little Emily for them one evening. Emily was the name they had given the baby. Lucy, who loved the child to distraction, would have been delighted except that it fell on a Wednesday night, which interfered with her courting schedule.

'So bring him here,' Jane suggested logically. 'Moses and me have got no objection.'

'That would be perfect if Dickie could be with me,' Lucy replied with a grateful smile. 'So where are you going?'

'We had a letter to say as Moses's Aunt Sarah's been took bad. The old dear's in her eighties and he reckons this is the end for her, so he wanted to go and see her, for she brought him up. But I don't reckon it'd be a good place to take our Emily if there's sickness about. Trouble is, the old woman lives at Priestfield, so it means going there on the train.'

So, before Lucy bid Dickie goodnight on the prior Monday, she asked that he call for her at the Cartwrights' cottage in South Street. 'And I'll have some supper ready for you,' she promised.

Wednesday night rolled round and Lucy, after her meal, made her way to her sister's house.

'The baby's had a good feed, our Lucy,' Jane informed her

before she and Moses left. 'So she should sleep sound. Put her in her new crib when you reckon she's ready.' Little Emily was familiar with her Aunt Lucy through her frequent attentions, so Jane had no qualms about leaving the baby with her. 'There's coal in the coal bucket and water in the kettle. Just mind what you'm up to,' she added with a wink, realising full well that Lucy would not. 'See you later.'

With her cooing baby talk, Lucy managed to eke out a toothless smile from Emily before she put her to bed. Anyway, there was no rush. She wanted Dickie to see the baby, how she had come on, how pleasant she was. But Emily fell asleep before Dickie arrived, and she answered the door to him with the baby in her arms.

'A babby suits you,' he said with a broad grin as she let him in. 'You'd make a beautiful mother. I love to see a young woman with a bab in her arms.'

'Do you now?' she answered perkily. 'I think it depends on the young woman and whether she's wed or no.' She offered her lips.

He kissed her and she stood aside to let him in. 'Whether she's wed or no,' he said, 'there's nothing to stop her doing the thing what causes kids, but so sure as she has one and ain't wed, there's all hell to pay.'

'Course there is. Because having a child before you'm wed, proves you've been naughty.'

'I like being naughty with you, Luce.'

She smiled affectionately. 'I like being naughty with you as well. But to my mind, the sin ain't in the doing of it, the sin is in being found out.' She swivelled her eyes down momentarily towards the child. 'What do you think of her now? D'you think she's come on since last time you saw her?'

'She's a little boster and no two ways. How long's she been asleep?'

'A while now. I suppose I should put her in her crib. You

should see her new crib, Dickie . . . Open the door to the stairs for me, please, and we'll take her up.'

He opened it and she ascended the narrow twisting staircase. Dickie followed her on tiptoe so as not to awaken the child with unnecessary clumping of his boots on the bare wooden stairs.

'There,' Lucy said, nodding into the corner of the bedroom where the crib stood. 'Isn't it lovely? Moses went and fetched it Saturday. Lord knows how he managed to carry it from Brierley Hill, but Jane reckons he did. He'd do anything for his daughter.' She took the baby to the crib and laid her in it carefully, making sure she was not too restricted with swaddling blankets. 'Oh, isn't she a picture, Dickie? Come and have a look at her . . .'

He stepped over to them and gazed at the baby, then looked into Lucy's pale blue eyes that were like saucers in the half light. 'She looks a bit like you, you know.'

'There's bound to be some family resemblance,' she answered logically.

'She could be your little daughter for all anybody knew.'

'Then she'd have to be your daughter as well, Dickie.'

He held out his hand to her and she took it. They were standing at the side of a bed that looked soft and inviting, and they turned to face each other. She rested her head against his chest, then he lifted her face to his and kissed her on the lips affectionately. Dusk was neutralising the colour of everything, but its subdued greyness managed to send enough illumination through the small window for them to see each other's expressions clearly. Looking deeply into her eyes, he undid the tie of her pinafore behind her and let it fall to the floor. Then he unbuttoned the front of her blouse and, when it opened, he pushed it back over her shoulders and down her arms, and that fell whispering to the floor too. He unfastened the waist-band of her skirt and that, as well, fell around her feet.

'I'll do the rest,' she whispered with a smile.

As she divested herself of the rest of her clothes he too took off his boots and got undressed. Naked, she shivered at the cool air of that May evening and jumped into the bed first, snuggling under the layers of blankets and sheets for warmth.

He got in beside her. 'I hope Jane and Moses won't mind us using their bed.'

'It's in a good cause,' she said softly.

'Oh, I know it well enough, my flower.'

'No, I mean looking after the baby, Dickie,' she quipped.

'That's what I mean. You're my baby.'

'Hold me,' she breathed. 'I'm cold.'

'I'll soon warm you.'

The warmth from his body was irresistible. It was almost as familiar to her as her own by now, yet she never tired of the feel of him against her own skin. His body was smooth and firm. She closed her eyes as she sensually brushed her soft lips over his shoulders and his neck, caressing his skin that was so smooth to her touch. He pushed himself against her and she held him there, her hand cupped around one firm buttock, holding him tight. Already he was hard and ready, and she could feel him pressed against her belly, such an exhilarating sensation. As she rolled onto her back submissively his hands gently skimmed first across her breast, over her stomach and settled within her mound of soft hair. They kissed again and she was feeling warmer already.

'I wonder who a child of ours would look like?' he remarked, his fingers gently probing the soft, warm place between her legs and making her writhe with pleasure.

'Like me,' she sighed.

'How do you work that out?'

'I would never say it looked like you . . . Unless we was wed. We'd have to get wed, Dickie . . .'

'Shut up and kiss me again.'

They kissed earnestly. His skilful touch and his smooth skin pressing against her lit her up like a gas lamp, as it always did. Sensuously, he rolled onto her and she let out a little sigh of anticipation, then a gasp of pleasure as she felt him slide silkily, familiarly inside her. There was no mistaking their mutual hunger as they rocked together in harmony, eking out as much pleasure as they could from the sensations they elicited in each other.

But there was something different about that evening. Something mystical.

The reddish-grey light of dusk outside was affording the room a suitably romantic amount of illumination, enough to see each other clearly, enough for him to appreciate the refined contours of her body as he raised himself up so that he could look down on her and admire her. Her beautiful eyes seemed even bigger in this gloaming, even softer as she looked up at him, her smiling love brimming over. Her nipples, standing proud, shimmered where he had smothered them in hot wet kisses. There was something magical about a beautiful baby lying there in the same room, as if it were their child and they were in their own marital bed. He remembered the way she looked holding the baby when she opened the door to him. He gazed at her glistening nipples again and imagined their wetness caused by the baby's gently sucking lips, and the thought aroused him way beyond his usual intensity. He began moving inside her more strenuously, fired by the sensuality of his thoughts, desperate to feel that sweet, sweet glow in his loins that would bring with it complete fulfilment and peace. That unmistakable sensation was building inexorably in the epicentre of his very being and this time he lacked the will to control himself. He screwed his eyes up, clenched his teeth and uttered a low groan of satisfaction and release as he emptied himself inside her. Then, he slumped back into her arms, spent and breathing hard from his exertion.

'Dickie, you let go inside me,' she breathed without admonishment, stroking him lovingly.

He nodded, his face wet with sweat against her hair. 'I couldn't help it, Luce,' he sighed. 'I just had to . . . I always knew it would end up like this with you.'

★　★　★

17

Towards the end of May, Arthur Goodrich received a letter from his brother Talbot, which read:

Dearest Brother,

I feel that I should write and let you know that Father's health is in rapid decline. Over the past few months he has been unwell and getting progressively worse. He needs constant attention, which has occupied Mother to the detriment of all else. Magnolia too has been spending much time helping to nurse him while Albert has been at school. Dr Walker says the old man has a malignant growth in his bowel and that his time on this earth is going to be short, although he cannot say how short.

Because of Father's illness, the business has suffered. I have much more work than I can cope with and whilst Moses Cartwright is a godsend helping with all the necessary tasks that have to be done around the yard and the workshop, he is by no means either a skilled letter cutter or a mason, although he tries hard and in the fullness of time I'm sure he will become very able within the limits of his incapacity. Certainly he is very willing, especially nowadays.

Mother is in a perpetual tizz, not only with Father, but worrying about you as well. I know you write to her from time to time but she is your mother after all and she can't help worrying about you. I think it's about time you returned home, Arthur. I am desperate for your help and skill in the business. Besides, I earnestly believe you should make your peace with Father before he passes on. It would be the honourable thing to do, especially as he keeps asking where you are. It goes without saying that Mother would welcome you back whole heartedly into the bosom of the family.

Arthur, please respond to this letter by return, so that I may present Mother with some news a little more heartening. Magnolia sends her love (as does Albert) and says she looks forward to seeing you again very soon.

Yours truly, your brother,
Talbot Goodrich.

Arthur replied by return of post.

Dear Talbot,

It was good of you to write and let me know how things are at home. I am very sorry to hear that Father is so unwell and I feel dreadfully sorry for Mother who must have her work cut out looking after the miserable old wretch. The trouble is I am so busy doing my own job on the restoration of St Mary Redcliffe that it allows me no time yet to take a day or two off to travel to Brierley Hill and see him. As you know, Talbot, Father and I never hit it off when I was at home. When I was a tiddler he never cared tuppence for me and never ever showed me any affection. As I grew up he never gave me any encouragement in my schooling or my work. He was almost a stranger to me and yet he expected me to work for him as if I was beholden to him, and for next to nothing in remuneration. Do you know, Talbot, that here in Bristol, doing a job of work that I love for a gaffer who is as good as gold, I earn nearly twice as much as what Father used to pay me. My health and temper are both better down here as well, save for a bit of indigestion now and again,

226

since I don't have to sit on cold gravestones in draughty churchyards any more catching my own death.

No, I find myself disinclined to visit him even though he might be very ill, because he would never have put himself out for me. I have no wish to make my peace with him. It is my hope never to cast eyes on him again. I believe you know this, Talbot, because you were always his favourite, not that I hold that against you. I don't.

I suppose you having so much work is a good thing. If you find you have too much, as you imply, then maybe you'll have to set on a new skilled man. There must be plenty about. There is only one thing I would do for Father now, and that gladly: with glee would I cut the letters on his headstone. Perhaps you will allow me that pleasure when the time is ripe.

I am what you might call courting these days, a very pretty girl called Miss Dorinda Chadwick. Her family are strong churchgoers and very respectable. Her father is the manager of one of the pits in Bedminster, not far from where I lodge in Totter Down. I work with her brother Mr Cyril Chadwick, and it is through him that I met Dorinda. I consider myself very lucky to have found a girl so lovely, which is another reason why I am not inclined to leave here, if only for a few days.

I hope you understand how I feel.

Your ever-loving brother

Arthur.

Coincidentally, Arthur received another letter the very next day, which came as a complete shock, sent as it was by Lucy Piddock. To his bewilderment, he felt himself go hot and his pulse quicken as soon as he saw the handwriting on the envelope. He opened it with fumbling fingers and read it twice, the first time quickly, the second more studiedly. It said:

Dear Arthur,

I dare say it will be a surprise for you to get a letter from me after so long and I shoud of writ sooner but I have been so bizy what with one thing and another. But I am writing now becuz I wanted you to know that our Jane and Moses had a daughter in March and they have called her Emily. Moses delivered the baby himself without another woman there. She is such a lovely baby, so pretty and such a sweet nature and I love her to pieces. I just love to hold her. Oh, Arthur, I wish you cud see her. Jane is quite beside herself with joy and Moses is like a dog with two bones over his daughter: I don't think I've ever seen a happier couple. I go to there house a lot more often these days becuz of the baby, specially every Wednesday night when I look after her for our Jane when she and Moses go to visit his sick aunt who lives in Priestfield. I think they go and have a drink somewhere after, before they catch the last train back. Still, I don't blame them. It's a change for them to get out and I love to go and look after Emily while they are out as I say. I'm just sorry as I can't feed her.

Well, Arthur, it's getting on for a year since you went to live in Bristol and since I haven't heard from you for such a long time I thought it would be nice to write to you again. What happened with that girl Dorinda you said you liked? Did you ever start courting her? I hope you did, and I hope she turns out to be a very suitable girl, just right for you. Don't forget to invite me to the wedding.

How are your toothaches these days and all your other ailments? I hope they are better. I heard from Moses that your father is very ill. Moses says he hasn't seen him for weeks even though he goes to the yard every day bar Sundays, so he must be ill. Maybe you'll come home to see him. If you do don't forget to come and say hallo. My mother wood love to see you again and so wood my dad,

*they often talk about you. In the meanwhile I'll see if I can
find ten minutes to go and see your mother. There might be
an errand or two as I can run for her if she's so tied up with
looking after your father. She might also give me one of her
lovely pork pies.*

*Well, Arthur; it wood be nice to hear from you if you feel
like writing back. Keep well.*

Your friend,
Lucy Piddock.

★　★　★

It was late afternoon when Dorinda took an omnibus from
Bedminster to Redcliffe, having arranged to meet Arthur at
the church after work. He had sought permission from Mrs
Hawkins, his landlady, to invite her to tea, keen that she should
meet Dorinda since the girl occupied so many of his evenings.
This particular day, a Friday, was deemed by all to be suitable
for such an occasion.

Dorinda also encountered her brother Cyril leaving work
and asked him to tell their mother and father that she had
arrived safely to meet Arthur. Then they parted company,
Cyril to walk towards Bedminster via Redcliffe Hill, Arthur
and Dorinda heading for Totter Down, first by way of Pump
Lane. Arthur carried with him his dusty tool bag while
Dorinda took his arm.

'What have you been working on today?'

'More gargoyles. Sprucing 'em up, touching 'em in here
and there.'

'Trying to make 'em handsome?' She chuckled at the
thought. 'You can't make gargoyles handsome, Arthur. By
their very nature they're ugly.'

'I know. Try as I might I can't make them pretty.'

She laughed again. 'And you'd very likely get into trouble
with the sexton if you succeeded. It would be a strange church
that had handsome gargoyles. It's funny, isn't it, how some

things that are meant to adorn are like gargoyles, and yet other things are so pretty? And I'm sure that *adorn* is the right word.'

'How do you mean, Dorinda?' Arthur asked, a look of puzzlement on his face that was soiled with the dust of masonry.

'Well, I mean, St Mary Redcliffe is *adorned* with gargoyles, and gargoyles are supposed to look fearsome and repulsive, whereas the trimmings that *adorn* my bonnet, for instance, are supposed to look pretty. Which is a peculiar sort of difference for just one word to express, I believe, Arthur,'

'Why is it peculiar, Dorinda? I don't understand what you'm a-getting at. Bonnets *are* supposed to look pretty.'

'Course they are. That's what I'm saying. But not gargoyles, yet the word *adorn* is used to describe both conditions. Don't you see? Anyway, you wouldn't love me half as much if I wore bonnets dripping in fearsome gargoyles, would you?'

He laughed at the absurd image his mind conjured up. 'So do you think I like you less when you don't look nice?'

'I think you like me better when I do . . . which amounts to the same thing, I suppose. And why put a strain on your affection with bonnets dripping with gargoyles when I can ease it with pretty ones? After all, if we ever get married, you'll promise to love and cherish me in sickness, and poverty and all manner of unpleasant things. There's nothing in the marriage service that I know of which says you'd have to cherish me in awful bonnets.'

'You'd look pretty in anything, Dorinda.'

She beamed a grateful smile at him for saying so, and they walked on in silence for a while, crossing the bridge over the New Cut which was constructed in the first decade of the century to divert the River Avon.

'I had another letter yesterday,' Arthur said, striking up another topic of conversation. 'From Lucy Piddock.'

'The girl you used to be in love with?' Dorinda queried with a hint of apprehension in her eyes.

'Yes. To let me know her sister has had a baby daughter.'

'Ouch! How painful. But why should that be of concern to you?'

'Well . . . because I like Jane . . . and her husband Moses was my friend. I always got on very well with them . . . Oh, and he delivered the baby himself.'

'Goodness me, how terrifying! You mean without a midwife?'

'So I understand. It's all the more an achievement when you consider he's only got one leg.'

'He would have had to hop about a bit then.'

'He uses a crutch.'

'But not to deliver a baby?'

He grinned at her. 'Don't be daft.'

'What happened to his other leg?'

'He lost it in the Crimea.'

'And couldn't find it, you mean?'

He looked at her sideways, not knowing whether to admonish her for unwarranted flippancy or to laugh. She began to giggle girlishly and he realised she was teasing him.

'But I don't like the idea of her writing to you, Arthur,' she added, serious again. 'Did this Lucy say she was still courting?'

'She didn't say.'

'Then maybe she's not.'

'She says, if I return home to see my mother and father I am to call on her and say hello.'

'It sounds to me as though she ain't courting no more, Arthur, and she's trying to wheedle her way back into your affections. Do you intend to write back to her?'

'I suppose so,' he answered defensively. 'It'd be rude not to. Anyway, she says she's going to see my mother, to ask if she wants any errands running while my father is so ill. I think that's very kind of her. But she *is* kind, is Lucy.'

'She sounds a bit of a busybody, if you ask me. She'll be writing you love letters next . . . I can write you love letters, Arthur, if that's what you want. Heaps of them.'

'It's not what I want, particularly. But if you want to . . . Perhaps if I have to go back to Brierley Hill, you can . . . If my father died, I mean. I would have to go back for a while to comfort my mother if my father died.'

The very notion was too painful a reminder of how she had lost Philip. He had gone away from her, manifestly sad at the prospect of being apart, promising ardently that they would wed on his return, yet he returned already married to a Maltese girl. She could never allow such a thing to happen again and similarly lose Arthur, yet it was ever likely to happen, since there was another woman patently interested in him, with whom he had already been in love. Goodness, no. If he had fallen in love with this Lucy Piddock once, he could fall in love with her twice.

'You don't think I would ever let you go back to Brierley Hill without me, do you?' Dorinda said assertively. 'I'm not letting you within ten miles of that Lucy Piddock.'

'I don't think you have anything at all to worry about, Dorinda. Lucy never was that devoted to me. I don't expect she will have changed. Anyway, I suppose she's still courting. I reckon she was very taken with the chap, whoever he is.'

★ ★ ★

The house in which Mrs Hawkins lived had a neat and tidy back garden that was overgrown since her husband had died. She had endeavoured to interest Arthur, her lodger, in tidying it up and, on a few occasions, he had set about it with a spade and fork and applied himself somewhat. But since Dorinda had appeared in his life he barely had time any more. Mrs Hawkins was a regular churchgoer and considered herself religious. Indeed, a crucifix bearing a bronze casting of Jesus stood on the mantelshelf and several allegorical prints adorned the walls.

She had prepared a fish pie for her guests, a recipe which she knew Arthur enjoyed, and she loved to see him enjoy it, for it made the whole exercise worth while. She was also looking forward to meeting Dorinda, about whom she had heard snippets from her lodger and, since she considered herself a sort of foster-mother to him, was concerned on behalf of his real mother that he should associate with the right sort of girl.

'I understand you attend church regularly, Miss Chadwick?' Mrs Hawkins asked her guest as they sat down to their meal overlooking the window of her small dining room that looked out onto the back garden.

'Every Sunday, morning and evening,' Dorinda replied. 'We feel obliged really, because the owner of the mine my father works for is churchwarden.'

'So you don't attend out of a sense of piety or duty to our Lord, more out of a sense of duty to the mine owner?'

Dorinda pondered the question a second or two, deciding to overlook what could have been a slur. 'Mmm . . . I would agree with that assessment on the whole. But I do enjoy singing some of the hymns. Some of them are very jolly, with decent jolly tunes and all that.'

Unfortunately, that admission did not meet with Mrs Hawkins's absolute approval, but she kept her opinion to herself, since she did not know Dorinda well enough to say what she really thought.

'I assume, since you are here, Miss Chadwick, that your parents approve wholeheartedly of your courtship with Arthur?' She smiled to reaffirm her goodwill.

'Oh, yes, of course. Otherwise, of course, I wouldn't be here.'

'Your father is what at the coal mine?'

'Manager, Mrs Hawkins.'

'Mmm . . .'

'Do you see a problem with that, Mrs Hawkins?'

'Oh, certainly not,' Mrs Hawkins replied, and dabbed her mouth with her napkin. 'But dear Arthur here is but a stonemason . . . Not to demean you at all, dear Arthur; stonemasonry is a skilled craft and shouldn't be demeaned . . . But I would have thought, Miss Chadwick, that your father being a mine manager – or at the very least, your mother – would have preferred you to have taken up with somebody of a higher station – somebody with a carriage at least.'

'Well, no, that's not the case at all, Mrs Hawkins.' Dorinda was trying desperately to hide her indignation at such a notion as she picked half-heartedly at her food. However, it was necessary to explain her parents' position, for she was sensible enough to recognise that it might seem odd to anybody who was not familiar with the circumstances. 'My parents are not high-born, Mrs Hawkins, although my father has done quite well as the son of a mere working-class family. My brother and I have each had a decent education as well, thanks to my father's endeavours but, you see, my brother is also a stonemason, as perhaps you are already aware. They could hardly condone their son being a *mere* stonemason, and not a prospective son-in-law. Besides, I was once disappointed by a naval officer who I was engaged to . . . whose family actually owned a carriage,' she added scornfully. 'You might consider a naval officer to be of a higher class, Mrs Hawkins, but I would have to disagree with you.'

'My husband was a sea captain . . .'

'But he was most likely a decent man,' Dorinda was quick to suggest. 'Anyway, my family and I are less concerned with class than we are with integrity. We are all agreed that dear Arthur is brimming with integrity.'

'Indeed he is.' Mrs Hawkins looked at him with admiration. 'I mentioned it only because I see myself as responsible for Arthur while he is in my care. I am sure his mother would expect such a duty of care from me, and it would break my heart to feel that I had let her down.'

'Oh, I understand perfectly, Mrs Hawkins. But I do sincerely hope that you find me entirely suitable for dear Arthur.'

'It must have been awful for you to have been disappointed once before,' Mrs Hawkins remarked, taking refuge in a side issue.

'Oh, it was. It gives you a different perspective on men, believe me. Thank God there are still men about like Arthur who are decent and honest . . . with heaps of integrity.'

'I see that you're not eating much, Miss Chadwick,' Mrs Hawkins observed. 'Don't you like my fish pie?'

'Oh, your fish pie is exceptional, Mrs Hawkins, and entirely suitable for a Friday,' Dorinda replied sincerely. 'And I really do believe that Arthur is fortunate indeed to be lodging at the home of such an able cook. But as for myself, I really don't eat a lot.'

Mrs Hawkins turned to Arthur and looked at him questioningly. 'And yet she looks as if a good feed would do her good, Arthur, wouldn't you agree? Why, if she turned sideways I'm sure we would have to mark her absent.' She smiled to show that she meant no offence.

Arthur smiled politely back and swallowed what remained in his mouth before he opened it to speak. 'Dorinda is worried about getting stout, Mrs Hawkins.'

'Stout? Upon my soul, she's got a long way to go before ever she gets stout.' She turned to Dorinda. 'If I were you, Miss Chadwick, I wouldn't worry myself at your age about getting stout. I am stout, but I'm content to be stout, but then I'm considerably older than you. Stoutness is more inclined to come with age.'

'But my mother's very stout,' Dorinda said, feeling the need once more to justify her stance. 'Stouter than you are, Mrs Hawkins, and I witness every day the difficulty she has in moving between the chairs in our parlour, how it pains her to have to flop into a chair, then how her stays dig into her when she has to stand up again. It all looks decidedly uncomfortable, you know, and stoutness makes a woman very clumsy. I remember my father being poorly in bed once and my poor stout mother turned round in their bedroom and upset his medicine bottles. I had to go to the apothecary to fetch some more. So I am determined to avoid such a condition myself. To my mind, stoutness is the grimmest of all women's curses. I'd rather be dead than stout any day of the week.'

'But my dear Miss Chadwick, I can't see the sense in that,' Mrs Hawkins declared, determined to defend stoutness. 'I mean to say, there would be no point in being thin if you were dead.'

'Come to think of it, Mrs Hawkins,' Dorinda replied, 'what would be the point of being alive if you weren't thin? That's the way I view it.'

'Well, I am perfectly content to be alive and I am not thin . . . as I have already pointed out,' she added, as though it were not apparent.

'I am content too, to take up a smaller amount of space. So, as you have noticed, Mrs Hawkins, I don't eat a vast amount, in order to accomplish it.'

'Perhaps when you are married and have children you will not feel so strongly about it,' suggested Mrs Hawkins tentatively, feeling peeved at being rebuked by this pretty but vain and much younger woman, and unable to let it go.

'Oh, but I don't intend to have children, Mrs Hawkins. Too many women become stout when they have had children and I know I should, because it runs in my family . . . on my mother's side at any rate. I'm afraid it would have to be a condition of my marriage that I should not have children.'

'Then you would miss out on so much that life has to offer, Miss Chadwick.'

'Please call me Dorinda . . .'

'And besides, I don't see how you can prevent children when you are married.'

'Presumably by not doing the very thing that causes them.'

Mrs Hawkins emitted a gasp of horror. 'But my dear, the whole point of marriage is for the procreation of children, as ordained by God Himself, and clearly stated in the marriage ceremony.'

'Yes, and I know from hearsay what goes on in the marriage bed, Mrs Hawkins. Nor does it sound exceptionally ladylike in any case. I imagine it is something that I could easily dispense with.'

'But maybe your husband, whoever he turns out to be . . .' Mrs Hawkins glanced at Arthur '. . . might have more to say about that.'

There followed a prolonged silence when each avoided the other's eyes and concentrated on the food on their plates.

'And all this in the name of staying thin,' Mrs Hawkins said at length, breaking the uncomfortable silence, but feeling obliged to pursue the issue for Arthur's benefit for fear he was loath to. 'I can honestly say that it was only after my first baby was born that I could understand the joys of mother-hood, the joys that the good Lord sends in the form of children. After that, stoutness never crossed my mind. Stout-ness became irrelevant, Miss Chadwick.'

'Do please call me Dorinda.'

'Besides, I don't believe that having children makes a woman stout, you know. I know many women who have had several children, and yet they are as slender now as the day they were wedded in holy matrimony. I believe other factors come into play.'

'As far as I can make out, most women over the age of thirty weigh more than nine stone, yet so few ever admit to being more than eight. Anyway, I'm interested to hear your views, Mrs Hawkins.'

'Diet, of course . . . And activity. You say the women on your mother's side are stout?'

'Yes. Very.'

'But what about your father's side? Do the women on his side of the family run to stoutness?'

Dorinda shook her head. 'No, they don't, as a matter of fact. They are generally small and dainty.'

'Then I suggest you will also remain small and dainty. I think if you were going to be stout, there would be signs of it already. But I see none. You are small-boned, with not an ounce of excess fat upon your person. I truly believe you will retain your slenderness even if you have a dozen children.'

'Do you really think so, Mrs Hawkins?'

'I most certainly do . . . Dorinda.'

'All the same, I can think of nothing more horrid. Can you, Arthur? I mean just imagine having to wipe their smelly little bottoms and such, then having to contend with their vomit all over you when they've been fed.' Dorinda's lovely face exhibited a look of distaste.

'Well, I certainly hold with wives having children, Miss Chadwick,' Mrs Hawkins attested. 'It finds them something to do between Sunday's sermons and Saturday evening's liver and onions.'

'And I must say,' Arthur interposed diplomatically, 'Mrs Hawkins attends to her liver and onions with the same zeal that she harkens to the Sunday sermons. I just wish that I liked liver and onions . . .'

★ ★ ★

Saturday 29ᵗʰ May 1858

Dear Lucy,

It was a lovely surprise to get a letter from you after so long and I thank you very much for it. Thank you for letting me know the excellent news that your sister Jane and brother-in-law Moses now have a little daughter. I have no doubt that they are thrilled, so please pass on my very best regards.

As for Dorinda, yes, we are courting and have been for some months. She is very pretty and quite clever for a girl. At least she keeps me on my toes. Her family seem to have taken to me as well. It's a bit early to say whether we shall ever get married but I like her enough although I haven't asked her to marry me yet. She has mentioned it in passing a time or two, though. Dorinda came to tea yesterday and we discussed having children. She says if we ever get married, she is not of a mind to have any and I can see her point of view. So, it is likely that we shan't. My landlady Mrs Hawkins says that it is a childish attitude for a young woman to take and maybe she is right. What would I know? I am but a man.

How is your love life, Lucy? Do you still see that chap you took up with after I left for Bristol? If so, no doubt you are already thinking about getting married.

You ask about my health. Well, I have never felt better than I do down here. I seldom get the toothache nowadays, nor catch so many chills, but I do get a bit of indigestion lately and constipation. Mrs Hawkins has plenty of remedies for such ailments though and dispenses them liberally. She really looks after me.

Thank you for being so kind as to visit my mother. I imagine she would be delighted if you ask if she wants any errands running. I know my sister-in-law Magnolia helps her out while Albert my nephew is doing his schooling, but

*she has her own home to look after, them not having a maid.
As for her pork pies, it sounds to me as though she won't
have had time to make any, fetching and carrying for the old
man.*

*As for coming home, it would be good to see your mother
and father again, and Jane and Moses and the baby, but I
can't see my way clear to doing it. My work keeps me very
busy and I don't think it would be fair to ask for the time
off. As you can very likely tell, I am very settled here in
Bristol, although I do miss some of my old friends, and I
confess it would be lovely to see you again, Lucy. I still have
dreams about you (but don't tell Dorinda) and I can picture
those beautiful blue eyes of yours quite clearly still. Whoever
this chap is who is courting you, I think he is very lucky.*

*Well, I must close now, as I have to go out to see Dorinda
and her family. This afternoon I went ferreting with her
brother Cyril but we didn't catch anything – again. Tonight
I am eating at their house, then Dorinda and me might go
for a walk after if the weather stays fair.*

Look after yourself.
Your friend,
Arthur Goodrich.

★ ★ ★

The weeks passed by with no significant events occurring.
Lucy did not respond to Arthur's letter, but Arthur received a
weekly bulletin on the decline of his father. It was on Saturday
21st August 1858 that an important letter from Talbot was
awaiting him when he returned to Mrs Hawkins's house after
work that morning.

Dear Arthur,
*It is with great sadness and a heavy heart that I write this
letter to let you know that our dear father passed away at
five to ten this morning, Friday 20th. There has been no time*

as yet to make funeral arrangements, but as soon as I know when it is to be I shall write and let you know.

We are all distraught, but Mother is bearing it well and I trust she will continue to do so. Her grief, I am sure, would be lessened if you could see your way clear to returning home, if only for a short while, to bring her some consolation.

Yours very truly,
Talbot.

★　★　★

18

Monday 23rd August was a holiday. Lucy awoke to a morning that was fine, sunny and warm, with inoffensive white clouds skipping across the sky like lambs across a meadow of cornflowers. The day promised so much. At half past nine, Jane and Moses called for her with Emily, and they made their way to Brettell Lane station. Lucy relieved her sister of the baby while they waited for their train and Jane, in turn, took the picnic basket from Moses. While they talked desultorily the southbound platform was filling up, cheerful with excitement and the ringing of laughter.

'What time did Dickie reckon the train would get here?' Moses enquired as he repositioned his crutch under his arm.

'It was due to leave Wolverhampton at quarter past nine.'

Moses eyed the station clock. 'Then it should've been here by now. The clock says quarter to ten, look.'

'Have a bit o' patience,' Jane muttered. 'If there's a lot o' folk to get on at every station it's bound to be delayed. Anyroad, what's the rush?' She turned to Lucy who was adjusting the shawl around the baby attentively. 'Is Dickie gunna be working today, our Luce?'

'He said not. He said he'd got the day off. But he did say he'd travel here in the guards' van with his mate, then with us in one of the carriages.'

The occasion was a special excursion to Worcester, organised specifically for the Black Country's Sunday School children and their teachers. Fares were offered at special cheap rates – only a shilling for a return ticket from Brettell Lane – and such bargains created a wave of interest all along the line. Thus, tickets were sold to anybody and everybody, whether they were attached to a Sunday school or not. After all, it was commercially expedient so to do, and any number of carriages could be attached to the train to fulfil the demand.

It was almost ten o'clock when the locomotive came huffing and hissing round the bend, hauling the longest train any of them had ever seen. It was considerably longer than the platform. Lucy looked for sight of Dickie, and wondered how he would get to them from the guards' van which was further up the line and actually out of sight. So she lingered, and Jane and Moses lingered with her.

Then she saw Dickie strolling casually towards her beyond the station platform, waving, his usual matey grin adorning his handsome face. Her heart quickened and she smiled with relief at his arrival.

'Which carriage should we get in?' she asked when he'd given her a peck on the lips.

'Suit yourselves.' He gave Moses a chummy pat on the back in greeting. 'See if there's one with nobody in yet. Not that there's much chance of it, and there'll be even less chance of keeping it to ourselves the more passengers we pick up.'

With a clear conscience, they settled themselves in a second-class compartment. All class restrictions had been lifted in view of the across-the-board fares.

'What held the train up?' Moses asked Dickie when they were seated.

'We had to put on eight more carriages and another engine at Dudley. That makes thirty-two carriages so far and two engines . . . Oh, and then a coupling broke. We had to stop and change it.'

'D'you keep spare couplings in the guards' van then?'

'Chains and shackles. The shackles are them thick chains

243

what attach to the staples at the centre between the buffers,' Dickie explained. 'There's a smaller chain either side as well, so it's secure enough.'

Moses nodded his understanding.

'Should be a good day out, this, with all these folk going,' Dickie said, rubbing his hands together in anticipation. 'I'm looking forward to a tankard or two in Worcester, and a stroll along the river. Maybe we can hire a rowing boat. How's the bab, Jane?'

'A golden child. Look at her. Comfortable as an old shoe, she is.'

All eyes were on the baby as Lucy rocked her gently. 'I daresay she'll be waking up soon,' she remarked, looking at her sister for confirmation. 'What time was she awake this morning, our Jane?'

'Just as it was getting light,' Moses answered for her, ever the attentive father. 'She's been asleep about an hour now.'

The train slowly pulled out of the station. First stop was Stourbridge. There they picked up many more day trippers, and five further coaches were attached. Next stop was Hagley. Almost as soon as they left Hagley station they all felt a harsh bump, making Jane and Moses lurch forward. The train stopped and they looked at each other with trepidation. Dickie opened the door of the carriage and jumped down to the side of the track to investigate.

'Another coupling come adrift,' he explained dismissively when he returned a minute or two later. He smiled as if to reassure them. 'Only a side chain. Nothing to worry about. It's fixed now.'

'Is that 'cause there's too many coaches being pulled?' Moses asked.

'No, I don't reckon so. Just one of them things. It can happen from time to time.'

They travelled on to Kidderminster without any further

hitches, passing fields gold with ripening wheat and barley, and meadows cropped short by cows and sheep. By this time they were sharing the compartment with other passengers, and some lively banter broke out, which had them all entertained for the rest of the journey. With no further delays they arrived at Shrub Hill Station in Worcester, at half past twelve. Nearly two thousand people, adults and children, alighting from forty-five carriages, funnelled through the station's exit into the city's welcoming sunshine.

First thing Dickie wanted to do was find a tavern, claiming he was parched. Moses had no objection and, not knowing the city or its inns, happened upon one called the King Charles situated in the Cornmarket. Jane and Lucy decided to remain outside and enjoy the sunshine with little Emily. Presently, Dickie delivered them a tumbler of beer each, then went back inside, to Lucy's discontent. They stayed for an hour replenishing their tankards and tumblers a couple of times, before deciding to make their way to the river. There, in a field which abutted the water's edge and overlooked by the cathedral, they sat and ate their picnic, and Jane discreetly fed Emily hers.

'I'd like to have a look around the cathedral,' Lucy suggested.

'What for?' Dickie scoffed. 'You going all religious?'

'Me? No, I just think it would be nice. You have to admit it's a beautiful building. I wonder how long it took them to build it.'

'What does it matter?'

'I'd like to go in, that's all.' She was disappointed with his abrasive attitude, probably caused by the drink. 'I've never been inside a cathedral. I want to see if it's any different to the Methodist chapel in Brierley Hill.'

They all laughed at the absurd comparison.

'Oh, I know it's bigger,' she said defensively. 'If you won't come with me Dickie I'll go with our Jane . . .' She looked at her sister pleadingly. 'Come with me, Jane. I'd rather go in with somebody else, in case the vicar's there and asks me what I'm doing.'

Dickie looked at Moses. 'Shall we let 'em go, mate? Me and thee could find another alehouse and have a few more, or we could see if we can hire a rowing boat for an hour.'

'You won't get me in a rowing boat,' Moses jibed. 'How do you think I'm gunna get in a rowing boat? The bloody thing'll be bobbing all over the place and tip me up. I'll end up in the river.'

'No, I'll get help to hand you in.'

'All right. But only if I can row.' Moses wore a look that told of his joy at the prospect of a challenge.

'Can you row?'

'Better than you, any day of the week.'

'Then that's settled.' Dickie turned to Lucy and Jane. 'We'll see you in about an hour by the door of the cathedral.'

Jane and Lucy thus made their way to the cathedral. A small group of children in rags and tatters were begging in a tranquil area called College Green and Lucy handed them each a penny.

'Poor souls,' she commented, 'with no soles in their boots and no backside in the lads' trousers. I wonder what the vicar thinks of them?'

'Shoos 'em off, if he's anything like most vicars I've ever happened across. Anyway, our Luce, I don't think they have vicars in cathedrals. They have bishops instead.'

'Vicars, bishops, what's the difference? Anyway, I just wanted to go inside the cathedral and sit quiet for a minute or two to think. I thought it'd be a good place.'

'You turning to religion, am yer?'

'Lord, you sound just like *him*. No, I just want to be quiet so as I can think.'

'Think about what?'

'Oh, just things,' she answered wistfully.

Inside it was cool and Lucy was aware of the ancient, musty smell of the nave. Plenty of other people were in there too, the Sunday school children from the same excursion among them. Their in-bred reverence meant it was exceptionally quiet save for the occasional whisper, or scuff of a heel, which echoed off the tiled floor and into the high vaulted roof. It was evident that some serious restoration work was in progress if the wooden scaffolding was anything to go by. Lucy marvelled at the stonework, the stone pillars deeply fluted with Purbeck marble, and the sweeping arches that held the roof up miraculously.

'Arthur Goodrich would be in his element,' she whispered with a smile as she remembered him. 'Good old Arthur . . .'

Jane was cooing softly to the baby lest she cry and draw attention to them. 'What made you think of Arthur?'

'All the work they're doing here. All the work that's ever gone into it over the years. I suppose, when you think about it, the work Arthur does will last for donkeys' years, like this cathedral. I mean, stonemasons must have worked on it, and look how long it's lasted . . . Centuries . . .'

They ascended a short flight of steps into that part of the cathedral called the Quire, and happened upon the tomb of King John. Lucy gazed at the carving of the ancient warrior in his centuries-long slumber and thought again about Arthur Goodrich, wondering if he was happy, whether he was surer of Dorinda than he had been of herself. She looked up at the high, vaulted ceiling and gasped with admiration at the intricate patterns painted on it. Then she turned away, leaving Jane to wander around slowly with just Emily for company.

Lucy descended some stone steps and found herself in the crypt and all alone. It was so cool in there, with light pouring in from side windows. It had an air of ancient mystery and devotion, and she could imagine monks in olden times chanting psalms that echoed all around the forest of pillars. She spotted a bench. When she reached it she sat down and shut her eyes, so as to exclude everybody from her thoughts right then.

She needed to ponder her love for Dickie Dempster, and his love for her. She adored him with all her heart and soul, but she could not help wondering lately if his love matched hers in intensity and commitment. Oh, he loved her in his own rough and ready way; he made love to her good and hard, with an ardour that made her toes curl from the pleasure of it. He was tender and affectionate afterwards, not like some of the men she'd heard about from her friends at work. Lately, though, he had not been so attentive when they were in company and she wondered whether he was tiring of her.

Her faith in his love for her was under pressure. Was he the marrying kind after all? She had given him complete access to her body, willingly, and was amply rewarded with breath-taking pleasure in return. She considered what might have happened if she had withheld her favours, whether it would have spiced up his interest if she'd kept him dangling on the promise of what might be. But she could not have withheld herself, for she wanted him as much as he wanted her, and what was the sense in denying yourself that which you wanted and needed more than anything else in the world?

It irked her that she knew plenty about his brothers and sisters, his mother and his father, but she'd met none of them yet. From what he'd told her she didn't really know what to make of the situation; whether he was too ashamed of them to allow her to meet them and be put off; whether they were too rough even for her, whose father was but an ironworker? On the other hand, she did not know either whether he was ashamed of her, whether she was too lowly, the same mere ironworker's daughter, to grace the home of his family, if only for a fleeting visit. He'd never given her any such inkling on either count and she was confused. On the face of it, he and she seemed to be of equal standing when it came to class, an ideal match as far as that was concerned. Perhaps it was because he knew that if he took her all the way to Wednesfield Heath where he lived near Wolverhampton, he'd only have to accompany her all the way back to the station. It was unsettling, this being kept apart from his family, and it was gnawing at her. It had been worrying her all the more these last few weeks; she had become mightily sensitive about it, although she had mentioned not a word to him, or to anybody else for that matter. But the time would come when she must, for her own peace of mind. Soon she would have to talk to him very seriously.

Irreligious as she was, she offered a little prayer to her Maker, fervently seeking His help in securing this man Dickie Dempster, the love of her life. And so earnest, so poignant was her prayer, that she felt tears prickle her eyes, then trickle down her cheeks.

'What are you crying for, our Lucy?' Jane whispered.

At once Lucy opened her eyes. 'Oh, I didn't hear you, our Jane. How long have you been sitting beside me?'

'Only just. I wondered where you'd got to. I've been looking everywhere for you. You'm weeping, our Luce. What's up?'

She sighed, a deep shuddering sigh. 'I was just thinking, praying that Dickie loves me as much as I love him, if you want to know the truth.'

'Have you got any doubts? You must have doubts if you've asked yourself the question.'

'Yes, I've got doubts . . .' She wept silently out of respect for the quiet ambience of the crypt. Her face was an icon of anxiety, and she withdrew a rag from the pocket of her skirt to wipe her eyes.

'I reckon you'm just being a bit over-sensitive, our Luce,' Jane whispered. 'I reckon it's that time o' the month, eh?'

'Oh . . . maybe . . .' A fresh flood of tears streamed over the soft curves of her cheeks. 'I need to know whether he loves me enough to want to marry me.'

'So soon?'

Lucy nodded. 'I'm pregnant, our Jane.' Tears welled in her eyes again and she tried to stem them by wiping them on her sleeve. 'That's why I need to know if he'll marry me.'

'Oh, Lord . . . Have you told him yet?'

'No.'

'Don't you think you should? And soon?'

'Yes . . . I'll have to tell him soon.' She sniffed and wiped her eyes again.

'Tell him tonight.'

Lucy shook her head resolutely. 'No, I don't think so, Jane . . . Not tonight. I don't want to spoil his day out to Worcester. I'll talk to him Wednesday night. We'll be on our own. I'd rather be on our own when I talk to him.'

Jane nodded her understanding. 'Dry your tears, eh? Don't let him see as you've been a-crying, else he'll wonder what's up.'

Lucy forced a smile. 'I know . . . But we've got another half hour yet before we'm due to meet them. I'll be all right by then . . . I feel better already for having talked to you, our Jane.' She rose from the pew and put her rag back in her pocket. 'Come on, let's see what else there is to see. Shall I hold Emily for you? Give your arms a rest?' She held her hands outstretched to receive the child and forced a smile. 'I've got to get used to holding a baby.'

★ ★ ★

The train home was due to leave Worcester at quarter past six that evening and they arrived at Shrub Hill station just before six, in plenty of time to make sure they could get a seat in a decent carriage. With the hundreds of people milling about, all with the same intention, it was pandemonium.

Dickie scanned over the heads of the throng to look at the train, and turned to the other three. 'I'll try and find out what's going on.' He left them and made his way towards the guards' van, where he saw his workmate Fred Cooke.

There were two guards' vans and Fred was in the end one, accompanied by others who seemed in a festive mood, joking among themselves and laughing. Dickie approached them.

'What's going on, Fred?'

'The powers that be have decided to split the train into two,' Fred told him, and drew on his pipe. 'This is the first part and it's due to leave here at quarter past six. The second will leave about ten minutes after.'

Dickie glanced round at the other men, strangers, who were evidently set to ride in the van with the guard. One of them came out of the gloom of the interior and spoke to Fred.

'I ain't going back with you, mate.'

'Why not?' Fred asked.

'I stood up all the way over here and I ain't standing up all the way back. I'll get a seat on the next train.'

'You'll have to give me a guinea.'

The stranger did not know whether Fred Cooke was joking or not. 'A guinea?' he queried. 'You'll be lucky. On the other hand it might be worth it get a seat.' He wandered off and was lost among the folk milling about on the platform.

'So how many carriages are there to this train?' Dickie asked, resuming his conversation.

'Twenty-eight, with the guards' vans. I imagine we'll have to stick on another engine at Stourbridge for the climb up to Round Oak and Dudley.'

'So what engine are you starting with?'

'A mighty one to pull twenty-eight coaches, mate,' Fred replied with a grin, and looked at the assembly around him seeking approval of his astonishing wit. One or two duly laughed, and it was obvious they had been drinking.

'What about the second train?'

'It'll have fewer coaches, so it'll use the smaller engine.'

'You having a party in there or summat?' Dickie at once displayed some interest. He could see a row of stone jars lining the floor.

'They've got some jars of beer.' He nodded towards the men. 'If you want to join the party you can put in a shilling and drink till it all runs dry. When we get t'Ampton we intend to call in a tavern for a few more. Then I'll be able to have a drink.'

'But I'm in company,' Dickie said regretfully.

'Bring 'em along. The more the merrier. Any women among 'em?'

Dickie guffawed with bravado. 'Yes, two. And one's mine. The other's got a babby in her arms, and an 'usband with only one leg. He ain't gunna be able to stand up all the way in a guards' van, specially if he's sunk a few.'

'So he's already legless,' Fred quipped and guffawed at his own joke. 'Listen, tell 'em you'll meet 'em at the station at the other end and come on your own.'

The thought of all that beer was very alluring. 'I might just do that, Fred. Give me a couple of minutes and I'll be back.' He pointed his forefinger at Fred. 'Don't leave without me.'

Dickie made his way back to Lucy and the others, shoving his way through the crowds who were jostling each other in turn as they tried to board the train.

'It's a damned pity that I went to check what's going on,' he said, his face a portrait of disappointment and regret. 'They've split the train into two. The first one . . .' He wagged his thumb over his shoulder in its direction. '. . . is long – twenty-eight carriages – and they've had to put on an extra van. They want me to work on it. That means I'll have to see it right through to Wolverhampton. I'm ever so sorry, my flower, but they'm short o' men.'

252

'Oh, Dickie,' Lucy sighed with frustration.

He shrugged as if he had no choice in the matter. 'Can't be helped, Luce . . . Now I reckon this train is gunna get very crowded with everybody anxious to get home, so if I was you, specially with the bab, I'd get on the second 'un. It leaves ten minutes after this.'

'But it means I shan't see you again tonight . . .'

'I'll see you Wednesday as usual, eh, Lucy?' He smiled brightly to ease her disappointment. 'Meet me off the train Wednesday, as usual.'

With reluctance she nodded but rolled her eyes, peeved that he should have to work when she needed the reassurance of his arm around her, his kisses to allay her doubts, before he went home.

'I'd better go then, afore they bugger off without me. See you Wednesday.' He gave her a kiss on the cheek.

Resignedly Lucy watched him go, and waved her fingers as he turned to leave her.

★   ★   ★

By the time the second train arrived at Brettell Lane it was almost dark. Lucy, carrying the baby again, left the station unhurriedly with Jane and Moses. They stopped to talk at the junction with the Delph before Lucy crossed the road to go home.

'Well, it's been a grand day and no two ways,' Moses declared, entirely satisfied with his outing, 'but I confess I'm buggered now, with all that walking and larking about on the river.'

'You shouldn't have been larking about on the river, you daft bugger,' Jane admonished. 'I'm surprised as you was potty enough to even get in a boat. What if you'd have fell in the water?'

Moses grinned. 'I'd have got wet.'

'And you'd have got no sympathy from me.'

253

The engine that had hauled them from Worcester wheezed and hacked bronchially in the cutting below as it took on the challenge of the incline to Round Oak.

'But you'd been drinking as well. That made it all the more dangerous. Why are men so stupid, Luce?'

Lucy shrugged disconsolately.

Moses said, 'I can handle me beer, wench . . . Now I'm clammed to death, so let's get home so's I can get a bit of fittle inside me.'

'Oh, and just what d'you fancy?' Jane asked.

'A bit o' cheese and some onion will do me.'

'I hope we've got some onion, that's all I can say.' Jane rolled her eyes in mock irritation and Lucy smiled at their affable banter. To enjoy such an easy relationship with the man you loved, and be able to sleep with him all night long without having to get up to go home . . . Oh, she longed to be in the same situation with Dickie.

'Mother will have an onion, I'm certain,' Lucy said. 'Come and take one of ours.'

'No, I've got some onions, our Lucy.' Jane smiled brightly. 'I was just plaguing him.'

Suddenly, the peace was shattered by an almighty crash that made the ground beneath their feet shudder. Never had they heard such a horrendous assortment of sounds orchestrated into one simultaneous eruption. It was like several tons of iron bars being dropped into a monstrous iron bucket from an appreciable height, combined with the splitting of a thousand oaks and the sibilant smashing of a thousand window panes. The terrifying noise resounded ominously through the still evening air of Silver End, and sent shudders up Lucy's spine.

'What the devil was that?' she shrieked with apprehension.

'Sounds like the furnace at the glassworks exploding,' Moses suggested. 'It came from that direction.'

'I'm off to find out what it was.' She handed the baby back

254

to Jane. 'Are you coming, Moses? It might even have been the train.'

'Yes, I'll come.' He turned to his wife. 'Go and stop with your mother a bit and I'll come back for you later.' Jane said she would and they crossed Brettell Lane together. 'I never heard a bang like that before in all me life. All the guns in the Crimea never sounded like that. I hope to God nobody's hurt.'

At the bridge over the railway Lucy ran down the side of the cutting and waited while Moses slid down on his backside. There was a bend in the track and they couldn't have seen around it even if it had been still light. Then as they started to make their way round it, Lucy could see the guards' van of the second train.

It was stationary.

Further on she saw a lamp being swung as somebody, probably the guard, made his way to the front of the train.

'Hurry up, Moses,' Lucy called apprehensively. 'Something's happened to the train.'

'You go on,' he called back. 'I can't go any faster. I need a steam driven crutch to get me along quicker than this. I'll see if I can invent one.'

Lucy ran as fast as she could. Frightened passengers were leaning out of the windows trying to glean what had happened. Some even asked *her* what was wrong. She could see steam rising from the engine ahead of her and hear the incessant hiss of its boiler, growing louder the closer she got. But, in front of the engine, there were many more coaches where there should have been none at all . . . and those that were closest to the engine were like matchwood – smashed to smithereens . . .

Her heart was in her mouth. She ran on in a blind panic as fast as she could, impeded by the track bed's gravel that crunched as it yielded beneath her boots, slowing her down. She was unaware even that she was crying out, only conscious that it might be the earlier train from Worcester they had run into. Pray God it was not so . . .

Mayhem had broken out. Lucy let out a cry of disbelief when she saw the mangled mass of twisted metal and wood that was once a guards' van and a passenger coach. If these were the rear coaches of the first excursion train . . . She could hear clamours for help and groaning from within the mess, voices tortured with pain and fear.

Dickie . . .

It was a Sunday School outing . . .

All those children . . .

The engine driver of the second train was one of the men standing and watching, evidently transfixed and perplexed, seemingly oblivious and too stupefied to understand fully what was going on.

'What happened?' Lucy enquired.

'Get back in the train, miss,' he replied mechanically. 'Everything's under control.'

'Under control?' she shrieked. 'There are folk hurt, look . . . Listen, you can hear them . . . There might be little children there, dying. Why aren't you helping to pull them out?'

The man with the lamp was peering about in a panic, using its meagre illumination, looking here and there for injured people, apparently counting them. Others joined, some from the forward train, some from the neighbourhood perhaps, who had heard the crash and rushed to the scene. She noticed another man in guard's uniform, hobbling about as if hurt. She ran to him.

'What happened?'

'I ain't sure,' he answered, dazed.

'Have you seen Mr Dempster?'

'He was in the guards' van with me, but I jumped out before the up-coming train hit us. I don't know if he did.'

As she wandered about, feeling utterly helpless, Lucy found

herself standing in the darkness alongside another man who was bending over something or somebody. Her heart was thumping fast, her head seemed to be spinning with fear and apprehension as the realisation of what this all meant came to roost. Dickie must be here somewhere. He just had to be. Where was he? She prayed swiftly and silently that he was not hurt. She prayed he had jumped out also.

'Is there somebody under all that wood and glass?' she asked the man who was leaning over, earnestly attending to something.

'Yes,' he replied, and his voice was agonisingly familiar. 'When the guard shone the lamp on him I recognised him straight off.'

She looked in disbelief at the man who had spoken. So far, he had not looked up, but she did not need to; she knew at once who he was. Then, as if he recognised her voice too, he turned to face her with equal astonishment.

'Lucy!'

'Arthur!'

'Lucy, thank God you've come to help. I know this poor chap.' He spoke quietly, his voice full of sadness. 'I've got to help him. Do you remember when I fell asleep on the train from Kidderminster and ended up in a siding at Wolverhampton?'

Lucy felt her legs go weak, knowing very well what was coming next, as if she had been through all this before in a dream.

'This is the chap who looked after me, Lucy. I told you about him, remember? Dempster, his name was. Dickie Dempster. He seemed a decent sort . . . The least I can do now is to help him . . . Lucy . . .'

Arthur's words . . . She'd heard him utter them before. Was she reliving something that had already happened, or had she dreamed all this? She fainted and lay in a heap on the gravel.

'Lucy, are you all right? . . . Lucy?'

More and more people were milling around, some in a daze of bewilderment, some desperate to help, a confused mix of passengers and onlookers. Then Arthur saw a man rushing towards him on a crutch.

'Moses!' he yelled over the raucous hiss of the engine.

Moses was peering around with anxious curiosity.

'Moses . . . Lucy has just fainted. See if you can bring her round while I tend to this chap here.' Another man was meandering about aimlessly. 'You, sir . . . Can you and a couple of others go to the inns on Brettell Lane and Church Street and get help as quick as you can. And see if you can get some boards or something to carry the poor injured and dying back to comfort and safety.'

The man seemed to come to his senses and acknowledged what was wanted of him. He set off at a run.

'What happened?' Moses asked as he tried to bring Lucy round.

'Some coaches came adrift from the train that went up the line first, then rolled back down again . . .'

Arthur turned his attention back to the man lying badly injured, whom he knew as Dickie Dempster, and began clearing the mass of debris that held him trapped. He discerned that he was still breathing and began working even faster. Dempster's face was lacerated but still easily recognisable; his clothes were torn and even shredded in places. Then, as he cleared away more broken and splintered wood he saw thick blood oozing darkly into the fabric of the poor man's trousers. He began to roll up a trouser leg to try to estimate the extent of his injuries. The material was warm and wet, tacky with fresh blood. But in the semi-darkness, all Arthur could discern was a morass of torn flesh and fractured bone poking through it in shards. He felt the urge to vomit.

He turned away to rid himself of the awful sight and remembered Lucy. She was coming round, sitting up on the gravel, but still evidently in a daze. She in turn saw Arthur and lurched anxiously towards him, as the significance of his presence revisited her.

'How d'you feel now, Lucy?'

'Oh, Arthur . . . How is he? Is he still alive? Please tell me he's still alive.' There was panic in her voice.

'He's still alive, but he's unconscious . . . which is just as well. His one leg's smashed to a thousand pieces, though. Like pulp. I can't see as how they'll be able to mend it. We need to get him to a surgeon, and quick.'

'Is he going to be all right, d'you think?'

He looked at her with apprehension, surprised how avid her interest was in this man, yet unable to assimilate why. 'I couldn't say, Lucy. I ain't a doctor. But I hope to God that he is. He was good to me when I was in a spot. This is my chance to repay him.' He could see tears of fear, hysteria and anguish in Lucy's eyes. It began to dawn on him that maybe she knew this poor injured man also, so he asked her the question.

'Yes, I know him, Arthur.' She gave a great sobbing sigh. 'This is the man I fell in love with . . . This is the man who's been courting me . . .'

'Dempster?' he queried with amazement. 'Then let's get him out quick if we're going save him. He needs medical attention.'

'It's Dickie?' Moses queried with consternation. 'Jesus Christ! D'you reckon he's still alive?'

'Yes, but for how long . . .'

Moses knuckled down to helping as best he could, struggling to shift the splintered planks and the thousand shards of broken glass with the rest of them. Although Lucy was devastated by the fact that Dickie was seriously injured, she realised she must do something to help if they were to save him. Arthur, too, was all at once acutely conscious of her

259

emotional suffering because of it, and wished to divert her mind. For once, he had no difficulty in leading a conversation with her that he hoped might succeed in distracting her from the horror, if only for a minute.

'What brings him in the guards' van, Lucy, when that don't look like a uniform he's wearing?' He struggled with a splintered plank of wood, freed it and cast it to the side of the cutting.

'We'd been on an excursion to Worcester,' she answered evenly, stooping to clear more. 'He had to do the return journey in the guards' van, 'cause they wanted him to work. I was in the second train and got off at Brettell Lane.'

'Count your blessings that you didn't travel with him. Others did, by the looks of this . . .' He could smell beer, but did not remark on it. 'There's other poor souls trapped under the rubble, look . . . Anyway, we've gotta pull him out quick. D'you want to give me a hand?'

'Course.'

More lamps had arrived so that it was becoming easier to see the extent of the wreckage and the people trapped, some of whom were still conscious and groaning with agony beneath it.

'What d'you think happened, Arthur?'

'I saw exactly what happened. Me and Dorinda was walking over Moor Lane Bridge and we saw about fifteen coaches hurtling back down the track – part of the same train as we'd seen go up on the same line just a minute earlier. They must've broke away as they pulled into Round Oak, and just rolled back down the incline. It's a one in seventy-five incline, this, you know Lucy.'

'What's that mean?'

'That it's steep for a railway track. They ran into the engine coming the other way with a tidy force.'

'Did you say you were with Dorinda?'

'Yes.' He was pleased his side-tracking was working.

260

'So where is she?'

'I sent her back to mother's.'

'I 'spect she's here to help with your father's funeral,' Lucy suggested.

'She would insist on coming with me.'

'I was sorry to hear about your father . . .'

Lucy stepped back and saw for the first time the mass of dark blood seeping up into Dickie's trousers, glistening ominously by the light of the oil lamps. She shuddered. Tears stung in her eyes again, and she choked on a great sob of grief that was tearing its way out of her chest. She stooped down, the better to see her love, and was appalled when she saw his face cut and bruised, lumps of flesh gouged away horrifically from his neck, an ear torn. Terror struck her. Her beautiful Dickie with the confident, cheerful, laughing face was viciously mutilated and maimed. It was a sin. It was a dark and dreadful sin. She threw herself upon him and wailed piteously, and would not leave him until Arthur, watching silently and patiently and with an infinite fund of sympathy, tapped her on the shoulder to tell her softly that they had a trestle at last, on which they could convey him to the Whimsey.

'He'll be comfortable there,' he said kindly. 'And they've sent word to all the doctors in the area, so somebody will tend to him soon.'

'Can I go with him, d'you think, Arthur?'

'I would . . . if I were you.'

★   ★   ★

19

Haden Piddock was already drinking at the Whimsey when the crash happened. As soon as word reached the inn, he and others rushed to the scene to offer what help they could. On the way, he saw his daughter walking towards him alongside two other men bearing a trestle, on which lay an injured victim. Haden's heart rejoiced that Lucy was not a victim, aware that she had been on the same excursion train.

'It's Dickie,' Lucy informed him tearfully. 'He's hurt bad. They're taking him to the Whimsey. I shall stay with him, so tell Mother not to expect me back.'

'How's our Jane and the bab?' he asked anxiously.

'We all got off the train before the crash, Father. Except poor Dickie.'

'Thank God.' Haden inspected the injured man cursorily. He had no special regard for Dickie Dempster, actually resented the fact that he'd beguiled his precious daughter. 'Thank the Lord you ain't one o' them hurt, bab.' He hugged Lucy tightly, half in thankfulness, half in consolation, for he was well aware how distraught she was. 'Is there anybody else there helping?'

'Quite a few. There's Moses . . . oh, and Arthur Goodrich. Arthur's been as good as gold. It was him who found Dickie and got him out of the rubble. He's back here for his father's funeral, you know.'

Haden acknowledged the fact with a sympathetic nod. 'Get on then, my angel, and look after Dickie Dempster.'

She smiled tearfully and turned to catch up with the trestle-bearers and her injured sweetheart, calling over her shoulder, 'I'll see you when I see you, Father.'

At the Whimsey, they took Dickie to a bedroom reserved for travellers and gently lifted him from the trestle to install him in the bed. He was as pale as death and still unconscious.

'There'll be a doctor along to see him soon, my flower,' one of the trestle-bearers kindly consoled. 'Keep him comfortable till he comes, eh?'

Lucy nodded and thanked the men for their help, then they left with the trestle to find and convey another victim to the safety and comfort of one of the local inns. When they had gone, she loosened Dickie's collar, carefully avoiding touching the lacerations and gouges in his neck, which were still bleeding. Some of the blood was congealing and she dabbed at it lovingly with her handkerchief. If only she could clean him up more, and see better the extent of his injuries. She picked up the oil lamp and lifted the leg of his trousers carefully to inspect the damage done. With horror she saw how his shin was smashed to a rough pulp of ground muscle, sinew, and shards of bone, how his foot was set at an incongruous angle almost detached from the shin, and she heaved at the sight. She had to turn away. It was the most gruesome, grisly sight she had ever seen. Surely, nobody – not even the most skilled surgeon – could save his leg. No wonder he was unconscious; the pain would be unbearable if he were conscious.

She stroked his face lovingly and imagined him as another Moses Cartwright, getting about on a crutch but not allowing himself to be hindered greatly by the handicap. If he ended up like Moses she could put up with that. But would Dickie face the challenge of such a handicap with the same spirit that Moses had? He might end up helpless, unwilling or unable to fight it. It wouldn't make any difference though; she loved him enough, she would help him and look after him. With only one leg he would need her. He would depend on her like never before, and she would be so good to him, so utterly reliable. Things might not be so bad. Jane had married a one-legged man, and loved him as much as when he had two.

Always, however, she had envisaged being married to Dickie as a fit man, manoeuvrable, and all his faculties intact. The possibility of him being crippled had never before entered her head. Anyway, she was carrying his child and her child needed its father.

It occurred to Lucy, as she sat thinking, her eyes never leaving Dickie for signs of consciousness, how fate and events not only change our values and our perceptions irrevocably, but how quickly they can do it. She had privately scoffed when Jane announced that she was going to marry Moses, because he was no longer perfect, because he was minus one limb. It was beyond her comprehension how anybody could commit themselves to somebody who was not whole. Indeed, she could not understand how anybody could be satisfied with a man who was not entirely perfect to behold in every way, even down to the evenness of his teeth or the set of his shoulders. Dickie had been perfect . . . but not any more. Not after this. Yet what did it matter? He would still be the same person, the same delightful character, with or without his right leg, whether his face and neck were scarred for life or not. How could she stop loving him, just because he did not look the same?

Then Dickie stirred.

She peered intently into his eyes, hovering over him like a guardian angel. 'Dickie, my love,' she whispered. 'Can you hear me? Can you see me?'

He rewarded her with a faint smile, muttered something unintelligible, then drifted off into unconsciousness again. Tears clouded her vision once more and she wiped them away with the backs of her hands. Weeping would do no good. Weeping would not make him better.

'Dickie, if only I could bear the pain for you I would,' she breathed, touching his hand. 'I just want you to get well, and I'll help you do it. I'll look after you, I'll make you well again. When the doctor has seen you I'll ask if I can have you taken to our house. You can have my bed till you're better, and I'll sleep on the settle downstairs. I promise I'll look after you.'

She heard a renewed commotion on the landing and went to the door to investigate, lest it was somebody seeking her. More victims of the crash were being brought in. Three bodies were put into a room opposite.

'Are they hurt bad?' she asked the men who carried them.

'They'm dead,' one of them answered. 'And more to come, I daresay.'

'How many dead?'

'There's more than half a dozen been pulled out so far,' the other man replied. 'Some of 'em have bin took to the Crown in Brettell Lane, others to the Swan in Moor Street, along with other poor sods what am injured but surviving.'

'Isn't it tragic?' Lucy commented ruefully. 'All that needless loss of life, all that suffering.'

'Aye, and there'll be plenty more yet, believe me,' the first man said. 'Lord knows what the death toll will be. But we shall know soon enough. Already they've started clearing the lines so the trains can start running again. And would you believe it, there's even some damned harpies been looting the pockets o' them poor devils lying hurt. I'd have 'em shot.'

'What about doctors?' Lucy enquired. 'I'm waiting for a doctor to come to see Mr Dempster here.'

'I've heard as they've telegraphed Dudley and even Worcester for doctors – and Lord knows where else. Already Dr Walker has showed up with his assistant.'

'I wish he'd come here.'

'Somebody'll be here as soon as they can be, my flower, rest assured.'

It was approaching midnight when a doctor finally arrived carrying his bag of mysterious instruments and potions, tired and distressed at the extent of the carnage and the injuries he'd had to deal with. He examined Dickie, looking at his mangled leg with extreme concern and an ominous shaking of the head.

'Has he regained consciousness at all?' the doctor asked Lucy.

'He opened his eyes just for a second or two and smiled at me.'

The doctor looked at his assistant woefully. He turned to Lucy again. 'Are you this man's wife?'

'I'm engaged to be married to him,' she replied, exaggerating the truth.

The doctor spoke very quietly and very solemnly to Lucy, explaining what he had to do, then asked her to leave the room. He would call her back when it was expedient to do so.

'Will I be able to have him taken to my home when you've treated him?' she enquired.

'Maybe in a few days. But for now, he must stay here. For now he must not be moved.'

She left with fresh tears in her eyes.

★ ★ ★

Dickie Dempster's smashed leg was amputated above the knee that very night, during which time he did not regain consciousness. Lucy returned to the room when the surgery was finished and his stump had been dressed. She wept for the man she loved and what he would have to endure from that moment on, merely from a psychological point of view, never mind the physical pain. Why had her world and his suddenly been turned upside-down when there had been so much to look forward to, so much to live for? What had either of them done to be so radically and cruelly punished?

As she sat on the chair at the side of the bed weeping, she bent forward, laid her head on the pillow alongside Dickie's, and cried herself to sleep.

★   ★   ★

The next day revealed the extent of the carnage. Eleven dead were extracted from the wreckage. Another passenger died a few hours later. Several more were so severely injured that their recovery was in doubt, and only time would determine whether they lived or died. In addition, a hundred people had been attended to by the doctors, and all bar two or three were expected to recover fully. Mercifully, only one child out of all the Sunday schools present, a girl of twelve, suffered any injury, and that only slight.

★   ★   ★

When Lucy awoke, it took a second or two to assimilate what had happened. She was in a strange room . . . Dickie was with her . . . Dickie . . . So the nightmare was real after all . . . She looked at him for signs of life, but he was still unconscious and as pale as death, but he was breathing. Outside on the landing she heard signs of activity and went to the door. Mrs Elwell, the landlord's wife was heading downstairs.

'Mrs Elwell . . .'

Mrs Elwell stopped and turned around. 'Lucy,' she answered gently. 'How is he?'

'Still breathing, Mrs Elwell, but there's little sign of anything else.'

'You've been here all night with the poor lad, in't yer? Can I get you some breakfast, a mug of tea or something?'

'What time is it?'

'Just gone seven.'

'Have you got time to sit with Dickie for a few minutes while I go home? I could do with a swill and cleaning my teeth. My mother could do me some breakfast, save you the bother. You must've had a hard night of it as well.'

267

'I have, but I got nobody hurt, Lucy, like you have. You go on home and spruce yourself up, and I'll pop in every five minutes or so and keep my eye on him for you.'

'Oh, thank you, Mrs Elwell. I won't be more than half an hour.'

So Lucy returned home. Briefly she told her mother about Dickie's amputation while she washed and changed her clothes. She drank a mug of tea and ate a piece of buttered toast done in front of the fire, before hurrying back to the Whimsey.

'I've been to see him a few times, Lucy,' Mrs Elwell reported, 'but there's no sign of him coming round yet.'

'Think I should try to wake him?' Lucy asked.

'Why don't you just try talking to him and see if that brings him round?'

Lucy ran upstairs to the room where Dickie lay and sat at his bedside once more. She felt his forehead and thought he seemed feverish.

'Dickie,' she whispered. 'Dickie, can you hear me? . . . There's so much I want to tell you, and now would be a perfect time if only I thought you could hear me . . . D'you remember the very first time we saw each other? I fell for you straight away, you know, and I knew from that moment that we'd always be together . . . that I'd marry you. Well, I'm going to marry you when you get better and we're going to start a family right away . . . So please get well, my love . . . Please . . . I don't mind how long I have to wait. I'll wait for ever if need be, only please, please get better. I'll look after you well and make sure you do get better . . .'

Somebody tapped on the door.

'Come in . . .' The door opened. 'Arthur!'

'Hello, Lucy. I hope you don't mind me coming so early this morning.'

'Course not.'

Last night she did not get a proper look at him because of the panic and the darkness. But now she saw him in broad daylight and he had changed. She had not seen Arthur for nearly a year and in that time his image had become distorted in her mind. During his months of absence she had decided he was stupid and a chump, and these mentally afforded attributes had assumed exaggerated proportions. Despite her grief over Dickie, she could see just how wrong her pet perceptions of him had been, that they had been distended to favour Dickie in her mental comparisons. She was immediately aware that Arthur was decidedly better looking than last time she saw him. He was swarthy now and his frame seemed bulkier, a picture of health . . . He seemed more confident, too, more assertive, and more manly. Bristol, or Dorinda – or both – had done him a world of good.

'I just wondered how he was, Lucy. I've hardly slept all night thinking about what happened. I'm so sorry, you know. I do hope he recovers soon.'

'The doctor amputated his injured leg, Arthur.'

'Oh, no . . .' He regarded her with sincere compassion. 'But I'm not surprised. It was a mess and no mistake. How does he seem after it?'

Lucy's eyes filled with tears, as much because of Arthur's genuine concern than because of her own grief. 'Last night he looked at me and smiled. Only for a couple of seconds. He hasn't come round since, not even when the doctor took off his leg. And that must have been painful –'

'Very likely no more painful than what he was already feeling,' Arthur suggested. 'If you can feel anything when you're unconscious like that.'

She considered the possibility for a second or two. 'I hope you're right. But he seems a bit feverish now . . . Feel his forehead. Tell me what you think, Arthur.'

'But I ain't no doctor, Lucy,' he answered quietly. Nevertheless, he felt Dickie's forehead. 'Yes, he feels hot. But at least he's alive, and where there's life . . . Maybe we should open a window, to let some cool air in.'

She agreed and he opened the sash for her.

'How many other poor devils are here at the Whimsey?' he asked.

'They brought in three dead last night that I know of, and two or three others badly hurt, a woman among them.'

'It's a tragedy and no two ways, Lucy,' Arthur said, shaking his head.

'You're telling me . . .'

Dickie moved his head a little and murmured something, again unintelligible.

Lucy looked questioningly at Arthur. 'Do you think he's coming round?'

'Who knows? He might be. But then, he might just be delirious. Fever brings it on . . . Listen, d'you want me to do anything for you, Lucy? For Dickie?'

'Do you think they'll have told his folks that he's been hurt?'

'Oh, I expect so. He's an employee of the Oxford, Worcester and Wolverhampton. They'll have told his family by now. I reported his injury to the duty stationmaster myself, after they brought him here.'

'That was thoughtful, Arthur. I can't thank you enough. It would never have crossed my mind.'

'Course, we couldn't identify all the other poor devils I helped to get out. I don't think many of 'em came from round here, thank God.'

Dickie was grunting again, mumbling, but showed no signs of opening his eyes, or regaining consciousness.

'I just wish there was something more I could do,' Lucy whispered, with an earnest expression. 'I feel so helpless.'

'He's a big strong chap, Lucy. I reckon he'll get through this. But it'll take time. You'll have to be patient.'

As she nodded, there was another knock on the door, gentle, tentative.

'Come in,' Lucy called.

The door opened and a young woman, possibly twenty-four or twenty-five years old, poked her bonneted head round it.

'I was told Mr Dempster's in here.'

'Yes, he is,' Lucy affirmed. 'You must be his sister . . .'

'Sister? No, I'm Mrs Dempster. I'm his wife . . .'

Lucy gasped with disbelief and indignation, and looked at Arthur for his reaction to this astonishing claim. The woman was patently a fraud.

At once the young woman went to Dickie's bedside and peered at him anxiously. Lucy saw that she was decently clothed in a dress of good quality and a light Paisley shawl that matched it well. 'Have you been looking after him?' the young woman enquired, looking from one to the other.

Arthur immediately sized up the situation. Gently but firmly, he laid his hand on Lucy's arm and, with his eyes, flashed a warning to her that she should allow him to explain their presence. 'Miss Piddock here and I pulled Mr Dempster from the wreckage last night, Mrs Dempster,' he said convincingly. 'We are engaged to be married, you know . . .' He looked at Lucy apologetically, but he understood that Mrs Dempster's emotions would already be stretched to breaking point when she was made aware of the extent of her husband's injuries, without being further troubled by implications of his infidelity. 'We have been here all night keeping an eye on him.'

'Then I can't thank you enough,' Mrs Dempster replied, having no reason to doubt Arthur's words. 'I received news of the accident early this morning. An officer of the railway got me up at just turned five. I knew something was wrong when I awoke and saw that Mr Dempster was not in bed beside me.

Then the officer broke the news. I had to get my neighbour to look after my children so as I could come here to see him.'

Arthur squeezed Lucy's arm as a sharp reminder to be restrained.

'You have children?' she queried, shaken rigid, but trying to keep her voice even.

'Two. A boy and a girl. They're only very young, but they'll be devastated all the same when they know what's happened to their father. I dread telling them.'

'His leg was very badly injured,' Arthur said, as gently as he knew how. 'Unfortunately, the doctor who attended him in the early hours of the morning realised there was no way of saving it . . . I'm afraid, Mrs Dempster, that he had no alternative but to amputate it . . .'

'Oh, my God . . .' Her hands went to her face in horror and tears filled her eyes. 'Oh, the poor, poor man.'

'Now, it looks to me as if he's feverish, but that isn't really surprising, I suppose, after what he's been through. He's becoming delirious. I imagine the doctor will be around to see him again soon. Maybe he'll be able to give him something . . .'

'I need a cold damp cloth to put on his forehead to help cool him down,' Mrs Dempster said decisively.

'Lucy will fetch one, won't you Lucy?' Arthur nodded to her, indicating that she should do as he suggested, and she left the room, but with great reluctance.

'When Lucy comes back I think we should go, Mrs Dempster, and leave you to give you time with your husband. I recognised him last night when he was lying injured,' he felt compelled to say, should she wonder. 'I had occasion to be in his company once before, you know . . . He was very kind to me and believe me, I needed help. Helping him last night was the least I could do. I hope he recovers satisfactorily, Mrs Dempster.'

'I can't thank you enough for what you've done. Mr . . .'

'Goodrich. Arthur Goodrich, ma'am. I'm only sorry I couldn't do more. But if Miss Piddock or myself could call again later today or tomorrow, to see how your husband is faring, I would deem it a privilege.'

'Of course. I would be obliged if you would.'

'Thank you, Mrs Dempster. Meanwhile, if there is anything I can do for you, please don't be afraid to ask. Anything at all. I'll do whatever I can to help you and your husband.'

Lucy returned with the dampened cloth and handed it grudgingly to Mrs Dempster, who thanked her.

'I've just told Mrs Dempster that we'll be leaving her now, so she can spend time alone with her husband. But she's very kindly agreed to let us call again later to see how Mr Dempster is progressing.'

'That's very kind,' Lucy said, and left the room with tears in her eyes yet again.

★ ★ ★

Outside in the cool air of morning, Lucy laid her head on Arthur's shoulder and wept bitterly, while he consoled her in his arms. He understood what she was going through, the mixture of emotions that were tormenting her, and he pitied her. The tighter he held her and the greater the manifestation of his sympathy, the more she cried. Nor was she the only person crying in the streets of Brierley Hill that morning as bereaved relatives of the dead arrived by train to identify and claim the bodies.

'Come on, Lucy,' Arthur said kindly. 'Let's go and sit on one of those benches in the churchyard. Have yourself a damned good cry and talk to me if you feel like talking. You'd be surprised how much it helps, just talking. I don't suppose you feel like going home yet.'

'I don't,' she whimpered. 'Oh, Arthur, I want to die . . .'

'Then the churchyard will be very appropriate . . . I feel quite at home in churchyards myself.'

273

So they walked up the steep hill to the old redbrick church of St Michael, and Lucy snivelled into her handkerchief as she tried in vain to stem her weeping. What had happened was unbelievable, a sudden sequence of unanticipated events, with which she could hardly come to terms in so short a space of time. It was bad enough Dickie being injured so hideously. Now this . . .

Arthur walked beside her. He did not put a comforting arm around her while they walked lest she should think him presumptuous, or harbour the false notion that he was still struck on her. They walked up the broad steep path that cut through the churchyard. A wooden bench situated on the west side of the church looked out from its high vantage point over the parishes of Kingswinford, Wordsley and beyond, and they sat on it. The atmosphere was hazy and everything in the distance, including the horizon, was confused and indistinct.

Lucy looked up from her weeping with eyes that were red and puffy. 'I feel such a fool, Arthur . . . You can't imagine . . .'

'It isn't such an exclusive feeling, Luce,' Arthur replied gently. 'You're not the only one who's ever felt a fool. We all make fools of ourselves sometime.'

'D'you think that woman really was Dickie's wife?'

'Why should I have any doubts? Why should *you*? She seemed genuine enough. She looked appropriately anxious about him. And she was wearing a wedding ring.'

'But Arthur, he would have married *me* . . . I know he would.'

'How could he possibly, if he's already married? Did you have no inkling at all that he was married?'

'Never. Not even once . . . But looking back now . . .' She sniffed and gave a great sob of grief. 'There were clues enough if only I'd been clever enough to interpret them . . . The fact that he never took me home to meet his family was the strongest, but I never gave it a thought. Instead, I thought he was either ashamed of me, or he'd think I'd look down on *them*. I was never sure which.'

'I liked him, Lucy. I told you. I only met him the once, but I liked him. I never dreamed that he was a cheat. I'm as shocked as you are.'

'That time you met him . . . Did he ever say anything to you about being married?'

'No, nothing, but I assumed he was.' Arthur shrugged. 'Anyway, when did you start courting him?'

Lucy flashed her puffy eyes guiltily at Arthur, and shook her head, winding her handkerchief around one slender finger in her preoccupation.

'If you don't want to tell me it doesn't matter.'

'If I tell you, I'll only sink lower in your esteem.'

'All right . . .' He shrugged again. 'What if I suggest to you that he was the reason you could never commit yourself to me . . . eh? What would you say to that?'

She nodded her head, avoiding his eyes. 'I'd say it's true,' she said in a small voice. 'Although I'm not proud of it. I'm not proud of the way I treated you, Arthur. Especially now. Especially after this . . .'

He shrugged again. 'What's done's done. It can't be un-done.'

'But I must have hurt you . . . I know how much you thought of me and I treated you so bad. Only now can I begin to appreciate what you went through. I'm so sorry . . .' She began weeping again, and put her handkerchief to her eyes. She would have given the world for him to hold her right then, to put a comforting arm around her, but he did not. Nor would it have been right to ask him to. She had caused him suffering, now she must likewise suffer, and suffer alone. Nobody else could suffer for her. Not even Arthur.

'I loved him so much,' she cried. 'I still do . . . I can't

imagine even now, that he was already married . . . and to *that* woman . . . that I was nothing more than a mistress. Can you imagine, Arthur? Me? A mistress? This is my comeuppance.' She considered confessing that she was carrying Dickie's child, but thought better of it.

'You're not the first woman ever to be deceived by a handsome man, Lucy . . . nor will you be the last . . .'

Her crying came in plaintive wails during which Arthur said nothing, allowing her to weep to her heart's content. He wisely figured it was something she must do to get Dickie Dempster and the conflicting emotions of love, shock and anger out of her system and eventually out of her thoughts, though it might take months and even years to expunge the hurt.

When eventually her sobbing subsided, Arthur said, 'I didn't see any point at all in letting Mrs Dempster into your secret, Lucy. The poor woman was shocked and stunned enough over her husband being so badly injured. To have let her know he was deceiving her with another woman would have been a wicked unkindness. I hope you thought I acted properly.'

She nodded, allowing herself a glance at him when their eyes met briefly. 'Yes, I think it was dead right of you. You showed admirable concern for her feelings, and steered me in the right direction, when I could have been the cause of a rumpus –'

'Which would have been very untimely.'

'Yes.'

'And pointless.'

'I know.'

'And very inappropriate.'

'Oh, very . . .' She sniffed and wiped away an errant tear. 'You seem to like those words a lot, Arthur.'

'Which words?'

'Appropriate . . . and inappropriate. Did you pick them up in Bristol?'

'Not that I'm aware of. Well, they're not words that I've *just* learnt anyway.'

'Bristol's changed you, Arthur. You're much more sure of yourself now. Maybe it's Dorinda's doing.'

He shrugged. 'Maybe. But I don't feel any different.'

'You even look different. Did you know that?'

He shook his head. 'I ain't aware of it. You look much the same, though, Luce. Still the same beautiful eyes, the same slender figure.' He smiled encouragingly.

'I'm a wreck, Arthur, look at me. I'll be a wreck for a long time yet . . . Wreck of ages . . . cleft for me, let me hide myself in thee . . .'

'That's very witty, Lucy,' he said softly, 'for somebody in the throes of heartbreak.'

'Witty or not, I have to thank you, Arthur, for being so kind to me now, and so patient. I'm sure I don't deserve such consideration. I don't know what I'd have done if you hadn't been there when that *Mrs* Dempster arrived. I think Dorinda's a very lucky girl to have found you.'

'I think I'm lucky to have found Dorinda.'

'That as well.' She forced a brief smile. 'Just think, if you'd never gone to Bristol, you wouldn't have met her.'

'Life's like that, Lucy. Unpredictable. Putting people in our way, offering us challenges and calamities that I suppose must shape our lives, whether we like it or not.'

'That's very deep, Arthur . . .' Lucy sniffed again. 'See? You have changed. You never used to be as deep as that.'

'Maybe I'm deeper than you've ever given me credit for . . .'

She nodded. 'Oh, more than likely.'

'A bit later today, Lucy, I'll go back and see Mrs Dempster, to ask how Dickie is,' he remarked, changing tack. 'I'll go to your house and let you know. Unless you want to go yourself and ask . . .'

She sighed profoundly. 'I think it best if I don't show my

face. If I start crying in front of her, it'll give the game away and, as you say, there's no sense in upsetting the poor woman further. She's got enough on her plate.'

'That's very noble, Lucy.'

'No, I'm not trying to be noble, Arthur. If it seems that way, I can tell you it's not for her benefit. I'm trying to protect myself. I just have to accept that she's the one with first call on him, not me. However much I might resent it. So yes, I'd like to know how he is. Course I would.' She sniffed again and wiped her eyes. 'By the way, when's your father's funeral?'

'Thursday . . . At twelve. They're burying him here . . .' he pointed to a spot in the graveyard.

'Are you putting the inscription on his gravestone?'

Arthur smiled roguishly and Lucy thought how very appealing he looked. 'No, our Talbot won't let me . . . in case I inscribe something too irreverent for the rotten old sod. I would, you know.'

She chuckled. It was the first time he'd seen her laugh since his return to Brierley Hill and he thought how appealing she was too, despite her puffy eyes and red nose. Yes, he thought, time and events hurl their vicious trials and tribulations at us, and these very incidents do shape our lives. What effect those events, so especially tragic for Lucy, would have on her in the long run, only time would tell.

★   ★   ★

20

An inquiry into the cause of death of the twelve persons killed in the railway accident at Brierley Hill was opened on the Wednesday, before T. M. Phillips Esq., Coroner. The location was the Whimsey Inn, where a jury was empanelled, among them Talbot Goodrich, Arthur's brother. As soon as they were sworn in, they proceeded to view the bodies, then the Coroner adjourned the enquiry to the Bell Hotel, in more spacious and convenient rooms than were available at the Whimsey.

When formal identification of the accident victims had taken place, witnesses were called and duly sworn in. Arthur Goodrich would be required to give evidence at some time, having considered it his public duty to put himself forward as a witness, for he and Dorinda had been kissing on Moor Lane Bridge at the time of the accident and he had seen everything. Lucy decided that since she was not at work it might behove her to go along as well to hear other people's versions of events, and give evidence also if she felt the need, or was called to do so, since she was one of the first on the scene.

They sat together, attentive to what was going on and the testimonies of various witnesses. Already, there were indications as to where blame for the accident was likely to be apportioned, particularly when a William Skeldon, a boiler-maker from Coseley was called.

William Skeldon claimed that he had ridden in the guards' van all the way from Wolverhampton to Worcester, along with other passengers, and that some of those passengers, his seventeen-year-old brother among them who later died in the accident, were allowed to operate the brake.

'So what was the guard doing all this time,' the Coroner asked.

'He was smoking his pipe most of the time, sir.'

'Had he been drinking?'

'Not so far as I could tell.'

Skeldon claimed to have made the return journey from Worcester in the first coach of the second train. He went on to say of the crash, 'When we were between Brettell Lane and Round Oak I felt a very severe shock and was thrown against the side of the carriage. It quite took my senses away for a long time. My tongue was badly cut and my nose crushed and I got two black eyes. I've had a pain in my head ever since. As soon as I could recover my senses I went to see what was the matter. The first thing I saw on getting out of the train were the funnel and buffers from the engine lying on the rails. I saw the engine driver wandering about and asked him what was the matter. He said 'What the devil do you want here out of your carriage? Go and get in again. There's nothing serious the matter. We shall be off again in a minute or two.' I didn't get back in the train, though. I saw the guard I rode with in coming, who had travelled back on the first train, and then I knew we must have run into it. Two or three carriages were all smashed to pieces. The guard wasn't hurt at all, but my father and mother were in the last compartment of the first train, next to the guards' van.'

'Then I suppose you went to look for them?' the Coroner suggested.

'Yes, but I didn't find them. I looked for two or three hours before I found my father at Mr Noden's. My mother and brother I haven't seen at all. My brother wasn't dead then. He died the next morning after his legs were amputated. He was quite sensible when I saw him. His feet were cut off by the train and he was badly bruised about the hands and face.'

'Was he aware of his situation?' the Coroner asked. 'Did he express any belief that he should live?'

'He only enquired about our mother,' Skeldon replied sadly. 'He was afeared he would never see her again, because he said as how she'd been crushed under the carriage. He only lived twenty minutes after the operation, they told me. I wasn't with him when he died.'

'Was your brother familiar with the workings of a guards' van, Mr Skeldon?'

'No, sir. Although the guard directed him to work the brake he'd never been a railway servant, nor was he acquainted with such matters, never having travelled so far on a railway in all his life before. There were several other passengers besides my brother and me in the van when we arrived at Worcester.'

'What about the return journey?'

'The guard asked me to ride back in the van when he saw me, and anybody might have heard him ask it, even officials of the company. I said I wouldn't, but he told me if I wanted to ride in a coach I would have to pay him a guinea for the privilege. I said as I didn't mind, for the sake of a comfortable seat. I think they had some sort of party organised for the journey back. I saw about a dozen people get into the guards' van of the first train before it started.'

'Thank you for your deposition, Mr Skeldon.'

Arthur cast a glance at Lucy to see her reaction to this allegation, since it patently did not concur with what Dickie had told her. She remained passive, however.

Arthur was next to be called, and he was duly sworn in.

'You saw the accident happen, I understand, Mr Goodrich,' the Coroner said.

'Yes, sir,' replied Arthur, feeling very important. 'My lady friend and me were taking the air Monday night just after eight and we'd stopped to talk on Moor Lane Bridge. I didn't take much notice of the train what went up the line, except that it seemed to be very long, but when I saw a dozen or more coaches coming down the same line again without an engine, it made me stop and look, especially when I could hear the panic of the people inside them.'

'Did you think the coaches had become unhitched from the rest of the train?'

'That's how it looked to me, sir.'

'How fast were these unhitched coaches travelling?'

'At least as fast as when they went up the line. I wouldn't like to say exactly how fast. I'm not really any judge of speed like that.'

'Then what did you see?'

'I saw the coaches go under the bridge and on down the line, and then I heard the crash. It must have happened four or five hundred yards beyond the bridge.'

'Did you hear any whistle from the on-coming engine?'

'No, sir, only the crash. It was so loud I was afeared it would affect my hearing. I have very sensitive ears, you see.'

'Did you see any sparks coming from the wheels of the guards' van, which might suggest the brake was being applied?'

'No, sir,' Arthur replied honestly. 'I didn't see any sparks.'

'Then what happened?'

'I bid my lady friend return to sit with my mother who has just been widowed, telling her that I ought to go and see if anybody was hurt. When I got to the place I could see that another train coming up the line had hit the runaway carriages, and some of them were smashed to pieces. At first I saw a man with a lamp and heard a lot of screaming. Lots of people were lying under the debris with broken arms and legs and cuts, many of them dead, I imagined. I immediately began to get out the survivors. I believe I helped in getting out every one of them.'

'Have you any idea what might have caused the accident, Mr Goodrich?'

'No sir. I wouldn't like to speculate, for speculation it would be, coming from me.'

'Thank you, Mr Goodrich. You may stand down for now, but I would like you to hold yourself in readiness to give further evidence if required, to answer such questions that might crop up over the next weeks, as the inquest proceeds.'

'I see, sir.'

Shortly after six o'clock, after evidence from other witnesses, the inquiry was adjourned until the following Wednesday.

* * *

The hearse arrived sharp at quarter to twelve the following day to convey Jeremiah Goodrich to his final resting place. Friends and relatives followed it along the Delph and up Church Street's sharp incline, with heads suitably bowed. Dorinda, statuesque in a black satin dress and bonnet to match, ambled deferentially alongside Arthur. Although it was not common practice for women to attend funerals, Dorinda was sufficiently defiant of convention to wish to do so, leaving Magnolia to remain with Dinah, preparing pork sandwiches and fishing pickled onions from a jar for those mourners who wished to return afterwards to celebrate Jeremiah's life. Besides, Dorinda wished to see the inside of St Michael's church, which had been denied her so far, before she returned to Bristol.

'That's the Whimsey, where that Dickie Dempster's recovering,' Arthur informed her as the sombre pageant of bearers and mourners trooped by. 'I'll try and get in there later to see how he is. I heard at the inquest that one chap who had both his legs amputated died twenty minutes after the operation.'

'Then that was a bit of waste of everybody's time, wouldn't you say?'

'But, Dorinda, surgeons have to try and save lives, however hopeless it looks.'

283

'Hmm . . . Perhaps . . .' She looked pensive for a moment. 'You know, Arthur, for obvious reasons I don't think I could ever be enamoured of any old flame of yours . . . And yet I do feel very sorry for Lucy over what's happened to her beau, and how she was so cruelly deceived.'

'It's tragic, and no two ways,' Arthur agreed with a nod. 'Especially as she daren't show her own face in there to see how he is. It's a double blow to the poor girl, him being wed already.'

'Fancy not knowing he was married,' she whispered. 'I can't conceive of anybody being so naïve. Of course, they must have been lovers . . . in the most lurid sense of the word, I mean.'

'Do you think so?'

'Don't *you*? I mean, married men don't have mistresses just for walks in the park.'

'I really don't think poor Lucy is that sort of girl, Dorinda.'

'Pooh! Then I believe you have an overblown opinion of her, as if she's some inviolable, impenetrable nun living in a very strict convent. Even if she refused to consent to such things with you – which she must have done, else you wouldn't labour under the opinion you hold,' Dorinda gloated, 'it doesn't mean she wouldn't consent with another. Some women can't help themselves with some men. It's a question of chemistry, I believe.'

'I wouldn't know, Dorinda, not being a chemist.'

'Oh, Arthur, don't be silly. You don't have to be a chemist. You just have to be a student of human nature . . . as I am. Still, it is very tragic for her.'

Suddenly she grimaced and lifted the hem of her skirt as she side-stepped a trail of steaming dung that one of the hearse horses had just dropped. 'Ugh! How disgusting . . .'

They were silent after that, as they walked up the steep, broad path to the church, saving their breath. The vicar met them at the main door and headed the procession as it entered the church.

'*I am the resurrection and the life, saith the Lord,*' he intoned with due solemnity. '*He that believeth in me, though he were dead, yet shall he live: and whosoever liveth and believeth in me shall never die . . .*'

Never die? The notion of his father never dying, just for believing in God, even though he had seemed plainly dead before, troubled Arthur. He reassured himself that Jeremiah was not that fussed about God, or anybody else for that matter, so God had more than likely got the measure of him and would keep him dead.

Arthur noticed that Lucy had come to pay her respects, and was already standing in a pew as the entourage swept slowly up the aisle. He acknowledged her with a smile of compassion.

'*We brought nothing into this world,*' the vicar droned on, '*and it is certain we can carry nothing out. The Lord gave, and the Lord hath taken away; blessed be the name of the Lord . . .*'

The service progressed very satisfactorily. As they made their way to the graveside to see Jeremiah happily in his grave, Arthur looked up at the sky and reflected on what a splendid day it was for a funeral. His mind ran on to the sort of inscription he would choose for the old man's headstone. Not listening to the monotone incantations of the vicar, he quickly came up with one. He took out his notebook and blacklead from his jacket pocket and wrote it down before he forgot it.

Affliction sore long time he bore,
Physicians were in vain,
Till God did please death should him seize,
And ease Arthur of his pain.

Quite clever, and spontaneous, Arthur thought and smiled smugly to himself.

The service finished and everybody stood peering, in a

285

reverential manner, into the precise rectangular hole which contained the coffin, then started drifting away, making or resuming conversations. Arthur felt a gentle tap on his shoulder and turned around to see Lucy standing there.

She looked first at him, then warily at Dorinda. 'Could I have a word with you, Arthur?' She had been crying and her eyes were puffy.

'Course you can . . . Oh, by the way, this is Dorinda Chadwick . . . Dorinda, this is Lucy Piddock.' The two girls nodded to each other uncertainly and with tentative smiles. 'Excuse me a second, Dorinda.' They moved a few steps away.

'I only wondered whether you'd been to see how Dickie is.'

'Not today, Lucy. Not yet at any rate. I was saying to Dorinda before we got here that I must go today and enquire. You could always go yourself. Mrs Dempster thinks you're my intended, remember.'

'I couldn't, Arthur. I'd be all weepy and she'd know there was something going on. Besides, what if he's come round? It would put us both in a fix.'

'Then you could tell him what a swine he's been.'

Lucy was taken aback by this surprising change in Arthur's attitude. 'Do you think he was a swine then?'

'He was to you, leading you on the way he did.'

'I don't know what to think. I swear he loves me, even if he is married. I swear he'd rather have me than her.'

'You'll probably never know the truth of it, Lucy. I don't suppose you'll ever go spooning with him again to find out.'

Dorinda had been left alone in the graveyard too long for her liking, and decided it was time she joined the whispered conversation her man was holding with his erstwhile paramour. 'How long are you going to be, Arthur? Everybody will be waiting for us. There are guests to look after.'

286

'Maybe Lucy would like to come as well, eh?' he suggested, turning to her. 'Help take your mind off things.'

'I'm not dressed for a wake,' Lucy replied. 'Besides, I'd be no company.'

'She wants cheering up, Arthur. How can you hope to cheer somebody up at a funeral? Really, Miss Piddock, he does not think at all clearly sometimes,' Dorinda said apologetically.

'Well, I'm cheered by it,' Arthur proclaimed. 'I've been waiting for this for years. Now it's come, I intend to make the most of it.'

'I do believe, in some things Arthur has a heart of stone, Miss Piddock, wanting to see his poor father dead. I suppose the material he works with rubs off on him and gets into his blood stream, and sets his heart rock hard, like Portland cement. My brother's just the same and he's a stonemason too. It certainly seems to have an adverse effect on them both.'

Despite her aching heart Lucy smiled, somewhat amused both by Dorinda's prattling and her strange accent. 'Thank you for the offer, Arthur, but I shall go back home and wait for news of Dickie. I hope he's making some headway.'

They began walking together unhurriedly, lagging way behind the rest of the mourners. Dorinda took Arthur's arm proprietorially, putting herself between him and Lucy, which Lucy noticed of course.

'I heard at the inquest that another chap who had both his legs amputated. died twenty minutes after the operation.'

'Oh, thanks, Arthur, for telling me that.'

'But I only mention it to show that Dickie survived it, Lucy, and still has, as far as we know. So there's hope.'

'Hope for Mrs Dempster.'

'Look at it this way, Miss Piddock,' Dorinda chimed. 'Mrs Dempster is the one who'll be beset with all the trouble. If he's unable to walk and do the simplest things, she'll have to wait on him hand and foot—'

'Literally,' Arthur added tactlessly.

'I wouldn't mind that,' Lucy said quietly. 'I hope for his sake, that she won't mind either. Maybe she won't, if she loves him.'

'I couldn't do it,' Dorinda admitted. 'Not if you crowned me with gold and anointed me with oil, and not necessarily in that order. And, doubtless he'll be unable to work. She'll have to rely on parish relief or charity, and that won't bring in many nice new bonnets and new frocks. I think you should count your lucky stars, Miss Piddock, that he's not your responsibility after all. I believe you had a lucky escape.'

'You speak your mind, Miss Chadwick,' Lucy said.

'Oh I do. I do not believe in calling a spade an implement for excavating.'

'I only know I'm going to miss him.'

'Then consider just what you *are* missing,' Dorinda added pointedly.

'My brother-in-law has only one leg, Miss Chadwick. He manages very well, has full-time work, and even delivered my sister of her first child.'

'Then that is remarkable.'

'He's a remarkable man.'

'But I would question his intelligence in wishing to involve himself in delivering his wife of a child. I'm sure it would put me off ever having children if I had to witness it. Not that I'm enthusiastic about the prospect in any case, as Arthur knows well enough.'

'Fancy . . . So how do you feel about having children, Arthur, if and when you ever get wed?' Lucy enquired, spotting an opportunity to maybe score a point off Dorinda.

'I don't believe I ever could,' he answered, straight-faced. 'I certainly couldn't breast-feed, anyway.'

'Oh, you!' she exclaimed. 'You know what I mean.'

'He can be such an unbelievable idiot sometimes, can't he, Miss Piddock?'

'It could be a bone of contention between Dorinda and me,' he admitted. 'If we ever get to the stage where marriage is in the offing, I would try to change her mind.'

'But children are such a trial,' Dorinda stated flatly. 'And actually giving birth to them must be an even greater trial. I yearn for neither. Especially knowing what it can do to your figure.'

'I hope I'm never quite so vain,' Lucy said.

★ ★ ★

'How very nice of you to call, Mr Goodrich,' Mrs Dempster greeted when she answered his knock. 'I was just thinking about you, how hard you must have worked on Monday night releasing Dickie and others from the wreckage of the train.'

'So how is he?' Arthur peered curiously at the pale, un-stirring patient.

'He regained consciousness this morning for a few minutes. He was very disorientated and spoke not a word. He is very weak, you know, but his fever seems no worse. The doctor called in as well. He told me that Dickie lost a lot of blood. He said it could be weeks if not months before he recovers. I know I shall have to be very patient, Mr Goodrich, and that'll be difficult with two small children to look after as well.'

Arthur watched her as she spoke. She seemed very gentle and sincere, her soft eyes expressive, often putting extra meaning into the words she spoke. Studying her again, he put her age at a couple of years younger than himself and Dickie. She was an attractive young woman, yet not immediately striking in the way that Dorinda was. With a wife like that, Arthur wondered why Dickie could not be content. Why he would wish to seek pleasure elsewhere, chaotically disrupting the lives of others into the bargain.

'So when do you think you will be able to take him home?'

'Oh, tomorrow if all goes according to plan. The doctor is trying to arrange for a litter and two men to carry him to and from the train and see him safely home. At least when he's home I won't have to worry about the children. I imagine they're fretting already with neither of us there, and their not knowing how their father is.'

'How are you going to cope with two children and a husband who will be a cripple for the rest of his days?' Arthur asked, concern evident in his face.

'I haven't paid it too much thought, Mr Goodrich. I daren't think about it too much yet. One of the officers of the railway called in earlier today. He said there might be some compensation payable, but he was at pains to stress it was only a possibility. A lot depends on the outcome of the inquest, who was at fault. All the same, money will be tight.'

'An inquest was held yesterday, Mrs Dempster, but was adjourned till next week. No doubt you heard. Some of the passengers weren't so lucky, you know. Some sustained even more terrifying injuries.'

'Maybe they were luckier. At least in death they're not suffering.'

'But I'm sure their relatives are suffering their loss.'

'Oh, yes . . .'

'I'd appreciate it if you would allow me to call and see your husband from time to time, Mrs Dempster.'

'I'd be very pleased if you would.'

'Perhaps I could make a note of your address . . .' She told him what it was and he wrote it in his notebook. 'As I mentioned yesterday, your husband was very kind to me on one particular occasion.'

'I'm intrigued as to what that was all about, Mr Goodrich.'

He told her, and they both enjoyed the tale.

'I remember him mentioning it. Wasn't it about a year ago?'

'Nearly, but not quite.'

'Well, it was fateful that you happened upon him so quickly

the night of the accident. If he'd lain trapped for very long he might not have survived at all.'

'That's possible, I suppose.' Arthur took his watch from his fob and glanced at it. 'I'd better go, Mrs Dempster. Thank you for letting me see your husband.'

'Thank you for coming. I shall look forward to seeing you at some time in the not too distant future.'

'Rely on it.' He went to the door and opened it.

'Oh, and Mr Goodrich . . .' He turned round to catch a glimpse of those expressive eyes again. 'Please give my sincere thanks and best wishes to the young lady who looked after Dickie with you . . . You two are engaged, I think you said, unless I dreamed it.'

'Yes . . .' He nodded. 'Thank you. I'll tell her . . .'

★ ★ ★

As Arthur headed for the Piddocks' cottage on his way back home, he pondered Mrs Dempster. He was full of admiration for her. There was something more genteel about her than the usual women from the working classes. In many ways she reminded him of Lucy, her innate reserve, her quiet demeanour. Maybe Dickie Dempster had perceived the similarity as well, and that was the yeast which had fermented his interest in Lucy in the first place. It certainly made some sense.

Lucy answered the door to him and asked him in. Hannah was evidently delighted to see him, and said how sorry she was that his father had passed away. Haden, too, seemed pleased to see him, and shook his hand firmly. Yet there was a strained atmosphere in that house which was normally so pleasant.

'What dost think of all this business, Arthur?' Haden asked, before Arthur had had chance to sit down.

'A terrible tragedy, Mr Piddock. So much loss of life, so much hurt and suffering.'

'Aye, it's a tragedy and no mistake, but I mean the fact as this bastard Dickie Dempster has turned out to be a married

291

man and he's bin leading me daughter astray. Why, if he wor' lying unconscious with ne'er a right leg I'd goo and knock his block off. You know, I've a good mind to see his missus when I goo up the Whimsey after, and tell her what he was up to.'

'But it wouldn't solve anything, Mr Piddock.'

'It'd gi' *me* some satisfaction, though. I never liked him.' Haden grimaced. 'There was summat about him as I dai' like.'

'There's his poor, long-suffering wife to think about,' Arthur replied, anxious to protect the poor woman. 'Why make her more unhappy than she already is? She's no idea what Dickie was up to, and I must confess she seems a very decent young woman. She reminds me of Lucy and I feel very sorry for her. She's got enough on her plate as it is.'

'He's right, Haden,' Hannah said, sewing a button on a shirt as she sat. 'The poor wench must be at her wits' end already. If she's innocent of everything, why mek her life more of a misery for summat as she knew nothing about?'

'What do you say, our Luce?' Haden asked.

'I agree with Arthur. We've already talked about it. No good will come of raking up muck with Mrs Dempster.' She sighed deeply. 'Anyway, how is he?'

'He regained consciousness for a few minutes, she reckons, but he didn't or couldn't speak. Then he drifted back into sleep. His fever's no worse, so maybe he's on the mend. Although it'll take months, according to the doctor what went to see him.'

'Be glad yo' ai' got all that to contend with, our wench,' Haden said.

'Oh, and she's taking him home tomorrow. The doctor's arranging for a litter and two men. I daresay they'll get a hansom in Wolverhampton to carry him from the station to where he lives.'

Lucy began weeping at the news and Haden put a fatherly arm around her to comfort her. 'That's it,' she whimpered. 'I've seen the last of Dickie. I'll never see him again.'

'I shouldn't think you'll want to,' Hannah said.

'I shall go and see him from time to time, Lucy.'

'But, Arthur, how can you?' Lucy asked. 'You'll be going back to Bristol in a few days.'

'Yes, tomorrow. But I've got to come back for the inquest when it's resumed next week, since I'm a witness. Who knows how many weeks that's likely to go on? I'll have the chance to visit Dickie Dempster, have no fear.'

★ ★ ★

21

Arthur returned to Bristol with Dorinda the next day. They bade his mother farewell and he told her he would see her again Tuesday night when he came back to attend the adjourned inquest on Wednesday. Dinah was tearful, but grieving more over Jeremiah than over Arthur's leaving. They then went to the workshop to say goodbye to Talbot and Moses.

'I, er . . . I want you to think about coming back to work with me, Arthur,' Talbot said just as they were about to leave. 'Give it some thought over the next few days and we'll talk about it more when I see you next week.'

'I'm happy where I am, Talbot,' Arthur replied, conscious of the time and that their train was due in a few minutes. 'Besides, I have Dorinda to think about.'

Talbot looked at Dorinda admiringly. He could see where the attraction lay. 'Well who's to say as she can't come with you?'

Dorinda looked at Arthur for his reply, which she thought might indicate more clearly his intentions towards her. Perceiving that he was reluctant to make any comment, however, she decided to give the answer he might have given had she not been there. 'I think you are presuming too much, Talbot,' she said bluntly. 'Moving from Bristol to be up here with Arthur would mean nothing less than marriage. So far he hasn't proposed it, and neither would I expect him to so soon into our courtship. Neither am I sure that I could accept him anyway . . . yet at any rate.'

Arthur stood and listened impassively. She had got it about right.

'Then can you spare him to be away from you for weeks on end?'

'Oh, for a week at a time, yes, I suppose so. That would be no great hardship. It's not as if he would be going to sea for months or even years on end.' She thought of Philip and his going away, and his returning with a Maltese wife. 'So long as he can return to Bristol for a Saturday and Sunday . . . We would be glad to put him up at our house Saturday nights.'

'I'm thinking in terms of a partnership, Arthur,' Talbot went on, not disheartened by Dorinda's response. 'I know you always had a raw deal with Father, and I mean to make amends. Together, we could build up the business, we could look at other aspects of stonemasonry that might help us expand. Even church restoration, as and when it's called for. There's a big project under way at Worcester cathedral, folk tell me. I know you enjoy that sort of work, Arthur, and you have some valuable experience. And as for remuneration . . . well, we would be equal partners.'

Arthur glanced first at Dorinda, then at Talbot. 'I told you, I'm quite content in Bristol.'

'But you're not a partner in the business there, our Arthur. And stone is stone, whether you're in Bristol or Brierley Hill.'

'He'll think about it, won't you, Arthur?' Dorinda said, perceiving the social advantages and respectability that would be afforded her man as a partner in a prosperous family business. Besides, if Talbot and Arthur could set their own wages, they could be quite well off. 'We'll discuss it, Talbot, and Arthur can let you know next week.'

So, on the train journey to Bristol, Dorinda and Arthur discussed Talbot's proposal.

'Just think,' she said. 'You could earn much more money than you are now. As gaffer of your own business, you could pay yourself what you want.'

'So long as the work's there to pay for it,' he countered rationally.

'Then there's all the social esteem that goes along with such a position. You could join the township commissioners, become a bigwig in local society, hobnobbing with all the dignitaries and other important people. You could become an important person yourself in the community, have your own pew in church, maybe even become a church warden . . .' As his attractive young wife she would also come in for some socialising and admiration.

'I don't think that's necessarily the life for me, Dorinda. I'm a man of simple pleasures.'

'You're a stick-in-the-mud,' she said impatiently. 'You lack imagination. Arthur. *And* you're stubborn. Can't you see the advantages in going along with it? I've a good mind to recommend our Cyril to Talbot. He'd jump at the chance of being his partner. But then he always was enterprising, even if he is a bit dense.'

'But what about you?' Arthur asked. 'We wouldn't be able to see each other so often.'

'Well, we'd have to grin and bear it, but I'm sure the sacrifice would be worth it in long run. Especially if we do decide to . . . to get married, that is. In any case, those times you couldn't come to Bedminster, I could come and stay with you and your mother, or even Magnolia and Talbot, in Brierley Hill. I'm sure they wouldn't mind. My mother and father wouldn't mind, as long as somebody was there to chaperone us. Brierley Hill's no worse than Bedminster, believe me, and a bed's a bed, wherever it may be situated.'

'I'll sleep on it . . .'

'Oh, very funny. I want you to think very seriously about

this, Arthur. It's for your own good that you should accept your brother's very generous offer.'

★　★　★

Miriam Watson, on her way home from work on the Friday, called to see Lucy. The rumour mill had been grinding away relentlessly and there was plenty of speculation as to her affair with the railway guard who had been critically injured in the crash, and Miriam wanted to seek out the truth so that she could put the gossipmongers out of business.

'Let's go outside into the sunshine,' Lucy suggested when Miriam had exchanged pleasantries with Hannah. 'We can talk out there.'

'I'll bring you out a mug of tea apiece,' Hannah said, acknowledging Lucy's wish for privacy in discussing her lost love with her close friend, and set about boiling the kettle while she cooked Haden's dinner.

So the two girls went outside, sat on the hard front step of the cottage and soaked up the late afternoon sun. They spoke in lowered tones so as not to be overheard.

'So is it true as that this Dickie Dempster's married?' Miriam asked, getting straight to the point.

'Yes, he's married,' Lucy responded resignedly. 'I could have died when this woman came in to the room where he was lying hurt, and announced she was his wife. I could scarcely believe it.'

'I think it's terrible as the poor chap was hurt so bad,' Miriam said. 'I wouldn't wish that on anybody. But when I think how he pulled the wool over your eyes, I could kill him.'

'Oh, my father would've killed him anyway.'

'Nobody would've known he was wed but for the accident, would they, Luce? Did you have no inkling at all as he was married?'

'No. None. I trusted him, blind fool that I was. I trusted him to be honourable.'

'So how do you feel about him now?'

Lucy shook her head. 'I don't know how I feel, and that's the truth, Miriam. I'm just numb. When we started courting, as you know, I was as happy as a pig with a big potato. He was perfect for me, I thought, and I loved him . . . and he loved me – I know he loved me. I honestly believed it was just a matter of time before we'd get wed. But lately I started having doubts about him. Not that he was married already, but that he was getting tired of me, and it worried me – I didn't want to lose him, 'cause I knew it would break my heart if I did.' Lucy spoke in a whisper so as her mother shouldn't hear. 'Maybe I'd been too easy for him after all. I suppose I was no challenge once I'd let him have his way, whenever he wanted it . . .'

'I told you, it's always that way with men.'

'Oh, I know you did, Miriam, but to me, lying with him was always the best part of our courting.'

'It's generally the best part of anybody's. It's what courting's for.'

'Well, when we went on that trip on Monday, I went into the cathedral in Worcester and prayed. Well, you know I'm not normally the praying kind, Miriam . . . Dickie had a few drinks with Moses. Anyway, to come back home they'd split the train into two, and Dickie said they'd asked him to work, so he came back in the guards' van of the first train. Now, after the inquest, I'm not so sure as it wasn't all a tale. One of the witnesses said as how there was a dozen folk in the guards' van and they was having a party. To me, a party means drink.'

'I daresay they'll get to the bottom of it, Luce,' Miriam said.

'But, you see, it all adds up. Everything that happened up till the time of the accident tells me something. Knowing what I know now, I'm beginning to see what he was like. If they was having a party in the guards' van on the way back, and Dickie was intent on going to it, it was easy for him to lie to me about

298

it and say he was working. And if he could lie about something as petty as that, he could lie about anything.'

Miriam tutted appropriately, indignant at what she was hearing.

'I'm heartbroken over losing him, you know, Miriam, but I'm starting to get angry as well, because he used me as nothing more than a rubbing rag, as somebody just to . . .' She began to cry. It was so easy to cry. The slightest thing, the least reminder of Dickie and how he had treated her, quickly brought on tears. 'I'm starting to ask myself whether I meant anything to him at all . . .'

'Oh, Luce . . .' Miriam turned to Lucy and held her hands consolingly. 'What can I say? I'm so sorry . . .'

'But there's worse, Miriam.'

'Worse?' Miriam regarded Lucy with alarm and apprehension.

'Can you keep a secret?'

'If you don't think I can, then don't tell me nothing else.'

'I'm pregnant.' Lucy admitted. 'I'm having his child.'

'Oh, Lord above! Oh, Lucy . . . Have you told anybody yet? Does Dickie know?'

'I was going to tell him Wednesday night . . . I haven't told anybody else. So don't you, Miriam.'

'Oh, I won't, I swear . . . I did try and warn you off him, Lucy. There was summat about him as I just couldn't take to. He was too full of himself. He was handsome and he knew it. I wonder how many other wenches have been took in by him? How many others he's babbied.'

'I don't know . . . Maybe quite a few. There was somebody called Myrtle . . . He mentioned her once or twice, told me she was after him all the time, even after he'd given her up.'

'But that might have been a tale as well, just to make you jealous,' Miriam suggested.

'I hadn't thought about that.'

'Anyway, for the sake of Dickie Dempster you lost the best chap any wench could want – Arthur.'

Lucy sighed and wiped her tears. 'I know . . . It's stupid now I think of it, but I wouldn't commit myself to Arthur because I thought he wasn't handsome enough, because he always seemed a bit of a twit. But, you know, Miriam, he's got two legs, two arms, two eyes, two ears, a nose, ten fingers, ten toes and a heart of gold. Dickie hasn't. Not now . . .'

'In a way,' Miriam said, unsure of the ground she was treading, 'It might be a blessing in disguise Dickie turning out to be married.'

'Oh? How do you work that out?'

' 'Cause I can't imagine you wanting him anyway with a leg missing.'

Lucy sighed ponderously. 'I have thought about that, Miriam . . . But I can't admit to myself that I could be so shallow.'

'But if you do start to admit it to yourself – 'cause you know what you was like before . . . even Arthur wasn't perfect enough for you – it'd prove that you didn't really love him anyway. I mean, look at your Jane . . . Moses has only got one leg and yet she loves him to bits. She wouldn't look at another man, would she? That tells me something about real love . . .'

'I've thought about it, Miriam.'

'And what conclusion did you come to?'

'None.'

'Well, there'd be no shame if you did think it. Not compared to the shame he should feel at putting you in the family way when he's already wed. He should be locked up in the work-house for it.'

Lucy shrugged. She could understand her friend's point of view, even though she dare not subscribe to it.

'They reckon Arthur's courting though now,' Miriam went on. 'So you've missed your chance there anyway. They say as how pretty she is. Them as saw her walking behind the hearse yesterday said as she looked really beautiful dressed all in black.'

'Oh, she did and no two ways, Miriam. And it makes you realise that if a chap can win a girl as pretty as that, he must have something about him after all. Mind, you, she knows she's pretty. I've never met anybody so vain.'

Miriam regarded her friend suspiciously. 'I never thought as you'd be catty, Luce.'

'I'm not being catty. It's the truth.'

'You met her then?'

'I went to the funeral as well, just to pay my respects. Arthur introduced us . . . He's been as good as gold you know, Miriam. He's been like a brother to me these last few days. I don't know what I would've done without him. I'll miss him now he's gone back to Bristol.'

Hannah delivered two mugs of tea and put them on the step next to the girls. 'Did I just hear Arthur's name mentioned?'

'I was just saying, Mother, as how I couldn't have done without him these last few days.'

'It's a pity as you tried to do without him in the first place, our Lucy. Things might have turned out different. Because you didn't want him, he's took up with another young woman now, a bobbydazzler an' all, by all accounts.'

'He's coming back next week for the inquest. If I know Arthur he'll come and ask how I am.'

'Yes, at least you know you can count on him. Not like that other sod . . . I got no sympathy at all for that other sod, you know, Miriam.'

★ ★ ★

As the adjourned inquest was not due to resume till one o'clock on Wednesday 1st September, Arthur commenced the journey early that same morning, having consulted his copy of Bradshaw to ascertain his rail connections. He arrived in good time to say hello to his mother and enjoy a sandwich. He and Talbot walked to the inquest together and resumed their discussion on the proposed partnership.

'I need you Arthur,' Talbot said. 'I've got so much work, even before Father took ill, that I need at least one extra pair of hands. I take it you discussed it with Dorinda?'

'Yes, we discussed it.'

'And?'

'In principle I think I'm for it,' Arthur said. 'But I refuse to spend my life in draughty churchyards like I did before. We can get some younger chap just out of apprenticeship for that. We should start an apprentice of our own as well.'

'I told you I wanted to make amends, Arthur. I won't ask nor expect you to spend your life in draughty churchyards any more than I would myself.'

'Well, if we can agree on how much money we can pay ourselves and draw up a suitable deed of partnership, then I'm prepared to give it a go.'

'Oh, Arthur, you've taken a load off my mind. You belong in the business anyway. It's half yours by right of inheritance. That you should not be getting the benefit for the sake of working in Bristol is plain stupid. I'm glad Dorinda's been able to talk some sense into you. Let's shake on it.'

They shook.

'But it ain't Dorinda's doing, Talbot,' Arthur protested. 'Oh, she's all for it, but I agree with you. Half of the business is mine by right of inheritance, and it's the only way I'm ever likely to get anything out of the old bugger. I never did when he was alive.'

'So you'll give in your notice with Pascoe's?'

'Course. When I get back. While I'm away, if you can get Mr Burbury to draw up a deed of partnership . . . If he ain't too busy looking after the claims of clients hurt in the accident.'

'We'll very likely see him at the inquest,' Talbot said. 'We'll ask him then.'

★ ★ ★

It was announced at the inquest that another life had been lost due to injuries sustained as a result of the accident on Monday 23rd August. Mr Richard Dempster, a servant of the Oxford Worcester and Wolverhampton Railway, employed as a guard, passed away the previous evening after a valiant fight. He had been off-duty at the time of the accident. His loss would be felt by his family and colleagues and deep sympathy was expressed for his widow and their two children.

The witnesses that day were largely confined to employees of the railway and definitions of their duties – who was responsible for checking the state of shackles and chains. One of the witnesses, Mr Adcock, secretary and superintendent of the railway, denied that the train had been split into two at Worcester for the return journey because of chains and shackles breaking under the strain on the outward journey. It made sense to draw a lesser weight in order to avoid similar occurrences on the way back, but the reason the train was divided so unequally, he said, was because one of the engines was a six-wheel coupled engine, and was capable of hauling more than the other less powerful one. There were more technical questions and answers regarding shackles, and the duty of the chief guard, Frederick Cooke, in respect of them.

But all this technical talk was of no interest to Arthur. He was shocked yet hardly surprised to learn of Dempster's death, and his mind was filled with sympathy for poor Mrs Dempster. He would make it his business to visit her and express his condolences tomorrow, rather than return to Bristol straight away. Tonight he would visit Lucy. It was entirely possible she had not heard of Dickie's demise, yet he did not relish the prospect of telling her in case she hadn't.

Eventually, after a day of bone-dry technical evidence and

even drier opinions, the inquest was further adjourned until the following Tuesday, 7th September.

★ ★ ★

After he had eaten and freshened up, Arthur made his way to the home of the Piddock family to see Lucy. As usual they made a great fuss of him, which was all very gratifying. He thought Lucy still seemed greatly troubled, but it was early days yet.

'Do you fancy a walk?' he asked her. 'It's a pleasant enough evening out.'

'Yes, all right,' she answered without hesitation. 'Give me a minute.' She trotted upstairs.

'How's the inquest gone today?' Haden asked. 'Anything fresh come up?'

'One or two interesting bits . . . Plenty of technical stuff today, Haden.' He related briefly the thrust of the inquest, but could not bring himself to say that Dickie Dempster had passed away. The Piddocks might not have been Dickie's most ardent admirers but if they knew, they would of course tell Lucy, when he would prefer that such news was broken to her gently, and possibly withheld until the initial pain of heartbreak had eased or been mollified. If she must learn of it, let it be from somebody else. No doubt if they took the trouble to buy the Birmingham Daily Post tomorrow they would see an account of it, but he doubted whether they would.

Presently Lucy came down and looked altogether very presentable. She'd changed her dress, and brushed and tied up her hair. He looked at her agreeably.

'I'm ready,' she said.

Arthur bid goodnight to Hannah and Haden and stepped outside with Lucy.

'It's good of you to come and see me while you're up here for the inquest,' she said.

'It's the very least I can do,' he answered with a smile.

They crossed the street, heading towards Brettell Lane, as if to walk downhill in the direction of Hawbush Farm and Audnam, the route they took the very first time they walked out together.

'Have you heard how Dickie is?' she asked.

'Have you?' he said, returning the question.

'No.'

'I'm going to visit Mrs Dempster in the morning before I go back to Bristol.' He sidestepped her question, and thus avoided a lie. 'I'll report back to you, but it'll have to be by letter, because I'll travel directly to Bristol from Wolverhampton.'

'Back to Dorinda . . .'

'Back to Mrs Hawkins, my landlady, to be more accurate. But she won't be my landlady for long . . .'

'Oh?' Lucy looked up at him as she walked alongside. 'How come? Are you getting wed then?'

'No, it's because I'm leaving Bristol. I'm coming back to Brierley Hill to set up in partnership with our Talbot.'

Lucy's face lit up like a lamp and her eyes, which had been so lacklustre of late, sparkled again like they always used to. 'I'm happy for you, Arthur,' she said, smiling. 'I'm happy for myself as well. I might see a bit more of you. I expect Dorinda will be sorry to lose you for weeks on end.'

'Oh, I'll go back most Fridays or Saturdays, depending on what work there is. She'll only miss me for a few days at a time. I'm sure we can both endure that without too much hardship.'

'She's very pretty, isn't she, Arthur?'

'Strikingly so, I always think.'

'Fancy you ending up with a girl as pretty as that.'

'I know. Sometimes I have to pinch myself to make sure it's not all a dream.' He seemed to say it with his tongue in his cheek, and she wondered whether he meant it.

'She's very blunt, isn't she? But amusing with it.'

'If you don't know how to take her, I suppose she could easily upset you. I hope she didn't upset you, Lucy. Actually, she was greatly troubled by what you were going through over Dickie.'

'That was good of her.'

'So how have you been this past week, Luce?'

'Oh, a bit better. I'm getting over the shock a bit now. I still miss Dickie though.'

'You're bound to. You were in love with him. Your life revolved around him.'

'I'm amazed at you, Arthur,' Lucy said frankly. 'The way you harbour no resentment at all over the fact that Dickie usurped you.'

'Who am I to complain? You loved him more than you loved me.' He was conscious of using the past tense with regard to Dickie, but hoped she wouldn't read anything into it. 'I didn't see any point in competing.' He smiled generously. 'Anyway, I had other fish to fry in the shape of Dorinda. Once you released me, there was no point in grieving longer than need be.'

'I can't say as I blame you . . . I wonder how long I shall grieve, Arthur . . .'

'It depends whether somebody else comes along to divert you, I reckon. They always say the best cure for a broken heart is to fall in love with somebody else. I heard somebody else say – I think it was Mrs Hawkins – that a broken heart lasts about three weeks in the town and five weeks in the country. Well, you live in a small town, so maybe a month in your case.'

'So soon?' She sounded surprised. 'But why only three weeks in a town?'

Arthur laughed at her failure to understand the joke. 'Because there's more chance of meeting somebody else in a town to take your mind off things.'

'Oh, I see . . . But there's nobody else in this town that I'd be interested in . . .' Lucy knew that to be a lie, but a deliberate one. She would certainly be interested in Arthur when she'd fully got over Dickie, if he were not so wrapped up in Dorinda . . . Oh . . . and if she were not carrying Dickie Dempster's bastard child already, which would put any chap off.

'Then it'll take five weeks, as prescribed by Mrs Hawkins.'

'Tell me more about this partnership with Talbot.'

'He just wants to make amends for the way my father was with me. It's a very noble gesture when you think about it. Dorinda and me talked about it and we agreed it would be the right thing to do. My mother, as well, will be glad of me living there, I think. I'll be a bit of company for her. Somebody she can cook for. So, like you said, Lucy, you might be seeing a bit more of me.'

'Well, that can only be a good thing, Arthur.'

'So what do you intend doing about your job at the Whimsey? Shall you keep it on?'

'Oh, yes. If I want my broken heart to last for only three weeks or less, I'd better.'

He noticed a sparkle in her lovely eyes when she said it. Maybe the hurt Dickie Dempster had occasioned her by his deception might, in time, significantly outweigh the pain of his loss. After all, *Heaven has no rage like love to hatred turned, Nor Hell a fury like a woman scorned . . .*

★ ★ ★

22

Greatly looking forward to seeing Mrs Dempster again, Arthur took a hansom to Wednesfield Heath from Wolverhampton's Low Level station. He was barely able to acknowledge that it was for the mere pleasure of seeing her, rather than a wish just to convey his condolences. He did concede, however, that he would almost certainly be encroaching on her grief at this time and, from that aspect, debated with himself the folly of his visit. Thus it occurred to him to ask the driver to turn around and return him to the station, so that he could be on his way to Bristol. But it was not in Arthur's nature to turn his back on somebody who he thought might need his help, and perhaps even some support. If it was evident that Mrs Dempster was indeed sorely grieving and plainly did not want any intrusion he would quickly offer his condolences, then promptly leave. After all, the poor widow might be surrounded by other relatives, eager to comfort her and her two children.

The driver took Arthur to the house in Frederick Street and was asked to wait. Frederick Street, which adjoined the Wolverhampton Road, was lined with recently built terraces of houses. Everywhere was as yet unpaved, pock-marked with holes and bumps and littered with unkempt children who were hurling house bricks and any other debris they could lay hands on at a cat, to occupy themselves. Wednesfield Heath had all the characteristics of a village whose heart and pleasant pastures were in the process of being swallowed up and regurgitated by its rapidly expanding industrial neighbour Wolverhampton.

The curtains were drawn as the mark of a house in mourning, and Arthur hesitated to go further lest it really was a bad time to call. But then he reminded himself that he should be trying hard not to be the tentative, hesitant person he was; he'd come all this way on a visit, he would show his face, whatever the outcome. So he rapped on the front door.

He heard footsteps in the entry at the side and craned his neck for a glimpse of who it was. Mrs Dempster presented herself before him with a smile of surprise and welcome.

'Mr Goodrich!' She looked and sounded pleased to see him. 'It's good of you to call, I'm so glad you haven't forgotten me. Forgive me for coming down the entry to greet you, but I don't want to open the front door. Do come in and let me brew you some tea.'

'That'd be very acceptable, Mrs Dempster. Thank you.' Having been so welcomed, he followed her with a broad smile into the entry feeling greatly relieved. At the top, it opened up into a party yard with a brewhouse and a privy.

'Come in, Mr Goodrich.'

He stepped inside. Everywhere was clean and tidy, and very neat.

'I heard about your husband's death at the inquest yesterday,' he began. 'I came to offer my sincere condolences, to tell you how sorry I am. It must be a bitter blow for you.'

'That's very thoughtful, Mr Goodrich.' She gestured that he should sit down.

He perched himself on the settle facing the fire-grate. 'If there's anything I can do for you, Mrs Dempster, just say the word. I realise how hard it must be at the moment with two children to care for, on top of all the other considerations.'

'Oh, I'll manage, Mr Goodrich . . . There's already some water in the kettle, enough for a pot of tea, I think . . .' She shifted the kettle from the hob, assessing the amount of water in it, and hung it over the fire from a gale hook. 'It won't take long to boil, it's hottish already.'

Arthur had expected her to be a picture of misery and grief, but although she conducted herself with solemnity and grace, she seemed hardly miserable. 'So this was Dickie's home,' he mused aloud. 'Aren't your children here?'

She sat down primly at the other end of the settle, inclining herself towards him. 'My mother's taken them for a few days. While Dickie's body is resting here I think it's sensible, because they're too young to understand what's going on. Dickie's in the front room, which is the reason I didn't want to open the front door, in case you didn't fancy the idea of seeing him. Would you like to see him, Mr Goodrich?'

'If you don't mind, Mrs Dempster, I won't . . . I'd prefer to remember your husband as the helpful chap I met at the station . . . So when is the funeral arranged for?'

'Next Monday at noon.'

'I'll try and arrange to be there. I imagine there'll be lots of people from the railway company . . . Relatives as well. Did Mr Dempster have many relatives?'

'A few brothers and sisters, but they weren't particularly close. I expect most of them will be there, though.'

'Have you had any further contact from the railway company?'

'Yes, Mr Humphries the stationmaster called only yesterday, as soon as he'd heard of Dickie's death.'

'I imagine he was upset,' Arthur suggested.

'He was very sympathetic.'

'No doubt they're looking into the question of compensation.'

'Well . . . It's strange that you should mention that, Mr Goodrich—'

'I'd much prefer it if you called me Arthur, you know . . .'

She smiled, and for a second those expressive eyes lost their look of solemnity and actually twinkled. 'Thank you . . . Arthur . . . Then would you please call me Isabel?'

He returned the smile and their eyes met. 'Thank you, Isabel. It makes life so much easier if you're less formal, I always think.'

'And I agree.'

'Anyway, you were saying . . .'

'Oh, the question of compensation . . . Yes . . . There might be a problem. Since you're here . . . Arthur . . . perhaps you wouldn't mind if I asked for your opinion.'

'What sort of problem?'

'Well, Mr Humphries claims that Dickie was not on duty on the day of the accident, which will almost certainly affect any compensation payment. But I swear, Mr – I mean, Arthur –' She smile apologetically. '– that he left this house in his uniform. I understood him to be working that day.'

'Ah . . .'

Oh dear. A tricky situation.

'Mr Humphries said that if he'd been on duty there would be no question, but since he was travelling merely as a passenger, any claim for compensation would have to be treated differently.' The kettle began steaming and spitting and Isabel stood up to make the tea. 'I'm anxious about this, you know, Arthur.' She reached into a cupboard for her tea caddy. 'Why should Mr Humphries claim that Dickie wasn't working when he was supposed to be? Can you throw any light on it?'

'Me?' Arthur took a second to consider how to answer her question. He had no wish to incriminate poor dead Dickie, any more than he wished to burden Isabel with the knowledge of his deceit. 'I take it you've checked to see if any of his clothes are missing?'

She spooned tea leaves into a brown enamelled teapot then

311

followed it with boiling hot water and gave it a stir. 'Strangely, Arthur, there's a pair of trousers and a jacket missing. Mr Humphries says they found his uniform in his locker. That suggests he took other clothes with him on the day of the accident, perhaps to change into. In which case, he'd lied to me.' She sat down again.

Arthur looked down at his boots and the navy blue podged rug beneath them, unable to look Isabel Dempster in the eye. Of course he knew why Dickie had changed from his uniform into his own clothes, but how could he possibly reveal it to her?

'To tell you the truth, Arthur, I think I *do* know why,' she said evenly.

'Oh?' He regarded her apprehensively. 'But I'm sure it's not something you want to talk to me about.'

'I do if you've a mind to listen . . . You see, even though I don't know you that well, I feel I can talk to you easily. Sometimes it's easier to unburden yourself on somebody you don't know too well. You seem to have a very sympathetic ear, Arthur, somebody I can confide in. And believe me, I do need to confide in somebody . . .'

At last he witnessed tears trembling on the lashes of her lovely eyes, and a tear trickled gently over the soft curve of her cheek.

'Please don't upset yourself, Isabel.'

'Forgive me, Arthur, but I've been upset a long time. This is nothing new, you may rest assured.' She lifted her apron and wiped her eyes. 'Forgive me for blubbering like a schoolgirl.'

'Oh, don't mind me. But whatever it is, are you sure you want to tell me?'

'Oh, yes . . .' She sniffed and dabbed her eyes again, endeavouring to compose herself. 'You see, Dickie was often unfaithful to me. Whilst he made sure that his children never went short, he had affairs with a whole string of women over the five years or so since we've been married. After a while you recognise the signs, you know. The distant looks, the not listening when you talk to him, the changes in routine which are obviously made to suit somebody else's, the starting to go out on different nights of the week. And, as you might guess, Arthur, the lack of interest in me when he's in the midst of his current adventure.'

'I find that hard to understand, Isabel. I find it hard to understand why he should have bothered with other women in the first place when he had you.'

She flashed him a grateful smile. 'I'm certain he was involved with another woman at the time of the accident. That's why, I imagine, he led me to believe he was working when it's obvious now that he wasn't. I suppose the poor girl he was seeing was on the train with him. I only hope to God that she wasn't maimed or killed as well.'

'There were no women in the guards' van that Dickie travelled in, Isabel. I know it for a fact.'

'Then that's a good sign . . . for her, I mean, whoever she might be. Let's hope she's unhurt.'

'Oh, I doubt whether she will have emerged from it scot-free,' he replied, thinking more of Lucy's broken heart. 'There was something going on, though, according to one or two of the witnesses. I think there was some drink. It seems there were about a dozen men in that guards' van that night. Some of them were drinking . . .'

'Oh, Dickie would have been one of them if there was drink about. He was very partial to a drink. Too partial . . .'

'So what other women did he have affairs with, Isabel. Do you know?'

'The last one I know about was a girl called Myrtle Collins. She was unmarried and fairly well presented. She was neat and tidy, and attractive to look at, although not immediately striking. I think she came from a respectable family. I know this, because I met her. I think all his women fitted that description. But Myrtle was a bit more defiant than the others. She was not going to be put off. Dickie must have got tired of her and told her he wanted to finish with her, but Myrtle followed him home one night unbeknownst . . .'

'Followed him home? That must have been a trial for you.'

'In the finish it was really more of a trial for him. As far as I was concerned she was just another of his women, but she considered herself entitled to more than just a mistress might expect, and I don't blame her. He'd made her pregnant, you see. Evidently, he'd promised her marriage, a promise he obviously couldn't keep. Myrtle kicked up quite a fuss and even brought her father along on another night. Some time later she gave birth to a daughter. Dickie's bastard . . . It ended up with Dickie having to pay her something every week if he didn't want his nose broken by Myrtle's father.' Isabel sighed and stood up. 'I think the tea must be ready by now . . .'

She lifted the lid off the pot and gave it another stir, then went to the cupboard and withdrew two cups and saucers, which she placed on the scrubbed wooden table under the window.

'You've had a rough time, by the sounds of it, Isabel,' Arthur remarked caringly. 'Fancy. Who'd have thought it.'

'You don't strike me as being anything like Dickie, Arthur,' she said, pouring the tea. She looked up at him and smiled approvingly. 'I can't imagine that you'd treat your young lady like that when you get married.'

'No, I wouldn't dream,' he asserted.

'I think she's a very lucky young woman to have got somebody like you.'

He grinned self-consciously, feeling himself blush at the compliment.

She sighed. 'It's a pity there aren't more men like you . . . Sugar?'

'One spoonful, please.'

She handed Arthur a cup and saucer then sat down again. 'So you see, Arthur, my marriage wasn't a particularly happy one. The problem for women, in this day and age, is that there's no practical remedy for us against husbands who are unfaithful or unkind. Did you know that a man's horse has more rights than his wife? I think that's silly, don't you?'

'Daft, I agree. The law needs changing.'

'So, although I never wished Dickie any harm, I cannot be so hypocritical as to grieve over him now he's gone. I feel very little grief. What love I had for him when we were married, he sort of knocked it out of me with his affairs . . . and his drinking.'

'Was he ever unkind to you? I mean, did he ever strike you?'

'Oh, yes.'

'I'm so sorry, Isabel. I had no idea, I would never have dreamt. I can understand how you feel. It seems to me that this girl who you reckon he was seeing lately had a lucky escape.'

'I'd love to know who she is. I could save her a lot of heartache. I could certainly put her wise.'

'Isabel . . .' Because of the way he said her name she looked at him expectantly, placing her cup back in the saucer. 'I'm a stonemason in my family's business . . . I can't remember whether I told you that or not . . . You'll probably want a decent grave for Dickie . . . Let me provide it, will you? It'll save you a lot of expense and trouble if you will leave it all to me. I mean, if the compensation you're likely to get falls short of your expectations as well . . .'

'Arthur, that's very, very kind. Certainly, you can construct the grave. As you say, it will relieve me of a lot of time and trouble, but as for letting you pay for it . . . I wouldn't dream.'

'Well, let's say that, in view of your stretched circumstances, I'll not press you for payment.'

'That's more than considerate, Arthur. Thank you.'

'After the funeral, I could call and see you again and show

you some designs. I could help you choose a suitable grave and together we could come up with a suitable inscription for the headstone.'

'I'd be grateful if you would, Arthur.'

★ ★ ★

Arthur left Isabel Dempster almost as soon as he had finished his cup of tea, wondering whether or not to reveal to Lucy what she had said. He travelled back to the station debating with himself on this very point. If Lucy got over Dickie fairly quickly there might be no point in telling her, but telling her might speed up the mending of her broken heart. He did not know what to do for the best. Perhaps he should seek Dorinda's advice . . . Then again, perhaps not . . .

On arrival at Temple Meads Arthur went directly to St Mary Redcliffe. Mr Pascoe was in the hut his men used as a base while they worked restoring the beautiful old church, and Arthur tapped on the open door to draw the man's attention.

'Oh, you've decided to grace us with your presence, Mr Goodrich.' He leaned back in the chair he was occupying and drew on his clay pipe, appraising his employee. 'I was expecting you first thing.'

'I only just got back, Mr Pascoe . . . Sorry. As a matter of fact, I'm due at the inquest again next Tuesday. It's been adjourned again.'

'D'you think you'll ever put in another full week for me?' Pascoe asked sarcastically.

'Well . . . Maybe not, Mr Pascoe.' Here was the perfect opportunity to tell his gaffer he was returning home for good. 'The truth is, I have to tender my notice. I'm moving back to Brierley Hill to be an equal partner with my brother in the family business, now that my father's passed on. If you could see your way clear –'

'Equal partner . . .' Mr Pascoe scratched his chin. 'Mmm . . . Well, I can't compete with that, Mr Goodrich, much as I appreciate your work . . . when you're here to do any. So, I reckon I got no choice in the matter. Just so long as you don't go poaching my best men, mark you.' He wagged his clay pipe at Arthur admonishingly.

'Oh, I wouldn't do that, Mr Pascoe.'

'Do you intend to stay and inspire us for the rest o' the week, then?'

'Oh, yes, sir,' Arthur replied.

'Then I'll have your wages made up till Saturday dinnertime. You can collect 'em then.'

'Thank you, Mr Pascoe.'

★   ★   ★

'Now look after yourself, dear Arthur,' Mrs Hawkins said as the pair stood together saying goodbye. 'And give my sincere good wishes to your mother. I do hope you'll give her a tolerable account of me and the way I've tried to look after you all these months.'

'Oh, I have already, Mrs Hawkins. As a matter of fact, I've already told her how good your fish pies are and everything.'

'Bless you. Well, if your new venture doesn't work out to your satisfaction, and you feel like coming back to Bristol, you'll be very welcome to lodge here again. I shall miss you, Arthur.' Tears welled up in the old lady's eyes and she dabbed at them beneath her spectacles with a small handkerchief.

Arthur was touched by this spontaneous glimpse of her genuine affection. 'Oh, I'll be back to see you many a Saturday or Sunday, Mrs Hawkins. I shall come to Bristol at the end of most weeks to see Dorinda, 'cept when she comes to stay with me and my mother in Brierley Hill. You'll very likely get tired of seeing me.'

'But won't the expense of travelling to and fro be too much for you? I mean, if you're saving to get married, you won't be able to save much if you're travelling by rail to Bristol and back every week.'

Arthur scratched his head. He hadn't considered the matter before. 'Maybe so . . . Maybe some weeks I won't come . . . But when I do, I promise I'll call and see you, and bring you some of my mother's best pork pie. She makes the best pork pie in the world you know, Mrs Hawkins.'

Mrs Hawkins smiled through her tears. 'Tell her I'm looking forward to it.'

'I will,' Arthur grinned, trying to be cheerful. He planted a kiss on the old lady's cheek, picked up his travelling bag. 'Thank you for everything, Mrs Hawkins.'

Mrs Hawkins opened the door for him, but Arthur hesitated to put on his hat.

'Can I ask you something, Mrs Hawkins?'

'What do you want to ask?'

'Well . . . I'd like your opinion. To me, you're the sort of woman who sees things clearly and I want to know what you think about something . . . from a woman's point of view.'

'Is it going to take long? You might as well put your bag down and come back inside . . .'

Arthur did as he was bid, and followed Mrs Hawkins into her small sitting-room where they sat facing each other on comfortable padded chairs.

'So what do you want my opinion about?'

'You know the railway accident I told you about—'

'Yes. I read about it too, remember.'

'You know the widow of that chap Dickie Dempster I told you about – Isabel . . .'

'Yes . . .'

'She knows her husband was a rogue where women were concerned. Well, she stopped loving him because he was such a rogue, and she says she doesn't grieve over his death . . . She's troubling me, Mrs Hawkins. Sorely. She seems such a decent, gentle soul. She never deserved to be treated the way he treated her. She's got a couple of children, very young, although I don't know their ages, because I haven't seen them – and I never thought to ask.'

'You mean you feel sorry for this Isabel,' Mrs Hawkins suggested.

'I feel sorry for her, yes . . . but I think it might be more than that. I'm drawn to her. She's so much like Lucy . . . But the children—'

'Does this Isabel like you in the same way?'

Arthur shrugged. 'I can't say. She seemed happy to see me. We talked for ages and she confided quite a bit to me. And she wants me to visit her again after the funeral . . .'

'It would be totally inappropriate to go calling on a young widow so soon after the death of her husband, Arthur, however much of a rogue he's been,' Mrs Hawkins counselled.

'I'd be calling in a professional capacity though. She's asked me to design and make his grave.'

'As long as it is only in a professional capacity. But it sounds just an excuse to me.'

'I suppose it is,' he conceded. 'But what I want to know is whether it's wrong that a man should be wary of taking on another man's children . . . If it ever got that far, I mean.'

'I would have thought there's more to it than just that. There's nothing wrong with taking on another man's children, and it could be considered a very charitable thing to do, as long as you remember that just because they are another man's children doesn't mean that they should not be loved and nurtured as if they were one's own. You see, children seldom have any choice in the matter of whom their widowed parents might re-marry. I was such a child myself, you know. My mother re-married after my father died. I was very wary of how my life would turn out. I was very wary of the man. I did not know him, I did not know whether he would be cruel or kind to me. Even though I was so small I worried about these things. I can remember it all so clearly. Nonetheless, it

319

transpired that my new step-father was very kind to me. He showed me affection and I loved him for it . . . as much as I loved my real father. Other men are cruel to their step-children – women too – and that can only lead to a child's misery, and adversely affect the way they grow up. And who in their right mind would want to make a child miserable, and ruin their futures because of it?'

'I wouldn't,' Arthur affirmed.

'I know you wouldn't, Arthur, because you are a kind, gentle and considerate person. But to answer your question more fully, the real issue is not whether you should consider taking on another man's children, it is really whether you wish to take on that man's widow, since the children are an inevitable part of the legacy.'

Arthur perceived the wisdom in Mrs Hawkins's words. 'I don't know whether I want to take her on or not. I hardly know her, but, like I said, I am drawn to her. She might not like me in that way anyway, but if it became obvious that she did . . .'

'So what about Dorinda?'

'That's where I'm all at sea, Mrs Hawkins. I love Dorinda. She's a beautiful girl.'

'And do you love her for her beauty, or for her heart?'

'What's wrong with loving a girl if she's beautiful?'

'Nothing, so long as she is blessed with other virtues as well. But if Dorinda was a widow and had a child already, and that child was a horrid little brat, would you still be inclined to marry her and take on that child?'

'I think, Mrs Hawkins, that if a child is a horrid brat, then there's a reason for it. If I loved the mother, then why not try and help the child mend its ways and show it some affection? But I don't think there's much chance of Dorinda having a child anyway, so it's a pointless question. She don't want children, as you know.'

'And that, surely, is another consideration, Arthur.'

'I know,' he conceded quietly. 'When a girl is as beautiful as Dorinda is, a man feels something and wants to exercise his marital rights – if you'll pardon me for speaking so blunt, Mrs Hawkins. It's nature's way, I reckon. But that ain't part of Dorinda's agenda from what she says. I don't reckon I can go through life being celibate, and if I marry I don't see why I should. So when I see another girl I fancy, like this Isabel, who already has children, I know she ain't averse to doing the very thing what causes them in the first place. I know I wouldn't have to be celibate.' He smiled his apology at using such liberal talk with Mrs Hawkins.

'Then I think you need to have a heart-to-heart with Dorinda before you do anything, Arthur. A girl cannot live in cloud-cuckoo-land when it comes to marriage and what is expected of her in the marriage bed. That is naïve in the extreme. But only you can sort that out. Dorinda must be aware that marriage was ordained for the procreation of children, and she must be persuaded to accept it.'

Arthur nodded pensively. 'Thank you, Mrs Hawkins . . . I'm sorry to have burdened you with that, but there's nobody else I can talk to.'

'As long as it's helped.'

'Yes, it's helped. And I'll think about it some more. Thank you.'

Sadly, she watched him go. She knew he was going to the Chadwicks' house to spend the night before he returned on Sunday to his mother's tender mercies and his new venture in Brierley Hill. She hoped he would return to Bristol regularly to visit her, despite Dorinda. On the other hand, she hated the thought of him being married to that vain, idiotic girl. Men were such fools where a pretty face was concerned, but their folly was not necessarily chronic if the girl had no heart and no common sense. She wished Arthur could meet somebody else. But preferably not a widow with children already.

★ ★ ★

That same Saturday evening, the Chadwicks wanted to make an event of it, to mark Arthur's departure, and they had a substantial dinner with some decent wine, and all became quite merry. Arthur was due to catch his train when he'd had his Sunday dinner the following afternoon. Dorinda decided to walk with him to Temple Meads, and would take a hansom back to the family home in Bedminster.

'It's always a benefit to the system to have a walk after Sunday dinner, I always think, Arthur,' Dorinda chimed as they strolled alongside the New Cut approaching the station. 'It helps my digestion recover in time for tea. If I don't, I find myself thrust upon my tea before I've forgotten my dinner, and there always seems something indecent in that . . .'

'I don't suppose I shall get any tea,' Arthur ruminated morosely. 'I'll still be on the train.'

'It wouldn't hurt me to do without it either. I think I've eaten quite enough for one day already. I have to think of my figure.'

'Yes, I think of your figure quite a lot as well,' Arthur said experimentally, affecting a gleam in his eye.

'Oh, well, we know what you are thinking, don't we?'

'I daresay we do, and what's wrong with that?' He looked at her with annoyance over her predictable response.

'Well, thinking can do no harm, I suppose. It's the doing that causes the problems. And there's not much chance of you actually *doing anything*.'

'Shall I come to Bristol next week?' he asked, changing the subject. 'Or would you like to come to stay with Mother and me?'

'Oh, I'm not going to stay at your house, Arthur. The place gives me the creeps, it's such a shambles. I'm sure I should pick up fleas. I hardly slept last time I was there, wondering

322

how long it had been since that bed I was made to sleep in had been changed.'

'It was changed just before you arrived,' Arthur answered defensively, cut to the quick at her contempt for his home. He was well aware their house was no palace, that it was unkempt, but it was not up to Dorinda to say so, and she should show more tact. He could say what he liked about the place, but she could not, and she should not take for granted that she could.

'Well, it didn't seem like it,' she went on. 'If you want me to stay there again get your mother to clean the place up. Or employ a maid to do it. I'm sure you can afford it. I shan't come otherwise.'

'The trouble is, Dorinda, I don't think I can afford to travel to Bristol and back every week. Not if I'm trying to save.'

'Are you trying to save?'

'I think it's sensible, don't you?'

'Not if it stops us being together on Saturdays and Sundays I don't.' She strutted on, her pretty nose in the air in her indignation. 'So not only do I have to give you up week nights, I have to give you up Saturdays and Sundays as well. You might as well be the man in the moon, Arthur.'

They sauntered on without speaking for a while.

'You are very dull this afternoon, Arthur,' Dorinda claimed derisively, breaking the silence. 'And I can't abide dullness in a man. You've hardly spoken this afternoon, except to mumble a few responses. Is it because you are sad that you won't see me for a week or two?'

'I don't know.'

'Oh, I do wish you wouldn't say "I don't know" when I ask you things. It annoys me to death. I'll ask you again . . . Are you upset because you won't see me for a while?'

'Yes,' he responded, taking the easy way out, and so avoiding a further chastisement.

'Well, you have a strange way of showing it, that's all I can say.'

'Do you love me, Dorinda?' Arthur asked directly.

'When you deserve to be loved, of course I do. You know I do.'

'Then you have a strange way of showing it as well. You are a beautiful girl, Dorinda, full of high spirits and good company most of the time, but I ask myself sometimes whether you're capable of deep affection.'

'What a thing to say!' she exclaimed haughtily. 'I love you to distraction.'

'But I think you love yourself more.'

'How can you possibly say such a thing, Arthur?'

'Because if we were to get married, you've already said that you would not have children.'

'I hate the little blighters. I hate the thought of childbirth.'

'And because having children would spoil your figure, you said.'

'Yes, that as well,' she pouted.

'So you're thinking only of yourself. You're not in the least concerned with what I'd want. And I've decided . . . I'd want children . . .' He transferred his travel bag to his other hand, causing Dorinda to change sides and take his other arm. 'Furthermore, I'd expect to do in bed with you what normal young married couples do, and as often as I wanted . . .'

'Arthur, you are the limit! I really don't think I shall walk any further with you if you are going to be so indelicate.'

'Well, I can quite manage the rest of the walk on my own.'

'I don't know what's got into you, Arthur Goodrich. I never heard such things before in my life. Ever since you went back to Brierley Hill you haven't been the same. I think the Black Country air has addled your brain, I really do.'

'Well, maybe that terrible accident did it,' he said evenly. 'All that suffering I saw, all that agony. People dying before my eyes just because they were in the wrong place at the wrong time, other people grieving over their dead relatives. Maybe that's had an effect on me. Because when I hear you harping on about how having a child might upset your figure, I think just how pathetic that is compared to what the poor victims of that accident suffered. It's plain childish talk, Dorinda. Anyway, I won't stand for it. So, if you have any hopes of us ever getting married, you'd better change your tune.'

Dorinda looked at him in speechless astonishment.

★ ★ ★

23

Low, racing clouds, ominously dark, threatened to jettison their cargo of rain, but so far that September morning they had contrived to hang on to it. The wind had freshened and turned, swaying the tops of the tall elms, ripping away twigs and leaves not due to fall for some weeks yet. Roses and other late flowers, lovingly placed on neighbouring graves, were violently spun and twisted as the wind caught them in its restless commotion.

The slow march of railway men in uniform, shouldering Dickie Dempster's coffin, solemnly made their way to the neat oblong hole in the ground that waited to receive him. They passed Arthur Goodrich and Lucy Piddock who stood together yet apart from the chief mourners, thinking their own thoughts, alternately pondering moments of pleasure the deceased had provided and the pain he had inflicted. The vicar, unknown to either Lucy or Arthur, conducted the service at the graveside, his white surplice rippling over his cassock in the wind like a flag of surrender to the overwhelming bluster.

Arthur had his arm around Lucy's waist to comfort her. As she leaned against him for support she tried hard to shed tears, for she felt that she ought; but no tears came. She had no more tears left to cry. God knew she'd spilled enough already. She watched the coffin, which held what remained of the man who'd said he would marry her, being lowered into the grave, and recalled the first time she had ever cast eyes on him, and her instant love. Oh, it had been love at first sight all right, but such downright folly. Conflicting feelings of regret, love, anger, and grief were tormenting her, and had been from the moment she knew of his already being wed. Her heart had been broken, her soul had been violated, but her anger would surely be the healing salve. The bitter frustration she felt was unappeasable, as unappeasable as the giving of herself to a man who never could have been hers was futile. Little wonder she could not weep at his funeral.

Lucy resented more than anything the irrevocable changes in so many lives Dickie's death had wrought, changes that were attributable only to him. Yet she also resented this unexpected, tragic end that made a nonsense of everyday living. However much of a rogue Dickie had turned out to be, two children had depended on him, and they presumably loved him and looked up to him simply because he was their father. Those children did not deserve to be left to the whims and devices of an unsympathetic social system that might see fit to incarcerate them, wrenching them from their mother's care and placing them under the dubious custody of some workhouse, especially if it was believed she could not now afford to look after them without a man's wage being brought in.

As the funeral service drew to a close Lucy at last felt a tear roll down her cheek. But it was a tear for herself, for the doubts, the misgivings, the wasted love she'd given Dickie Dempster which, unbeknownst, had been spurned anyway. It had taken the catastrophe of a railway accident and his death to reveal the truth, but the truth had not come in time to save her. There had been other women; she knew one of those women was called Myrtle. But that was all she knew. Yet that knowledge never prevented her from loving and trusting him, even though it had anguished and plagued her beyond measure.

When the heavy earth thudded onto the lid of the coffin

Lucy slumped against Arthur, belying her anger and frustration. He held on to her tightly. Caring, dependable Arthur, who had once been hers for the taking but who plainly she did not deserve. In her hand she was already holding a small lace handkerchief. She dabbed the tears that were stinging her eyes, and felt a squeeze of sympathy from him. She looked out across the churchyard, saw Dickie's widow and felt a great surge of sympathy for the woman. Mrs Dempster seemed to be bearing her loss well, with grace and dignity. Neither did she appear to shed a tear, to Lucy's amazement.

Lucy paid no heed, however, to another young woman carrying a child in her arms, no more than a spectator standing at a discreet distance from the proceedings, also with a grace and dignity that belied her own anger, her own frustration and sadness. But Arthur saw her . . . and wondered . . .

The service was over and people began to drift away. The wind gusted once more, and Lucy held on to her black bonnet with one hand and held her shawl clutched around her neck with the other. Arthur smiled anxiously at her, uncertain of how acute and confused her innermost emotions might be. He simply saw beautiful tear-filled eyes, yet he had no doubts as to her suffering, and led her away before the other mourners reached them.

Some day – Lucy did not know when, but when it no longer hurt nor angered her to think of Dickie and what might have been – she would return to this churchyard and lay flowers on his grave.

★　★　★

From St Barnabas's churchyard Lucy and Arthur made their way back to Wednesfield Heath station, owned and run by the Grand Junction Railway, where they took an omnibus back to Low Level station. They conversed little. He knew she was best left to her thoughts uninterrupted, and that she would speak when she felt like talking.

Low Level station held so many poignant memories for her, memories of Dickie meeting her there on Saturday afternoons before taking her to the Old Barrel at Boblake, and their delicious love-making sessions in that upstairs room. It also reminded her of the unpalatable fact of his marriage, and that he wilfully seduced her to satisfy his own lusts, to boost his own ego, knowing that he could never marry her, yet never allowing her to know it, never giving her the opportunity to walk away. And yet she wondered: even if he had told her, would she have walked away?

Eventually they boarded the train. At that time of day it was hardly crowded and they had a compartment to themselves, in which they sat opposite each other next to the windows.

'I'm glad that's over,' Arthur said as they pulled out of the station, hoping to begin a conversation that might divert Lucy.

Lucy nodded glumly. 'I'm glad you took me. There were quite a few women there.'

'Yes.'

'His wife didn't seem to shed a tear that I saw. Did you notice, Arthur?'

'Maybe she's done plenty of crying already.'

A pause. Lucy was fiddling with a piece of thread sticking out from a finger of her glove. She stopped, and looked up at Arthur.

'You never told me Dickie had died, Arthur, but you must've known.'

He regarded her guiltily. 'Yes, I learnt it at the inquest. To tell you the truth, I couldn't bear to be the one to break it to you. I knew you'd hear about it anyway, since it was announced at the inquest.'

'Thank you.' She nodded and returned to her stray thread. 'I understand.'

'I went to see Mrs Dempster the day after . . . to offer my condolences.'

'That was thoughtful.'

He shrugged. 'She told me one or two things . . .'

'Oh, what about?' At once there was an urgent curiosity in Lucy's eyes.

He shrugged again, not at all certain how to proceed, not at all certain that he should. 'Oh, about their married life . . .'

She looked at him expectantly, but he stalled. 'What about their married life?'

'Oh . . . their children . . . how Dickie was not particularly close to his side of the family.'

'But he always told me he *was* close to them.'

'Maybe he lied . . .'

'Maybe he did,' she allowed. 'He lied about other things, why not that? But I can't imagine why.'

'To deceive you? To use them as the reason he couldn't see you when really it was his wife and two children that held him back?'

'His wife and two children!' Lucy repeated with resignation. 'It might be hard for you to believe, Arthur, but I feel sorry for his wife and two children. I imagine *she* loves her children like any mother would, but if the authorities think she can't look after them, they'll very likely put them all away in the work-house, and she might never see them again.'

Arthur gulped. 'I never thought about that, Lucy. D'you think they would?'

'They could, I suppose. I suppose it depends whether she's got any family that can help them.'

'And how much compensation she's entitled to,' Arthur speculated. 'She's got a mother, but I don't know whether the woman could afford to take them in or keep them.'

'Course, I suppose she'll get some compensation from the railway company, him being on their books,' Lucy conjectured.

'Some, maybe, but Dickie wasn't on duty at the time of the accident. He was travelling as a passenger.'

'He told me he had to work on the journey back.'

'But he lied about that as well, didn't he?'

'Lord knows what he didn't lie about . . .' Tears filled her eyes again. 'Oh, what have I done, Arthur?'

He leaned forward and took her hands in his. 'You fell in love, Lucy. Love excuses all.'

She looked into his eyes with an earnest expression. 'Oh, Arthur . . . You are so good, so understanding . . . Why didn't I fall in love with you, instead of falling in love with *him*? You'd have been so much better for me . . . for everybody . . . I rue the day . . .'

'Life is never that simple, Luce,' he replied consolingly. 'We all have to experience pain so as we'll appreciate better the good times when they come.'

'The good times seem a long time coming . . .' She sniffed and forced a smile for him, pushing back tears. 'What did Mrs Dempster tell you about her marriage?'

'It was told to me in confidence, Luce. I'm not sure that it'd be fair for me to say.'

'I see.'

The train rattled over a bridge and Lucy peered out of the window. In the lane beneath, a man was thrashing an ill-kempt horse that was hauling a four-wheeled cart loaded with metal pails.

'I can tell you she wasn't happy,' Arthur revealed after a pause, drawing Lucy's attention again. 'Dickie had been having affairs with different women all their married life. She knew about them.'

Lucy was filled with horror. 'Did she know about me?'

He shook his head and smiled reassuringly. 'She'd sussed he was having an affair, but she doesn't know it was you. No, she believes you are engaged to me, remember?'

331

She smiled again, sadly. 'He was forever telling me about a girl called Myrtle. Harking back now, I suppose it was to make me jealous. Did she know about Myrtle?'

Arthur nodded. 'She knew all about Myrtle . . . Myrtle had Dickie's child . . .'

'Myrtle had his child?' Lucy's face was an icon of wide-eyed astonishment.

'Yes. There was a young woman with a child in arms at the funeral. Did you see her? She looked to be the sort that Dickie would fancy. A bit like you. I reckon it was Myrtle.'

'I didn't notice anybody . . . Oh, Arthur, just what have I done? I've ruined everything. I've ruined my life, yours, hers . . . everybody's . . .'

'Well, Luce, just count your blessings that you haven't ended up like Myrtle . . . that you haven't ended up with another of Dickie's bastards to contend with. Then it could truly be said that he'd ruined your life.'

She did not have the mettle or the heart to tell him that indeed her life was already ruined, and that soon it must start to show.

★   ★   ★

When she returned home, Lucy saw that her mother was not there and made straight away for her little bedroom that overlooked fields towards Audnam and Wordsley. She laid her shawl neatly over the bedrail, placed her bonnet on a chair, and took off her boots. As she eased herself onto her bed and lay down her mind was filled with little incidents which had occurred while she and Dickie had been together, many of which had amused her at the time, though now they seemed so trivial. She stared blankly at the whitewashed ceiling and wished with all her heart that she could turn back the clock.

In one of the drawers of a chest was a small albumen print of Arthur, mounted in a brass frame. He'd given it to her when he'd had his likeness taken early on in their courtship, mistakenly thinking she might cherish it. Ever since, however, it had lain in the drawer forsaken and unseen. She got up from her bed and retrieved it, gazed at the photograph through misty eyes for a long time, then clutched it to her and lay down again. She started weeping once more, but this time whispering Arthur's name to herself. When the flood of tears abated she fell into a light but troubled sleep.

Hannah came in and roused her. Tentatively she asked her if she wanted any dinner. When she saw her distressed state she put her motherly arms around her to console her, and succeeded in making her worse.

'I knew from the beginning as that Dickie Dempster was a scoundrel,' she said. 'Your father couldn't abide him either.'

'I'm not crying over Dickie,' Lucy retorted through her tears. 'I've done crying over him.'

'Well, and I'm glad you'm done with it so soon, our Lucy.'

'I'm crying over the damage as I've done to everybody, the hurt I've caused, by being drawn in by him. I've been such a fool, Mother. *Such* a fool . . .' She sobbed again, and Hannah gently stroked her daughter's hair. 'You can't imagine how I feel, Mother . . . I'm bereaved because I've lost the man I really did love, but I hate him for what he's done, and I'd like to punch him on the nose. And yet he isn't here to punch . . .' She screwed her eyes up and clenched her fists in anger and frustration. 'And I feel so riled and so foolish . . . Everybody must be talking about me behind my back.'

'Sticks and stones,' Hannah consoled. 'Even if they are, it don't matter none. But I don't think as folk am talking about you – not nastily. I think they feel your pain. There's very few of us go through life without making big mistakes. It's how we learn our lessons. And the bigger the mistakes, the better we learn not to repeat them.'

'Well, if folk aren't talking about me now, they soon will be,' Lucy said, drying her eyes and sighing, ready for her big confession.

Hannah looked at Lucy warily, half dreading, half expecting what was about to break.

'I'm carrying Dickie's child, Mother.'

Of course, Hannah had already considered the undesirable possibility. She had carefully thought through the problems and consequences of such an eventuality so, to some extent, she was prepared for this admission. She looked at her daughter with sympathy and understanding, and gave her a squeeze. 'I wondered if you were.'

Lucy was expecting a tirade of calumny and revilement from her mother, but all she saw in her eyes was compassion and understanding. 'Aren't you going to rant and rave at me, and tell me what an evil whore I am?'

Hannah took her daughter's hand and stroked the back of it. 'Why should I do that, our Lucy?'

'Because of what folk will say. Because of what your friends at the chapel will say, especially behind your back.'

Hannah sighed. 'Sticks and stones again. Folk can say what they'd a mind, but you're my daughter, and 'cause you're me own flesh and blood I shall always be here to look after you . . . And woe betide anybody who has the effrontery to say anything about you, either to me face or behind me back.'

Lucy smiled her astonished thanks. 'Oh, Mother, it's such a weight off my mind to hear you say that. But what about my father? Will he feel the same as you?'

'Don't think as we ain't talked about it happening, our Lucy . . . Your father will be no different to me. There but for the grace of God would be a damned good many young wenches, and some not so young. Your bad luck, our Lucy, is that you've got ne'er a fellow to make an honest woman of you.'

'Nor am I ever likely to get one,' Lucy replied. She picked up the picture of Arthur again and studied it for a second or two. 'I had my chance with him . . .' she nodded at the frame.

'But I let him go, certain that my contentment lay with Dickie Dempster . . . Oh, I do wish I could turn back the clock, Mother . . .'

'Yes, it'd be a handy skill to own if you could do it. Just think of all the clocks you'd be turning back. You'd have a full time job going round to everybody's houses, turning back their clocks so as they wouldn't fall into the same traps as they fell in afore.'

'I could put an advertisement in the Brierley Hill Advertiser,' Lucy grinned, warming to the welcome absurdity. It made such a quickening change to be so nice and silly after all the weight of grief and anguish of the last few days. 'I'd make my fortune putting folk back on the right track by turning back their clocks and returning them to a point in their lives just before they made a big mistake.'

Hannah smiled, having allowed Lucy to indulge in her nonsense long enough. 'But in this life there's no turning back clocks, our Lucy. Clocks can only move forward, and we have to move forward with 'em. You'll have to move forward with your child, when it's born. It'll re-shape your life and no two ways, but you won't resent it for a minute. You'll love it, the same as any mother loves her child, whoever the father is. And we'll be behind you, your father and me.'

'Oh, how can I thank you, Mother?' Lucy beseeched. 'I've been dreading telling you I was carrying for fear you threw me out.'

'Why would we want to throw out our own daughter at a time when she most needs us? Who in their right mind could be so heartless?'

'It just makes everything so much easier to bear, knowing that you don't condemn me.'

★ ★ ★

At the inquest next day the jury heard evidence from the guards. Frederick Cooke was named as the head guard on the

335

excursion to and from Worcester. There was much technical evidence about the state and quality of the shackles that had broken and why passengers had been allowed to travel in the guards' vans. Cooke himself then gave evidence for some considerable time before the inquest was again adjourned to the following week.

Arthur resumed his working at the business of which he was now an equal partner. He and Talbot agreed to retain the trading style of Jeremiah Goodrich & Sons, Monumental Masons and Sepulchral Architects, since it was already well established and recognised as such. At once Arthur wanted to advertise in the local news sheets for a skilled letter cutter and an apprentice. Within a week they had employed Shadrak Beardsmore, a Gornal man who gladly walked the three miles there and back every day. Shadrak would be the person sent on letter cutting expeditions to cold and remote churchyards in lieu of Arthur.

Arthur was delighted to renew his friendship with Moses Cartwright, and was pleased to learn that Moses too was making headway with his masonry skills. In his more idle moments he had watched Talbot at work and picked up some of his techniques and was allowed to apply them on straightforward tasks. Arthur believed Moses had a latent gift and began to encourage him, calling him over to watch how he performed certain things.

'You and the new apprentice can learn together, when he arrives,' Arthur suggested as he washed his hands after a day's work.

'Aye, as long as he's the one to brew the tea and not me,' Moses replied. 'Unless the poor bugger has only got one leg like me, and then we'll do turns,' he added with typical good humour.

'Talking about folks with one leg, Moses, have you seen much of Lucy?'

'Why? She ain't got one leg now, has she? She hadn't last time I looked.'

Arthur grinned tolerantly. 'I mean, that Dickie Dempster she was courting would've had one leg if he'd survived the accident. That's what reminded me to ask about Lucy.'

'Lucy seems to be getting over things well enough. But *him* I never liked him.' Moses shuffled agitatedly on his crutch. 'Our Jane used to insist on us pair visiting me sick aunt in Priestfield of a Wednesday night, just so as young Lucy and that Dickie bloody Dempster had got somewhere warm to do their courting.'

'Well, that was thoughtful of her.'

'Oh ar, it was thoughtful as regards Lucy and him, but he warn't very bloody thoughtful in return – he only ever thought of hisself. Why, when I used to get into bed of a Wednesday night it was still warm from them pair . . . And still bloody wet sometimes.'

'You mean . . . they used to go to bed together?'

'No two ways about it.'

'Lucy?'

'Course Lucy. Who d'you think?'

'With Dickie Dempster?'

'Course with Dickie Dempster. You know when some-body's bin in your bed, Arthur.'

'I never thought she was like that.'

Moses gave a hollow laugh. 'I tek it as you never poked the wench then . . .'

'No, I never did any such thing. I never thought she was like that, so I didn't press my luck. I don't think she—'

'Pity, that's all I can say. What did I tell you that time we talked about it? I said if you didn't start poking her somebody else would. And I was right, 'cause that Dickie was poking her up hill and down dale.'

'I don't think I want to know any more, Moses. Spare me the vile details.'

'That's a tasty bit o' fluff you got now though, Arthur, eh?

That piece from Bristol. I hope as you'm poking *her*. I bet she's a heap o' fun between the sheets, eh?'

'Oh, she's a heap of fun,' Arthur repeated absently, neither confirming nor denying the suggestion.

'Christ, you could make a pig o' yourself with *that*, I'll be bound.'

It was unlike Moses to show disrespect, but Arthur could forgive him easily enough, for he didn't believe he meant any. It was just his way, his camaraderie, no doubt the kind of talk that went on between soldiers in the Crimea when they were all billeted together. Arthur should have resented his loose talk, especially when it was about Dorinda, but his thoughts were on what he'd just learnt. So he just smiled absently and took his leave of Moses, preoccupied with mental images of Lucy in bed with Dickie Dempster.

★　★　★

24

Dearest Arthur,

I considered it best to wait a day or two before writing, to punish you after your little outburst while we were walking to Temple Meads. I do hope you have calmed down by now and are duly ashamed of the appalling way you spoke to me. You upset me so much I cried nearly all the way back home in that hansom. Indeed Mother was convinced we had fallen out for good, I was so upset. I know how much that dreadful accident has affected you and I can understand why, having myself seen it happen and heard the horrid crash. But I do think you should consider my point of view from a perspective that does not involve the accident. I fail to see what not wanting to have children has to do with a railway crash, so I am giving you the benefit of the doubt because I think it has affected your powers of reasoning. To say that my not wishing to go through childbirth is trivial compared to what those poor accident victims suffered is not a fair comparison. I <u>choose</u> *not to have children if we ever get married; those poor people did not* <u>choose</u> *to be involved in that accident. That is the difference.*

I suppose I am presupposing a great deal here again though, since of course you haven't yet asked me to marry you, even though we have talked about it a number of times. I've a good mind to break with convention entirely and ask you, but my mother would castigate me for being a hussy, and I suspect that you would offer a whole host of excuses that you are too busy with the new partnership or you have an inquest to attend or a cricket match to play in. Frankly, I don't see why you have to attend any more inquests since you gave your evidence at the first one, and surely the cricket season is coming to an end now that the nights are drawing in so.

It has crossed my mind to give you an ultimatum – that we make arrangements to get married by this time next year at the latest. Although I agreed to your going into partnership with Talbot, it is a peculiar sort of courtship we must endure because of it. I see no point in us remaining eighty or ninety miles apart when we can be together. Anyway, it's something we can discuss when you come to stay with us the Saturday after next. Of course, I hope the partnership works out well. It will provide such a stable base for our future prosperity together.

Tomorrow I am going riding with my friend Bunty Fisher who I was at school with, whom you have not met. My mother said that she would like to come too, but I told her there isn't a horse in the county that could bear her weight for more than a few minutes at a time, and that I thought it best that she relinquishes all such vain notions at once and concentrates on her household duties. She seemed to quite take the hump at that. Clearly, one cannot speak one's mind without somebody getting all upset about it, which I deem to be very immature on the part of some people, namely Mother.

Cyril says that Mr Pascoe is looking for another stonemason to fill the vacancy you created when you left. But it is such a skilled craft, I know, and I doubt whether he will fill it quite as quickly as he would like. Of course it means extra work for Cyril, but with the nights drawing in now he cannot usefully work very late. I mean, it would be terrible if he chipped the nose off Saint Peter or St Paul as they lurk petrified above the main door, just because it was too dark to see what he was doing. Mr Pascoe would have something to say about that, I'm sure.

I must close now, Arthur. Mother is about to call us to table for our meal and my father must have already changed and put on his good shoes, for I can hear him clumping around upstairs. I await your letter with longing and hope you will be able to write to me by return of post. I am so looking forward to seeing you again (even though I have been so angry with you in your absence), and to giving you a long juicy kiss under our porch, so please hurry to me and let's make up.

Your ever-loving and long suffering sweetheart,
Dorinda.

★　★　★

Arthur wasted no time in visiting Isabel Dempster to discuss with the young widow her requirements for a grave for her late husband. He decided that Saturday afternoon after work might be an appropriate time. He would strip down to the waist and wash, thoroughly spruce himself up and generally sweeten himself in readiness, and be in time to get the five past two to Wolverhampton. He had mentioned nothing as yet to Talbot about his plan to bear the cost himself until such time as Mrs Dempster could afford to pay, once her compensation had been settled.

Rather than waste money on a hansom, he took the first omnibus to Wednesfield Heath station and sniffed the robustly disagreeable stench that emanated from the neighbouring night soil lagoon. From there, he walked to Frederick Street. The weather was not much to shout about, dull and dreary, but the high winds had eased since the day of Dickie's funeral.

Isabel Dempster, wearing a plain but becoming black day dress, was talking to a neighbour in the back yard when he arrived and was quick to explain who Arthur was, to allay at

341

once the possibility of any mischievous and speculative gossip. Evidently she was pleased to see him and invited him in. She explained that the children were at her mother's again, and sat beside him on the settle.

'I've brought some drawings for a few graves so you can see the sort of designs I thought might be suitable,' he began, and reached down for the case he had taken with him, to get them out and show her.

'I'm deeply indebted to you, Arthur,' she said sincerely, and leaned over towards him in anticipation of having a peep at them.

Arthur opened out a detailed sketch he'd done. 'This would look very impressive in polished black granite with gold lettering . . .' She shuffled along the settle and inspected the drawing over his shoulder, her shoulder familiarly pressed against his from behind, her bosom pressing into his arm. Arthur found her warmth and proximity not only very disconcerting, but also extremely pleasant . . . as was the spontaneity of his erection. 'It could be just as effective in white marble with blackened letters, though,' he struggled to utter with any conviction. 'Course, if you preferred something less extravagant . . .'

She turned her face to him and smiled, her eyes sparkling, attractive creases at the corners of her smooth lips. 'Oh, yes, something a bit less extravagant I think, Arthur. After all, why should I reward Dickie with such a handsome tombstone after the way he treated me and all his other women?'

'That's your prerogative,' he replied, stumped for any other reply.

'Well, wouldn't you?' she asked. 'I mean, if it was your wife who'd been killed and you knew she'd been having affairs with various men, and you couldn't be sure that the children she'd had were yours or somebody else's, wouldn't you think twice about spending a fortune on her grave?'

342

'If I knew it for certain, I suppose I would be a bit reluctant.'

'I would, Arthur. And if, as a result of her love affairs, she withdrew her favours from you at bed time as well, would you not be even more inclined to have her encased in a grave that was less than flamboyant?'

'I'm sure I would.'

'Then you understand how I feel . . .'

'I think I do,' he agreed.

'Oh, Arthur, I truly feel that I can confide in you, that I can discuss anything with you . . . Anything . . . My innermost feelings.'

'I'm flattered.'

'Dickie and I never could discuss intimate things. That's how it was, because of his affairs. He only wanted me between affairs. My children were conceived on such occasions as that. Now that he's gone . . . now that he's dead and buried, I feel as if a weight has been lifted from my shoulders and it's such sweet relief.' She linked her arm through his as they sat together and his erection pushed insistently against the material of his trousers, mercifully hidden beneath his drawing. 'For the only time ever in my life I feel free . . . You know, Arthur, I began to resent so much his other women that I used to shrink at his touch. I just couldn't bear him to touch me. Now that's not the kind of woman I am. Such a pattern of behaviour is contrary to the way God made me. I'm a loving and passionate woman, you know, Arthur, given the chance to show it with a man I can love and respect.'

Arthur felt his throat tightening and swallowed hard to lubricate it. 'I'm sure you are, Isabel . . . Shall we er . . . look at another idea I had for Dickie's grave?' His voice seemed high-pitched with constriction.

'Yes . . . Forgive me for pouring out my troubles . . .'

'Oh, there's nothing to forgive, Isabel.' Feeling inordinately hot, he opened out another drawing. 'I feel flattered that you should confide such secrets to me. I feel flattered that you're able to tell me things that are so . . . so private . . .'

'I should be equally flattered if you were to confide such things in me as well, Arthur. You know, I feel very close to you . . . Do you mind if I am very honest with you, Arthur?'

'No, course not.'

'The truth is, I'm drawn to you. Please don't mind me admitting it. But it's wonderful to feel that there's somebody after all who you can share secrets with. Especially a man.'

'I . . . I feel drawn to you as well, Isabel,' Arthur hesitantly admitted with a tentative smile, urged on by the obstinate ferment going on inside his trousers. 'I shouldn't, I know . . . I have a sweetheart who loves me . . .' An image of Dorinda flashed into his mind, and then he realised that Isabel knew nothing of Dorinda. As far as Isabel was concerned his sweetheart was Lucy, whom she had met. And then, for no accountable reason, pictures of Lucy and Dickie romping naked all pallid and white in Moses's bed invaded his consciousness. Wouldn't it be ironic, and such poetic justice, if he and Isabel were to engage in similar activities? But vindictiveness was not a word that existed in his vocabulary. In any case, his mind was running too fast, his imagination was far too wild in thinking such outrageous thoughts, no doubt driven by his insistent erection.

'Do you and your sweetheart ever . . .?' She failed to finish the question to enhance its meaning.

'Ever what?'

'Well . . . I mean, do you share a bed at any time?'

He gulped. 'Lord, no . . .'

'No? How can she keep her hands off you, Arthur?'

'Off me?' he queried, confused by such a notion. 'Well, she manages to quite well.'

Still overlapped behind him, Isabel rested her chin on his shoulder. He could smell something very fragrant on her,

344

some perfume perhaps. Very pleasant. Strands of her rich brown hair were tickling his cheek.

'Arthur, you know I'm not grieving over Dickie. You know I'm content to see the back of him, although I would've preferred that he hadn't been killed, that he might just have run away and left me, with one of his women. I don't see any reason at all for the customary two years of mourning over *him* – not inwardly – although I'll have to be seen to abide by it outwardly, I suppose. I fancy kicking my feet up. I swear, when this grave of his is finished I shall dance on it . . . and if you want to dance on it with me, I'll welcome you with open arms.'

Arthur turned around to better see her face, induced by the innuendo in her last phrase. She was smiling, all her admiration for him blatant in those clear expressive eyes of hers. On impulse he leaned his head towards her and kissed her on the lips, a brief but very telling kiss.

'That was nice,' she remarked, evidently surprised.

Arthur could feel the blood coursing through his veins. 'I'm sorry. I shouldn't have done that. Lord, I don't know what came over me . . . You've been a widow not five minutes. I should be ashamed taking advantage like that. I didn't mean any lack of respect.'

'Lack of respect? Ashamed? Is that what you feel just because you kissed me? And so nicely? I feel flattered, Arthur. I feel no disrespect, only admiration . . .'

'There's another person I have to consider, Isabel,' he heard himself say. His conscience was fighting back, damn it.

'Lucy . . . Oh, yes.' She lowered her eyes and he was moved by the way her long lashes rested with such femininity on the curve of her cheeks. 'I keep forgetting about Lucy.'

Again he was plagued by the image of Lucy and Dickie in bed. He lifted Isabel's chin and their eyes met. Slowly, deliberately, almost defying his own nature, he tilted his head

345

to kiss her again. This time they lingered. Isabel's lips on his felt so soft, so cool and so pleasant, and he felt that inexorable stirring in his loins again that usually left him feeling so empty and so frustrated once the excitement had been thwarted by Dorinda's innate prissiness. They broke off and Isabel changed her position on the settle, so that she was sitting beside him but with her back towards him. Then she leaned back and he had no alternative but to take her in his arms. They kissed again, and there was no doubt where this was leading.

'What time are your children due back?'

'When I fetch them.'

His heart was pounding, his head throbbing as they kissed again. Encouraged by her responsiveness, his hands roamed over her breasts, skimming over the material of her dress. She offered no resistance. He took a peep at her and saw that her eyes were closed, concentrating on extracting maximum pleasure from his lips. There was something about her. Oh, there was definitely something about her that stirred him. He was helpless in her arms, lost, unable to resist, despite the guilt he felt over deceiving Dorinda; guilt which was inexorably decreasing in direct proportion to his increasing desire.

'I want you, Arthur,' Isabel breathed into his ear. 'Oh, I've waited so long for you.'

'For me?'

'Yes, for you. We have an affinity, you and me. Two lost souls who have found each other. I knew it from the moment I first set eyes on you. For years I've known that eventually you'd come along. I never dreamed that it would take Dickie's death to bring us together, but somehow, somewhere there was always you.'

'You know what real love is all about, Isabel – in bed, I mean. You've been married . . . I'm no dab hand at that sort of thing, having never been wed.'

'Well, you don't have to have a diploma,' she smiled.

'There's not a fat lot to it. Some folk reckon it's overrated anyway, but it's something that drives us all, whether or no. It's the point all lovers have to get to, to be real lovers.'

'I'd like to get there with you,' he whispered.

'Then let's not wait any longer,' she said softly, an appeal in her eyes.

She swung her feet to the floor and stood up, holding her hand out to him. He needed no second bidding, took her hand and allowed her to lead him up the narrow twisting staircase to her bedroom.

Dickie's bedroom. The *late* Dickie's bedroom.

There were two doors off, which opened into two smaller bedrooms, the children's. In her room stood a wardrobe, a dressing table with a mirror, a piece of embrioidery or a sampler of sorts adorned one wall, and a podged rug lay at the foot of the inviting brass bed. She sat on the edge of the bed and bade him sit beside her, her eloquent eyes following him minutely.

'Have you never been with a woman before then?'

'Never,' he answered honestly.

'Goodness, how dull for you.' She smiled warmly. 'I suppose there has to be a first time for everybody. But does the prospect of being taken the first time by a recently bereaved woman put you off?'

'Not since that woman is you, Isabel. I wouldn't be here if it did. Anyway, you make yourself sound like an old woman, which plainly you're not. I believe you're younger than me.'

'How old are you, Arthur?'

'Twenty-seven.'

'I'm two years younger. I met Dickie when I was eighteen.'

'I wish I'd known you when you were eighteen.'

'I wish you had as well.'

She tilted her head and allowed him to kiss her again. It was a hungry, searching kiss. Never had he kissed a woman like

347

this before, so ravenous was he for her, and her avid response lit him up, increasing his desire.

'Let's undress ourselves and slip into bed,' she whispered tantalisingly. 'Can you unhook the back of my dress?'

She turned her back to him and lowered her head. He fumbled with the hook and eye, more intent on admiring her slender elegant neck and the fine little hairs that populated it below the mass of her dark hair that was swept up and pinned up on top of her head. But in a few seconds he had undone the dress, and she thanked him. Tenderly, he kissed the back of her neck, sending a shudder of pleasure up and down her spine before she stood up to undress. He watched mesmerised as she slipped off her black dress and it lay like an inky pool around her feet till she bent down and scooped it up, to lay it over the chair which stood at her dressing table. He began undressing himself, unable to take his eyes off her as she undid ribbons and buttons, took off her petticoats and chemise and removed her stockings. As she stood before him naked and quite unabashed, he was moved by the sight of her breasts like full peaches, by the smooth firm skin of her midriff, the gentle feminine curves of her waist and her hips and the perfect triangle of dark hair. Her thighs were slender and unblemished and he saw how smooth and perfectly round were her buttocks.

She leaned forward to pull back the bedclothes and got into bed. Then, she threw back the sheets on his side as an added enticement, and he slid in beside her acutely conscious of his wagging erection and attempting vainly to hide it from her vision. At once they were in each other's arms and the feel of her warm, smooth skin, her breasts pressed against him, was the most glorious sensation he had ever experienced.

'Kiss me,' she breathed, and he kissed her.

While their lips were interlocked, his hands roamed the soft contours of her body at random, and he thought his

348

overworked heart would burst from its relentless pounding, pounding, pounding. He ventured south and located that delicious mound of soft warm hair. She uttered a little sigh of pleasure as he gently advanced beyond it and tentatively rubbed her between her thighs at her delectable butter-soft place, which made his fingers all wet and slippery.

'Don't stop,' she whispered earnestly.

He bent his head and ran his mouth over her breasts, and could smell the sweet, musky, natural scent of her body, a delight he had not anticipated. He lingered at a nipple before he eased himself gently upon her. She parted her legs to accommodate him and reached down for him, took him in her hand and guided him into her with a little gasp of pleasure. They rocked together slowly, tentatively at first, experimentally, as if they were both first time lovers, probing, sensing, appreciating the sweet sensations they provided for each other. In his lack of experience, Arthur too soon reached his climax and instinctively moved to withdraw. Isabel, with her greater experience, anticipated him and held him close, pulling him hard into her, denying him exit.

'No, Arthur,' she sighed. 'I want every last drop of you.'

He groaned with the ecstasy and agony of profound orgasm, their rhythmic movement unstoppable, increasing in intensity until Isabel was sighing vocally and repeating his name over and over.

She finally rested, also spent. 'Thank you,' she said.

They lay joined for some time afterwards, silently hugging and squeezing. Arthur did not know what was expected of him, so was glad to take his lead from her. He was content to lie quietly, still connected, until his wonderful erection subsided and he flopped out, which was the cue for each to come out of their reverie.

'I wonder what the time is?' he remarked.

'Why? Do you have to rush off to see Lucy?'

'No, not particularly.'

'Good. Then I'll go down and make us a cup of tea.'

'I'll come with you.'

She flashed him an impish grin. 'You mean, you're done with me so soon? You're casting me aside so early?'

'Not if you don't want to be.' He grinned in disbelief, for he'd reckoned that to have suggested more would have appeared greedy and ungrateful.

She shook her head, almost shyly, as she sat up. 'I think you have a lot of catching up to do, Arthur . . . But then, so do I . . .'

'Isabel, why did we never meet when you were eighteen and I was twenty?'

'Next week,' she said softly, looking up at him intently as they stood together by the back door. They were pressed against each other, holding hands at their sides. 'Can you come next Saturday afternoon again when you've finished work.'

'But I'm supposed to be going to Bristol next Saturday.'

'Oh . . .' Genuine disappointment registered in her eyes. 'Then come for tea on Sunday and meet my children.'

'I won't be back by then . . . No, I'll come Saturday,' he said decisively, realising he would have a lot more fun and derive a lot more pleasure here than he would with Dorinda. 'Hang it, I won't go to Bristol. I'll come to you instead.'

She smiled her gratitude. 'Oh, Arthur . . .' she sighed, and snuggled up to him. 'I'll make sure Julia and Jack are at my mother's again . . .'

'Well, I don't suppose it would do to let them see their mother with another man so soon after their father's death.'

'Not only them,' she said. 'We must be very discreet. Nobody must know about us. Not just for the sake of my reputation, but yours as well. You're engaged to be married, remember, even though it pains me to acknowledge it. You're promised to somebody else.'

He was tempted to admit that it was actually a lie, that he was not engaged after all, but he sensed that somehow, for her, it added to his appeal in the sense that stolen fruits taste sweetest. So he did not deny it. Let her believe it. For the time being it could do no harm. And besides, if he denied that Lucy was his intended, Isabel might begin to wonder what the girl was doing attending Dickie when he was first injured, and he was keen to protect her from any insinuations.

★   ★   ★

Sunday 12th September 1858

Dearest Dorinda,

I am so sorry that you cried in the hansom on your way back home from Temple Meads. I certainly didn't intend to upset you that much. But, for the life of me, I can't understand your argument about you <u>choosing</u> not to have children and the victims of the railway accident <u>not</u> <u>choosing</u> to be victims. I don't understand your logic. All I meant was that you worrying over childbirth was petty compared with what those poor folk suffered, and I still think it. Nothing will change my mind. It also applies to me. My toothaches and chills that I used to moan about are nothing compared to that.

Also, I don't know what you are trying to achieve by setting a time for a wedding as an ultimatum. I presume that if I don't agree, then you wish to break off our courtship. Why the rush? I'll ask you to marry me when I'm good and ready, if at all. Not when you issue me with an ultimatum.

Anyway, I can't get down to Bristol as we'd planned. Talbot and me have far too much work. It's amazing how the deaths from that accident have meant us picking up new orders for graves. It only wants another outbreak of cholera and we could make our fortunes, if only we could cope with the orders. So I'll try to get to Bristol the week after if I can. The invitation would still stand for you to come to Brierley

351

Hill but for your silly notion that you'd pick up fleas. I never picked up a flea from my bed in all my life, only ever from that stupid old dog of ours. But it's your decision.

Keep well, and give my best to Cyril, and your mother and father.

Arthur.

★ ★ ★

25

All the following week, Arthur could not expel thoughts of Isabel Dempster and the two hours they spent together. Not only was she constantly on his mind when he was awake, but he also relived their passion over and over in his sleep, wakening from his dreams every morning with an ardent and renewed desire for her. He could scarcely believe what had happened, or that she should find him so irresistible. At the same time it concerned him that a woman so recently bereaved should allow it to happen. Maybe *he* should not have allowed it, maybe he should have been more honourable, holding her mourning in greater reverence, but he felt he'd had little choice. At the time, though, he'd had very little inclination to stop it, and even less courage, since it all seemed to have occurred at her initiative.

He wrote again to Dorinda, motivated by guilt.

My dear Dorinda,

I think I was a bit too short with you in my last letter and deem it fit that I apologise. Nothing would ever induce me to be mean to you and upset you, and I don't know what came over me. I hope you will forgive me. Anyway, when I see you on the 25th you can scold me for being so vile and I will accept it willingly, knowing that I fully deserve it. I am due to arrive at ten to six, so I hope you will be at the terminus to meet me.

Talbot sat on the jury again when the inquest was

resumed yesterday. I attended myself for a short time but when it was obvious they were not going to call me into the witness stand again I left. Talbot told me what had gone on and it doesn't look too good for that head guard, Frederick Cooke. All evidence suggests that he failed to put the brake on to try and stop the runaway coaches, but they say he was sober for all that. The engineers ran some experiments, letting the same number of coaches containing the same weight as the excursion train run free down the incline, and applied the brake at different times. Each time the coaches were pulled up before the place where the crash happened. It certainly suggests Cooke did not do his job, and he jumped out of the guards' van before they crashed.

Of course I miss you, Dorinda, and I am looking forward to seeing you. Give my fondest regards to your mother and father and Cyril.

Yours very affectionately,
Arthur.

★ ★ ★

Despite feelings of guilt, Arthur could hardly wait till next Saturday when he was due to visit the extraordinary Mrs Dempster again. He arrived with more sheaves of designs for her dead husband's grave as his decoy.

As soon as she closed the back door behind them she slid the bolt across and they were in each other's arms. In less than five minutes they were in her bed, which put paid entirely to his feelings of guilt.

On this their second session, he was even more hungry to learn from such a comely young woman, who had acquired her experience so respectably in the marital bed. After their initial earnest embraces, he decided to let her make the running and lay submissive, contentedly yielding to her whims and fancies. She kissed him lingeringly all over, teasing him with her tongue and her soft lips till he was aching with desire.

354

Then there was the blissful moment of contact when she slithered her naked body across him slowly, like a cat stalking her prey, and their bodies aligned. She wriggled her hips to line him up for a perfect, well-executed entry that had them both gasping.

As they writhed together in glorious synchrony, he imagined for a few private, experimental moments that he was Dickie Dempster. What a lucky fellow Dickie had been in so many ways, having unfettered access to this woman who was so desirable and responsive. Yet he had spurned her for others. Those others must have made her worth the spurning. Lucy, for instance. What would it be like in bed with Lucy? Dickie had obviously found her entertaining. Would she be as deliciously pleasing as this woman, his widow, whom he was enjoying now for all he was worth? For that matter what would Dorinda be like?

Isabel raised herself on her arms and looked down at him, her dark hair falling in loose waves around her face. The expression in her wide eyes told of the fun she was having. Clearly, she was enjoying herself, which was, in itself, something of an eye-opener to Arthur; he had only ever suspected that women did this sort of thing under sufferance. That a woman should manifestly relish the sexual act suggested to his limited imagination somehow that she was debauched. He pictured the outwardly pious women he saw at church and tried to imagine them doing what Isabel was doing to him right then, and with such abandon. He tried to imagine Dorinda again, that Isabel was Dorinda, but it was not an illusion he could easily feign, because he realised that for Dorinda the whole business would be far too messy and distasteful. Lucy, on the other hand . . .

'I've waited a whole week for this,' Isabel murmured softly into his ear through strands of her own hair.

She lowered her face and kissed him tenderly, her nipples

lightly touching his chest, tickling him. He pulled her to him, so he could better feel the fullness of her breasts against him, then gripped the cheeks of her bottom, drew her hard onto him and thrust more vigorously into her. It was wickedly pleasant, this, virtuous or no. It was evidently no less pleasant for her. Somewhere deep inside he was aware of that familiar tingling. Did women get this same irresistible tingling too? It began to glow, intensifying, and he groaned at the exquisite sensation radiating from the depths of his groin through his entire body, from head to toe.

'Don't stop,' Isabel sighed, on the cusp of ecstasy. She increased the speed and intensity of her rhythm, maintaining it until she emitted a series of whimpering moans and slumped upon him, spent. Strands of hair, wet from perspiration, clung to her forehead and her flushed cheeks as she nuzzled her face into the curve of his neck with a deep sigh of contentment.

'Thank you, Arthur,' she whispered.

'There's no need to thank me,' he responded after a moment pondering her gratitude, which seemed misplaced.

'Oh, but there is.'

'Why? I don't understand.'

'Because you give me such pleasure.' She wriggled on him, still joined, to emphasise what she meant.

'You still don't have to thank me . . . Did Dickie give you pleasure?'

'Not often enough. He was too stuck on his ladyloves to worry about me.'

'I reckon he must've been mad.'

She wiggled her bottom again and kissed his chest. 'Do I give you pleasure, Arthur?'

'Lord, yes.'

'It *should* be pleasurable . . . For both of us.'

'I never realised that women got as much pleasure from it,' he said after another pause.

'Why shouldn't they?' she asked, feigning indignation that he should consider it a male-only entitlement.

'I don't know. It seems too sinful. I always thought women were supposed to be pure and chaste.'

She laughed, amused at his naivety. 'Like how we fondly assume our mothers to be, you mean?'

'I suppose so.'

'But even our mothers were young once, Arthur. And I daresay they were given to the same pleasures as us, once they'd got the taste for it. It's human nature.'

'I can't imagine my mother . . .'

'Not even on her wedding night? Nor for weeks and weeks after till the novelty had worn off? How do you suppose you came to be born? By immaculate conception?'

He smiled, acknowledging his ignorance of women, and stroked her hair. 'I suppose not.'

'Course not.' She slid off him and lay at his side, turned towards him, her hand gently fondling his belly. 'It's just possible that your mother enjoyed it too. Anyway, just because something is pleasurable, does it follow that it must therefore be wrong, sinful, as you suggest? Who cares anyway if it is? It's only sinful when you're unmarried and anybody finds out. What two people do together away from the prying eyes of the world is up to them, I would've thought, married or not. And nothing to do with anybody else. Besides, we're not hurting anybody.'

'My sweetheart would be hurt.'

'Then don't tell her. What the eyes don't see, the heart doesn't grieve about. Anyway, I haven't asked you to give her up for me, have I?'

'No . . . Would you want me to?'

She fingered the tiny hairs that populated his chest. 'Only if *you* wanted to. But I wouldn't dream of pressing you . . . I like you, Arthur, but there are other things to consider first anyway.'

'What things?'

'My children, for instance. You're still a single man. You might not take to my children. They might not take to you . . . Anyway, you wouldn't want to fall into the trap of marrying a woman out of lust, just because you enjoy bedding her, would you? And living to regret it when you grew tired of her . . . and her children . . .'

'This feels like more than just lust to me.'

She looked into his eyes, smiled, raised her head and kissed him on the mouth. 'You're a romantic, Arthur. This is a lovely way to spend a Saturday afternoon, but let's not fool ourselves that we're in love.'

'How d'you know I'm not in love?' he asked.

'I wouldn't like to think you're that susceptible and so easily diverted. Anyway, you're in love with your sweetheart.'

They remained silent for a few minutes, each contemplating this conversation and all that it implied. Arthur's mind had traversed to another aspect of this relationship with Isabel that had been troubling him, and he broke the brief lull.

'One thing worries me about you, Isabel.'

'Oh? What's that?'

'What are you going to do for money without Dickie's wage coming in?'

'Go on the streets, very likely,' she said with a little chuckle.

'You wouldn't! I wouldn't let you.'

'I didn't mean it, Arthur. It was a joke.'

'It wasn't a very funny joke. Jokes are meant to be funny. So how shall you manage?'

'I don't know yet. I'll have to find work of some kind, maybe with my father . . . Unless I can tempt some widower with more money than sense to marry me . . .' She chuckled saucily.

'Would you do that?'

'Yes, if I liked him enough.'

'But that'd be like selling yourself, Isabel.'

'That's what women do. All the time. Why do you think women get married? Because they're in love?'

'Aren't they?'

'Some, yes, but not all. Some get married so that they can be kept, and the more comfortably the better. In return, they are expected to give themselves wholly. Those that do have to put up with certain things they might find unsavoury, but they're generally prepared to go along with it, else they wouldn't subject themselves to a marriage of convenience.'

'Not all marriages are for convenience. Isabel. I would only marry somebody I loved.'

'But you're a man. *And* you're a romantic. But then, you can afford to be . . . You're not an impoverished duke or earl who needs a handsome dowry to restore his fortunes . . .' She paused and raised herself, resting her head in her hands, and resumed gently fingering the tiny hairs on his chest. 'I envy the girl you will eventually marry, Arthur, because I know you'll make her an excellent and loving husband . . . And I know she'll love you just as much as you love her.'

'I don't know about that, Isabel . . . Anyway, I want to help you with money. To help you keep your children.'

'I won't take money from you. Good gracious, are you trying to turn me into a whore? Your whore?'

'Course not.'

'But that's what I'd be. Oh, Arthur, I have too much pride to let you do that, and too much faith in myself.'

'I only said I wanted to help. You can't stop me helping you if I want to. Anyway, what if you had my child after all this?'

'If I had your child that might be different.'

'Then we'd have to marry.'

'If convention had its way,' she commented evasively.

'Would you want to have my child?'

Isabel sighed. 'You do ask some questions, Arthur. I

359

wouldn't be afraid to have your child if it ever came to it, in or out of wedlock. I'm old enough to know that what we're doing could cause me to have a child, of course, but it's a risk I don't mind taking because I've never been hidebound by rigid convention. Anyway, there are ways and means of avoiding pregnancy . . .'

'I wouldn't want you to have a child of mine out of wedlock . . .'

'That would be up to me.'

'I would expect a say in the matter, Isabel.'

'You could say what you liked.'

'Lord above, you're an independent madam, aren't you?'

'I'm headstrong, Arthur. It's what kept me going when Dickie was having his affairs.'

'Tell me about how you got to know him.'

'There's not much to tell really. My father was an apothecary in Wolverhampton – and still is. I used to work for him sometimes in his shop, at busy times. One day Dickie came in for something – Dover's powders, I think it was, for his sister – and we got talking. Oh, he was such a charmer . . . He asked me to meet him sometime, so I did and we started walking out regularly . . . And that was it. I fell for him . . .'

'Did your folks approve of him?'

'Not at all. His family were nothing, after all – harpies, some of them, although I didn't know it at the time – whereas my father was considered something in the town, being a respectable trader. But, you see, my father didn't know me half as well as he thought he did. He tried to stop me seeing Dickie, which only succeeded in fanning the flames of my love for him. I suppose he believed I would lose interest in Dickie and give him up. But of course, I didn't. He failed to realise I was headstrong enough to defy him and elope.'

'And you call me romantic. So how soon was it that Dickie started messing about with other women?'

'Looking back now, I think it was from the start. I'm sure now, that there was another girl he was seeing right at the beginning. Eventually, I fell out of love with him, as I told you, tired of playing second fiddle to his love affairs, tired of competing. But I was still trapped in this house with his children. Now that sounds awful, Arthur, but in truth the children were the only saving grace. His death has been an escape for me, and I'm not sorry it's happened, even though that might sound callous. It's why I can't grieve. It's the reason I'm content to lie here with you so soon after his death. Not because I'm a strumpet particularly – although you might think I am, Arthur – but because I detected in you something that Dickie lacked. I wanted to get to know you better and find out what it was. I quickly realised that you are a gentle, caring man and I wanted you to make love to me. I wanted to feel cared for, for a little while.'

'And I wanted you, Isabel. From the moment you entered that room at the Whimsey where Dickie lay injured, I wanted you.'

'Do you want me now?' she said softly, looking at him with an impish gleam in her eyes.

'Again, you mean?'

'Yes, again, Arthur.'

'I think I can manage it.'

'Bless you. Then you can be on top this time . . .'

★ ★ ★

Because Arthur was due to go to Bristol the following Saturday, he arranged to visit Isabel Dempster on the Wednesday evening prior. Her children had been put to bed by the time he arrived so he had no opportunity to meet them. They made love on the hearth rug in front of the fire, not risking her bed in case either Julia or Jack woke up and happened upon them, for they were prone to sneaking into her bed if they woke up, Isabel explained.

So, Saturday arrived and, when he had finished work, eaten and washed, Arthur made the journey to Bristol and Dorinda, taking a bag containing his things. He was in half a mind to confess about Isabel and be done with it. He was not sure that he could carry off deceit in the way Dickie Dempster had, but it struck him how like Dickie Dempster he had become, with two lovely women in his life. For Arthur, it certainly was quite a novelty. All his adult life he'd struggled to win the admiration of one woman, let alone two. How life had changed. So he decided he would not tell Dorinda, but make the most of his duplicitous good fortune. Since his self-confidence was much higher these days than ever before, he might even attempt to seduce Dorinda if the opportunity presented itself.

Dorinda was at the station to meet him off the train. She was wearing a new shawl, an emerald green bonnet and dress that complemented the titian of her hair and matched her eyes. She smiled hesitantly when she saw him step down from the carriage, their argument and the subsequent coolness of his letters inhibiting her from rushing to him. So she waited until he had spotted her, and waved.

'Hello,' she greeted simply when he reached her.

'You look pretty,' he remarked, smiling, reminded at sight of her just how beautiful she was, rekindling his admiration and interest. 'I haven't seen that outfit before, have I?' He gave her a brief kiss.

'Oh, of course you have, Arthur. I've had this dress ages – the bonnet too. It just goes to show you never take any notice of what I'm wearing. I could wear an oilskin hat and hobnail boots, with gentlemen's breeches up to my armpits as well, and I swear you wouldn't notice.' She smiled affectionately, glad to see him, and took his arm as they walked out of the station.

'Yes I would,' he protested. 'That shawl. That's new.'

'Oh, you noticed that. Wonders will never cease. Yes, it's

new. Mother said I should have it to cheer me up, after you were so horrid to me. It's Parisian cashmere.'

'Not British?'

'Why should I wear common Manchester goods?'

'Because I can't believe that foreign goods, especially French, are better than British.'

'Well, you don't wear shawls, Arthur, so you're not likely to be able to tell the difference.'

'Except in the price. What's wrong with a shawl from Norwich or Paisley, if Manchester's too common?'

'As long as my father can afford to buy me better and more exclusive shawls, that's what I shall have. Are you going to be argumentative all day and evening, Arthur? If so, I shall leave you here to wait for a return train.'

'Oh, in that case, I'll try to behave,' he answered sarcastically.

'Have you had a good journey?'

'Till I changed at Didcot. Then this woman got in my compartment with a screaming brat.'

Dorinda made no comment about the screaming brat. To comment about a child might have been to invite another disagreement about children in general, and the bearing and birthing of them in particular.

'How are your mother and father?' he enquired.

'Mother gets fatter by the day, and father gets thinner. She got herself wedged in the door of an omnibus last Wednesday.' Dorinda rolled her eyes in scorn. 'It must have been mortifying for her, but it didn't stop her devouring an enormous dinner that same evening. You'd think she must've starved all day she ate so much, but I know very well that she ate half of a huge pork pie as well at midday, *and* a great *wodge* of fruitcake at tea.'

'I'd hate to follow her into the privy.'

'Oh, don't be so revolting, Arthur. I hate you talking like that. It's my mother your referring to.'

'It was your mother *you* were referring to.'

'But she's *my* mother, so I'm allowed. You're not. Especially comments of a sanitary nature.'

'Or insanitary, as the case may be.'

'Arthur, you don't like it if I say things about your mother. Look how you jumped down my throat when I mentioned that I might pick up fleas in your house.'

'Then if we have fleas, like you suggest, maybe I've got one of 'em in my drawers, which I shall transfer to the bed I sleep in at your house.' He defiantly scratched his backside for effect.

'Then you'll have to be fumigated.'

'It was a joke, Dorinda.'

★ ★ ★

Dinner at the Chadwicks' house that evening was a little more sumptuous than usual, in honour of Arthur's visit. They had roast beef done to perfection, with roast potatoes and apple pie to follow. Before the meal they drank amontillado, which had lain in their cellar for years and, during it, Mr Chadwick dispensed two bottles of claret he'd bought specially for the occasion. So by the time the meal was over, Arthur was feeling a little light-headed.

Conversation afterwards was frivolous, but the family decided at about half past eleven that it was time for bed, since church would beckon next morning.

'Have a glass of whisky with me before you go up, Arthur,' Cyril suggested.

Arthur agreed, and Cyril poured him an ample measure. They talked about work on the church of St Mary Redcliffe, about their craft, and how Arthur's partnership with Talbot was proceeding. While they conversed, their words becoming more slurred, Arthur's mind began to wander, his thoughts as ever these days turning to Isabel Dempster and their delicious love-making sessions. He knew better than to mention her to Cyril, however. Close friend as Cyril was, he was still Dorinda's brother, and blood was materially and metaphorically thicker than water. But Isabel would not go away, and Arthur decided it was time he went to bed anyway so he could contemplate her undisturbed, and maybe even dream about her, in the quiet and privacy of his bedroom. So they finished their drinks and retired unsteadily with a lamp each to light their way.

Arthur undressed himself tottering about, inebriated. But persistent thoughts of Isabel had cursed him with a serious erection that would have been admirable at the appropriate time. He stood naked, eyeing it by the glow of the oil lamp, and pushed it down speculatively with the palm of his hand. But it sprang back again with the resilience of some defiant, erotic jack-in-the-box. Arthur looked inanely around the room for something to flick into the air with it, but saw nothing, so he put on his nightshirt. The protuberance, shrouded beneath the material, stuck out majestically before him. When he half closed his eyes it was the bow of a clipper, and he was seeing it from the top of the foremast.

He blew out the lamp, pulled back the sheets and blankets and flopped falteringly into bed, still contemplating Isabel. There he lay for a full half hour or more, wide awake despite the drink. His troublesome erection showed no signs of subsiding. Of course he could masturbate, but such self-gratification was not only wicked in the extreme and almost certainly injurious to the health, but it was impolitic as a guest in somebody else's house; he knew from experience that ejaculation was difficult to control from a directional aspect, especially in the dark, unless smothered in some sort of absorbent material, his nightshirt, for instance.

So he decided to creep along the landing to Dorinda's bedroom. She, after all, had not had the benefit yet of his sexual expertise, and it was time she had.

He swayed from side to side along the landing conscious of, but ignoring, the creaking floor boards that might easily have given him away. In the darkness he found the door and tried the knob. It turned with a metallic clunk and the door sprung ajar. Breathing rather heavily by this time in anticipation of a sublime first coupling with his beautiful and deserving sweetheart, he closed it behind him, and the same metallic clunk registered that it had shut properly. The fullish moon shed an appreciable amount of light into the room and he could see Dorinda asleep in bed, her hair loose and flowing over her pillow like an inky flood. She was angelically beautiful in the silvery light. The décolletage of her fashionable nightgown gave a tantalising glimpse of the soft curve of her throat and her creamy breasts, and he imagined how delightful it would be to nuzzle his face in their spongy smoothness.

Stealthily, he slid into bed beside her, anxious not to alarm her. Slowly, he inched his way towards her, and could feel the enticing warmth of her body radiating towards him. While she had been sleeping, her nightgown had ridden up, so that when his thigh came into contact with the bare flesh of her long legs his head was throbbing with the promise of the sensual delights that were now his for the taking. His hand ventured to her bare thighs and luxuriated in the silky sleek feel of smooth, feminine skin slightly moist from her natural perspiration. Encouraged, he roamed smoothly upwards and reached her mound of soft hair. She stirred, turned towards him and sighed, and his heart pounded with anticipation. He lifted his nightshirt so that the hem was around his chest, to better appreciate her body when hers was likewise up around her breasts at their coupling. Then he leaned forward and kissed her on the mouth, such a gentle sensual kiss.

She opened her eyes and emitted a piercing scream. There was man in her bed. She screamed again.

'It's all right,' he whispered. 'It's only me.'

'You?' she shrieked. 'What do you think you're doing in my bed, for goodness sake?'

'I mean to make love to you.'

'What? I never heard anything so scandalous. Have you no shame? Have you no regard for my honour? Get out at once.'

'Shh! You'll wake everybody up.'

'I don't know what's got into you, Arthur Goodrich,' she pronounced, her tone a mixture of alarm and anger. 'Ever since you've returned to Brierley Hill you've changed for the worse. Please get out of my bed and go back to your own at once.'

But it was too late. The door opened and an oil lamp flickered, illuminating the concerned face of Dorinda's father.

'What is going on in here?' he rasped, seeing Arthur leaning on his elbows in his daughter's bed. 'For goodness sake! Arthur, how dare you abuse my hospitality by behaving like this, by sneaking about in my house and invading my daughter's bed.'

'I'm sorry, Mr Chadwick.'

Mrs Chadwick loomed large and wide behind him, a ship in full sail in her white nightgown. 'Oh, my goodness gracious!' she uttered in panic. 'It's Arthur . . . Oh, Lord! Has he penetrated her, John?'

' 'Tis to be hoped not indeed. How dare you abuse my hospitality,' he ranted again, 'and my daughter to boot!'

'I never touched her, I swear, although I admit it was my intention.'

'What if he's made her pregnant?' Catherine Chadwick shrilled, overwhelmed with angst. 'Oh, my goodness.' She threw her arms up in her anguish. 'The shame! The shame!'

'I never touched her,' Arthur repeated, his voice a high-pitched whine. 'I swear, I never touched her.'

'I'll never be able to live this down,' Mrs Chadwick whined with intensifying melodrama.

'Arthur,' John Chadwick pronounced ominously, 'I am going to have to ask you, in view of your abominable behaviour and your thoughtlessness in compromising my daughter, to either marry her at the earliest opportunity, or leave my house forever, never to darken my doorstep again. Perhaps you would like to return to your room and stay there till morning, when we shall decide what is to be done.'

'Has the maid heard anything, do you think, John?'

'It is to be hoped not indeed, my dear. Because if she has, there can be only one outcome to this fiasco . . . And I'm not so sure any more that I relish the prospect of Arthur Goodrich as a son-in-law, having manifested such overbearing disrespect.'

★   ★   ★

Arthur slept little that night. As the effects of the alcohol wore off he grew ashamed of what he had done. He was full of remorse, having never intended to show any disrespect to his hosts, who had always treated him with the utmost kindness. Indeed, they had welcomed him almost as one of the family. He would offer his sincere and abject apologies for his drunken behaviour to John and Catherine Chadwick, and for the suffering he had caused them. As for poor, innocent Dorinda, he owed it to her to formally request her hand in marriage after all, if she would still deign to have him.

Grossly unsettled, he arose early, washed and shaved in cold water and went downstairs. He could hear the maid at work. She entered the room and set about lighting a fire where he was sitting preoccupied, absently turning over the pages of a county journal.

'Morning, Jenny.'

She bobbed a neat curtsy. 'Mornin', Mr Goodrich.' She spoke with a pleasant Gloucestershire burr. 'It's a chilly one this mornin', don't you reckon?'

'In more ways than one,' he commented wryly, and

returned to the journal while Jenny raked out the ashes from last night's fire and laid another.

'Did you sleep well, Jenny?' he asked.

She looked at him askew from under her mobcap. 'Oh, aye, sir, I always d'sleep well. Runs in my family to sleep well, so it does. My father, God rest his soul, worked on a collier, but he often used to miss the sailing for want of waking up in time. He could never get his back off the bed. My mother reckoned as he nailed himself to it somehow.'

Arthur nodded his understanding.

It was a dull morning with dark rolling clouds that threatened rain. Jenny lit the fire, and held a draw tin to it then, when she was satisfied it was alight, she left the room. Presently, John Chadwick came down and Arthur was charged again with apprehension at what faced him.

'Good morning, Arthur,' he said stiffly. 'I trust you slept well after your nocturnal adventure?'

'I didn't sleep at all, Mr Chadwick.'

John Chadwick raised his eyebrows scornfully. 'And little sympathy you'll get from me.'

'I'm truly sorry for what happened last night, Mr Chadwick. Truly, I am. I had too much to drink, and in my inebriation I mistakenly believed I was entitled to something that clearly I'm not . . . not yet anyway. But nothing happened. Believe me, Mr Chadwick, nothing at all happened. It frightened Dorinda the moment I slipped into bed beside her. That's why she screamed out.'

'All the same . . .' John looked at him squarely. 'You intended to take a liberty with my daughter. And would no doubt have done, had we not intervened, possibly using rape as your method—'

'No, never,' Arthur protested vehemently. 'I'd never stoop to that.'

'Well, I'm glad to hear it. But so far I only have your side of

369

the story. I am interested to hear what Dorinda has to say on the matter.'

'She'll tell you the same as me, sir.'

'I sincerely hope so . . . Do you love my daughter, Arthur?' John Chadwick asked after a brief and chilly pause.

'Er . . . Yes, sir. I suppose I do, sir.'

'You suppose you do?'

'Yes . . . I do. Course I do.'

'Do you respect her?'

'Course I do.'

'Then why did you see fit to violate her?'

'I was drunk, Mr Chadwick. I told you . . . And I didn't violate her. I only thought to violate her.'

Suddenly, there was a violent scream from upstairs. There was no mistaking Dorinda's frantic shrieks, familiar after last night's dismal episode. John and Arthur rose from their chairs at once and looked with alarm at each other. They heard her footsteps as she rushed down the wooden stairs in her bare feet, still howling in a wild panic. She entered the room. Her hair was unkempt, her face bore a look of horror. She looked at Arthur with wild, angry eyes.

'I am *covered* in fleabites,' she caterwauled. 'Thanks to you, Arthur Goodrich, I am literally covered in fleabites, and shall be scarred forever . . .'

26

At two o'clock on Thursday October 5th, Arthur and Talbot made their way together to the Bell Inn to attend the further adjourned inquiry into the cause of the late railway accident near Brettell Lane. As usual, it was held before T.M. Phillips, Esq., Coroner, and the jury, previously empanelled, of which Talbot was a serving member. Mr Sherriff the general manager, Mr Adcock the secretary, and Mr Wilson the engineer, all of the Oxford Worcester and Wolverhampton Railway were present, along with other notables, legal advisers and church ministers. The verdict was due, and was awaited with considerable interest in Brierley Hill.

The Coroner called upon Frederick Cooke, the guard, and enquired if he had any statement to make about his evidence, which had been read over to him.

Cooke replied that he had no other statement to make.

The Coroner then proceeded to sum up, and directed the jury to the evidence of the various witnesses which had been brought before them. He read over the depositions of the witnesses, describing the excursion, the accident, and the causes which led to it, and the various expert opinions given.

'Now, gentlemen, that is all the evidence that has been taken before you at this enquiry. I must beg of you to divest your minds of anything that you may have heard out of this room, and return your verdict only on such evidence as has been taken on oath before me.' The Coroner rambled on in his legalese, then went on to say, 'Almost all the scientific men agree in thinking that if Cooke had applied his brake in a proper manner when the carriages separated at Round Oak Station, he would have stopped the train and prevented the collision, and avoided the deaths of the several persons who are the subject of this enquiry. If you believe that Cooke could have stopped the train in the ordinary performance of his duty on that occasion, and did not do so, Cooke would be guilty of manslaughter. It is for you, gentlemen, to consider what is your verdict. You have heard the evidence, and if there is any question you want to ask me, I shall be happy to answer you. Perhaps you would like to consider your verdict in a clear room?'

Several of the jury agreed that they should, so the Coroner and jury then retired at four o'clock. Two and a half hours later, they returned.

'What is your verdict?' the Coroner enquired.

The Foreman stood up. 'We are unanimously of the opinion that a verdict of manslaughter be returned against Frederick Cooke.'

There was a murmur of resignation at the outcome among those attending before Frederick Cooke, the guard, was called.

'Frederick Cooke,' the Coroner said when the man appeared, regarding him over the top of his spectacles. 'The jury, after carefully considering the evidence in this case, has returned a verdict of manslaughter against you. Therefore you stand committed.'

Cooke stood stock still, head bowed, accepting his fate.

In the streets afterwards excitement prevailed. A number of people had lingered for hours before the end of the inquest, evidencing their deep and abiding interest in the result. Arthur and Talbot, along with others who had attended, made for the taproom of the Bell Hotel to quench their thirsts, and chew over the day's events.

★　★　★

It was in the middle of November when Lucy Piddock decided to risk a trip to St Barnabas's churchyard in Wednesfield Heath to place some flowers on Dickie Dempster's grave. One of the patrons at the Whimsey, George Bakewell, a keen rose-grower, had boasted that he still had some that were in bud and Lucy asked if she could buy a bunch. She collected them on Saturday afternoon, before catching the train to Wolver-hampton.

The weather was bleak, but she was prepared to suffer it to pay a final homage to the man she had loved and lost. As she rode in the train her mind was full of Dickie again and the times they had shared. Lucy had come to accept his fate and hers, and was largely at peace with herself and the world. The heartbreak of losing her love had been mollified, the anger she'd felt over being cheated and used had been quelled. Dickie had brought her misery, he had also brought her joy albeit temporarily. But his most useful legacy was that of inducing her to ponder the hard realities of loving and living, which finally brought her to her senses. Now she realised the mistakes she had made, the immaturity of which she was guilty, her blind impetuousness and defiance of everybody's advice and goodwill. It was this gift in particular which she wanted to thank him for now. Placing flowers on his grave was something she would do only once, a token not just of her gratitude, but of the love she'd given him. It would undeniably be a test of her strength also.

She stepped from the train at Low Level station and walked past the bench she used to sit on while waiting for Dickie. It was a poignant moment. As she left the shelter of the station's blue brick hulk she readjusted the shawl around her shoulders and made for the omnibus that would take her to Wednesfield Heath. She took a seat and placed the bunch of roses on her lap, hoping she could remember the way to the church when she'd alighted. Soon, she heard the scrape of horses' hoofs and felt the omnibus lurch forward on its way.

Finding the church and its graveyard presented no problem, but Lucy struggled to recall exactly where the grave was located. She scanned the churchyard to get her bearings and believed she had a notion of where it might be. As she made her way along the rough earth path towards it, past the monumental graves of the expired wealthy, she could see a workman who seemed to be digging a grave for some less affluent soul. On Saturday afternoons many people had to work. As she got closer she could see that it was no ordinary workman. His stance and the way he moved were agonisingly familiar; it was Arthur Goodrich, whom she had not seen for some weeks. What was he doing here?

She was in two minds whether to go on or run away. What would he think of her, after all that had been said, if he realised she had come all this way to put flowers on the grave of a man who had caused her so much misery? Then he turned, and saw her.

'Lucy!' he called amiably. 'Fancy seeing you here.'

He smiled, that unassuming smile of his, which had the combined but contradictory effects of putting her at her ease and making her heart flutter. Only Arthur could do that. She smiled back and waved, and approached him with a quickening step.

'What brings you out here on a cold day like this? Come to pay your respects to Dickie?'

Rumbled, she held the bunch of roses she was carrying defiantly in front of her. When she first saw him she'd half-hidden them under her shawl, but now they usefully disguised her growing belly.

'I came to lay these on his grave,' she admitted.

'You'll be able to in a minute or two,' he said with no hint of condemnation for what he might perceive as sentimentality.

'I've all but finished it. Your Moses, and Shadrak Beardsmore, that other chap we've got working for us, brought the grave over here this morning on the cart and put it together. I was just putting the finishing touches to the inscription.'

'You been cutting the letters on it?' she asked, surprised.

'Yes.'

'Fancy.'

'I know. It's ironic, don't you think, that me, who thought I'd progressed beyond cutting letters, should be carving the inscription on the grave of the chap who pinched my woman.'

'I don't mean that,' she said. 'I'm just a bit surprised it should be you, when there must be perfectly good monumental masons in Wolverhampton who could do the job.'

'But Mrs Dempster asked me to do it, when she knew I was a monumental mason.'

'I see . . . So let me read the inscription . . .'

He stepped aside, giving her a clear view.

' *"Richard Dempster born 28th October 1830, Died 31st August 1858 as the result of a tragic railway accident. Guard on the Oxford Worcester and Wolverhampton Railway, husband to Isabel, father to his children"*.' She looked at the verse carved below in smaller letters and began to recite it slowly.

> *'Life's railway's o'er, each station passed,*
> *Between death's buffers I rest at last.*
> *Farewell dear friends and do not weep,*
> *In God's guards' van I'm safe, I sleep.'*

'It's a good poem, Arthur,' Lucy commented. 'But don't you think it's a bit sarcastic?'

'Not sarcastic, Lucy. Just slightly irreverent. I think he would've appreciated it.'

'Maybe he would've. Who made it up?'

'Isabel and me.'

'Fancy *Isabel* asking you to do his grave,' she remarked, emphasising Mrs Dempster's Christian name and the fact that he was on first name terms with her. 'And helping her to compose his epitaph. You must have seen something of her over the past few weeks.'

'Yes, course.' He felt his colour rise.

'How is Mrs Dempster? Is she bearing up?'

'She's bearing up very well. Much better than anybody thought she would. But then she has good reason not to grieve.'

'Yes, I suppose so.'

'I've only got to clean up the letters, Lucy,' he said brightly. 'Listen, I've got a bottle of tea in my bag. I daresay it'll be cold as ice by now, but would you like to share it with me? You're welcome to.'

She smiled graciously. 'Thank you.'

'Here, you might as well sit down on the grave.' He made room by shifting his trankelments over, then took the bottle of tea from his tool bag and sat beside her. He drew the cork out. 'There's a tin mug in here somewhere . . .' He ferreted around with his free hand. 'Here it is.'

'Thank you,' she said again when he'd filled the mug and handed it to her. She drank the cold tea, smiling at him with her lovely eyes over the rim of the mug. 'You have the rest,' she said, handing it back, still more than half full.

He took it and quaffed some of what remained. 'I haven't seen you for a bit, Lucy. Have you been keeping well?'

'Yes, thank you,' she answered, as if she wasn't really sure. 'How about you?'

'Yes, I'm all right.'

'How's the new partnership with Talbot working out?'

'Oh, it's good. I'm glad we did it. We get on well. I'm much more content than I used to be?'

'And how's the beautiful Dorinda?'

He shrugged. 'I don't know.'

'You don't know?' she queried with astonishment.

'We sort of parted.'

'Oh, Arthur, I didn't know. I had no idea. Are you hurt? Are you upset?'

'Upset? No.' He laughed reassuringly. 'It was for the best.'

'What happened? Do you want to tell me?'

'I sort of disgraced myself . . .' He gave a mischievous chortle.

'How?'

He told her. He told her how he'd invaded her bed when he was drunk and was caught red-handed by her father. He made it sound hilariously funny, and Lucy chuckled.

'It's just your luck to do something like that and get caught,' she said. 'So then what happened?'

'Well, because I'd compromised his daughter, Mr Chadwick said as I should either marry her or leave their house come morning, never to return.'

'So you left?'

'Well, I didn't intend to. I was sorry for what I'd done, making a fool of myself and all. I intended to do the honourable thing and ask Dorinda to marry me, so that everybody would be satisfied. But, unbeknownst to me, I'd committed an even greater sin in Dorinda's eyes. She came screaming down the stairs before breakfast covered in fleabites. She was adamant the fleas were off me and that I'd transferred them to her bed when I got in it. She called me all the names under the sun. Lord knows where I picked up fleas from, the train most likely, but I never got a fleabite anywhere. Anyway, she said what with that, and me sneaking into her bed in the middle of the night like some demented Casanova, she never wanted to see me again. So I packed my bag and left . . . And I haven't heard from her since . . . Nor do I want to.'

'And you're not upset?'

'No, I'm not upset, Lucy. I was beginning to realise she wasn't the girl for me. She said if we ever got married she never wanted children—'

'I know, I heard her say it once.'

'Well, if I ever get married, course I'll want children. To be honest, it's hard to see how you'd stop 'em, barring never coupling, and that wouldn't do for me.'

'Nor me either,' Lucy agreed.

He looked at her with added interest at that response, but made no comment.

'Would you ever consider marrying a girl who'd already got a child?' she asked experimentally.

'It would depend.' He was reminded of his discussion with Isabel on this very subject. 'A widow, maybe,' he hinted with a shrug. 'Who can tell? A lot would depend on whether I could take to her children, I reckon.'

She nodded but decided not to investigate the issue. Instead, there was a topic she did want to discuss. 'Listen, Arthur . . . There's something I want you to know . . . I've been meaning to tell you for ages . . .'

'What?' He swigged the rest of the tea. 'Fancy a drop more?'

'If you've got some left.'

He poured the remainder of the contents of his bottle into the mug and handed it to her. She thanked him and drank.

'So what do you want to tell me?'

'Oh . . . that I'm . . . having a child . . .' She lowered her eyes, unable to look at him.

'You?' he snorted disdainfully. 'You're carrying a child? Whose?'

'Whose d'you think?' she returned, indignant. 'Dickie's.'

'Oh, Lord above!' he exclaimed, and there was no mistaking the contempt in his tone. 'So how far gone are you?'

She shrugged. 'Five months. Maybe six. I can't be that certain.'

'Are you showing yet?'

'A bit.'

'God's truth, Lucy! Moses said you and Dickie had been using his and Jane's bed. Well, that's what you get for being so . . . *so loose.*'

'I'm not loose, Arthur,' Lucy protested. 'I was in love. I did it for love, not because I'm a loose woman. I'm not a strumpet. You know I'm not . . . Wait till I see that Moses . . . telling you that . . .'

'Do your folks know?'

'They're the only ones I've told, apart from you. I'd have a job to hide it from them. Yes, they know. Course they know.'

'I bet your father's pleased,' he said sarcastically.

'Well, if Dickie had survived the accident, my father would've killed him anyway. So you'd still have been doing his grave . . . But Father's been as good as gold to me. So has my mother. They'll look after me.'

'Hmm!' he scoffed. 'Then count your blessings. A good many wenches in the same position aren't so lucky.'

'I can't help that . . . You disapprove, don't you, Arthur?'

'I thought you were different, Lucy. I always thought you were more virtuous.'

'I'm only flesh and blood, Arthur,' she said earnestly. 'I'm no saint, nor have I ever pretended to be.'

'You were a saint with me.'

'Because I wasn't in love with you then. I was in love with Dickie. Anyway, haven't you ever done that sort of thing with a girl? I bet you have, a man of what? Twenty-seven? You've had plenty of time.'

'It's different for a man.'

'But not for the girl? Aren't girls allowed to have feelings or desires?'

He thought about Isabel. Perhaps all women were the same

as Isabel, blessed or cursed with those same feelings and desires. 'Yes, course they are . . . I suppose.'

'Well then . . .'

'But it's girls who bear the consequences, Lucy. God's truth, I'm so angry with you. . . . No, *angry's* the wrong word . . . I'm *disappointed* in you. I thought you had more about you than to let the likes of Dickie Dempster have his way . . . and him a married man.'

'I can see there's no point in talking to you,' Lucy retorted. 'I can see I shall get no sympathy from you.'

'If it's sympathy you want, yes, you'd better go and talk to somebody else.'

She looked at his face, turned side-on to her, and saw that he was actually sulking. 'You're jealous.' She grinned with pleasure at the realisation. 'Arthur Goodrich, you're jealous.'

'Yes, all right, I'm jealous,' he admitted, and his face reddened again. 'Course I'm damned jealous. He got between your legs when I didn't. Well, I'll make sure I have the last laugh on him . . .'

'What do you mean by that?'

'Oh . . . nothing . . .'

'Yes, you do. What do you mean?'

'Nothing, I told you.' He threw away the dregs from the mug with annoyance, and stuffed it unceremoniously in his bag along with his empty tea bottle. 'I'd better finish my letter cutting, then you can put your precious roses on the arsehole's grave.'

Lucy sat passively, mildly amused but gratified at his surprising attitude, while he silently blackened the last letters of the lengthy inscription. She decided to fetch water from the butt the church provided, while she waited for him to finish his work, returning just as he was sweeping away the chippings from the carved lettering. She put the grave vase on the grave and he, impatiently but out of an innate pride in his work-manship, lined it up by eye and centred it.

'There,' he muttered morosely. 'Stick your roses in that. And when you've done it, I'll dance around the bloody things.'

She effected a look of disdain to disguise her amusement. 'You wouldn't be so disrespectful.'

'Oh, wouldn't I? I got no respect for *him*.'

'You thought the sun shone out of his backside once,' she said, and began arranging the roses as she leaned over the grave. 'That time you were in trouble . . .'

He waited till she had stepped back, her task completed, then he stood on the grave and did a comical jig around the vase of roses, which elicited a wry smile from Lucy.

'Is that how you have the last laugh?'

'It's one way,' he replied.

'Do you feel better now?'

He stepped down, took a deep breath and stood erect, smoothing his jacket with the palms of his hands. 'As a matter of fact, I do.' He smiled and smoothed his hair, his fit of pique rapidly receding.

'Good. So now you've sweetened up a bit I'll allow you to accompany me home, since we're both going the same way.'

'I'm not going home, Lucy,' he was forced to admit.

'Why not?'

'I . . . um . . . Isabel Dempster's expecting me,' he stuttered. 'So's I can let her know the grave's finished . . . She's cooking me some dinner . . .'

'Cooking you some dinner?' Lucy queried, her eyes wide with sham mockery. 'Fancy . . . Is that another way you have the last laugh? Or are there even more ways that you wouldn't want me to know about?'

'I don't know what you mean, Lucy,' he replied scornfully.

'Oh, I bet you do, Arthur Goodrich. I *bet* you do.'

'What is it to you anyway?' he jibed. 'You've had your fill of the Dempsters . . .'

'And now you're having yours, eh?'

★ ★ ★

Lucy returned home to Brierley Hill alone. She had fulfilled her purpose. It was certain she had got over Dickie Dempster, because throughout the return journey her thoughts were focused entirely on Arthur. She'd been so delighted when she realised he was jealous, but despondent again at the thought that there had to be something going on between him and Isabel Dempster, especially in view of the fact that he had finished with that silly girl Dorinda. It was strange how she never felt jealous of Dorinda, beautiful as she was, because the girl didn't seem right for him. It was only ever a matter of time before he realised she was not for him. But she *was* jealous of Isabel. Isabel was dangerous. What if Arthur married Isabel and settled down with her and her two children? Dickie's children. That would be the ultimate irony, the ultimate snub to herself, and the final straw in her hopeless quest for happiness.

The problem was that now, with a belly growing ever larger, there was nothing she could do to entice Arthur away. Without the child she was carrying, she felt she would have had a chance. Furthermore, Isabel was a fine-looking woman and had obviously benefited from a decent education. Lord knows how the girl had ever got mixed up with Dickie anyway.

Lucy finally and irrevocably accepted that with Arthur she had once had the most decent man imaginable, hers for the taking, but she had spurned him for the sake of a man who was marginally better looking, outwardly more confident, but with the integrity of a fox. What a fool she had been, and look how she was now paying the price. Everybody had warned her to steer clear of Dickie, but she had not listened, driven to that disastrous love affair just as surely as the birds in the trees are driven to build nests and mate in springtime. Everybody had told her she would never find a more honest and forthright man than Arthur Goodrich, but she had not listened. His quirkiness had not suited her, his little ailments had annoyed her, his finickiness at the table she had scorned. But where was his quirkiness now? What had happened to his petty ailments? There was no sign of them any longer. Always she had perceived him mistakenly. Never before had she seen how comical he could be, how unassuming he was, never boastful about the things he could do well. He was exceptional at his work, adept at cricket, as others had unfailingly informed her. He could be eloquent when the need arose, and he was not inhibited about showing his emotions, as his dancing on Dickie's grave had proved. People shunned him, and her own father used to gently mock him, but only because they had not taken the trouble to get to know him. Her mother had seen the real Arthur, though, long before her father, long before she had seen it herself. Her mother had thought the world of him, recognising his virtues at once. Why had she not heeded her mother? Why had she not heeded Miriam Watson, her friend, when Miriam had told her she was a fool to look further than Arthur for a husband?

Well, it was too late now. She had missed the finest opportunity ever to come her way. Fate would never smile upon her quite so benignly again. The life of an unmarried mother was the best she could hope for, albeit loved and supported by an understanding family. At least she was not so badly off as some. But her illegitimate child would always be a barrier to her meeting somebody else and getting wed. If only she had tried to overcome her immature prejudices over Arthur and stayed with him . . .

★ ★ ★

The weeks and months passed, Christmas came and went, and 1859 ushered itself in with bitter cold weather. On Tues-

383

day 22nd February, Lucy gave birth to a daughter. The child weighed seven and a half pounds, had very dark hair, and was instantly loved.

Moses passed on news of the birth next morning and Arthur, when he had finished work, decided he would call on Lucy and pay his respects. He left work early and bought some expensive imported flowers from the florist in Brierley Hill, which he took with him, wrapped in a cone of brown paper Hannah and Haden greeted him warmly and plied him with beer before he was allowed to go upstairs to see Lucy and her baby.

He clumped ungainly up the twisting wooden stairs and found her in her tiny bedroom. The child was lying in a new crib bought by Hannah in anticipation a week before the event. Lucy had heard his voice downstairs when he arrived and sat up in bed now awaiting him, putting a last stray hair back into place, smoothing it down and pinching her cheeks to add a bit of colour to them.

'Lucy!' he greeted warmly. 'How d'you feel? Is the baby all right?'

'The baby is so beautiful, Arthur,' she replied softly. 'I love her to bits. And I feel well too, considering. Thank you for coming to see us both.'

'Did you have a hard time of it?' He peered curiously into the crib, then sat on the bed beside her.

'It was bad enough,' she smiled serenely, 'but I'm all right. Our Jane was a brick. She and mother were here for the birthing.'

'Moses gave me the news this morning.'

'Have a peep at her,' Lucy suggested. 'See if you can see who she's like.'

He leaned forward and gently pulled down the baby's swaddling to get a better look. 'She's like you,' he beamed. 'The spitten image . . . Well, that's a relief. What are you going to call her? Have you decided on a name?'

'Julia.'

'Julia?' he queried, incredulous.

'Yes, Julia. Don't you like it?'

'Oh, yes, yes. I think it's a fine name, Luce.'

'To tell you the truth, it's a name Dickie said he liked for a girl. He is her father, so I see no harm in choosing his favourite name for her. It's the only relevance he'll ever have to her now.'

He smiled affectionately. How could he possibly inform her that Dickie's daughter by Isabel was also called Julia? Not that it mattered particularly, but it might make her feel foolish and cause her to change her mind, when Julia was a good name after all. 'It's a lovely name,' he conceded. 'I think it suits her well. What does your father think of her?'

'Oh, he's in love with her. I'm sure he's in love with her. I know he'll be like a father to her. She won't need her real father with him about.'

'It's good to see you looking so well. It's good to see you looking so content.'

'I feel content now. I'm glad it's all over. I'm glad the baby's all right. How have you been? It's been weeks since I've seen you.'

'Me? I'm all right. Keeping busy. Plenty of work to keep me out of mischief.'

'Talking of mischief, have you seen much of Isabel Dempster?'

'I, er . . . I do see her occasionally, Luce. She pays for Dickie's grave in instalments.'

'You've given her credit?'

'Her compensation for Dickie's death hasn't been sorted out yet. They're arguing that he died as a result of surgery, not of his injuries directly. I think they're trying to wriggle out of paying. So it seemed a charitable thing to do to afford her some credit.'

'And you go to her house and collect the payments?'

'Yes.'

She noticed how he had reddened, and felt that same stab of jealousy she'd felt before. What else did he collect from the woman, she wondered?

'I'm sure she's fortunate to deal with a stonemason so kind and considerate,' Lucy said, effecting a detachment she did not feel. 'I hope she appreciates it.'

'Oh, I think she does . . . So what of you, Lucy?' he asked, changing tack. 'Shall you try and find work after?'

'I might. In the long run. It depends on Mother. But not till Julia's weaned.'

'It might be a good thing for you to find work in the long run. When you're good and ready. It'll give you a bit of independence, won't it?'

'I suppose,' she said quietly.

'Shall you still work at the Whimsey nights?'

'I don't think so. I'd rather be looking after Julia. She'll need feeding at all odd hours. Especially while she's very small.'

'I expect so . . .' He imagined Lucy breast-feeding the child, and was stimulated by the notion. 'Listen Luce, I won't take up any more of your time. I expect you're tired. Can I call again and see you . . . and the baby?'

'I'd love you to, Arthur. Come whenever you want.'

He smiled warmly. 'I will. Later in the week. I'm glad you're all right.'

He bent down to give her a kiss on the cheek, and said goodbye.

When he'd gone, Hannah came up the stairs bearing a vase of assorted fresh flowers.

'Look at these,' she said. 'Aren't they beautiful?'

'Fresh flowers at this time of year?' Lucy queried. 'Where did you get them?'

386

'Arthur brought them.'

'Arthur?' She was touched by the sentiment.

'It was very thoughtful of him, wasn't it our Lucy?'

'Very . . . Oh, isn't he just the nicest person you ever met, Mother?' Tears welled up in her eyes. 'That's so kind of him . . . and so typical . . .'

★ ★ ★

27

Just a few days after Lucy had had her baby, Arthur returned to the house from his labours and found his mother unconscious at the bottom of the stairs. Her head was bleeding profusely and he could smell drink on her. He tried to rouse her, but to no avail, and ran back to the workshop to catch Talbot before he left for home. Talbot came rushing.

'Has she been drinking?' he asked as they rounded the path to the front door.

'I can smell drink on her,' Arthur replied. 'I know she has a tipple in the afternoon.'

'Mornings as well. She's been worse since Father died.'

Arthur shoved open the front door and they went in.

'I wonder how long she's been like this?' Talbot said.

'Lord knows. Let's get her into bed.'

They tried to lift her and at once Dinah roused and squealed in agony.

'She's hurt,' Arthur said. 'Maybe she's broke something. It's better if I lift her myself. She can't be that heavy. If I can get my arms under her . . .'

Arthur scooped up his mother, thankful that she was not as unmanageable as Catherine Chadwick would have been, else they'd have needed a block and tackle. To Dinah's agonised groans, he took her to her bedroom and laid her carefully on her bed. Talbot followed.

'I'm going to fetch Dr Walker, Mother,' Talbot said. 'We think you've broken a bone. It'll need to be set.'

Meanwhile, Arthur fetched a basin of warm water and cleaned the blood from his mother's head. There was an angry looking gash near her temple and she was pale.

'You shouldn't be drinking in the daytime, Mother,' he reprimanded.

'What else is there to do?' Dinah mewled.

'Something useful for a change. A bit of housework wouldn't come amiss now and again.'

'I've never bin one for housework, our Arthur. Housework is maids' work.'

'But Father would never employ any maids, would he? So it fell to you to do it.'

'I couldn't cope, what with cooking, maiding and mangling and the smoothing iron. Then there was the business and everything. Leave off complaining at me, Arthur. I feel like death . . . Oh, the pain is vile . . .'

Dr Walker eventually arrived in his dog cart. He examined Dinah thoroughly and pronounced that not only had she broken her leg above the knee, but she'd fractured both wrists as well. 'She'll be out of action for some weeks, I'm afraid. Is there somebody who can look after her? She won't be able to do much for herself with both arms in slings.'

Arthur contemplated the odious implications for a second.

Talbot said, 'My wife Magnolia can be here to look after her most days. Arthur and I will be on hand anyway, should anything extraordinary arise. But in the evenings . . .' He turned to Arthur. 'I suppose it falls to you to do your best . . .'

'I daresay I can cope,' Arthur replied.

Talbot put his hand on Arthur's shoulder. 'It goes without saying that anytime you need help from me . . .'

'Maybe, from time to time. Who knows?'

They left Dr Walker to set Dinah's broken bones and went downstairs.

'I hope she'll be all right,' Talbot remarked. 'Serious falls like she's had can start so many other things in train, especially in a woman Mother's age. She's no spring chicken.'

'She's never looked after herself properly,' Arthur said. 'And I blame Father.'

'Aye, Father was to blame for a lot of things. But what's done can't be undone . . .' Talbot looked at his watch. 'I'd best be off, our Arthur. Magnolia will wonder what's become of me. Anyway, expect her in the morning. She'll do all she can to help.'

So after Talbot had gone, and Dr Walker had been paid and had departed, Arthur was alone with his mother, who was all trussed up like a chicken. He tended to her conscientiously, bringing her tea to drink.

'Bring me a drop o' whisky, our Arthur.'

'You've had enough drink, Mother. And look where it's got you.'

'It'll help me sleep. I'll sleep till morning.'

It was an attractive proposition. So Arthur fetched an ample measure of whisky, laced with a couple of drops of laudanum, and held it to her lips while she sipped. When it had all gone, he left her, leaving the oil lamp burning lest he had to go to her in the night.

It soon became clear to Arthur that he would be unable to visit Isabel for some time, and felt he should write explaining his absence. So he penned her a brief note and posted it next day.

He thought much about Isabel during the first few evenings that he was confined to the house. Theirs was a highly sexual affair, and he acknowledged that it existed just for sex. They never spoke of love, indeed, to mention the word would have spoiled everything. But Arthur liked Isabel. He liked her immensely. He admired her independent, indefatigable streak, her intelligence, her demeanour. And Isabel liked Arthur just as much, and for very similar reasons. Often he puzzled over what had ever possessed her to get mixed up with the likes of Dickie Dempster. She wondered it herself, now that she was older and had more sense. The stubborn prejudice of youth had motivated her, the determination to defy her parents if necessary had amplified her unhealthy adolescent obsession for Dickie.

By this time, however, Arthur had met her children and was not particularly enamoured of either of them, the three-year-old son Jack especially. Jack evidently regarded Arthur with some suspicion and scowled at him most of the time, despite his mother's assurances. Julia, however – five years old – was a different kettle of fish, intelligent but petulant. Like her mother, she was self-willed but prone to demanding her own way, which she normally got. It was the line of least resistance for Isabel to simply give in, in the short term at any rate, whereas Arthur would have been inclined to give her a smack, which he regarded as a longer term solution.

Arthur managed to sneak away from his mother's bedside for half an hour one evening to pay a visit to Lucy. He enjoyed Lucy's company, more now than when they were courting. He felt easier with her than he used to, because there was no pressure on him any more to try and impress her. In trying to impress her he generally succeeded only in making a fool of himself, so perhaps it was no surprise that she was drawn to Dickie Dempster who was better looking and did not act like a fool, even though he turned out to be a more stupid fool than anybody ever imagined.

He tapped on the door of the Piddocks' cottage and was let in by Hannah.

'Why, it's Arthur,' she greeted with a smile of affection. 'Come in, my lad. Our Lucy's defied me and got up. She's down here now, and feeding the babby.'

Arthur was a little embarrassed to witness Lucy with the

child at her breast. He tried not to look but she smiled up at him from her chair with no inhibitions.

'You won't mind if I don't get up, Arthur?' she said.

He smiled amiably. 'No, I can see you're busy, Luce. How are you both?'

'We're both very well. Look at her, Arthur, isn't she beautiful?' She eased the child away from her nipple and turned her towards him. 'Don't you think she gets lovelier every day?'

Of course he had no choice but to look and agree. The baby was indeed very pretty for one so young. Already her pinched redness had gone and her baby flesh was pink and smooth. She opened her eyes momentarily and he saw how blue they were. He also saw how pink and smooth and very appealing was Lucy's exposed breast, but Lucy did not seem to mind. She returned the child to it and Julia continued suckling keenly.

'Mother's bad,' he announced. 'Had you heard?'

'Moses mentioned it,' Hannah said. 'Broken some bones, he said.'

'Her leg and both wrists. She fell down the stairs. She was a bit shook up.'

'I bet she was,' Hannah replied. 'Poor soul. Is she getting over it?'

Arthur shook his head. 'Not so far. I think she's running a fever.'

'It's shock, Arthur.' Hannah pressed her lips together and turned down the corners of her mouth ominously. 'You must keep your eye on her.'

'Well, our Magnolia comes over in the day to look after her, and I do it at night.'

'Can you manage all right?' Hannah asked. 'I bet your mother's a handful.'

'The worst is when she needs to use the commode,' he

admitted. 'I never thought as I'd have to hold my mother while she did . . . that.'

'That's no life for a young chap, Arthur. There's no joy in seeing your mother all undignified. Why not let me come and help yer out? I could pop up of a night and give yer a lift.'

'Or I could,' Lucy offered.

'I wouldn't dream of putting either of you to all that trouble. Especially you, Lucy, now you've got Julia to look after. No, I can manage. It's only for a few weeks till her broken bones mend and she can start to do things for herself. She'll be able to get about on a crutch afore long, like Moses.'

'Not with two broken wrists she won't,' Hannah said. 'How's she gunna support the crutch with ne'er a good arm? She'd be in agony.'

'I hadn't thought about that, Mrs Piddock.'

'No. So why don't you let me come and give you a hand for half an hour of a night? I can get your mother on and off the commode. It's more in a woman's line than a man's.'

'I hate to put you to all that trouble,' he said again.

'What trouble? It's what friends and neighbours are for. To help one another. I'll come back with yer when you're ready to go, and I'll have a run at it, eh?'

Arthur smiled gratefully. 'That's very good of you, Mrs Piddock.'

Arthur stayed about half an hour, talking to Lucy and Hannah. He was impressed with Lucy's natural ability with her baby, her instinctive mothering of the child, her ready response to her needs. Secretly, he wondered how he would feel if the child were his. She really was a lovely little bundle, apparently not prone yet to squawking and mewling like some children, obviously contented.

'Can I hold her?' he asked when the baby had been fed and her wind coaxed up.

Lucy looked at him with an expression of astonishment and delight. 'Are you sure?'

'Yes,' he said. 'I'd like to hold her.'

Lucy passed Julia to him. He held her gingerly at first, then with greater confidence when she did not struggle to escape his arms. She seemed to have very little weight and even less bulk.

'She's so light,' he commented.

'See if you can say that in another six months,' Hannah said, laughing.

He rocked the baby very gently, looking down with wonder and admiration at her little face. 'She's the image of you, Lucy. You can't imagine how glad I am she isn't like Dickie.'

'Oh, thank the Lord she ain't like *him*,' Hannah proclaimed with disdain. 'We'd all commit suicide if the babby looked like *him*.'

'You shouldn't speak ill of the dead, Mother,' Lucy chided mildly. 'We know Dickie was no angel, but we shouldn't be too hard on him now he's gone.'

He held Julia for the rest of the time he remained there, handing the child back to Lucy just before he left. Hannah put on her shawl and accompanied Arthur back to the Delph.

'I do wish you two had never parted,' she said as they crossed over Brettell Lane. 'Just think, you might even have been married by now.'

'Oh, I don't think so, Mrs Piddock. Lucy wouldn't have me. I asked her.'

'Well, she'd have you now, Arthur, mark my words.'

'D'you reckon?' Arthur smiled modestly. 'I can't imagine it for a minute.'

'I know it. Our Lucy's growed up a lot since she learnt about that swine Dickie Dempster, and she'll grow up a lot more still, now she's got the bab. But I told her. "You've missed your chance", I said to her. "Why would Arthur want yer now, now as you've got somebody else's bab?" I said.'

394

'She's a lovely little thing though, Mrs Piddock. Julia.'

'They'm all lovely when they'm that little. It's when they grow up as they bring trouble. I never thought as our Lucy would bring trouble, you know. But I could never have turned me back on her. Not when she needed me.'

'I know,' Arthur said. 'And I'm glad. You did the right thing.'

'I could never have lived with me conscience if I hadn't. But I do wish as our Lucy could find a nice homely chap who'd look after her and be kind to the babby. She's a good wench. She just made one saft mistake . . .'

'Maybe she'll meet somebody,' Arthur consoled. 'She's still a lovely girl, and nice-looking with it. She can still fetch the ducks off the water.'

'But it ain't ducks as she wants, Arthur.'

★ ★ ★

Arthur received a note from Isabel Dempster a few days later, written in a very neat and tidy hand. It read:

> *My dear Arthur,*
>
> *I am so sorry to hear of your mother's fall, and I sincerely hope she is well on the road to recovery. Of course, you must look after her and do all you can to help her and ease her suffering. If it means I am unable to see you for a while then so be it. I understand perfectly.*
>
> *I finally received an amount in compensation for Dickie's death yesterday. It wasn't as much as I'd hoped for, and certainly not as much as if he'd been actually working on the day of the accident. On a par with other passengers' compensation payments, I believe. But it's better than nothing at all, and it will enable me to pay you at long last for Dickie's grave. So, when I see you next time you shall have the money.*
>
> *Talking of Dickie's grave, I noticed when I went to the*

churchyard last, that there were some chips knocked out of it on two of the corners. Goodness knows how they got there, but if in the daytime you get the chance to go over and have a look, I am sure you would be able to repair them somehow. I do want the grave to look as pristine as possible. And while you are there, well, it occurred to me that perhaps you could see your way clear to calling on me to collect your money.

I shall not expect you for some time, in view of your mother's unfortunate condition, but please write to me in the meantime. When it is convenient for you to do the work, let me know beforehand and I will see to it that the children are elsewhere.

Affectionately yours.

Isabel Dempster.

★ ★ ★

It was towards the end of March, cold, and a blustery wind was howling outside. The month had roared in like a lion and was roaring out like one. It was dusk when Arthur prepared a cheese sandwich for his mother and took it upstairs to feed her. By the time he'd completed the task it was dark, and he sat in the parlour contemplating his lot by the light of an oil lamp.

This house . . . What a mausoleum. It wanted pulling down. Never had he known such a cold and draughty place. The window casements rattled at every gust, smoke blew back down the chimney and filled the room with choking sooty fumes. Paint was peeling off the doors, whitewash fell in flakes from the ceilings, plaster was coming adrift from the walls in places. The floors were uneven, silverfish and woodlice had evolved into several populous communities behind the skirting boards and trooped like miniature armies between the joins of the quarry tiles. Mice regularly flitted ever more boldly across any number of rooms and disappeared through unbelievably

396

tiny holes and cracks. To renovate this place would cost a fortune.

He thought about Dorinda and the fleas. He was sorry over what had happened and felt ashamed when he recalled that lunatic escapade of his, invading her bed in the dead of night hell-bent on seducing her. But he was beginning to see the funny side of it. Dorinda, he realised now, would not have suited him as a wife, pretty as she was. Looks were not everything in a woman. Of course, he could never tolerate an ugly bride, but as long as the one he eventually chose was reasonably presentable, sufficiently alluring and kept him happy in bed, he would be content enough. Nor would he stray. He had no wish nor desire to chase every pretty face he saw, like Dickie Dempster had. Chasing women must be expensive and time-consuming, and Arthur was blessed with neither of those resources to facilitate such an egocentric pastime.

Lately, though, he had had some measure of success with women. There was no doubt that Dorinda had been in love with him – a beautiful girl like her. Indeed, it was Dorinda who had made all the running. Then there was Isabel, to whom he had lost his virginity so willingly and so deliciously. Who ever would have thought that he and Dickie Dempster's widow . . .? And it was not over yet. They both enjoyed their times together cavorting in her bed. Isabel had taught him much about women in the six months they had been con-sorting, women's wiles, women's ways. Not that she had given him lessons; he had merely studied her and witnessed how she operated. Suggestions she *had* given, however, and in abun-dance on the most effective ways to please each other between the sheets. To her, bed was not only a place to sleep, but a place for recreation too. It was somewhere to shed all inhibi-tions, a temple for extreme pleasure.

Isabel was an enigma – she did not fit into the conventional mould of young women. In Arthur's limited experience, most of the women he had ever come into contact with – mothers, daughters, sisters, cousins, aunts, customers, women who went to church – he could not imagine any of them to be much troubled by sexual feeling. If they were, or ever had been, they hid the fact inordinately well. But then, he had never seen any of them in the privacy of their beds with their respective men.

It boiled down to this: Isabel was not the pure, sexually modest type of woman he ought to attach himself to on a permanent basis. She was no angel. She was not enduringly, incorruptibly good. In short, she did not meet his criteria for the perfect wife.

But then, judged by those standards, neither did Lucy Piddock. Only Dorinda qualified. Maybe he had been too eager to let go of Dorinda, too blinded by the physical and sensory delights that Isabel bestowed. Maybe he should write to Dorinda, try and reignite their courtship, raise it to a more serious level, make his intentions clear . . .

Just then, he heard a knock at the door and went to answer it, taking the oil lamp to light his way.

'Lucy!' he exclaimed, surprised to see her standing there. 'What brings you out on a blustery night like this all alone?'

She smiled with pleasure at seeing him. 'Mother would've come, but father came home from work with a torn jacket and she's had to mend if for him. So I offered to come in her place.'

'I could've managed Mother on my own. There's no need for you to be inconvenienced.'

'Can I come in?' Her bright eyes looked at him appealingly.

'Yes, course you can. Sorry. I didn't mean to leave you standing out in the cold. It's just a surprise to see you, that's all.'

'Are you sure I haven't called at a bad time?' she asked, uncertain of his welcome.

'No, it's as good a time as any.' He smiled to reassure her. 'Come on upstairs, Luce. I was just thinking what a bloody mess this house is. It's like a perishing morgue. A cold and draughty hole. It needs a mint of money spending on it. I'm ashamed of it. Just look around you . . .'

'I know what you mean,' Lucy agreed. 'It is a bit of a shambles.'

They climbed the stairs, Arthur lighting the way.

'And dusty,' he added. 'I'll have to give it a good spring clean, I reckon.'

'I could help you,' she said brightly. 'As long as I could bring Julia. She could lie quiet. She'd be no trouble.'

'You'd do that for me?' he asked, touched by her unselfishness.

'If it helped you.'

They reached Dinah's bedroom and he led Lucy in. 'Mother, Lucy's come to see to you tonight. Mrs Piddock couldn't make it so she's sent Lucy.'

'How are you Mrs Goodrich?' Lucy immediately enquired.

'I've bin better, my wench,' Dinah groaned dolefully, full of self-pity over her suffering.

Lucy looked at Arthur with a worried expression. She had not expected to see Mrs Goodrich looking so ill. The woman, never heavy, had lost weight since last time she'd seen her. Her skin was drawn and she was as pale as death.

'I'll help you lift her on the commode,' Arthur said. 'Then I'll leave you to it. I prefer to give mother a bit of privacy befitting a woman of her years, when she's on the commode.'

Lucy acknowledged his sentiment and smiled.

'When she's done I'll come and empty the slops.'

Together, they transferred Dinah to the commode, which stood at the side of the bed, and Arthur removed himself to his own bedroom to make himself scarce. It was woman's work, he acknowledged to himself, the work of a ministering angel. Only women were capable of being ministering angels. Well . . . most women. He could hardly imagine Dorinda doing what Lucy was now doing. Dorinda was too pernickety, too aloof, too high and mighty to lower herself to such ministering . . . Ah, well, maybe he would not write to Dorinda anyway.

He stood and gazed out of the window, watching the twinkling lights of the houses. The sky to the north glowed red, lighting up the low clouds, as it was frequently wont to do with all the earthly furnaces and hearths ablaze. Funny how Lucy had come to help tend to his mother. It was thoughtful of her. Funny, too, how they had remained friends, how they still had this healthy regard for each other, despite all that had happened.

He recalled what Hannah had said: *she'd have you now, Arthur, mark my words*. He'd thought little of it at the time, dismissed it as unlikely. Even now he was inclined to doubt it, to consider it the wishful thinking of a mother who regretted the scrape her daughter had got herself into with another, when it might otherwise have been avoided.

The door to his mother's bedroom opened and Lucy called his name. He went to her.

'We're done now, Arthur.'

Dinah was back in bed, neatly tucked in and comfortable.

'Thanks, Lucy. I do appreciate you coming.'

'Is there anything else I can do?'

'Stay here and talk to her for five minutes while I empty the slops and fetch some coal to make up her fire.'

'Course I will.'

'You can wash your hands in the bowl on the washstand. See it?'

She nodded, washed her hands and drew a wicker chair up at the side of Dinah's bed. 'I bet you're glad to see Arthur home, Mrs Goodrich, after his time in Bristol,' she said when Arthur had left them to talk.

'That I am, and no two ways. He's bin golden while I've bin bad. Lord knows what I woulda done without him. Course, I blame his fairther, God rest his soul the old sod, that he ever buggered off in the fust place. If the daft old bugger had bin fairer with him he'd never have left . . . And he'd never have met that flighty Bristol piece as he brought here. I couldn't abide her. I rue the day as he gi'd yo' up for her, young Lucy.'

'You didn't like Dorinda then, Mrs Goodrich?'

'Her was never the right sort for our Arthur. Thought too much of herself. Afeared o' getting her hands dirty. Hardly ate a thing while her was here.'

'I think she was frightened of losing her figure.'

'What figure? There was nothing of her. The wench could've sat and ate till kingdom come, and still never put weight on.'

'She didn't want children either,' Lucy remarked intently.

'Well, yo' can hardly blame her for that. Vile business, having kids.'

'I've got a baby now, you know, Mrs Goodrich?'

'You? By our Arthur, you mean? He never said. Wait till he comes back, I'll skin him alive.'

'No, not by Arthur. I met this other chap . . .'

'Am yer wed?'

'We never got wed, Mrs Goodrich. He died as a result of the railway accident.'

'So yo' was a widder afore ever yo' got wed. Fancy. Pitiful that. Still, you shouldn't have bin a-dabbling afore you got married. Then you wouldn't be saddled with a bab.'

'But I wouldn't be without my baby, Mrs Goodrich. She's my life now.'

'Well, I don't suppose yo'll ever land an 'usband now, with a bastard child trailing behind yer.'

'I suppose not,' Lucy agreed, determined not to take offence, for she knew how outspoken and tactless Dinah could

401

be. 'Shall I give you a drink of water before Arthur comes back with the coal?'

'Wairter? D'you want me to catch the cholera? No, I'll have beer. Or whisky.'

Arthur returned, with a bucket of coal. He raked out the fire and piled a few lumps on. 'I'll walk you back, Lucy, when I've washed my hands,' he said. 'She'll be all right for half an hour.'

Lucy smiled. 'All right. Thank you . . . She'd like some beer before she goes to sleep, Arthur.'

'I'll bring her some.'

Lucy turned to the invalid. 'Goodnight, Mrs Goodrich . . . I hope you're feeling better soon.' She followed Arthur downstairs and into the parlour.

'Would you like a crock of beer yourself, Lucy?' he asked.

'Yes, if you've got some. If not, I could go and fetch some.'

'I fetched some earlier. It might be a bit flat by now, but it'll be all right to drink.' He went to the pantry and retrieved a jug of beer from the cold shelf, and poured it out by the light of the oil lamp he'd been carrying about with him. 'Sit yourself down a bit, Lucy. You might as well.'

She sat down and sipped the beer, watching his face intently as he sat beside her.

'You've changed, you know, Arthur,' she said softly.

He took a gulp of beer and looked at her. 'Yes, I think I might have done.'

'You're so much more . . . I don't know how to put it . . . so much more sure of yourself these days . . . You don't complain about daft little ailments any more, either.'

'I don't seem to get any daft little ailments any more,' he responded. 'I think the railway accident and seeing all those poor folk suffering put paid to all that.'

She smiled disconsolately. She wanted to say more, to tell him how she felt about him these days, to make amends, but could not find the words. Anyway, he would most likely not be interested. He would probably laugh in her face. After all, she had a child now . . . But then, so did Isabel Dempster.

'Have you seen anything of Mrs Dempster lately?' she enquired.

'Not for a while. Not with having to look after Mother.'

'That's a shame. I imagine you've become very fond of Mrs Dempster.'

'In a way,' he answered.

'It's funny, isn't it, how I fell in love with Dickie, and when he died, you started seeing his widow. How ironic that is. Don't you think so, Arthur?'

'I can see the irony,' he conceded, 'but I'd hate you to think there's more to it than there really is.'

'Oh?' she exclaimed. 'But it was plain to see that there was something between you. Isn't it serious, then?'

'It depends what you mean by serious. I'm fond of her, Lucy, but I don't intend to marry her, if that's what you're getting at.'

Lucy sighed with relief. The possibility had been bothering her for some time, and she had not known either the strength or the weakness of the relationship. 'All the same, it's time a man of your age was thinking about marriage. You can't be tied to your mother's apron-strings for the rest of your life.'

'Hmm,' he mused, and took another draft of beer. 'Actually, I've been thinking about that myself. I've been thinking the very same thing. As a matter of fact, I was thinking only tonight of writing to Dorinda again.'

'But I don't think she suited you, Arthur. Nor does your mother.'

'No, it's a certain fact Mother wouldn't suit me . . .'

She thumped him playfully and grinned at his glibness. 'You know what I mean, Arthur Goodrich.'

'Well, I changed my mind about Dorinda anyway, Luce. I compared her to you tonight, helping Mother. Dorinda could

403

no more do what you did than fly in the air. Dorinda has no compassion, she only ever thinks of herself.'

'She's vain,' Lucy added for good measure.

'Yes, I know she's vain.'

'I used to be vain as well, you know, Arthur.'

'You? I never noticed any vanity in you particularly.'

'It was a different sort of vanity. I wanted the man I marry to be perfectly handsome in every way. Only handsome would do. I wanted to be the envy of all my friends with a fine, handsome husband. I was prepared to overlook any other characteristics in a man, just so long as he was wickedly handsome. Handsomeness was the be all and end all, just so long as he cared for me as well. And Dickie came along and I thought all my prayers were answered. Then . . . when he was so ill . . . and a wife suddenly appeared out of the blue . . . I realised then that looks are not everything. Dickie deceived me cruelly, Arthur, you know he did. It was then I began to realise that other qualities in a man are much more important than fine looks.' Arthur listened intently to this confession he had never expected. 'You, Arthur, for instance, are kind and considerate. You haven't got a dishonest bone in your body, an evil thought in your head. You wouldn't hurt a fly. You'd rather help somebody than hinder them. You're well-mannered. Dickie, by comparison, was neither use nor ornament.'

'So you've changed as well as me,' he remarked.

'I have. I know I have. Without question. I've grown up, Arthur. I've had to grow up. You know, Arthur . . .' She put her hand on his and he took it, holding it affectionately. Encouraged, she sighed and went on. 'You know, Arthur, I bitterly regret now that I never could give myself to you in the way I should've done. I'd give anything to be able to go back to where we were.'

'Would you?' He sounded surprised.

'I would. Things would be different . . . Knowing what I

know now, I would treasure you.' She squeezed his hand. 'Stop me if I'm making a fool of myself, Arthur . . .'

'You're not making a fool of yourself, Lucy.' His voice was stretched taut with emotion. 'For goodness sake don't think that. Say what you will.'

'Well . . . I just wish . . .'

'What do you wish? Tell me.'

'Oh . . .' She sighed nervously. This was about to become a very revealing confession with a great deal at stake, and she wasn't sure she could take rejection now if rejection were to follow, after all she'd been through. 'You'll think me mad if I say it. You'll think I've got the cheek of the devil.'

'I won't know until you tell me.' He suspected what it was she was trying to say, but for him to give any response she had to come out with it. She had to say what was in her heart.

'Well . . . I know it's just dreams now . . . because I've got Julia . . . but I do wish, with all my heart, that you and me could be together again . . .'

He remained silent, and Lucy knew she should have said nothing. Now she wanted to apologise for being so stupid, so emotional, but she'd said what was in her heart. How could she apologise?

'It's not dreams, Lucy,' he said at long last.

She looked at him in astonishment, suddenly filled with hope. 'It's not?'

'Why should it be just dreams? Why shouldn't it be real, if we both want it to be? I think the world of you, Lucy. Surely you must know it. I'd give anything for us to be together again.'

'Do you really mean that?'

'I wouldn't say it if I didn't mean it. I just never really thought you'd ever feel that way about me. I never dared hope.'

'But I do. I think I always have deep down. I always thought the world of you, Arthur. I just had to get Dickie Dempster out of my system first.'

'Hmm . . . I had to get him out of mine as well, Lucy.'

She looked at him, uncertain as to what he meant. Then the penny dropped. 'With Isabel, you mean?'

'Yes, with Isabel. By using Isabel.'

'How do you mean?'

'Can't you imagine?'

'You mean . . .'

He nodded. 'I mean we've been lovers, Lucy,' he admitted. 'I'm not proud of it, particularly, but I confess it. I confess it because I don't want any skeletons tumbling out of any cupboards later.'

She smiled, and her eyes by the light of the oil lamp looked large, exuding such an engaging expression of happiness. 'So, we're even,' she said contentedly. 'So you could never throw Dickie in my face for fear I throw Isabel in yours.'

'I reckon that's true,' he admitted with a chuckle.

'But what about Julia?' she asked.

'What about her?'

'Do you think you can accept her? Can you accept that I'm a fallen woman?'

'If you can accept I'm a fallen man. As for Julia, I think she's beautiful. It's not her fault she's Dickie Dempster's daughter.'

'But would you always be kind to her, Arthur?' she pleaded. 'Could you treat her as your own?'

'I reckon so . . . Hey, are you asking me to marry you, Lucy?'

She grinned. 'No, that's up to you to ask me. If it's what you want.'

'Shall we see how we get on?' he replied. He saw the look of disappointment in her eyes at his reply and realised at once that it sounded sceptical, and that she'd misinterpreted it. 'What I mean is, Luce, let's decide when my mother's recovered. The way she is now I couldn't make any promise about anything, and I wouldn't want to subject you to looking after her. That would be a punishment you don't deserve.'

'I wouldn't mind, Arthur.'

'No, it's best we wait till she recovers.'

'So in the meantime, have we started courting again?' She looked into his eyes expectantly.

He squeezed her hand. 'It seems like it. I'd better give you a kiss to set a seal on it, hadn't I?'

'I reckon so.'

As he kissed her, he pressed her backwards so that she was semi-reclining on the sofa. Her lips on his were so agonisingly familiar, but the way she kissed him was not. She kissed him with a delicious zeal that he had not known from her previously. It was far too pleasant to stop, so they lingered, wringing maximum pleasure out it.

'Did Dickie teach you to kiss like that?' he commented with a smile of approval.

'Did Isabel teach you to kiss like that?' she countered. 'Or was it Dorinda?'

'A bit of both, I reckon. As long as you approve.'

'Oh, I do. Kiss me again.'

They kissed again.

A weak voice could be heard from upstairs. 'Arthur, Arthur, where's that drop o' beer yo' promised me. I'm dying o' thirst up here.'

'Oh, bugger!' he exclaimed.

★ ★ ★

28

When Lucy and Arthur resumed their gentle courtship it had been barely seven months since she had lost Dickie Dempster, and little more than one month since Julia had been born. Without discussing it, both were mindful of the relatively short time that had elapsed between the monumental episodes and events, in Lucy's life especially, and the impact they had had on her. Lucy had had time to get over Dickie and he was now consigned to history. Because of her relationship with him her eyes had been opened to the realities of life, and she was all the happier and the wiser for it. Julia was the focus of her existence; then suddenly so was Arthur. Having Arthur's love again was the one prize she yearned for but least expected, for she believed that neither was there the remotest chance of it, nor did she deserve him. Now, she had a great deal to look forward to, and she relished the prospect, and her renewed zest for life became obvious to those around her.

Because it had been little more than a month since Julia's birth, Arthur was anxious not to press Lucy to consummate their new-found love. He had no idea what childbirth did physically to a woman's body, or whether Lucy was even emotionally ready for such intimacy. To him that level of intimacy was an important facet of life since he had been alerted to its pleasures, but he had no wish to rush things and spoil what promised to be an easy and undemanding relationship. He was beginning to realise that Dorinda had been merely a diversion, who had managed to overwhelm the grief he would otherwise have suffered over losing Lucy in the first place. He had never loved Dorinda with the same intensity as he loved Lucy. He rarely ever thought of Dorinda now.

Isabel, however, was still very much on his mind. It would not be easy to bid Isabel farewell. He liked Isabel, and would always hold her in fond regard. He could easily have allowed her to become a part of his life on a permanent basis, but for her children and her unconventionality. He did not like her children, and he saw no reason to suffer them since they were not his. Neither did he have any moral or social obligation to keep them. Isabel's children were Isabel's responsibility.

Nevertheless, it behoved him, as a man of honour – which, disregarding the occasional lapse in gentlemanly conduct, was how he liked to regard himself – to let Isabel know that their affair must end. It should not be too difficult; no undying love and devotion had been declared on either side, no promises made. The affair had existed only for their mutual pleasure, and both were sufficiently mature to understand that. All things, pleasurable affairs included, eventually arrived at a finality. In any case, Isabel still believed that he was engaged to be married. He had never told her otherwise. Now he perceived it as his means of escape, and he needed it. He would tell her that he and his intended – whom she still believed to be Lucy, since he had never revealed the truth of it – had finally named the day and were shortly to be wed. All right, it was exaggerating the truth a little, but in essence it was nearer truth than falsehood.

So, after only three days into their rekindled love affair, Arthur told Lucy that he had a loose end to clear up.

'I feel obliged to see Isabel Dempster,' he said as they stood together outside the Piddocks' cottage when he'd walked her home after helping him with his mother. 'It's only fair that I should.'

'Why do you need to tell her anything?' Lucy queried with some anxiety that the woman might tempt him away.

'Because it's only fair.'

'But you never made her any promises, you said.'

He held her to him and she leaned her head on his chest, filled with foreboding that she might lose him again almost as soon as she'd got him back. But it was only fair that he should be straight with Isabel. Arthur was not like Dickie Dempster; he had to play by the rules. It was not in his nature to be ungentlemanly. Well, she must be thankful for that. She'd seen enough of ungentlemanly ways.

'I trust you to behave like a gentleman with her, Arthur,' she said quietly.

'Then your trust is well-placed, Luce. What do you suppose I'm going to do? Jump into bed with her?'

'I don't want to know about it if you do . . .'

'There's no fear of it anyway.' He lifted her chin and he saw the troubled look in her eyes, so beautiful in the half light. 'It's you I want. Not her. I've only ever wanted you.'

'When will you go?'

'Tomorrow. Whether morning or afternoon, I don't know yet. It depends on what there is to do in the workshop. I have to go to Dickie's grave anyway. Isabel wrote to say there are some chips in the stonework that need repairing. I'll have a look at that first, then go and see her. In any case, she wants to pay me for Dickie's grave. I'll be back in decent time, whether or no.'

Lucy acquiesced with a nod and held him tight around his waist, snuggling into him. Arthur was touched by this new depth of her affection, so much more intense, more caring than ever she had been with him before. She was so much more willing to show it too. How things had changed. He found her lips and they kissed.

'You don't have to do *those* things with her, Arthur,' she breathed when they broke off.

'What things?' he asked, unsure of her meaning.

'Oh, you know what things . . . Those things you do in her bed . . . You don't need to go to her for that . . .'

'What do you mean?'

She avoided his eyes, uncertain of how she should say what she wanted to say, so as to secure him in her insecurity. 'Doesn't it occur to you that I have desires as well, Arthur?'

'You? Are you serious?'

'Course I'm serious.' She looked into his eyes now with such an appealing look of frankness, yet feeling sheepish lest he thought her too fast.

'But it's not been that long since you had Julia. Are you ready for such things?'

'Course I am. And you want to, don't you?'

'What do you think?' He held her tight. He had not expected this. But then, nothing Lucy ever did had he expected.

They stood in each other's arms for some minutes, content just to be together, silently contemplating this new understanding, the tenderness of the moment. Then, from inside the cottage, Lucy heard Julia's cry and realised that her child was hungry and had to be fed.

'I'd better go in, Arthur. I can hear Julia.'

'Your mother's got her, hasn't she?'

'But Mother can't feed her.' She smiled up at him. 'And you have to go back to see to your mother.'

'I'll see you tomorrow then.'

'Yes, I'll see you tomorrow.'

They kissed goodnight, and he went.

★ ★ ★

The weather next day was fair and the early spring sun was eager to impart some warmth to a landscape that for so many months had lacked it. Random daffodils lifted their yellow trumpets at the command of a breeze that was gentle now, compared to the chilly blasts of the previous week. Arthur

411

embarked on the train for Wolverhampton in the afternoon, armed with a bag of tools with which he could effect a creditable repair to Dickie's grave. His mind was full of all that had befallen him these last few days, the wonderful change in Lucy, and in his fortune, and the journey seemed over before it had begun.

He arrived at the grave and inspected it. Such damage as there was, was superficial, and he wondered whether Isabel had exaggerated it just to get him over there. No fresh flowers adorned the grave, just a posy of limp and decrepit anemones that looked forlorn and pitiful in the grave vase. It had been a while since anybody had visited Dickie, according to that. He took a sheet of emery cloth and stretched it over a wooden block. As he sat on the grave and began rubbing away the tiny chips, he pondered what he should say to Isabel, how he should couch his words . . . Until he was conscious of some-body standing behind him. He stopped what he was doing and turned round to see who it was, half expecting to see Isabel herself.

A young woman stood watching him, bearing a child of twelve months or more in her arms, and a bunch of irises.

'Good afternoon,' he said politely and smiled. 'The weather's picked up a bit, thank goodness.'

'Yes.' She nodded and returned his smile tentatively. 'It's warmer today. As you say, thank goodness.'

She showed no inclination to move on.

'Am I in your way?' he enquired. 'Do you intend to put those flowers on this grave?'

She nodded, and Arthur stood up so as to get out of her way.

'It's all right. I don't want to stop you working,' she said apologetically.

'No, I can wait,' he affirmed. 'I'm in no particular rush. There are some tiny chips out of a couple of the corners.

I received a letter asking me to come along and repair them.'

'Oh.'

She sat the child, a girl, on the flat part of the grave's construction in the centre, where she was content to flap her arms and gurgle, smiling pleasantly.

'I can watch her,' Arthur offered. 'Save her falling over and hurting herself on the hard stone.'

'If you don't mind . . .' She bent down and took the dead anemones from the grave vase, then sniffed the water in it. 'I think I'd better go to the butt and fetch some fresh water.'

'I'll do it,' Arthur said, and held his hand out to receive the vase.

'There's no need to go to all that trouble on my account.'

'It's no trouble, I assure you.'

'Thank you. That's very kind.' She handed him the vase with a grateful smile. 'Would you mind throwing these into the bin as well while you're there. They haven't lasted as well as I thought they would.'

'You brought them, did you?'

'Oh, yes,' she replied as if it were the most natural thing in the world. 'A fortnight ago.'

Arthur made his way to the water butt. He dropped the dead flowers in the bin and replenished the vase with fresh water, wondering who this pleasant girl could be who regularly brought flowers to Dickie's grave. Maybe one of his former women. But she seemed such a demure, refined young lady. Yet weren't all Dickie's women a cut above the average in refinement, and a little more reserved in demeanour? You only had to look at Isabel. You only had to look at Lucy. This girl was a similar type. Very appealing. Arthur's curiosity was aroused.

'Here you are,' he said, handing her the vase when he returned to the graveside.

'Thank you ever so much.'

'Oh, you're welcome . . . Are you a relative of Mr Dempster?' he asked experimentally, for the girl evidently had no idea he was connected with the family.

'No, not I,' she answered, and took the paper wrapping off her irises.

'A friend, then?' He turned his attention to the child, still sitting untroubled on the grave.

'Yes. I was a friend of Mr Dempster.'

'I take it the baby is yours? I mean, you're not looking after her for somebody else?'

'Yes, she's mine.'

'She's lovely.'

The girl smiled graciously, looking up from her flower arranging. 'She is, isn't she?'

'What's her name?'

'Julia.'

'Julia,' Arthur repeated, trying to hide his astonishment. Three daughters of Dickie Dempster all with the same name! Isabel's, Lucy's, and now this young woman's. 'It's a pretty name. I imagine her father's very proud of her.'

'I wouldn't know,' the young woman replied. 'Perhaps he might have been.'

'Oh.' Arthur was stumped for words. He could hardly ask her outright if Dickie Dempster was the father, although it seemed certain.

'To tell you the truth, Mr Dempster was her father,' she offered with no prompting whatsoever.

'So you are Mrs Dempster?' he asked, feigning a lack of any knowledge about his erstwhile lover.

She smiled. 'No. My name is Myrtle Collins. Mr Dempster and me were never married.'

'Oh . . . I see . . .'

'I'm not ashamed of it, Mr . . .'

'Goodrich . . .'

'I'm not ashamed of it, Mr Goodrich. I *could* have been Mrs Dempster. I was to have been.'

'But how?' He smiled sympathetically. 'I understand there is already a Mrs Dempster?'

'Ah, that's what everybody thinks. But there isn't.'

'There isn't?' Arthur looked at her, trying to hide his scepticism. 'I don't understand.'

'Oh, there's a woman who calls herself Mrs Dempster. Mrs Isabel Dempster. But she was not married to Dickie.'

'I'm . . . I'm confounded, Miss Collins. I fail to see how you can say that.'

'I can say it because it's true. Isabel Grosvenor defied her father and ran away with Mr Dempster within a year of their meeting. It was commonly supposed they had eloped, but I have a second cousin who used to work in service at the Grosvenors' house in Chapel Ash, and she was privy to everything that went on. Since Dickie's death Isabel and the Grosvenor family have become reconciled, by the way. Anyway, she was content to be his common-law wife, living in sin with Dickie in a house they rented – the house she still lives in now. It turned out to be an imperfect arrangement – for both of them. I understand their romance soon ran out of steam and they lost interest in each other. But while Isabel didn't want Dickie for herself any longer, she certainly didn't want anybody else to have him either. She had some sort of hold over him. The likelihood of inheriting her father's money, I suspect. She forbade him to have anything further to do with me when she found out he and I were in love. When she found out I was carrying Dickie's child she cited her children as having priority. I suppose she told him she was the cheaper alternative.'

'Isabel Dempster did all that?' he queried, astounded.

'Oh, on the outside she's very charming, is Isabel Grosvenor. I knew her when we were younger. She always disliked me, but I never knew why. She's very clever, you know, Mr Goodrich. Clever enough to know how to trap poor Dickie when he wanted to break free of her and marry me.'

'Well, fancy, Miss Collins. I would never have guessed. And you are sure the two of them never married?'

'You may take it as gospel, Mr Goodrich. You'll find no marriage certificate in that house. No church records of it exist anywhere.'

'But her children are his, I presume?'

'It's reasonable to presume so, but who can be sure?'

'It's a fascinating story, Miss Collins. I'm only sorry Mr Dempster was unable to make you his wife. Things might have turned out differently.'

'Perhaps it was for the best, Mr Goodrich. We shall never know. I'm a believer in Fate – that things happen for a reason. Our marriage was evidently not to be. Who am I to question the wisdom of Fate?' Myrtle held her arms out to the child, who looked at her mother with eager expectation and chuckled. 'Come on, little Julia,' she cooed. 'It's time we left Mr Goodrich to finish his work.' She collected the baby from the grave top. 'I hope I haven't detained you too long, Mr Goodrich.'

'You haven't at all. It's been very interesting talking to you. I'm so glad our paths crossed.'

★ ★ ★

Arthur did not call on Isabel Dempster after all. Instead, he went home to see how his mother was, and then to the workshop where he plied his craft deep in thought for what remained of the afternoon. That evening, before Lucy called, he wrote a letter to Isabel.

Dear Isabel,
I visited Dickie's grave today to assess and repair the damage you reckoned had been done. I must inform you that

it was of a trivial nature and was quickly and easily rectified. Unfortunately time was short and I could not see my way clear to call on you.

Having given the matter due consideration, I feel it best that I no longer call on you. My own personal circumstances have changed since last we met, which renders it impossible and inadvisable to make further calls upon you. I trust that you will understand my situation and forgive this very impersonal means of letting you know.

As regards payment for the grave, I have already settled the account, so there is no need to trouble yourself further on the matter. The compensation you have received for Dickie's injuries will be needed in its entirety, I have no doubt. It is best spent on yourself and your children and not on a cold tombstone.

It has been a pleasure and a privilege knowing you, and you may be sure that I shall never forget you.

Yours very sincerely,
Arthur Goodrich.

★   ★   ★

That night, Lucy called again, as they had arranged. They went through the motions of preparing his mother for a night's rest, getting her on and off the commode, giving her a tipple of whisky to help her sleep, laced of course with a drop or two of laudanum for good measure. Afterwards, they drifted into his bedroom and stood at the window in the darkness watching the same twinkling lights and the same glowing sky Arthur had seen so many times before from that vantage point. But having Lucy at his side made it all the more pleasurable. He felt for her hand and gave it a squeeze, and she looked up at him.

'I went to Dickie's grave today,' he said quietly so as not to disturb Dinah.

'You said you would.'

'I didn't go to see Isabel though.'

'Oh? Why not?'

'Oh . . . I decided to take the coward's way out and write to her.'

He could hardly tell her about Myrtle and what she had revealed. He could hardly say that Dickie Dempster was not married after all, and so insinuate that he could have married Lucy after all, had he lived – had the blighter mustered the courage to defy Isabel. No, all that was best left untold.

'But I thought you said she owed you money.'

'I told her to forget it. I told her I'd settled the account.'

'And have you?'

'Yes. I could hardly let our Talbot be saddled with half of it.'

'That's typical of you,' she whispered and put her arm around his waist. 'You're just too soft, even with money.'

'No, I'm not soft.' He turned round to face her, their bodies touching. 'It's amazing how quickly you've got your figure back. I was only thinking the other day, you look just the same as you did before.'

'Before what?'

'Before I went to Bristol and lost you.' He bent his head and kissed her on the mouth.

'You never really lost me . . . You know, Arthur,' she said reflectively, 'some of the things that happen to us seem so terrible at the time . . . and yet often, I think they happen for the best . . . Don't you think so?'

'Who are we to question the wisdom of Fate?' he replied, moved to use Myrtle Collins's words, spoken to him earlier that same day.

Lucy looked up at him, all her love in her eyes. 'That's very deep, coming from you.'

'I can be deep, Luce. Believe it or not.'

'Yes, I'm beginning to believe it . . . Anyway, as I was saying . . . I think things happened for the best for us. Don't you?'

'Unquestionably . . .'

'I do love you, you know, Arthur. Much more than I ever thought possible.'

'And I love you.' He gave her a squeeze as he looked out at the red, fiery sky, alight again with the reflection of flaring molten iron. 'Did you mean what you said last night, Luce?'

'About what?'

'When you said you had desires the same as me.'

'Yes. Course I meant it,' she said softly.

'Well . . .' A lump came to his throat. 'I want you . . .'

'I'm glad,' she said simply.

'Shall we then?'

'I reckon now is as good a time as any.'

They got undressed and clambered into Arthur's bed together. It was cool and she snuggled up to his naked body for warmth. He found her lips and they kissed ardently, rolling first one way then another. Both had wondered what it might be like to share a bed with each other, he more times than enough, plaguing, torturing himself with yearning. She had idly wondered it too, before ever he had mentioned what Moses had so coarsely advised him. She had laughed at that at the time, but in those days she could not take Arthur seriously. In those days she could twist him round her little finger. But things were different now.

His hand roamed her body inquisitively and lingered at her breasts, round and ponderous, full of the nourishment that Julia thrived on. He kissed her neck, as Isabel had taught him, scratching the tight skin slightly with his teeth. Lucy shuddered with pleasure. He continued south with his kisses, smothering her breasts. He found her nipple and lapped it hungrily, licking, sucking, tasting the very milk that Julia fed upon, the absolute, life-giving essence of her body. It was slightly sweet and sticky. The notion of sampling it, savouring it, stimulated him, arousing his passion to fever pitch as if it were some highly potent

419

elixir of love. He manoeuvred himself between her legs and kissed her stomach, so smooth and firm, yet so soon after the birth of her baby. Lucy rested her thighs against his shoulder while he lapped between her legs, drinking her in, tasting her, aware of the faint, sweet aroma of her wetness. She fingered the hair of his head, pressing him to her to feel his mouth, his tongue teasing her the more, the better to enhance the pleasure.

So this was Lucy. This was the precious, mystical, secret Lucy he'd wondered about, fantasised about. Here at last was the ultimate access to her love which had been hitherto denied him. Well, it was denied him no longer. She was his, he was hers. Yet neither were the pair of fumbling fools they might have been earlier. They had both acquired some worthwhile experience, they both knew what to do and what to expect. There might be something to be said for such amorous adventures after all, however much they were disapproved of by conventional society.

He eased his way over her belly again, skin skimming skin, leaving a trail of wet kisses in a line over her navel, between her breasts and at her throat. She reached down for him and took him in her hand. He felt so hard and so yieldingly smooth, and the knowledge that he was as eager for her as she was for him, exciting her further. With a sigh, she guided him into her, and felt his delightful weight upon her as he slid easily, lusciously inside her.

So this was Arthur.

Welcome home . . .

Funny the way things turn out . . .

★　★　★

Isabel responded to Arthur's letter by return of post:

> *My own dear Arthur,*
> *It pains me terribly that you are unable to visit me any more. I can only presume that your mother has taken a turn*

for the worse, thus making it impossible for you to get away.
I only wish there was some way I could help. Don't hesitate
to let me know if there is something I can do.

As for you settling the account for Dickie's grave, I'm
afraid my pride will not allow you to get away with that. I
have the money now, I can afford it, and I am adamant
that you should not be out of pocket. I would therefore deem
it a special favour if you would call and collect it. In any
case, there is another pressing matter that concerns me that I
wish to discuss.

I do hope that in the meantime your mother's health
improves, allowing you more time to pursue the things which
interest you, and I look forward to seeing you soon.

With fondest regards,
Isabel

The other pressing matter alluded to in Isabel's letter that
concerned her, was that she was carrying Arthur's child.

★ ★ ★

29

At the end of the first week in April Dinah took a turn for the worse. On the Friday, Arthur had noticed a deterioration in his mother so, after he had seen Lucy home – not late at just a few minutes after nine – he decided he would sit with her and keep his eye on her. Dinah's breathing was rapid but shallow and she was feverish, but at midnight she seemed more settled, so he retired to his own bedroom leaving a lamp burning, should she call him in the night.

He seemed to have been asleep only minutes when he heard Dinah's feeble calls and he dragged himself to her room.

'Are you feeling worse, Mother?'

'Fetch me a drop o' whisky, our Arthur,' she bleated. 'It'll perk me up a bit, and might send me off to sleep again.'

So Arthur fetched her a cup of whisky and held it to her lips while she sipped.

'I'll sit with you a bit,' he said consolingly. 'I want to keep my eye on you. Let me give your pillow a shake and make it more comfortable.' He eased her up and shook her pillow, then gently let her down again.

'Ta, my son.'

He dragged the wicker chair closer to the bed and watched, desperate for sleep, but forcing himself to stay awake. By the light of the lamp he watched the hands of the clock creep towards four, and seemed to know instinctively that this was a watershed in the life of his poor mother.

The clock, his father's clock, reached the hour and he heard its usual whirrings begin inside it. But the chimes had ceased to work years ago and his father, typically, would never pay to have them mended, so it remained depressingly silent, like a woman trying to gossip who had lost her voice.

Dinah snorted in her fitful slumber and roused momentarily. She was shivering so Arthur tipped some more coal on the fire. He rinsed his hands in the bowl on the washstand and felt her brow. She seemed hot, despite the shivering.

This was never right. This was never normal, even for a woman who had broken three limbs. So he watched her attentively, often glancing at the clock. Another hour passed. Dinah awoke. She was confused, mythered.

'I'll bring you some water, Mother.'

He went downstairs and filled a mug from a pitcher which they kept in the pantry.

'Here. You'd better drink this.' He eased her up and she sipped the water, pulled a face and he let her rest again.

Was there any sign of the approaching dawn? Arthur went over to the window and lifted one of the drapes. There was a glimmer of light in the eastern sky.

'I'm going to fetch Doctor Walker when it's light,' he said. 'You should be getting better, not worse.'

Dr Walker lived in Bell Street in a rambling rented property owned by the Earl of Dudley. It was handy for St Michael's church of a Sunday and for the Bell Inn at other appropriate times. Arthur made his way there hurriedly as dawn was breaking. Breathing hard from his rushing up the steep hill past the church, he turned into Bell Street and found the house, the front door of which opened directly onto the street. He hammered on the door.

The house and its neighbours, was set among tall elms, and the pigeons and magpies were already awake, flapping around and squawking, oblivious to the slumbering of their human neighbours. Arthur looked at the polished brass plate on the wall and sniffed while he waited for an answer.

At the umpteenth knock a window above him screeched open and a nightcap appeared over the sill like a cuckoo thrust from a clock.

'What the hell is going on down there?' an angry male voice enquired. 'Who is there?'

Thankfully, he had flushed the right bird first time. 'It's Arthur Goodrich, Dr Walker, from the stonemason's down the Delph,' he replied apologetically.

'Oh, Arthur,' he acknowledged irritatedly. 'What's the meaning of waking me at this time of the night?'

'It's morning, Dr Walker. It's nigh on half past five. My mother's taken a turn for the worse.'

'Your mother?'

'You know. You set her broken bones after a fall . . . Old Jeremiah's widow. You tended my father afore he died.'

'Yes, I recall.'

'I'd appreciate it if you'd come and take a look at her.'

'Now?'

'She's proper ill, Dr Walker, else I wouldn't bother you. She's been going downhill ever since she fell. I fear for her.'

'I'll be down in five minutes. Go back to your mother and I'll follow you there . . . Oh, and have the kettle on. The least I expect for my trouble is a tot of tea with a drop of whisky in it.'

Arthur grinned, relieved. 'I'll see to it, Dr Walker. Thank you.'

★ ★ ★

'How long has she been like this, Arthur?' the doctor asked when he'd examined Dinah.

'A few days, steadily getting worse.'

'Why didn't you send for me sooner?'

'We all thought that maybe it was just a chill she'd caught, weakened by the fall and that.'

424

'She's developed pneumonia,' Dr Walker announced bluntly.

'Pneumonia?' The very word delivered a ring of dread. 'So what are her chances?'

'If I said they were better than poor, Arthur, I'd be telling a lie. She's already shocked and weakened by her recent fall. I'll be surprised if she recovers at all.'

'So how long has she got?'

'Days, perhaps. It's hard to be precise. Normally, the tenth day is critical, but since we can't be sure when the first day was . . . In any case, she might well expire before that. I'll call in later and see how she's faring. Get her to drink plenty of water. She needs it.'

'I try, but she swears she'll catch cholera from it.'

'She should have no fear of cholera with what she's got. Cholera is the least of her worries. Now . . . that tea . . . Is it brewed?'

'It is, Doctor.' Arthur smiled. 'We'll have it downstairs, eh?'

★ ★ ★

Isabel waited more than two weeks for a reply from Arthur, but none came. The trouble was, she had no prior claim on him. She was aware he was engaged to another, so she must take second place in his affections. Their relationship had been one of sexual convenience only. He, she was now frustratedly aware, had once been on the point of declaring enduring love for her until she had stopped him, suggesting that surely he could not be that susceptible and so easily diverted. After that he could never admit his love anyway, and so they had continued lying with each other when time permitted, usually on Saturday afternoons and sometimes on Wednesday evenings, when Saturday afternoons and Wednesday evenings did not clash with her monthly bleeding or with cricket practice, rabbit shoots or his Bible class. Now she regretted ever having inhibited him from spoken expressions of love.

She knew as well as anybody that we all tend to believe our own propaganda, and if Arthur had spoken the words 'I love you', he would have lived them to the letter. But he had not, and so the opportunity had passed.

The changed circumstances of which he had written, she at first assumed was a reference to his mother's fall and the consequences of that. Never did it occur to her that he and his sweetheart had finally made an arrangement to marry. But it was all beginning to fall into place. That's what he must have meant. And, knowing Arthur as she did, he could never share two beds. He was the honourable kind who would forsake all others and keep him only unto her; '*her*' being that young woman she'd seen him with at the time Dickie lay injured. The one called Lucy. Pity all men were not like him.

All the same, she felt she should oblige him by letting him know of her condition, that she was carrying his child. She had always maintained that she would never press him to choose her over that girl called Lucy, but knowing he had a responsibility to herself now, she believed he should at least be given the choice. All right, it would complicate matters for him, but she owed it to herself as well as to the unborn child.

Isabel had always been shrewd when it came to avoiding pregnancy, or she thought she had. On reflection, though, there must have been times when she had forgotten to apply a douche, or simply have fallen asleep after making love. Certainly, there had been times on their evening encounters when she had woken up to find Arthur gone to catch his train home; she had rolled over and gone back to sleep, content to wait till morning to douche herself. This child growing in her belly was the price she was paying for her complacency.

There was only one thing for it; she must go to Arthur and tell him face to face. She had a perfectly legitimate reason to visit him anyway: to repay the money for Dickie's grave. She had his address, she would visit him at his workshop.

She decided not to wait till after Easter, but would go on the Thursday before it, Maundy Thursday, which fell on 21st April. Happily, the spring sun was shining, and it was warm for the time of year. So, during the morning, she collected her two children, washed them and dressed them in their second best clothes and bundled them into an omnibus which would deposit them at Low Level station. Railway travel was not strange to her; Dickie had taken her on an excursion once, and she'd had to go by train to see him when he was injured after the accident. Otherwise, it occurred infrequently. She bought return tickets for Brettell Lane station, unrecognised by any of the railway staff who saw her, and awaited the departure of the train. The children were excited about the journey, for neither had been on a train before, but she urged them to be more restrained in their exuberance and not to annoy other passengers.

When the train slipped into Brettell Lane station, they disembarked and, at the exit, she asked for directions to the Delph. Mercifully, it was not far to walk with two small children in tow.

As she approached what she thought must be the house and workshop, set back from the road in a yard littered with worked and unworked stone, she espied some activity and decided to stand and watch until she could discern what was happening. She wanted Arthur to catch sight of her, not to have to go looking for him. A pair of fine black horses emerged from behind the high wooden gate and it was obvious they were in harness. They were hauling a hearse that bore a coffin, a hearse bedecked with wreaths of spring flowers . . .

Horses and hearse slowly entered the street, followed by a procession of black-clad mourners. Isabel tried to find a nook or crevice to hide in until the funeral procession had passed, but there was nowhere to hide. So she stood motionless with head down, ostensibly as a mark of respect, but actually so as not to draw attention to herself. She warned the children to do likewise under pain of severely smacked legs if they defied her.

The cortège approached in solemn pageantry, and she could not help but glance up to catch a glimpse of the chief mourners. As she feared, Arthur was one of them. He was wearing a tall black hat, a black jacket and dark striped trousers. He looked sombre. At his side was the girl she just about remembered from the time of Dickie's accident, the girl called Lucy, his intended. Lucy was much prettier than she remembered, with big blue eyes that emitted a glow of contentment as she flashed them at Arthur, despite the gravity and stateliness of the occasion. He smiled back at the girl and Isabel enviously witnessed such a look of love and devotion beamed back at the girl, whose arm was linked affectionately through his.

Isabel sighed and turned away lest Arthur recognise her. She had not reckoned on this and she did not know what to do. Fancy having the ill luck to choose the day of a funeral to make her visit and stake her claim. She presumed Arthur's ailing mother had passed away.

But what should she do now? It was obviously not the best of times to see Arthur, even if she waited till they returned. So she resigned herself to tarrying a moment or two longer, till the procession had gone by and was out of sight.

When it had turned the corner, Isabel approached the yard, fired by curiosity. She stood at the open gate for a few seconds taking in what she saw. So this was Arthur's home and his place of work. It could be none other than a stonemason's yard with all the paraphernalia of the craft so liberally and so randomly strewn about. Blocks of granite, slabs of marble and slate, urns, vases, planks of wood, a rickety old cart with the shafts, paint peeling off, resting on the ground.

A one-legged man using a crutch lumbered out of the privy. He saw her, looked at her questioningly and then smiled at the children.

'Hello there, missus,' he greeted as he approached. 'Can I help you?'

'I . . . I was . . . I came to see Mr Goodrich,' she stuttered, unsure what to say.

'Which one?'

'Oh . . . Mr Arthur Goodrich.'

'He's just gone to the funeral,' Moses said, as if she must be well aware whose. 'You just missed him. I doubt whether he'll be back at work today.'

'Is it his mother's funeral?'

'Aye. Passed on last week, she did, poor soul. Pneumonia. Set in after her fall. I said it would. I said to Arthur – and young Talbot – I said, "You want to keep an eye on her", I said. "Queer things happen to old folk when they'n had a fall", I said. "Specially when they'n broke bones", I said.'

'I'm very sorry to hear of her death,' Isabel replied. 'Of course, I had no idea, nor that the funeral was today, else I wouldn't have come.'

'Can I give Mr Arthur a message for you, missus?' Moses offered. 'I might see him later.'

'No, no. I particularly wanted to see him personally . . . I have his score to settle.'

'I can relieve you of your money, missus. I do some o' the clerking. If you'll step into the office, I'll be glad to help.'

To her surprise, Isabel found herself following him as he hobbled in front of her, ushering the children along with her.

'How old am they, the kids?' Moses asked affably over his shoulder.

'Five and three.'

'Lovely, ain't they, kids? I got a little daughter meself, you know . . . *and* another on the way.' He arrived at the little office, untidy with papers strewn everywhere. 'Due next August, so my missus reckons.'

Isabel smiled back at him. 'You must be very proud.'

429

'Oh, I am.'

A dingy old dog was lying languidly and indifferently beneath a workbench, and the children, having spotted it, were immediately taken with it. At once they began prodding it and stroking it with the natural curiosity children have for animals, especially docile dogs.

'Leave the poor dog alone,' Isabel chided.

'Oh, they'll come to no harm with him, missus,' Moses affirmed as he sat down and leaned his crutch against the wall. 'He'll let 'em poke him and fuss him till kingdom come. It'll keep 'em amused a while. So, do you know how much you owe?'

'Not exactly.'

'What name is it? I can look it up.'

'There's very likely no record of it. It was all done as a favour.'

'Oh, I see.' Moses winked at her conspiratorially. 'I reckon he dain't want it to go through the books then.'

'I suspect that's the case.'

'So what sort o' grave was it? They can be anything from three pounds to a hundred.'

'It was just an ordinary stone grave. Not polished granite, nor marble, just stone.'

'Basalt,' Moses suggested. 'Rowley Rag, I daresay. Cheapest there is. A grave in that would be about four pounds maybe, pushing it.'

'Then I'll give you the five. Certainly it was not the more expensive kind. Perhaps Mr Goodrich can let me have any change I'm due.' She opened her bag and counted out the money.

'Who shall I say called?'

'Oh, tell Mr Goodrich it was Isabel.'

'Just Isabel?' he queried.

She smiled enigmatically. 'Just Isabel.'

'I'll tell him.'

'I . . . I think I saw him at the head of the cortège, Mr . . .'

'Cartwright. Moses Cartwright . . . missus . . .'

'He was walking with a young woman. Isn't her name Lucy?'

'Yes, our Lucy. She's me sister-law as a matter of fact . . . They'm reckoning on getting wed soon.'

'Oh? How soon?'

'July, I believe.'

'Well . . . July's a good month to get married, I imagine. Hot and sunny.' She smiled wistfully. 'Let's hope they'll be happy.'

'Oh, I reckon they'll be happy enough . . . especially after what they've both bin through.'

'Oh?' she asked, a look of curiosity on her face.

'Between you and me, missus, there's quite a story to be told.'

'I'd love to hear it.'

'If you've got a minute, I can tell it yer. Well, they was a-courting afore, like. Nigh on three years ago. But Arthur could get nowhere with Lucy then. Anyroad, he left home, 'cause he couldn't abide his father, and went to Bristol to live. He asked her to marry him and go with him, but she wouldn't. She'd took up with this other chap, see. A guard off the railway. Somebody called Dickie Dempster . . .'

Isabel felt her heart quicken. 'A guard off the railway?' she repeated, affecting to sound indifferent.

'Turned out to be a right bugger. Made her pregnant, then died after he got hurt in that railway accident we had here last year. As if that worn't enough, it turns out he was married anyroad.'

'So this girl Lucy . . . has had this . . . this Dickie Dempster's baby by now, has she?'

'February. A lovely little thing she is, an' all.' Moses grinned affably. 'The image of her mother. She calls the bab Julia,

431

'cause she reckoned as it was this Dickie's favourite name for a little wench.'

'Julia? Fancy . . . So then what happened? Because I thought Mr Goodrich was engaged to be married to her.'

'No, missus . . . Pardon me, but I've bin overrunning me tale . . . He met a wench in Bristol, a proper prissy little madam. Like a china doll, she was, and about as cold. She wouldn't have done for me. I'd have smacked her backside for her a time or two and no two ways, if she'd been mine. I think they talked about getting wed, but he gi'd her up when he come back to live up here when his father died.'

'So now Arthur's marrying Lucy? Do I understand you correctly?'

'Yes, you got it right, missus. Well, they both realise what a proper pair o' mawkins they was getting mixed up with others in the fust place. I can honestly say as I've never seen two folks more in love than seeing them pair now. And that Arthur loves that bab, that dirty Dickie's bab. By Christ, he does. He's content to bring little Julia up as his own, and I must say as I admire him for that more than anything in the world. When a chap's prepared to tek on another bloke's bab, it tells me as he's got some mettle. Mind you . . .' He winked waggishly. 'I daresay that afore long they'll have one or two babs o' their own to add to the collection.'

'Yes, I daresay,' Isabel conceded pensively. 'That's quite a tale, Mr Cartwright. I feel somewhat . . . different . . . for having heard it. Yes, he's quite a character, isn't he, that Arthur Goodrich.'

'Salt o' the earth.'

'Tell me, Mr Cartwright, how did you lose your leg? You weren't a victim of that terrible railway accident, were you?'

'No, missus. Gunshot wound. In the Crimea. Horrible job.'

'I can only begin to imagine . . . Well, I must go, else the

432

funeral party will be back. I'd hate Mr Goodrich to see me here.'

'I'm sure he'd be glad to see you, missus.'

'I'm not so sure . . . If you could just tell him, Mr Cartwright, that I dropped by to pay what I owed him. That will be quite sufficient . . . Oh, look at my children . . . I dress them in something decent, and look how they've managed to get themselves all dirty again.'

'Oh, we can easy give 'em a brush down, missus.'

'Come on, you two,' she called to them. 'Leave the poor dog alone. We have to go now, else we'll miss the train.'

★   ★   ★

Arthur heard nothing more from Isabel Dempster. He pocketed the five pounds she'd brought, but decided it best, out of deference to Lucy, neither to acknowledge it nor to contact her again.

★   ★   ★

The dwelling house, the workshop and the yard together comprised virtually the whole of the estate left by Dinah Goodrich to her two sons Arthur and Talbot. They agreed that, for the time being, Arthur should live in the house, and continue to do so after he and Lucy were married, but that when they were more prosperous they would demolish it, and possibly the workshop too, and build two fine houses on the plot of land, one for each of them. It was a proposal that they all thought fair.

Meanwhile, before they married, Lucy was of a mind to springclean the house and decorate it. After all, if she was about to live in it as the new wife of Arthur Goodrich, she wanted it spick and span, as her mother had always drummed into her. Anyway, there were some fine wallpaper hangings to be bought. They would invest in some new furniture; new furniture would be needed wherever they lived – if only they could afford to buy any.

433

In May, after a day's hard work, Arthur returned to the house. Lucy had been there much of the day with Magnolia, cleaning and clearing out the ancient and unwanted paraphernalia that Jeremiah and Dinah had accumulated over the years. He made up the fire and said goodbye to each of them as they left him to return home. Lucy, of course, would return, minus Julia, when she had eaten with her mother and father, and had fed the child.

Lucy duly returned. Over the weeks of their resumed courtship they had fallen into the pleasurable habit of going to bed most evenings to make love, which suited them both well, before she returned home to be mother to Julia and daughter to Hannah and Haden. However, that particular night they did not. They had involved themselves in some fairly serious and complex kissing downstairs on the hearth in front of the fire, and the hem of Lucy's skirt was up around her waist as darkness fell.

She felt herself trembling with excitement as he forsook her mouth to kiss those other soft lips between her thighs. His firm body felt pleasant and warm against her as he brushed down her. Her breathing quickened. His tongue probed her tormentingly. Comparison with Dickie Dempster was inevitable and she had to confess to herself that never had Dickie loved her as well and as exotically as Arthur did.

Somewhere in the back of her mind she heard a distant humming and thought her head would spin with pleasure. Within the darkness of her closed eyelids she felt his mouth working wonders on her. It was excruciatingly pleasant, radiating through her entire body. As his hands went to her bottom and drew her even harder to him she gasped, and shivers ran up and down her spine. The dreamy humming sound she could hear quickly turned to a pleasant roar. It increased with the sweetness of his caresses, rising, rising, to a magnificent crescendo. If ever she were asked, she could

434

never describe these wonderful sensations. Somewhere in the blackness of her closed eyes, where only the tactile senses mattered, she uttered a little moan of ecstasy as Arthur's grip on her backside tightened, drawing her harder into him. No wonder the girls at work, and Miriam were always talking about sex.

She was certain she could smell smoke, and swore she was smouldering with desire. He snaked up her prone body and found her mouth eagerly and, as the roaring continued, he entered her with such scintillating sweetness.

Suddenly, they were startled by the sound of the back door being unlatched.

'Hello!' a voice called from the depths of the house.

In panic, Arthur at once leapt up and clutched at his trousers that were half around his ankles, half beneath his feet. He stumbled as he raced against time to pull them up and so render himself decent before the intruder appeared. Most likely it was Talbot.

Lucy could see a bright flickering out in the Delph where a small crowd of people had gathered. The yard was bathed in a dancing orange light too, umber where the shadows fell, and the roar, which seemed to emanate from the chimney, was louder than ever.

'Hello!' called the voice again, followed by the clunk-clunk of a crutch as it struck the ground.

Arthur recognised Moses's voice.

'Hello!' Arthur called back. 'Is that you, Moses?'

'Ar. Where bin yer? It's dark out here. I cor see where I'm at.'

'We're here. In the parlour.'

The door opened. By the firelight Moses saw Arthur finalising adjustments to his dress having managed to pull his trousers up, Lucy was on her feet smoothing out the creases in her skirt and tucking away stray strands of hair.

'Sorry to interrupt,' he said with an audacious grin, 'but did you know your chimdey was a-fire?'

'Lord, no.'

'I heard this roaring,' Lucy said, 'but I never dreamt it was the chimney.'

'I could see it from our house. I guessed as you hadn't realised. Ten-foot flames am shooting out the top o' chimdey pot, and there's enough smoke to blacken out Dudley and Tipton. And you should see the folk what have turned out to have a look. Anybody'd think as they've never seen a chimdey a-fire afore.'

'What shall we do?' Arthur asked.

'Put the fire out for a start, and cover the hearth wi' summat. You don't want great chunks of red-hot soot falling on the hearth and setting the rug afire an' all. Wet sheets or blankets might help.'

'Luce, there's a cupboard upstairs in mother's room,' Arthur said in a panic. 'There's lots of old sheets and things. Take the lamp and fetch 'em while I go and fetch some water?'

'All right.'

He lit the lamp for her from a spill.

When Lucy had gone upstairs, Moses said, 'The most useful thing I can do here is piddle in the fire.'

'No!' Arthur yelled. 'You'll do no such thing. I'll fetch some water.'

Arthur rushed to the water pump in Silver End with two pails, parrying the comments of the onlookers as he went. He saw the flames shooting out of the chimney pot and thick plumes of inky smoke curling and writhing relentlessly into the inky sky. He returned, slopping much of the water over the sides in his haste. But enough remained to wet the sheets and blankets and lay them over the hearth. Sure enough, great lumps of burning soot fell down the chimney and rolled onto the hearth, to be shovelled up immediately and put onto the tiled base of the grate out of harm's way till they cooled down.

Eventually, the blaze in the chimney burned itself out and the roaring ceased. The bright orange glow outside diminished and the thick column of dark brown smoke thinned and dispersed.

'This could only happen to you, Arthur Goodrich,' Lucy exclaimed, seeing the funny side of it. 'I'm going back upstairs. I'll see you in a minute or two.' She left them and rushed out of the room.

'I can still smell smoke,' Arthur said.

'You will for days,' Moses answered. 'Still you've no need to send for the sweep now.'

'It's a good thing you come and warned us what was happening.'

'Aye, else you have had red-hot soot burning your arse.' He grinned knowingly. 'It's that what started the chimney ablaze, I reckon. All that red-hot poking you'm a doing lately.'

Arthur grinned proudly. 'You could be right, Moses. I never thought of that. But I was only taking your advice.'

'Aye, well, it's a pity you didn't take it sooner.'

'That's as may be, Moses. Anyway, for Christ's sake don't let on to her father. He'd skin me alive.'

Moses laughed. 'Have no fear. There but for the grace of God go I . . . Ah, well. I'll go 'um now. I'll see yer in the morning.'

'Yes, and thanks again, Moses. I'll see you in the morning.'

'Say ta-ra to Lucy for me.'

'I will.'

Two minutes after Moses had gone, Lucy, preceded by the oil lamp's glow, came back into the room excited.

'Come with me, Arthur,' she urged mysteriously. 'Come and see what I've found.' She took his hand and led him upstairs, into his mother's room. 'Here . . . Look.' She held the lamp so he could see into the depths of the cupboard; something tucked behind some old folded curtains.

'Lord above!' he exclaimed. 'I never would never have believed it. How much is here, do you reckon?'

'Hundreds, I reckon. All in five pound bills, by the looks of it.'

'And the old bugger swore he'd never got anything. Wait till I show it Talbot in the morning.'

'We'll be able to buy some new furniture after all, Arthur.'

'We'll be able to buy a whole new house, just with our share. Come on, Luce, let's count it.'

⋆ ⋆ ⋆

Lucy Piddock duly became Mrs Arthur Goodrich on 17th July 1859 at St Michael's Brierley Hill, the very same day that Isabel Dempster gave birth to his son, of whom he had no inkling whatsoever. The child would be christened Arthur, after his father.

AUTHOR'S NOTE

2003

The railway accident which occurred on the evening of Monday 23rd August 1858 on the Oxford, Worcester and Wolverhampton Railway, at the approach to the old Round Oak station, is a historical fact and happened in exactly the way I have illustrated it in the story. The jury at the inquest found the head guard, Frederick Cooke (sometimes spelled without the *e* in the records), guilty of manslaughter, and he was committed for his crime, although my research, at the time of writing this, has not revealed what sentence he served. One or two names quoted in connection with the inquest were actual personages, as was Ben Elwell, licensee of the Whimsey Inn, but all others are fictitious.

I was alerted to this incident by my old friend John V. Richards, whose extensive knowledge of the ancient and worthy public houses of the old Black Country, past and present, I have tapped on many an occasion. I was querying, during my research for my previous novel *Poppy Silk*, the history of the Crown Inn on Brettell Lane in Silver End, Brierley Hill, when the Whimsey entered into the conversation. 'That's where they took the dead and injured from the railway accident in August 1858,' John said. 'The Whimsey, the Old Crown and the Bell.'

Well, I researched it and from then on I was hooked. It is a forgotten but important part of the Black Country's heritage. The suffering that ensued is now unremembered. I just had to write a novel surrounding the event. Then I managed to obtain a copy of the transcript of the inquest, which was adjourned again and again. It ran for many weeks and with some interesting diversions, many of which bore no relevance to my novel, so which have not been touched upon. What did emerge, however, was the absolute integrity and unremitting thoroughness of the Victorians, their values, their engineering expertise, their indomitable 'can do' spirit, and their determination to get things right.